T3-BNJ-640

RIVEN'S PATH

ISADORA DEESE

WITHDRAWN
No longer the property of the
Boston Public Library
Sale of this material benefits the Library

Riven's Path by Isadora Deese

Part 2 of the *Roan and Judge Gorey Series*

ISBN: 978-1-938349-80-5
eISBN: 978-1-938349-85-0
Library of Congress Control Number: 2017957287

Copyright © 2018 Isadora Deese

This work is licensed under the Creative Commons Attribution-NonCommercial-NoDerivatives 4.0 International License. To view a copy of this license, visit http://creativecommons.org/licenses/by-nc-nd/4.0/.

Cover contains elements from:

Tree Of Life – Letunic and Bork (2006) Bioinformatics 23(1):127–8 and Letunic and Bork (2011) Nucleic Acids Res doi: 10.1093/nar/gkr201

and

Chapter graphics include schematic glyphs created by the *Synthetic Biology Open Language (SBOL) Working Group, http://sbolstandard.org/visual/*

Layout and book design by Mark Givens and Isadora Deese
First Pelekinesis Printing 2018

For information:
Pelekinesis, 112 Harvard Ave #65, Claremont, CA 91711 USA

www.pelekinesis.com

RIVEN'S PATH

ISADORA DEESE

PART 2 OF THE ROAN AND JUDGE GOREY SERIES

For grandmother Mary Belle Beam

and sons Curtis Nicholas,

Charles Franklin,

and Leo Howard

 **CHANGE IS THE ONLY** constant on the river. That's what his father said, anyway. Drifting downriver was like hitching a ride on the back of time itself. Fighting the upstream current was a fool's attempt to turn back the clock. He was partial to winking at Trevor when he got to that part, just before he announced himself, *therefore*, a bona fide time traveler. Trevor never really got the joke—if it was one—but he'd smile to be polite. Sometimes.

For Trevor, change was seldom and sudden. His mother was alive until she wasn't. He was the shortest guy in his class until he wasn't. He was going to college on a football scholarship, until he wasn't. As for the river, Trevor thought it looked mostly the same most of the time, until it didn't. It went from being a mass of green flowing through the gorge in summer to a dark thread rimmed by frosted glass in winter. The gradual states between extremes, those were lost on him. His father on the other hand could read the river so well he could tell you in summer when the algae bloom was high and the bass count was low, and in winter he could predict the thickness of the riverscour prairie and how many herons might nest there come spring. If something was in the river that shouldn't be, his dad was the first to know it. Matthias Skaggs was always there to receive the latest news from the river.

Until he wasn't.

From his hiding spot, Trevor watched the Feds crawl around Hawks Nest lodge like an invasive species. His legs were tired from the long walk here. His calves were starting to cramp from squatting so long. His stomach added to the list of complaints with an angry growl. He had some change in his pocket, enough for a candy bar from one of the lodge vending machines, but he couldn't risk it. After evacuating the residents along the river bank, the Feds set themselves up at the lodge where they could keep an eye on the river below, and keep everyone else out.

Trevor leaned heavily on the hemlock that grew at an impossible angle from the cliff side. Long before Trevor had been born, the massive tree had pushed its way into being by splitting a giant boulder into pieces. Even longer ago, the boulder had made the poor decision of settling down on top of the stubbornest seed ever to take root, and it had been paying the price ever since, chunk by diminishing chunk.

"What'd this dumb ol' rock ever do to you, sweetheart?"

His father had said that so many times, the words still hung in the air as if just spoken fresh. When Trevor was smaller they'd come to this spot just about every weekend to share the view and a sandwich, and that's how his dad would greet the tree, often with a loving pat to go with it. *What'd this dumb ol' rock ever do to you?* Sometimes, his father sounded like he was on the rock's side—accusing the tree of unnecessary roughness. Other times he sounded almost reverent, like he wished he could be so single-minded. So unapologetically determined. Most of the time he just sounded amused by the rivalry. After the ritual greeting, they'd sit in silence for a long while, enjoying whatever season it happened to be, until it was time to go home. To mark the end of the visit, his father would always say the same thing, as if he'd decided right then and there that it was just about the only thing in the whole world he was entirely certain about.

"One of these days, these two lovers are going over the edge together." And he'd make a cartoon falling sound to accompany a diving motion with his hand toward the river. "Kersplash!"

Trevor's usual spot was a section of boulder that had been carved smooth from runoff, but Trevor didn't sit in his usual spot today. Nothing was usual about this visit. His father's absence here dwarfed the open space beyond the rim of rock, like a black hole made of memories. Their spot wasn't even their spot anymore. The Feds had claimed it. Trevor was trespassing now in a quarantine zone, whatever the hell that was. The reverse 911 call had declared that something unnatural in the water posed an imminent threat. Residents were to abide by new Federal quarantine boundaries, or face prosecution.

In the West Virginia mountains, something unnatural in the water generally meant a slurry dam broke, or one of the companies upstream dumped something in they weren't supposed to. No one could remember the Feds ever getting involved, at least not in these numbers, so this time something was different. Feds invading Hawks Nest. Forced evacuations. Quarantine. It was enough to set off even the mildly paranoid. Feeding that panic even more was a crazy rumor about a giant crawfish created by toxic sludge, but Trevor didn't have time for crazy. The evacuation and quarantine meant the search for his father's body was suspended, and Trevor wanted to know what was really going on.

Trevor watched the dark-suited Feds watch the river with their high-powered binoculars. His fingers worked two small vials in his jacket pocket like a couple of lucky quarters. He'd discovered the samples of river water on his father's nightstand the day he died. For the last couple of years, whenever his father suspected contaminants in the river, he'd take samples and get their friend Caleb at the Appalachian Law Center to send them for analysis out of state. It was the only way to find a researcher not beholden to local industry. Results from one of those samples started an investigation into a waste water disposal company that had dug a well too close to Wolf Creek. Turned out a leak was slowly injecting a slew of nasty chemicals into the groundwater, and the creek obligingly gave the cocktail a lift to the New River, where pollywogs died in droves, river willow wilted, and a generation of striped bass turned belly up. *The Fayette Tribune* wrote up his father's role in the toxic discovery, but except for the local die-off, there wasn't much more to the story. The company paid a fine—a few thousand dollars—and was ordered to plug the hole. A few weeks later, his dad got jumped on his way home by some guys who worked for the company, said he nearly cost them their jobs. They roughed him up. Warned him not to stick his nose where it didn't belong.

Trevor wondered what secrets these new vials might hold. Could they be the reason his father never came home? He didn't know how the Feds factored into it, but that water sloshing around in his pocket was the only clue he had to what happened that day on the river.

"Hey, Trev." The voice behind him was accompanied by the sound of falling pebbles.

The loose sandstone carried Caleb Harper across the rock face until he caught himself on a low branch. He went pale looking over the cliff. "Whoa. Do we have to be so close to the edge?"

"You're late," Trev said. "I didn't think you were comin'."

"Traffic," Caleb said. He was so skinny his fleece jacket looked the same as it would on a hanger. "Everybody's stockin' up like it's the end of the world."

"Maybe it is."

"Oh, I doubt it," Caleb said. His skeletal face creased even with a weak smile. Trev wondered if it hurt, being that stick thin. "If it were really the Last Days, I doubt we'd spend it standing in line at the Walmart."

"Sounds like a good enough way to kick off the Apocalypse to me."

Caleb worked his way back toward Trev. He looked like he wanted to put a hand on Trev's shoulder, but he was unwilling to let go of the tree to do it.

"I was sorry to hear about Matthias, truly," Caleb finally said. "He was a good man."

Trev just nodded. He didn't want to try to speak about his father just yet.

"Where are you staying?"

"With the Bowmans," Trev said, trying to sound grateful, without much success. He'd rather stay in the empty trailer alone, but his father's best friend wouldn't let him. "For now."

"That's good," Caleb said with a nod. "They're good people."

"Yeah," Trev snorted. "We're all good people. It gives me a warm fuzzy feeling inside we're all so *good*."

Caleb shifted his weight, uncomfortable. Trev couldn't tell whether it was the tone of the conversation that caused the discomfort or the proximity to the cliff. Probably a share of both.

"What is it you wanted to show me?" asked Caleb, clearing his throat.

Trev pulled the vials from his pocket and held them out to Caleb in his open palm.

"More water samples?" Caleb sounded mildly disappointed. "You could've brought those to my office."

"They called off the search for his body," Trev said. "Did you know that?"

"No, I didn't," Caleb said.

"They're just going to leave him down there. Like he's not worth fishing back out."

"I'm sorry."

Caleb moved to take the vials from Trev, but Trev retracted his hand. The samples were a sad inheritance, but Trev found it hard to part with them all the same.

"Trev, you know the low esteem I have for our local corporate overlords, but even I can't believe those samples have anything to do with what happened to your dad."

"Howdy!" said a loud voice.

Trev snapped his head around to find one of the Feds standing casually with one hand on the hemlock and a big, stupid grin on his face. He looked like all the other Feds—dark suit, dark tie—except for his bushy brown beard, so long it covered his collar. How could Trev not have heard this guy sneaking up on him? Downright embarrassing.

"Sorry! I didn't mean to startle you," he continued, managing an even bigger smile. "It's just that this looked like a secret meeting, and I happen to *love* secrets. Though I have to admit, I'm lousy at keeping them. I am a *terrible* gossip."

"This is public property," Trev said, surprised by the anger in his own voice. "We're not doing anything wrong. You're the ones out of place here."

Caleb touched Trev's elbow and whispered, "Don't antagonize this guy. Remember, we are breaking quarantine."

"Oh, I'm sure you have a good reason," the Fed waved away Caleb's concern. "I mean, who in their right mind would come down here without a *really* good reason?" He whipped out his badge and ID. "Agent Woodrow Owens. What is that you got there, Mr. Skaggs?"

Trev froze. Agent Owens knew his name. How long had the Feds been watching him? Had they been watching his father, too? Frantic, Trev mumbled "Nothing" and tried to hide the vials behind his back. He fumbled. The vials dropped to the rock, clinked without breaking, and rolled toward the edge under the tree.

"No!" he shouted, and without thinking, Trev slid face first after the bottles, right over the rim.

There was a sickening moment when his brain caught up to his actions and he realized he had nothing to grab onto, because there was nothing beneath him but a whole lot of air, and the river hundreds of feet below. Lots of shouting and scuffling over rocks, and somebody grabbed his legs. His downward momentum stopped. Trev hung suspended there, like a dare to the death-defying hemlock. Caleb and Agent Owens traded a variety of cuss words while they regained their own balance, jostling him so much he thought they might lose their grip and let him fall after all. Beneath him in the vast empty space, the evidence that his father had so carefully collected spun like helicopter seeds toward the water. If they made a splash, he couldn't see it.

They pulled him up, and Trev slumped onto the rock, heavy

with revelation. The river was nothing but a greedy snake. Down there somewhere, his father was trapped in its muddy belly where he was bloating, rotting, turning into something unrecognizable. He was becoming part of the river, a broken down time traveler, cruising along the river's path through the mountains. And Trev was stuck here, alone.

"Well," Agent Owens said, breathing heavily and hanging an arm around a branch like he might drape an arm across an old friend's shoulders. "That was exciting! Please don't do that again, Mr. Skaggs. I am not so good with heights."

"How—how do you know who he is?" Caleb asked, looking green and backing further up the cliff into the woods.

"I have an inkling what brings Mr. Skaggs here, but *you*..." Agent Owens directed at Caleb, "...you, I don't know."

"He's my lawyer," Trev answered.

"Beautiful. I love lawyers."

"Are we under arrest?" Caleb asked.

"Goodness, no—"

"Because if we are, I'll need to call my colleagues at the Appalachian Law Center—"

"You're welcome to call anyone you like, but I just came down here to make sure you didn't miss the big show. Come on up to the lodge. We have coffee. Pop. One of the guys went out for burgers. You're welcome to join us, if you have an appetite."

Agent Owens started walking back up the trail to the lodge, but when he sensed Trev and Caleb weren't following, he turned back around to add in a more authoritative voice, "I insist."

Caleb and Trev still stayed put. Maybe Caleb was considering running for it, just like he was. Agent Owens looked genuinely frustrated. He rubbed his forehead. Shifted his weight.

"Ever heard of a man named Bradley Dimond?"

"No," said Trev, at the same time Caleb said, "Yes."

Caleb turned to Trev to explain. "CEO of Dimond Industries. Part of a global conglomerate. Oil, coal, natural gas, biotech, agribusiness, communications—"

"Everything a growing boy needs," Owens interrupted. "He's one of the guys at the top of the food chain, that's all you need to know. He's about to give a press conference that is supposed to have a major impact on national security, so as part of my job—the national security part—I have to watch it. And I figured, considering what happened to your father, you're going to want to see this for yourself."

"What does my father have to do with national security?"

"Your father? No, you misunderstand. Your father has nothing to do with national security," Agent Owens said. "But that monster in the water down there... the one that gobbled him up... that's another story."

Transcription of Bradley Dimond's "Right of Capture" Speech

Good evening, all. Thank you for joining us on such short notice. I will forgo formalities. You all know who I am. As the new CEO of Furst Enterprises, I stand before you today, along with Senator Nathan Hale, members of the Joint Chiefs, FBI Director Cheryl Santiago, and members of the White House Science Advisory Committee, to shed some light on strange phenomena that have become increasingly problematic around the world. While I don't have all the answers, I do have some, and it's time for me to share what we know. Today is not about me, or anyone else on this stage for that matter. Today is a day for all humanity to witness the new world that has opened its door to us.

This is a day of introductions. Please, take a moment to ponder this work of art I've kept under wraps until now. Some of you may recognize it, or what it once was before its recent alteration. René Magritte's self-portrait Son of Man. *I know, a bit on the nose to choose a surrealist for this demonstration, but it makes the point. Magritte painted a green apple where a man's face should be, but here, that apple has been swallowed up into nothingness. That nothingness, ladies and gentlemen, is a vak.*

Until now, we've been able to contain, for the most part, these things we call vaks. They won't suck you in like a vacuum, so at least we don't have to worry about that, but they are very dangerous.

If you ever come across one, for heaven's sake, don't try to get rid of it yourself. We have removal teams for that. Now I know what you're all thinking out there watching this on your TV or computer or phone, but this is no green-screened illusion. This is a real curiosity unlike anything the human race has ever encountered, which is probably why, if you stare at it for too long, you start to get queasy. It's unsettling, truly, so please, those of you who might be watching this with the elderly or weak of heart, please take care not to let them be overcome by the strangeness of it all. We're facing this together. All of us.

Like I said, we've been able to contain vaks to a certain extent, but that's not the case for streamers. Please shift your attention to this video taken during an attack on our California facility. Strange, sometimes beautiful creatures—otherworldly, sure, but not completely alien. Neither alive or dead. Not ghosts either, though they take the form of those who've been stolen from us. Streamers have been wreaking havoc in our world for over two years now, but their presence has been denied outright or dismissed as natural disaster. Folks, we must accept the existence of these mysteries in order to start protecting our own existence. We must find the courage to lift the veil of disbelief and denial, or face annihilation.

Now, it's true, we kept this knowledge to ourselves until now, because well, we thought there was a chance at a cure. A restoration of our reality. Such a sudden shift in the fundamentals of our universe has never happened before. No religious experience, no scientific discovery, no UFO sighting or ghostly encounter even comes close. Maybe it was misguided instinct to protect you all from the truth of our new reality, but we don't have time to litigate that now.

Let me share what we know for certain. Streamers are shape-

shifting, soulless machines that consume all biological materials, living or dead, processed or fossilized. It's DNA they're after, the very building blocks that construct all life as we know it. Why, we don't know. We call them streamers because—just like your wifi at home streams video received in data bytes—they stream DNA data as a three-dimensional, active manifestation. Here, in this slow-motion video captured outside our Ventura facility, you can see a streamer fluctuate from a moth to bacteria to a beetle. These changes are often imperceptible to the naked eye. Given the enormity of life on our planet, all animal, plant and microbes in existence now and extinct, streamers must be collecting vast amounts of information at any given time. For whatever reason, the streamer lingers on certain DNA, holding the pattern of that organism clearly for up to—I believe about 45 seconds is the longest materialization we've seen. I myself have borne witness to everything from a giant earthworm to massive fern plant to a Jurassic-age Eurobrontes—that's a dinosaur, folks. Our scientists may not be able to extract DNA from fossils, but streamers seem to have no problem doing so. Streamers are chaos incarnate. Completely unpredictable, they can pass through solid matter without disruption one second, and the very next can cause more destruction to our property and environment than an F5 tornado.

Now for our introduction to vaks. Vaks are static holes punctured in our reality, anchored by a kinetic firewall that fluctuates like flares on the sun. That firewall serves the same purpose to a vak as an event horizon does to a black hole. Anything that goes beyond that firewall is gone. Where does it go? We don't know. Inside the confines of a vak, our three-dimensional reality is flattened beyond recognition. Essentially, erased. In fact, the center of a vak looks like a clean blackboard, doesn't it? A black wall. We don't know where the information has gone. There is so much we still don't understand. The study of these phenomena is dangerous. Many of my dauntless employees have been lost to streamers, or have lost pieces of themselves to the deadly firewall that surrounds a vak. As for myself, I lost a finger. It's a constant reminder to the risks my people take, so in a way I'm grateful for the loss.

Like any phenomenon, vaks and streamers have a point of origin. A biological point of origin, in fact. This shock to our comfortable reality came from an alteration of the human genome on the quantum level. This quantum alteration was shared by siblings— genetic twins born twelve years apart—entangled beyond the confines of our dimension, beyond our scientific understanding of our universe. Roan Gorey is the source of streamers. Her brother Judge, the vaks. They hail from—locally, anyway—Barre, Massachusetts. Responding to a direct plea for help from parents Sophia and Paul Gorey, we have been housing these children in a secure facility where the best medical care was provided and the finest researchers worked the problem. For the past two years, Dimond Industries has financed the containment effort to protect your families from this environmental impact.

I'm here to report to you today that the Gorey children are in dire jeopardy, and their jeopardy imperils us all. They have been stolen. Taken from our facility by force, and at great cost.

Traitors are responsible for this kidnapping. Traitors to all humanity—no, to all life. This is an unforgivable betrayal, because it was not only meant to harm my company and our shareholders, but because it has put every human being on this planet at greater risk for extinction. Many of these extremists are former employees of Dimond Industries, a company I built from the ground up, now a first-tier subsidiary of global conglomerate Furst Enterprises. The ring leader, it pains to me to say, was the Head of DI's Biotech Divi-

sion. Our top biological engineer. When the discovery of the Gorey children became our burden, Dr. Berit Zook was a crucial member of the team assigned to researching streamers. Much of what we know about the connection Roan Gorey has to the creatures came from her experimental observations. Next on the list of traitors, one of my top security men, Sebastian Cross. We had an opportunity for recapture at the New River Gorge in West Virginia, but Mr. Cross instead enabled Roan Gorey to escape, leading to the tragic loss of one Mr. Matthias Skaggs, a river tour guide who simply was in the wrong place at the wrong time. And finally, Felix Kwan was a high-level technician on our vak team. He helped design and maintain the jetkill, the mechanism that has so far managed to contain the breach between dimensions that exists behind Judge Gorey's malformed eye. This breach is the source of vaks, and it's growing. Without a functional jetkill, a few seconds of malice or accident could cause our entire universe to be erased from existence. Despite this extreme risk, Felix Kwan threw in with this desperate lot when he helped Judge Gorey escape from our Ventura facility.

At this point, I must disclose the magnitude of my own liability, because that is ultimately why I stand before you today. As the new CEO of Furst Enterprises, in every way possible, I own this problem. As far as we know, this is the greatest threat our planet has ever faced. The asteroid that wiped out the dinosaurs was nothing. The Ice Ages were nothing. The threat of nuclear war was nothing. Earthquakes, volcanoes, tsunamis, hurricanes... all nothing compared to this. And this happened in my own backyard, folks. At one of my own biotech subsidiaries.

BioTeatro Labs in Maynard, Massachusetts was a site of sabotage and self-contamination by Sophia Gorey, mother to Roan and Judge. While a young and ambitious academic—if there is such a thing—Mrs. Gorey was conducting a cultural anthropology study on scientists working in the cutting-edge field of synthetic biology. BioTeatro allowed her access to their labs, believing—perhaps naively—that transparency was the best way to communicate their research to the public at large. BioTeatro should not have allowed the level of access that was granted to Sophia Gorey. We will be providing documentation of both Sophia and Paul Gorey's background in environmental terrorism and writings that show insight into the deeply disturbed, anti-humanity philosophy they shared. The details of her espionage at BioTeatro are limited, but this much is certain: Sophia Gorey purposefully exposed herself to contaminants that were part of a quantum biology experiment at BioTeatro. Why on earth would she do this? It's hard to imagine, but as best as we understand her motivations, Sophia planned to sacrifice herself in order to become a modern-day Cassandra. She believed if she shouted loud enough about the risks posed by genetic engineering, and then presented her self-inflicted damages as the undeniable proof of those risks, she might bring a halt to the entire technology. After her exposure, when her own health was not affected, she made no report of the contamination to BioTeatro. She no doubt believed her mission to undermine technological progress had failed. Unknown to the Goreys, the damage had in fact already been done, but not to her. To their unborn children. The conception of Roan and Judge came with a mutation that fundamentally altered their DNA. The double helix structure inside the Gorey twins is warped. Their DNA is not only held together by the usual covalent bonding of nucleotides, but by nanoscopic clusters of singularities. Tiny black holes, if you will. Bubbles in the line, each point an interdimensional entanglement. This otherworldly connection that exists trillions of times over in each of them has broken the rules of our universe. It is the delivery mechanism that has brought us streamers and vaks through Roan and Judge, and there is no cure. Only containment.

As some of you may know, The Human Genome Protection Act is a new law, signed by the President just a few days ago. The law was written to protect the natural state of our human genome from man-made biological alterations that threaten natural heredity, whether accidental or intentional. Sophia Gorey's actions were criminal, there's no denying it. Her contamination at our facility was unintentional, but Furst Enterprises accepts all liability for the unfortunate genetic aberrations that have appeared in her offspring as a result. We must contain these escaped biohazards. We must protect the integrity of humankind.

As long as these children remain at large, streamers and vaks will continue to kill and maim. They will destroy our property, our crops, the very infrastructure of our society. But despite this pervasive danger they pose, I want everyone out there to know, we wish no harm to these children. We merely want to save them from themselves, and to allow them to live their lives in a safe and supportive environment. Unfortunately, a group of extremists have kidnapped them and are holding them hostage, for what purpose, we can only imagine. We are offering a significant monetary reward for information leading us to the children. We need your help to bring this to a safe end.

We would encourage you to confirm this information with the Goreys, but that is now impossible. It saddens me to report this. Paul and Sophia Gorey were killed by their own son. The extremists interfered in our attempt to subdue Judge before he could hurt anyone, and the Gorey parents paid the price. It's a tragic, tragic turn of events. One that could have been avoided.

The Human Genome Protection Act obligates me to finance all efforts of containment and environmental remediation, and demands my leadership in the mitigation of this national security threat. Therefore, under Article Three, Section Two of the Human Genome Protection Act, I invoke the Right of Capture. This article endows me with the authority to direct the efforts of law enforcement to track down these—and forgive me, but this is the technical term most appropriate for these individuals—genetic pollutants. I remain deeply concerned about the danger facing us as a human race, but I am proud to lead Furst Enterprises into a new era of corporate responsibility. The aberrant DNA inside these children is our legal obligation to contain, and I assure you that I will stop at nothing until Roan and Judge Gorey are in our legal custody. If you come across these children, do not attempt to capture them yourself. Call me. This is my mess, and I'm not going to rest until I clean it up. Thank you.

SEQUENCE ONE

PART JUDGE_0001

Closed doors were a familiar feature in the architecture of Judge's world.

Raised in the basement warehouse of a retrofitted Atlas missile silo, Judge had grown accustomed to being stored like a weapon of mass destruction. He didn't take it personally. How could he, after what he did to his own parents?

Emerging from this particular hole in the ground would be magnitudes easier than breaking out of the silo. The door at the top of these stairs wasn't even locked.

The real deterrent had nothing to do with doors *or* locks. It was the Spaghetti Monster he knew was on the other side—or as everyone else called her, Roan. His sister. There was a time when he was more than a fair match for her, but right now he found himself at a distinct disadvantage. The robotic parts of his jetkill—the surgical implant he used to control the vaks—were on the fritz. He was in need of repair.

The misguided crew upstairs kept the basement door unlocked, but that didn't mean they weren't afraid of him. They considered themselves his liberators, so locking him up would clash with that image. Funny that *he* had helped *them* escape the silo, not the other way around, and even if he wasn't locked in down here, he wasn't remotely free. Not as long as the malfunctioning jetkill kept him tethered to their good intentions.

For now, Judge was forced to play the part of grateful refugee and let them believe he was accepting their protection, or guidance, or whatever it was that they were offering. He wasn't exactly clear on the plan, but pretending to defer to their wisdom was the only way to gain their trust. They had something he couldn't leave without: the remote that controlled him.

Less than a week after busting out of the silo, the deluded liberators brought him and the Spaghetti Monster here, a secluded farmhouse surrounded by acres of cranberry bog. The Monster was unconscious. She'd scrambled her brain while performing some kind of Monster rite of passage back at the silo, and for days she slept it off in one of the upstairs bedrooms. She was just as dangerous in a drooling stupor as she was in her usual wide-eyed and wigged-out state of being, because unlike Judge, the Spaghetti Monster had no off switch. She kept churning out those glow-in-the-dark chimera no matter what. 24-7 weird factory, his sister.

While the Monster slept, Judge allowed the grown-ups to care for him like the child they perceived him to be. He let Berit the bioengineer check him over for scrapes and bruises, even though based on her bedside manner, Judge was skeptical of her qualifications to tend to either. He sat nice and still while Felix the tech, hands shaking, assessed the damage sustained to the shutter-like mechanism of the jetkill, the shield that hid the hungry abyss that grew where his eye once was. He even ate the food the British guy U.A. cooked, despite the fact that it was harder to swallow than most of the injustices he'd suffered.

Judge refused, however, to sleep above ground with them. They aggravated him, every last one of them, the way they looked at him with that tedious mixture of concern and apprehension. It almost made him miss Bradley Dimond. Almost.

The soldier who owned the farm made a cozy corner for him in the damp basement. A cot with a sleeping bag next to a desk and a work lamp. Judge wasn't sure why Sergeant Griffith bothered with the desk and the light. Not like Judge had homework to do, or postcards to write. The thought of sending Bradley Dimond a postcard made him smile. *Sunny here. Making new friends and having the adventure of a lifetime. Thinking of you.*

Still, the desk was a nice gesture, even if it smelled of mildew. The rest of the basement was clogged by broken furniture and rusted old farm equipment, tied together by an intricate system of cobwebs. Busted metal claws and misaligned jaws of teeth from harvesting machines looked like leftovers of giant insects enduring a slow digestion inside this massive cocoon. Judge's quarters at the silo had been sterile, so this sudden introduction to rust and decay was as much of a shock to his system as anything else.

Judge had spent his life underground but had never actually smelled the earth. Dimond sealed him in with metal and concrete, separating him from the distracting sensations of life topside. Sure, he'd provided Judge with books and games to occupy his time—his DS was still his most prized possession—but most of his time was spoken for, training in the warehouse, learning how to become the discerning destroyer Dimond always knew he could be.

Even so, the silo had its spiders, too—not to mention bugs in the system. Judge would never have made it out of there otherwise.

Judge had been waiting for days as a reluctant guest in this makeshift B&B for a similar chance to take his leave, and based on the sudden drop in barometric pressure outside and the dust shaking loose from floorboards overhead, opportunity was knocking. Roan had called a streamer.

Judge turned off the work lamp and stood in the well of darkness at the bottom of the stairs, body tense and at the ready. Muffled sounds of an impressive struggle on the ground floor were unmistakable and getting louder. His subterranean territory would soon be under assault, and he knew who was coming for him. Judge's plan depended on his sister's homicidal predictability. She'd create something useful for once— the required distraction for him to steal back the remote. As long as he survived her tantrum, that is.

"Let me THROUGH!"

"She sounds really pissed," Judge muttered. "Beyond reason. Yep, this should work."

The Spaghetti Monster's unforgiving mood was brought on by the news of the atrocity Judge had committed at Point Zero shortly after escaping the silo. Point Zero was the charming nickname Dimond's people gave to the Gorey family home, a term borrowed directly from the CDC that was used to reference the origin of a disease. After he and his disease of a sister got the boot over two years ago, there wasn't much of a family left there. Now there was no one.

A slim blade of light marked the base of the door and cast a waterfall of shadows down the basement stairs. Judge's legs felt heavy as he took one step at a time, careful and deliberate, like he was wading through a strong current instead of rising one measly story. As much as he'd been waiting for this opportunity, he'd been dreading it. He dreaded seeing *her*, the psychotic meatball at the center of a million strands of cooked spaghetti that no one else could see but him. He dreaded seeing the way she always looked at him, like *he* was the monster, not her.

Except now, after what he did at Point Zero, he couldn't deny what he was. A killer.

Scuffling feet got close enough to break up the light slipping under the basement door. The darkened doorway could have been one of his simple vaks, and the strobe effect of light, the deadly firewall that marked its boundary. The last vak he created was anything but simple. His last vak was made not from the basic geometry of inanimate objects he'd practiced on for years, but from the depth and complexity of life. Two lives, to be accurate. Mother. Father.

The house shuddered, and debris from a sudden and strong wind outside battered walls and broke windows. It suddenly occurred to Judge that she may bring down the whole house and bury him down here, so he quickened his pace up the stairs. Adult voices shouting over each other became clearer, but he didn't bother trying to recognize who said what.

"You brought one of those *things* to my front door?"

"Why did you tell her Judge was downstairs?"

"I thought we weren't keeping secrets from them anymore."

"Argue later. Monster outside. In the trees. 50 meters. Getting closer."

"Are we sure it's a streamer? It could just be a storm."

"It's not a storm. I just saw it turn from a squirrel *to* a tree. Oh, and now it's a beetle or something. Yep. A very, very big beetle. Oh that makes my skin crawl."

Judge tried to tune out the growing panic. He focused on listening for one particular voice—his sister's—and for the familiar crashing and crunching sounds of her rambunctious pet playing in the yard outside.

"Can she risk releasing it?" Walt asked. Poor dumb Walt. "What if there's somebody inside?"

Yes, there's that. Judge wasn't the only killer under the roof. There'd been two people inside the streamer she sent packing outside the silo, and only one of them made it out alive when the ritual was complete. That poor sap was recuperating in one of the upstairs bedrooms. From what Judge had gathered from overheard conversations, the guy wasn't exactly free to go. Liberty was spread thin under this roof.

"She didn't bring it here for target practice." That was former security goon Cross, no doubt about it. "She brought it here to sic on Judge. If we get in the way, too bad for us."

"This could be unintentional. She can't control them completely. You know that." That had to be Berit, Roan's one-woman legal defense team.

"Maybe it'll pass us by." U.A.'s British accent was masked by how much his voice was shaking. "I watched the one that took my nephews stroll off into the desert. It left me alone."

"We're not in a desert. I have neighbors. Families." Judge heard something that could only have been Griff punching the wall. "She has to kill it."

"It's not alive."

"I don't care! We *are* alive and it's coming for us. She has to do something."

"So much for laying low." Felix must have been close to the door when he said that because Judge heard it as clearly as if he were standing right next to him.

"It's his fault. It's all his fault. JUST LET ME THROUGH. Just open the door. This has to end!"

"Roan, it was an accident."

"*He's* the accident."

"He didn't mean to kill them."

"He didn't *mean* to kill them?"

"Just like you didn't *mean* to kill Nuñez, right?" Cross again.

A window shattered, and the Spaghetti Monster seized the moment. She yanked open the door and stood eyes agape before him, hair disheveled like a cartoon mad scientist. She grabbed a fistful of his shirt and nearly knocked him back down the stairs. The sudden jerk to catch himself on the handrail popped open the jetkill. Felix snapped it shut again with the safety remote faster than any gunslinger could have, but not before Judge took a shot.

Cross was already pulling Roan back, and Griff had clamped down on her arm, so the vak claimed the shadows between the three of them. Shadow vaks were some of the strangest mind-benders he created, and that was saying something. Only the outline of what was remained, a coil of deadly light marking its territory. Despite the early name given to them, vaks were no vacuum. What vaks were *exactly* was still open for debate, but he liked to think of them as points of exchange. What existed was exchanged for its counterpart, what didn't. The hole in his head provided the trade route for the information, courtesy of the anchor dropped in the other dimension where he spent his first twelve years—or more accurately, his twelve *non*-years.

"Watch it!" cried Berit.

Griff arched away from the thin, jagged slice of abyss like he was trying to dodge a bullet. Judge had purposefully missed all of them—he'd even avoided stray threads on the cotton blends they wore—but did they notice? No appreciation for his skills.

Griff tumbled back into the part of his kitchen that still clung to its mundane existence, and Cross yanked so hard on the Spaghetti Monster she brushed against the firewall. Static-charged ends of her hair dropped to the linoleum, and she yelped in pain, falling into Cross and clutching her ear.

"Nobody move!" ordered Griff, arms wide as if he was parting the sea.

Nobody moved. Silence followed, as if the vak was a drain on all sound.

The streamer outside got jealous for attention and started breaking more windows and rattling doors. *What a prima donna,* Judge thought.

"That thing's going to tear this place apart," Cross said.

"*Which* thing?" Griff asked, eyes locked onto the shadow-vak. He turned quickly to Judge and added, "You took a shot at me in my own house."

Judge shrugged. "I missed, didn't I?"

"Am I supposed to say thank you?"

"Your call."

"Walt," Berit said calmly. "Get Roan's gear."

Walt bounced up the stairs. *Good boy, Walt. Good boy.* Walter Hale was the all-American, dopey-as-hell neighbor boy back at Point Zero, not to mention the Spaghetti Monster's long-suffering best friend—well, *only* friend as far as Judge knew.

"Roan," Berit continued sternly. "Let me see."

Cross peeled the Spaghetti Monster's hands away from her

ear. Blood streamed down her neck from a divot in her ear the size of a dime.

"Superficial," Cross assessed. "On your feet, kid. Work to do."

Cross yanked her up, and for a split second Judge met his sister's eyes.

Not all moments in time are equal. That particular one shared by Judge and his sister was weighted with grief and heated to an unbearable degree by pure hatred, the only warmth she'd ever sent his way. Judge felt scalded. Ashamed. He looked away.

The sooner he got out of here, the better.

Griff tried to work his way around the shadow-vak but gave up. He headed for the side door in the kitchen instead, yelling to Cross, "I'll meet you in the front. Sounds like it's coming from the northwest."

Cross started barking orders of his own. "U.A., you're staying with Judge. Felix, give him the remote. You're with me outside."

"No way," Felix said. "I'll take my chances with Judge, thanks."

Cross wrenched the remote from Felix and shoved it into U.A.'s shaking hands. U.A. aimed it at Judge like a gun. Judge thought that was funny, so he said "You got me" and leaned against the doorframe with his hands raised in surrender.

"Behave," Cross said to Judge. "No more misfires."

"If you'd just give me the remote—"

"Not a chance," Cross cut off Judge as he shoved Felix toward the front door.

"No no no," Felix whined. "What am I going to do out there? There's nothing *I* can do."

"I don't trust you enough to turn my back on you."

"I tried to make *one* phone call. Some of us still have families that worry," Felix protested. "That's no reason to treat me like a traitor."

"It's reason enough for me."

Cross half-carried the limp Spaghetti Monster toward the door, covering Felix's retreat attempts like a soccer player advancing a reluctant ball to the goalpost. Berit followed on his heels, trying awkwardly to keep a cloth napkin to his sister's bleeding ear. Cross finally nudged her back and said, "You stay inside."

"Why does *she* get to stay inside?" Felix complained.

"Because if I need to distract the streamer by tossing it some bones, I'd prefer to use yours."

"Real nice," Felix said.

"Keep your head down out there, Felix," Judge suggested. "It's what you're good at."

At the silo, Felix was the closest thing to a friend that Judge had. That is, until he went along with Dimond's orders and strapped him to a gurney in order to convert him into a remote-controlled robot. Very uncool.

Walt picked this moment to bound victoriously down the steps with a trumpet case and what looked like a hockey helmet.

"I found it in a closet upstairs," Walt explained, raising the helmet with a smile.

Felix grabbed it and said, "Thanks, man."

Before Felix could get it on his head, Walt grabbed it back and said, "It's for *Roan*."

While Walt and Felix argued over who needed the helmet more, Berit snatched the case and popped it open. The glow from the vak inside drew Judge closer. He allowed himself to admire his handiwork, even if it was the result of another misfire. During the silo escape, Judge had been faced with a conundrum: either target the axe-head of the Lakota tomahawk from Dimond's collection, or take out the dumbass-head of Walt who happened to be hiding right behind it. In that one discriminating second, Judge had inadvertently invented the hand-held device that would enable the Spaghetti Monster to conduct her barbaric ritual of slicing streamers open. He felt some regret about that, if only because he knew he'd never get the full credit he deserved.

The tomahawk was a thing of beauty. The wooden handle, still adorned by beads and feathers, supported the axe head-shaped hole in space-time as sturdily as it had the heft of sharpened metal. Judge did his best work under pressure.

The other apparatus in the case must have been what they called the amplifier, a tool Berit developed while playing super spy at the silo. Evidently, the amp gave the Spaghetti Monster a window into her own reality, the tangled mess she really was. Wearing the amp, she was forced to see herself as the true monster Judge could *and would* always see. How her disgusting tentacles spread out in all conceivable directions like a silly string road map to each and every streamer out there. And there were plenty out there. The amp highlighted the right string to cut, or chord to strike, as her team liked to put it, probably because it sounded more musical, less violent. That strike sent the streamer home and sent its guts flying all over creation.

Berit helped the Spaghetti Monster slip the tripped-out glove over her bloody hand and the matching belt around her waist. The amp lit up like Christmas.

"Roan, look at me," Berit said.

"I'm not finished with him."

"Come on, Sis, *focus*," Judge taunted. He just couldn't help himself.

"Please don't," Berit said to Judge, and then back to coaching the meatball. "You brought a streamer here. You have to do this."

Berit placed the tomahawk in her hand, and the Spaghetti Monster answered "First things first." She shoved Berit aside and leapt at Judge, aiming to take his head off.

"Whoops," Judge said, and he tried to shrink into the wall. He heard U.A. preemptively clicking the remote at him so much he sounded like a member of the paparazzi. If Judge could have taken a shot, he would have, but his stupid jetkill wouldn't respond.

Lightning quick, Cross jumped in front of Judge to block the attack. Cross forced the Spaghetti Monster back, keeping her tomahawk-yielding hand at arm's length.

"Thanks, Sebastian," Judge said. He was surprised by how much he meant it.

"Stow it, Judge," Cross spat. And then to Berit, with equal irritation, "Still think it was a good idea to keep them under the same roof?"

"What choice do we have?" Berit said.

They were poor surrogate parents, these two. Cross with his history of being one of Dimond's top security hounds and Berit one of his top bioengineers, now they shared the top two spots on the Most Wanted List of every law enforcement agency on the planet. It was bound to cause some friction in their romance. Bonnie and Clyde had a better chance of a happy ending.

Cross opened the front door and invited the wind inside. Griff's unopened mail on a nearby desk lifted off into the kitchen, some committing hara-kiri on the shadow-vak. Others stuck like glue to U.A. until he shook them off.

Felix looked like he might pass out as Cross shoved him out the door ahead of the Spaghetti Monster. Berit followed despite the disapproving look Cross gave her, and Walt chased them with the helmet. Poor dumb Walt.

U.A. rushed to close the door, still clicking the remote at Judge with trembling hands.

"You can stop that now," Judge said. "We're alone." *Alone at last*, he thought to himself.

"Oh, right," U.A. said, and he exhaled loudly. "I just didn't want you to... you know..."

"Accidently send the universe down the toilet?"

"Yes, that."

U.A. paced the foyer, checking the streamer's position outside but keeping one eye on Judge. Judge tried not to stare at the remote too much. He didn't want to telegraph his move and blow his chance. Besides, before he made a play for the remote, he needed his stuff.

"Be right back," Judge said suddenly, ducking down the basement steps before U.A. could say more than "Oi!"

Judge tossed his essentials into his messenger bag—DS, hoodie, stuffed bunny—gave a quick farewell to his second subterranean dwelling, and met U.A. at the top of the stairs.

"Did I miss anything?" Judge asked, slipping past him.

"N-no," U.A. said, raising the remote again. "I don't think

so. Hard to say."

Shouts outside got swallowed up by the howling wind.

"Yeesh. Sounds like she's got her hands full," Judge said, casually slinging his messenger bag over his shoulder. "She swiped your boy band away with one of those things, didn't she?"

U.A.'s demeanor changed in an instant, and Judge realized he made a miscalculation.

"*Boy band*?" U.A. challenged, letting the remote drop. "*Knotty Bits* are no boy band."

"My bad," Judge said. "I've been living under a rock my whole life. What do I know?"

"I'd be happy to educate you," U.A. said, "once this disturbance is over."

"Right," Judge said. "After Sis pops the balloon animal, everything should settle down, sure. But wait. Oh, man. Do you think there's a chance your nephews could be inside that very streamer outside right now? What happens to them if she lights the fuse and that bomb goes off? They could get squashed like bugs just like Nuñez back at the silo."

"I know what you're trying to do," U.A. said. "I'm not going to leave you alone in here."

"But you have to stop her," Judge said. "Don't you think?"

"Nobody else seemed to think so."

"I didn't hear a call for votes exactly. But I suppose debate takes time. Never much of that, is there? Not with the Spaghetti Monster setting her bio-traps around us every other second. But then again, that's probably how she likes it. Right?"

Judge finally got what he was waiting for. For a split second, U.A. glanced at the front door. Judge snatched the remote and shouted "Aha!" Again, he couldn't help himself.

U.A. lunged at him, but a wheelbarrow crashing through the window gave him the cover he needed to snake under the shadow-vak toward the kitchen exit. The vak might as well have been a force field for the effect it had on keeping U.A. at bay.

"Judge," U.A. pleaded from the other side of the divide. "No. Don't leave."

"Sorry, U.A," Judge said. "You don't get a vote on this either. And do yourself a favor," he added, tapping the remote against his closed jetkill. "Don't follow me."

PART ROAN_0001

RED. ROAN WAS SEEING RED.

Her heart pounded so hard there was a strong whooshing in her ears. Nothing was familiar. Not the house, not her clothes, not even the voices screaming at her to snap out of it.

The lit diodes of the amplifier gave her left arm fluorescent freckles while the waistband accessory drained her body of its warmth. The tomahawk glowed in her other hand, the space around its vak axe-head bending like a funhouse mirror. She ran her thumb across the crudely engraved word on its handle, Riven. It might as well have been carved into her own flesh.

She felt torn apart. The core of her, ripped out.

Her parents were gone. Really gone. She'd been so angry the last time she'd seem them, so hurt, they must have thought she hated them. Maybe she did, a little, for handing her over to Bradley Dimond so easily. One interdimensional tantrum. That's all it took. Still, not something that decades of family therapy couldn't repair. They'd had a good run, after all, before Judge turned everything inside out. She'd protected them as best she could. Now there was no future that included them. No awkward Thanksgivings where Roan would inevitably bring up her parent-sanctioned stint at the silo. No passive-aggressive birthday exchanges that would remind everyone of the two she'd spent as a science experiment. No future. All past.

Strong hands guided her outside. She just found out she was

an orphan, and they expected her to work. When the hands let go, Roan crumpled like a discarded marionette.

Something big flew over her head and crashed through a window. Might have been a wheelbarrow. A streamer in motion stirred up the turbulence of a tornado. All you saw was a whirlwind of debris until it was right on top of you, and by then your brain refused to accept what your eyes saw. If you survived long enough to snap out of *that*, it didn't help your fragile frame of mind that when you call 911 to report what is right in front of you, you'd get the same brush-off as a yokel reporting a UFO sighting, or a run-in with Big Foot.

Until ten minutes ago.

Ten minutes ago, the whole world was shown just how *real* streamers were and that she was the one who created them. In a news conference that took less time to digest than a pop-up ad, Chief Evil Operator Bradley Dimond had sold her parents down the river and set the entire human race after her. His version of events was now the standard explanation for streamers and vaks, and the two people who could have challenged the claim best—Sophia and Paul Gorey—were dead.

"Hey!" Felix shouted in her face. "That streamer got your invitation. This is your party. Do something!"

"She just needs a kick start," Cross said, moving toward her menacingly.

Walt stepped in front of her, knocking Cross back with a stiff arm to his chest. Cross looked like he was going to push back, but Berit inserted herself between them and said, "Stop it! Not now."

Cross backed off, waving his arms in frustration like a gorilla, and shouted, "Then let's just take a running jump into that thing and get it over with already."

"That guy needs some anger management sessions," Walt said, trying to smile despite the stinging wind. "Here," he added, trying to force what looked like a hockey helmet over her head. "Put this on."

She knocked it away. "Just get out of here."

"And go where?"

"You still have a home."

"Do I?"

Walt had a point. His mom and sister were missing. His father, Senator Nathan Hale, was last seen standing next to Dimond during the global declaration of war against her, nodding his head in time with the many anti-Roan points of propaganda. Mr. Hale had never been a fan. No doubt her history of getting Walt into trouble was a factor, but this alliance wasn't just about a mutual dislike of her. Playing the part of Dimond's wing man would keep Walt's face out of the Most Wanted line-up. For now.

Walt still had a chance at a family reunion, even if he didn't want to admit it. Keeping that streamer from making Walt part of its playlist in the meantime, that was on her.

The luminous creature bounced among the trees at the bog's edge, chasing the last fireflies of summer by *becoming* the last fireflies of the summer. It's what streamers do. Not alive themselves, streamers were shape-shifters fueled by life itself. Or so she was told. You'd think she'd know more about the things, since they wouldn't exist if it weren't for her, but she knew just as little about streamers as she did about the microbes living on her own eyelashes. She knew they were there, and she wished they weren't. That was about it.

Strange blue spheres of light ricocheted around the streamer's dark prison, looking like glow-in-the-dark pill bugs trapped in a mason jar. Roan didn't know what those things were, and she didn't care. Her only concern was the actual life held captive in there. Whatever the streamer absorbed left behind a 3D recording on the surface, like a holographic picture of the moment of capture, before doing a deep dive into another dimension. A streamer flashed between the lifeforms it collected so fast it was hard to distinguish microbe from mushroom from mouse, but every few seconds it would settle on a particular creature or plant and project it in complete perfection, down to the last scale or feather, petal or leaf, like it was showing off a prized possession.

"It's so beautiful," Berit said in a hushed voice. Cross pulled Berit back, like a grown-up might corral a Thomas-fanatic toddler away from a train approaching a station.

Roan did her best to ignore the streamer's light show. Her business was its trace, the umbilical between them. The amp worked its magic, turning the trace into a bright red line for her to distinguish it from all the other jumbled chords around her. For a split second she wondered how it would work if there were two streamers nearby. She shut down that thread before it paralyzed her.

The mess of information the amplifier showed her was nauseating. For one, it proved how accurate Judge's nickname for her was. *Spaghetti Monster.* The chords really were like tangled spaghetti strings, if spaghetti were made of an invisible material that could stretch to infinity and repair any damage instantaneously. And two, the amp revealed how suffocating her reality was. The chords afforded her no space. Wrapped up like a second-hand mummy, she was stuck in a constant struggle between freshly spun binds and unstoppable unraveling. As much as she wanted to puke, she knew she had no time for it.

The streamer had departed the far tree line and was creeping across the cranberry bog, its dense leafy collection giving it a thorny blob look. Plant life tended to slow a streamer down, but it was still coming their way.

She began to wade through the knotted chords to follow the streamer's trace, studying it for weakness. It wasn't enough to cut through the chord; the strike had to hit the right spot, a flyaway bend or loop, or the rest of the chords would instantly repair the cut.

A bight, her dad would call it. He knew knots from his time in the Boy Scouts. Thinking of her dad as a young Boy Scout gave her a sharp pain in her gut that she almost couldn't bear. She pushed the thought aside. No time for it. No time for pain or fear or puke.

"What are you waiting for?" Cross yelled. Man, she hated that guy. Maybe she could let the streamer take a nibble on him before she released it. What would be the harm in that?

She passed Griff as she pushed closer. He leaned into the wind as he watched the streamer's constant transformation, muttering, "Please please please don't be in there."

That interdimensional tantrum—the one that had convinced her parents to give her away—had delivered a streamer to the center of a crowded fairgrounds. Griff's wife and young son had been stolen from their Ferris wheel bucket. His hunt for them had led him to the silo, where he'd witnessed firsthand what happened to Nuñez during her first streamer eviction.

Crushed by a tree. As much as he wanted his family back, the odds were against both making it out safely. For now, limbo was the better option.

The anguished look on Griff's face was a harsh reminder that the streamer kept its collection secret, even from her. It was a wrong move, calling it here. Whatever happened next was *her* fault. If someone inside got hurt on the way out, she'd have to live with that.

"Stop him!" Cross shouted, just as someone shoved her, hard. She went face first into the grass, her nose centimeters from Riven's non-blade.

"He's going for my Chevy," Griff said, his priorities clear.

Matthias Skaggs charged over her, panicked as a jack rabbit. He jumped into Griff's 4x4 and fumbled to get the stolen keys in the ignition while Cross pounded on the glass. The old truck roared to life, and Matthias charged away. Cross kept one foot on the sideboard, doing his best to break the window. The wheels bounced over a hole, and Cross flew off, splashing down in the bog.

Berit ran to him, her voice calling his name getting lost in the wind.

"Oooh, that had to hurt," Felix said, not bothering to hide his smile.

"Where does he think he's going?" Griff said as he watched Matthias follow the hard angles of the road bordering the soggy fields.

"Home," Walt answered. "To his son."

"He'll never get past that thing," Felix said, more amused than anything. "He's toast."

"No," Roan said. "He's not."

If Matthias wanted out of here, she'd clear the way. He wasn't making it easy. He aimed the stolen truck straight at the streamer like he was on a suicide mission.

The red of the trace stood out like an artery flush with blood, and the idea of slicing through it made Roan even more nauseous. When a bight suddenly appeared, a nice fat loop, Roan swung at it like a major leaguer. The force of the disconnect sent her flying, and in that moment of weightlessness Roan found herself wishing she'd taken Walt up on that helmet.

PART MATTHIAS_0001

THE CHEVY WAS HELTER SKELTER ON TWO wheels before Matthias even registered the impact. A blast of small rocks smashed through the windshield like a giant scatter gun had opened up on him. He fully expected the truck to roll over into the bog, but the old girl found her balance again and bounced down to all fours.

Matthias punched the gas so hard his foot should've gone clear through the floorboard, but something was blocking the pedal. The engine lost steam, started to coast.

"That won't do," Matthias said, reaching down to dig whatever it was out of the way. Felt like slimy rocks.

He stomped on the pedal again and took off. A quick check in his mirror showed him the explosion had knocked his overbearing hosts off their feet, but he wasn't taking any chances. He would keep that Chevy at top speed until he was sure he was well and clear of them. They hadn't tied him up yet, but only because he was making out like he was more injured than he was. Didn't know what they had in store for him, and he didn't care to find out. When the boy, Walt, snuck him the truck keys and said it was time to go, Matthias took his chances and went.

Hurtling over the pockmarked dirt road, Matthias scanned the dark woods, scared as a pollywog in the shadow of a hunting heron. If one of those monsters was out here, there could be more. He'd done time inside one and had no intention of making a return visit.

What it had been like inside that thing—he didn't have the words. Maybe the closest thing was getting stuck in an elevator. Happened to him once, back at the Bentley mine when he was just a few weeks out of high school. Him and three other guys changing shifts. Lights had gone off. Lift motor ground to a full stop. Metal clunked when the elevator dropped a few inches from the sudden slack in the cable. Nobody'd said a word at first, then one guy cracked a joke, and the rest of them laughed even though it wasn't that funny. Elevator wasn't going anywhere, but their fear rose up the shaft, like a ladder made from pure panic.

Stuck deep in that strange beast's belly, there'd been no uncertain voices around him like there'd been in the elevator. No one's unsteady breathing, shuffling feet. Saying there was nothing didn't even come close. Nothing implies there'd once been something—dark where there'd been light, silence where there'd been sound. It wasn't like that, like *nothing*. He'd been reduced to a single point, like a dot on a piece of paper. It'd didn't hurt. He didn't feel a thing. No need of air or food or drink. Still had his thoughts, though. They buzzed around inside that tiny point, racing like the undercurrent of the New River, then flowing slow as coal slurry.

Had occurred to him that maybe he was dead or dying. Last thing he could remember was guiding the jet boat through the rapids to deliver that girl and her friend to safety, when he got hit by a tear gas canister and fell overboard. Couldn't recall fighting the current to reach the surface, and that just didn't make sense. He was a strong swimmer. Should've made it back up easily, even with busted ribs. Instead, he was stuck on another elevator, of a different variety. Put on hold between darkness and light. Nothing and something.

Certain thoughts would come to him like bait on a fishing line. Memories of his son Trev kept bouncing out of reach, frantic flies on an untouchable surface that sensed his desperation to catch them. But one thought dropped down to him on a sinker, and he latched onto it. That thought was of the girl, the one he'd tried to help. The one who got him into this mess. He tugged and pulled on the idea of tracking her down and forcing her to undo her strange magic. Convinced himself he was getting close to finding her. By some miracle, it wasn't a delusion.

The moment she sprung him from that prison was as painful and confusing as being born into this world must've been the first time.

Since then, memories of the nowhere place became muddled, like a puzzle of a dream that wasn't worth putting back together.

Matthias was snapped back into the now when the Chevy's wheels caught some air before meeting pavement. The dirt drive had emptied him onto a road, and Matthias jerked the steering wheel to stay with it, swerving all over. He had to clear rocks from under the pedal again to get the Chevy back up to speed, and Matthias drove like a madman to put distance between him and the nightmare behind him. A few minutes and ten miles later, he allowed himself a quick whoop of victory.

It was a short celebration. He discovered the gas gauge near empty and his wallet gone—either it was at the bottom of the river, or his kidnappers had taken it. Filling the Chevy meant finding a car that didn't have a lock on the gas tank. Older models. Hadn't siphoned gas since he was a teenager, but figured it would come back to him. Just like riding a bike.

If he drove all night, he should be home by noon the next day. No way to call home, but maybe that was for the best for now. Overheard enough from that upstairs bedroom to know that his captors were *wanted* with a capital W. He'd have to re-enter his life carefully, in case there was a misunderstanding about his role in all of it. Guilty by association was a phrase that came to mind. Contaminated was another.

Matthias found a tattered map stuck to the visor, and he studied it while he drove. He figured out pretty fast where he was and where he needed to go. Having a plan calmed him down enough to notice he needed to make a quick stop to clear out the cab. The same rocks that broke through the windows kept blocking the pedals.

Not rocks.

Clam shells.

PART JUDGE_0002

JUDGE WATCHED THE STREAMER EXPLOSION from the cover of trees behind Griff's house. When a giraffe— a *giraffe*—began to lope his way in confusion, Judge knew it was time to get moving. The strap of his messenger bag got stuck on something, so he gave it a yank. Turned out it wasn't snagged. It was clenched in U.A.'s fist.

"I can't let you go any further," U.A. said.

"Sure you can," Judge said, "because you like having two arms."

U.A.'s fingers reluctantly uncurled from the strap as he stepped from behind a tree.

"Henry, please—" U.A. stopped himself, dropped his head. "I mean, *Judge*. Blast it. You remind me of Henry."

"I don't remind anybody of anybody," Judge said. "But nice try."

"I just meant this isn't the first time I've chased down a runaway."

"I'm not running away," Judge said. "I'm walking. This way."

The crunch of the giraffe stepping into the trees behind U.A. gave them both a start. It wore a lei of seaweed around its neck.

"You see that too, right?" U.A. asked.

"Yep."

"How on earth did a giraffe get in the mix?" U.A. pondered.

"Streamers get around."

"Poor thing," U.A. continued. "Probably scared out of its wits."

Judge shrugged, suggested he "Call Animal Control," and took the opposite path. He could hear U.A.'s footsteps on the dried leaves behind him. Irritating.

"Fame can be overwhelming," U.A. mused, as if Judge had come to him for advice. "It's not for everyone. It's for no one, actually. It is an unnatural state for a single human being to be known by that many other human beings. It breaks our reluctant agreement with the universe that none of us really matter. Not in the long run. Not if we can just be snuffed from existence at any given moment, like an ant under your heel."

"Let me guess," Judge said. "U.A. stands for Unhappy Analogies."

"No."

"Unnecessary Altogether?"

"Not quite."

"Unfortunately Absent?" Judge shot a look over his shoulder to add some heft to that threat, but U.A. didn't flinch this time.

"It's for Uncle Archie," U.A. said flatly, as if it pained him to explain. He changed the subject quickly. "Henry wanted to run away from the spotlight, just like you."

"It's not the spotlight I'm worried about," Judge said. "It's the crosshairs."

"And you'd rather face that alone?"

Judge was alone even when he wasn't alone, but explaining that to U.A. would be a waste of breath. He knew the real reason why this guy was following him. He wanted his name to mean something. He still wanted to be an uncle.

"I can't bring Henry and the others back. Only she can. You don't need me," Judge said, pushing some low branches out of his way. "Besides, *she* wants me gone. The longer I stick around, the more collateral giraffe. You know?"

"But none of us stands a chance if something happens to you."

"I can take care of myself."

"You're unstable, Judge," U.A. said. Judge gave him a hard look, so U.A. tried to lighten the message by adding, "If there's one thing you need for a solo career, it's stability. The band won't be there to back you up."

"I don't need *the band*," Judge said, waving the remote in U.A.'s face. "I have this."

U.A. lunged for the remote, and Judge took a quick step back.

"Dear Uncle Archie," Judge said, trying to keep his voice under control, "I'm fighting a strong urge to give you a very close shave."

"I'm sorry. I really am. But I had to try."

"So tell me, U.A.," Judge said. "What makes you qualified to save the world?"

When U.A. gave no reply, Judge turned and stomped angrily through the undergrowth.

"What if you come back, and we let you keep the remote?" U.A. stammered. "I get it, okay? You've spent enough time under the control of others. But I hate to break this to you, Judge. Talent of your magnitude requires management."

"Are you actually pitching your services? Let me save you some trouble. I'm not hiring."

"Talent requires management and *maintenance*," U.A. said, more forcefully this time.

Judge knew what he was getting at. Judge was damaged goods. Literally.

"It's just hardware," Judge said. "It can be fixed."

"So you're going to pop into the local mechanic? Maybe you'll find a coupon for a free oil change while you're at it."

"Undeniable Ass. That's the one, I think."

"Seriously, Judge," U.A. said, sounding more and more desperate. "Do you really think you're going to find someone out there to trust? Who is going to fix you without claiming you as their prize, just like that other bloke did?"

Judge stopped in his tracks. He'd been so focused on severing ties with the group and getting as far from the Spaghetti Monster as possible that he'd ignored a critical problem with his plan. He needed a new jetkill, *yesterday*, and the only person qualified to install one was back at the house. Felix.

"Please. You have to come back with me," U.A. said. "I've lost too many boys on my watch. I can't lose another."

"I'm not yours to lose," Judge said.

PART CROSS_0001

TIME TO MOVE OUT. IF ROAN HADN'T CALLED a streamer, if they'd restrained Matthias, if Judge hadn't created a mini Grand Canyon in Griff's kitchen, if a dozen other things had gone their way instead of against, they could've stayed here a while, made progress on the forward strategy, healed from injuries.

But hoping for things not to go to hell around the Gorey twins was like hoping for time to stop. It was their nature, their instinct, to destroy. Cross didn't care if they were victims of whatever dimensional screw-up happened inside their nano parts just as they were making their way into being. He didn't even care if it was a cruel joke of Mother Nature, or if the truth was closer to what his former boss Bradley Dimond was peddling. No matter how it happened and whose fault it was or wasn't, Roan and Judge reminded him of just about every other teenager he'd ever met. Self-absorbed, spiteful, and in a lot of ways, just plain stupid. The fact that these two came equipped with tools capable of sculpting and swiping away life, in addition to the usual dose of hormones and bad attitude, made it crystal clear to Cross that there was nothing useful to be done in their vicinity but provide close-range target practice for them.

Sopping wet from getting dunked in the cranberry bog—twice—Cross dragged himself to where Berit knelt, absentmindedly brushing twigs out of her hair, and collapsed next to her.

"*Now* will you run away with me?" he said.

"She's getting better at it already," Berit said, and he could swear, even in the darkness, that he saw a smile on her face. *A smile.* "Did you see how fast she released that streamer?"

"Uh, no," Cross said. "I was too busy getting run over."

"Didn't anyone ever tell you not to chase cars?" Berit bent over to wipe some blood from his forehead and kissed him in the clean spot. "You okay?"

"Not remotely."

"We should check on the others," she said, standing unsteadily and offering him a hand up. He moved in slow motion on purpose, partly because that was the only way his stiff body wanted to move but mostly because he was in no hurry to check on the others. Scattered around the farmhouse, each of them was shaking off the experience of being tossed like a ragdoll by Roan's supernatural Rottweiler at their own pace. Griff was already back on his feet, Felix was recovering from a fetal position, and Walt was helping Roan detangle from a cluster of nets that had broken her fall. Cross knew he had a few more feet at most to speak his mind before the others would hear.

"It's only a matter of time, Berit. It's now or never. A buddy of mine lives in Gloucester, fishes for Atlantic Cod. He could smuggle us out, get us to Nova Scotia maybe. Maybe even Greenland."

"She needs to learn how to control them," Berit said, ignoring him. "But she looked like a natural with the apparatus, don't you think?"

"Oh sure, she'll be going pro soon," Cross said. He grabbed

Berit by the arm to give himself a few more seconds alone with her. "You got her away from Dimond. You've given her the tools she needs. The rest is up to her. I think what she needs most from us now is space. And a lot of it. She needs to find her own way."

"She's just a child, Sebastian. An orphan."

"Not our fault."

"There's evidence to the contrary on that one."

"You still feel guilty about the silo."

"I wish you felt a little more guilt, to be honest."

"It does no one any good to become sentimental about those two," Cross said, pulling her close to emphasize. "It's dangerous."

"You know me better than that. I don't have a sentimental bone in my body."

It was true. Her clinical detachment was what attracted Cross to her in the first place. Now she spent half her time playing mother, and she was predictably lousy at it. Saying Berit had been raised by wolves was an insult to the motherly instincts of a she-wolf.

"You're trying to be something you're not," Cross said.

"I know I'm not her mother, Sebastian."

"You're not her Yoda, either."

The blank look on Berit's face reminded him of her Amish upbringing. Most references to pop culture resulted in that look. She basically grew up in the 17th century and never bothered to fill in gaps that didn't involve microbiology. In some very real ways, Berit was as alien as the Bringer and Taker.

"You know, short green guy?" he tried again.

"Don't you mean Kermit?"

"No," Cross sighed. Forgetting their circumstances for a moment, he did his best Yoda voice, "Backward sentences, he speaks?"

"Did you finally hit your noggin' too hard, Cross?" Felix asked.

"I know who Yoda is," Berit chuckled, and she tugged on his harm playfully like they were on a date instead of slogging through God knows what. "Vijay had a Yoda on his desk that came to life whenever you triggered its motion sensor. Was really annoying."

"Vijay was really annoying."

"Poor Vijay."

Cross shrugged indifferently. He noticed the ground crunched beneath his feet like it would on a rocky beach. Mussel and clam shells. Sea slugs. And lots of crabs, some dead, some scurrying through the grass in search of shelter. The smell of ocean was overpowering. His proposed Gloucester to Greenland getaway seemed less pragmatic. Streamers were all over.

"What is that crap on my house?" Griff stood square-armed and lock-jawed in the yard, surveying the damage caused by the streamer's noisy exit.

Mixed in with the slimy salad of seaweed and algae, a strange blubbery substance oozed from the eaves and gutters and dropped onto the shrubs below. Jellyfish? Maybe part of a whale?

"Stand back," Cross ordered, pulling Griff back. Griff bristled at Cross bossing him around in his own backyard, but he took a few steps back anyway.

"*What is it?*" Griff asked again. "Streamer guts?"

"It's all over the trees, too," Felix observed. "And in the grass over there."

"Right along the perimeter of the blast radius," Griff said. "Why is it glowing like that? Is it radioactive?"

Cross's old instincts kicked in, and he scanned the scene for his young charges. Walt comforted Roan while she sobbed and hurled. They were too close to the questionable goo-cicles, so Cross relocated them to a safe patch of grass.

Berit crouched close to a pool of the strange substance. She poked it with a stick, then twirled some on the end in order to observe it closer.

"I think it's bioshell," Berit said.

"You've seen this stuff before?"

"On Griff and Walt," Berit said. "Those spots on their faces and hands. They must've been exposed outside the silo."

"Exposed?" Griff said, turning his hands over and inspecting his collection of shiny scars. "Exposed to what exactly? You said these scars were temporary."

"I thought they might be," she said dismissively. "I could be wrong."

Walt started to rub his jaw where he had a similar thin line of iridescent scar tissue, like he was trying to wipe it off. Understandable.

"Berit," said Cross sternly, taking her elbow. He could see she was in one of her obnoxious states of *I'm thinking too hard right now to help you catch up* and he needed to get her attention. "What the hell is bioshell?"

"Streamer skin," Felix said. When everyone looked at him, he shrugged. "Don't look at me. I just read her reports."

"*Bioshell* was the name our team gave to the exterior of a

streamer's anatomy," Berit explained. "The membrane—its boundary, its *skin*—separates our reality from whatever anti-reality exists *inside* a streamer."

"Looks like its anti-reality sneezed all over my house," Griff said, watching the bioshell drop in large slabs off his damaged roof. A quick survey of the extent of destruction to his family home slumped his shoulders into resignation. He mumbled, "I'm gonna do a quick recon of the debris field, confirm nobody was inside that thing."

"Good idea," Berit said, not looking up. Too obsessed by her swab of streamer skin to care about anything else. She lifted and lowered the sample, observing how the stuff moved. "Ignores gravity. Seeks out a break in the organic tissue to repair it. Or maybe not repair. Just bridge the gap. Fill in the hole. Mimic. *Wow.*"

"That's very scientific, sweetheart," Cross said, trying not to hurl, "but we need to discuss our extraction plan."

"Extraction?" she repeated, and then lit up with a loud, "Yes!"

She shot straight up so fast that some of the bioshell flicked off her stick in Felix's direction. He twisted his body around to avoid the volley.

"Watch it!" he shouted.

"The bus," she said, swinging around with the stick so that Cross had to jump out of the way. "We can store the bioshell in the baggage compartment."

"I don't give a rat's ass about the streamer snot," he said.

"He means we should extract *ourselves* from this location, because of the hillbilly on the loose," Felix said, kicking at the bioshell globs. "Only a matter of time before he leads the police here. We should split up. Go our separate ways. Become spectators like the rest of the world. Hope for the best."

Cross found himself in agreement with Felix, but his affirmation stuck in his throat. He knew Berit well enough that if he sided with Felix in front of everyone she'd never forgive him.

"You're not going anywhere until Judge's upgrade is complete," Cross said instead, playing the part of authoritarian. It was the part Berit had assigned him, and he'd play it until it got him killed. No doubt, she'll do just fine without him. But if he lost her, it'd be another story. He couldn't go through that again. He added, "But Felix is right. We can't stay here."

Before anyone could react to that declaration, the gutter tore away from the roof and splattered blobs of bioshell down on them. Felix leapt back in time, but Berit slipped on the wet grass. Cross gave her cover long enough to scramble away. He felt the weight of the goop land.

He was dropped to his knees faster than if a lion had pounced on him, but it wasn't claws and teeth he felt on his back and shoulder. The stuff felt like a million cold fingernails latching onto him, moving over him with intent. A giant frozen cat tongue giving him a bath. He tried to fling it off, but it resisted and oozed under his shirt without leaving so much as a water stain.

He ripped open his shirt just in time to catch a glimpse of the bioshell sinking through the gauze over his abdominal wound. It didn't hurt, not exactly, but he still let out a shout of alarm.

"Don't panic don't panic," Berit urged, and she helped him peel back the bandage.

"Easy for you to say."

The five-inch incision he'd suffered at the hands of his former work colleagues had been stubborn to heal, no doubt because he hadn't stopped moving since it happened. The wound had been closed by bioshell. Not healed, no. Sealed shut, like a cork in a bottle.

"Bioshell?" he muttered. "Try bio*spackle*."

The excess bioshell sloughed off him into the grass where it started to coat split blades of grass with the same speed and care.

"Is it painful?" Berit asked.

"It doesn't feel good."

"That's less than specific."

Berit couldn't hide her fascination. She didn't even try. She was looking at Cross the same way she looked at streamers. He suddenly found himself not appreciating her clinical detachment so much.

"Hey," he said softly as her hair brushed his cheek. "Am I going to be okay?"

"Hm? Oh, sure. Sure. Yeah. Probably."

"Probably? *Probably*?"

"Well, these are not ideal conditions."

"No shit."

"I mean," she continued with a smile, "we're unable to follow even the most basic biosafety standards. We should all be in biohazard suits, separated from this stuff by an airlock, but I don't even have gloves." She lifted her bioshell stick to make her point. "*This* is my pipette for god's sake. The fact is we're at ground zero all the time. We're all at risk, Sebastian."

"I just got *slimed*, Berit. Am I going to turn into...something?" Berit didn't answer him, probably because she didn't take his question seriously. Cross found a target for his fear and frustration. Sure, it was an easy target, but he took aim anyway. "You happy now?" Cross shouted at Roan, pointing at the bioshell sealant on his belly. "Is this how you plan to get your revenge on us? One at a time?"

Roan raised her head, mouth breathing because of her bloodied nose. No response.

"Sebastian, hush," Berit said, and she pulled him to his feet. "Come here. Into the light."

Berit led Cross into the house, dodging the occasional drip of bioshell from the roof. Griff's place looked better on the outside. Inside, broken glass and splintered wood littered the floor, clumps of ocean plants clung to overturned furniture, and a wheelbarrow was embedded in the brick fireplace. Not to mention the outside-in shadow in the kitchen.

U.A. and Judge stood together on the other side of the vak. The space around the vak was so skewed Cross got a headache trying to interpret what he was seeing. *U.A. was split in half.* His head and chest was a good three feet away from his legs. You'd think U.A. would be bothered by that, but he just gave a quick nod of hello.

"How are things?" Cross asked tentatively. "All in one piece?"

"Relatively, I suppose," U.A. answered, and by the way he cocked his head to the side, Cross gathered U.A. was seeing him through the effect of the zig zag trick, too. "Anyone pop out of that thing?"

"Don't think so," Berit said, still inspecting Cross's wound. "But Griff's checking now."

"Good, good," U.A. said, backing toward the kitchen door. "I'll join him."

"I doubt your boys would've been inside that one," Cross said. "Seems to have spent most of its time in the ocean."

"Except for the giraffe," U.A. said. "If those things can get to Africa and back, it could've skipped over our desert to get here."

"Franklin Park." All eyes found Roan in the doorway, glowering at Judge. "It's a zoo. Mom and Dad took me every birthday, before you were born."

"How sweet," Judge said flatly.

"*Judge,*" Cross warned, but he stopped himself. There was no point in getting between these two. The shadow-vak already separated them, a natural shield planted by Judge himself.

"They'd arrange for a special animal encounter," Roan continued. "I fed otters when I turned eight. Koalas when I was nine. Ten was a kangaroo. Dad got kicked so hard he cracked a tooth. We had to go to Roger Williams for elephants when I was eleven. No elephants at Franklin Park. But they have giraffe. I was going to feed the giraffe for twelve. But that didn't happen. I was in the silo for that birthday. And the next one after that."

"I'm sure someone else fed the giraffe," Judge said, "if that's what worries you."

Roan threw a blob of bioshell at Judge. He raised an arm to deflect the attack, but he didn't need to. His vak protected him. Its firewall split the blob and swallowed it up in its depths.

"What the—" Felix started.

Without dimming the firewall or hindering its strange dance, the clear goo wrapped around each ribbon of light. The bioshell stretched across the vak to leave a cloudy sheath across its emptiness, like a great white's eyelid.

"What did you do?" Cross heard himself ask, not sure which one of them he was asking.

Judge did the unthinkable. He touched the firewall. There was a collective gasp in the house, but Judge allayed fears by waving his wriggling fingers, still very much there.

"Incredible," Berit said, breathless. "Like rubber coiled around a live wire."

Judge sent a look his sister's way, as if he'd just read a surprising headline for the day: Bioshell Takes Bite out of Firewall. For a moment the look resembled respect, but then his eye narrowed. Hardened.

"I'll be in the basement," he announced, raising the remote for all to see, "and I'm taking this with me."

"Perfect," Cross mumbled. "The cyborg has control."

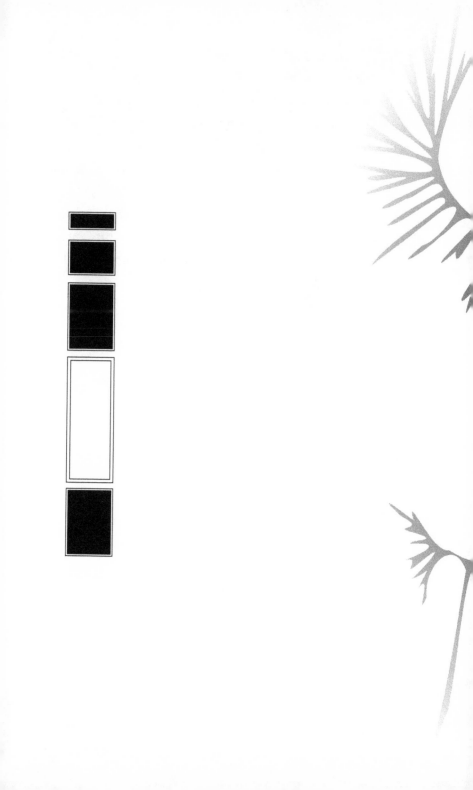

SEQUENCE TWO

PART DIMOND_0001

AMARANTA NUÑEZ WAS DEAD, AND DIMOND'S lost finger was killing him. Pain that registered from something absent shouldn't feel this real, he thought, and he flexed his remaining fingers to remind his brain he needed no reminder of the loss. He was there when it happened, saw the edge of the vak slice his index finger clean off with his own eyes. For some reason his mind felt compelled to revisit the experience.

He had no time for hallucinations. He had real nightmares to contend with.

Today was the exhumation of Amaranta Nuñez. Her family waited to receive her remains just beyond the blast radius of the streamer bomb, behind the plastic blue curtains installed on tall spikes to give Nuñez the privacy she deserved. A different sort of waiting room for a very different sort of delivery. Unfortunate, all around. No doubt about it. But what pained Dimond the most—aside from his own damaged nervous system—was the *time* all of this was taking.

"This is not a waste of time," Spencer Pirret said, reading his mind. Spencer was one of the few people who Dimond didn't consider replaceable, and he knew it. "Your people need to see that you'll put the screens aside for ten minutes to pay your respects while their remains are removed from your property. It's good for morale."

"Don't talk to me about morale," Dimond said. "It sounds

too much like *I told you so.*"

Spencer had been warning him for months that he smelled a revolt. Dimond had invited these people to his home—well, to the underground missile silo *under* his home—but still. It was the closest relationship he'd had to employees in years. The betrayal stung.

One former employee now held him hostage from under a tree that had flattened her. Amaranta Nuñez never had such power while alive. Imagine, to keep a man of his global stature *waiting*. He was stuck there until she was unstuck. No looking at his phone, no checking in with his project managers at the Elbowoods site. At Spencer's insistence, Dimond had put himself on display for his employees, to prove that he cared enough to show up when they got squashed by a sycamore and not to multi-task while bearing witness to such sacrifice.

Her body would have been returned to her family within hours of its discovery, if not for the bioshell contamination. His people first identified the stuff as part of some large animal that had been disorganized by its interdimensional travel, but when the glop was observed moving on its own, sticking like Velcro to anything organic, they determined it must be some sort of exo-structure. *Bioshell,* they called it. Dimond didn't think the name fit the gunk. Shells were rigid with structure, even the fragile ones. This stuff was more like blubber with a brain.

The former seacoast conservation area was littered with carcasses of long dead animals, glowing with the useless bioshell clots between tufts of matted fur, flaky scales, tangled feathers. His people spent days determining the safest way to strip mine the new material, and that plan included head-to-toe biohazard suits and an insufferably thorough—*slow*—method of bagging and tagging. Whatever had still been alive in the streamer had flown away, crawled off, or hitched a ride on a mystery bus that stole away Roan Gorey.

Nothing brought a scowl to his face faster than thinking about Roan Gorey, and he couldn't let his people catch him scowling over Amaranta's sacred burial ground. He must discipline his thoughts in order for this sacrifice of *time* to mean something, but it was hard not to think about the Gorey girl. And the boy. He'd had them both. They were his, by right—a right he'd worked *so hard* to earn—and now because of a group of his own people—*traitors*—his property was running loose. Up for grabs.

Someone had disabled the exterior cameras. Hacked the security system that would have been triggered into alert by the cameras being down. Reconfigured the master network that would have detected the breach of the security system.

"Schoop's team called it a Humpty Dumpty hack," Dimond shared while they watched the extraction from the sidelines.

"You don't say?"

"Humpty'd been put back together again without realizing he'd been broken into a million pieces in the first place."

"I don't think that's how the rhyme goes, boss," Spencer smirked. "You're sure they're not just covering their own tracks?"

"I'm not sure of anything," Dimond said.

"Oh, come on now," Spencer said, leaning forward on his crutches to give Dimond a rough pat on the back. "Don't go and get disillusioned on me. My whole world philosophy will crumble. Schoop seemed loyal enough, and he's not around anymore to defend himself. I'd put my money on the squirrely Asian. He had access to the jetkill that's gone missing, too."

"Felix," Dimond said. But then he dismissed the idea, "No, Spence. That puzzle piece is too forced. It had to be somebody else. Maybe even somebody on the outside."

Dimond rubbed the nub of his finger furiously as a stab of pain shot up his hand. The hallucination of his missing finger fluctuated between a bare bone protruding from the stump to a swollen abomination that made him feel like his arm ended with an elephant trunk. Maybe it was induced by the five-fingered glove he was wearing as part of his biohazard suit. Someone was getting fired over that.

"That crazy PT not working anymore?" Spencer asked.

"I've missed some sessions."

"No time to lick our wounds." Spencer tottered on his crutches to make his point. "Barely time to bury our dead. I suppose that's how an enemy like this wears you down. She creates those things even when she's asleep for Christ's sake."

"An aspirational efficiency," Dimond said, tugging at his plastic suit in irritation.

Even this early in the morning, the harsh valley sun was making the temperature in the suit unbearable, and his angry breathing kept fogging up the mask. He knocked his hood off, letting it hang down his back.

"Please, Mr. Dimond, your mask," Joachim urged from the debris field, behind his own thin wall of plastic. "We have no way of knowing what microbes were released."

"Never been much of a germaphobe," Dimond replied. "But I appreciate the concern."

Joachim was new enough to the position of team leader not to know if he should press the matter, so he gave a quick smile and returned to his work.

"I doubt he was talking about the common cold," Spencer chuckled.

"They'd be moving ten times faster if they didn't have these suits on."

"Not everyone shares your priorities. If they did, we'd have a planet full of people living on top of their own personal bunkers."

The bunker that Spencer referred to had been constructed decades ago to withstand a nuclear attack, and so it survived the slightly less destructive event of a streamer assault. The seacoast conservation area, on the other hand, suffered absolute obliteration. Acres of coastal grass were uprooted, and a grove of eucalyptus trees were stripped bare of leaves or knocked down altogether. The tall grass had served as the nesting ground for the endangered whippoorwill, and the eucalyptus as a natural windbreak to prevent erosion. Extinction and erosion were inevitable, but he had to admit he'd grown attached to the pleasant view of the wild patch. The extra acres of buffer between him and the general public down the beach were an added plus. When the state went bankrupt a few years back, Dimond had donated the funds to keep up the conservation effort. A visit from one of Roan's streamers had destroyed it all.

And people accused *him*—a humble oil and gas man—of being insensitive to the environment.

"Still no sign of the river guide?" Spencer asked.

"No. You're sure he went in?"

"I saw it myself. Hit him right in the chest with a gas canister, and he went straight over, right into that monster in the water."

"He could've drowned."

"I told you, I saw that thing turn into him, just like it turned into Nuñez after it took her. He was inside that thing. If he isn't here, he's with *them*."

The traitors, he meant.

"You're watching his family in case he shows up?"

"His son, yes. Dohanian's on it."

"It's the theft that really ticks me off. All those vaks," Dimond said angrily. During the mayhem of Judge's escape and Roan's break-in, dozens of his employees made away with untold numbers of crated creations. "They're building something."

"Let them. Let them expend their energy. Their resources. Then we'll tear it down. Leave them with nothing. It's worked for us in the past."

"This is different," Dimond said. "We're in a race, Spence. With some of our own. My financial liability is growing exponentially."

"You've done the calculation. That liability will hurt at first, but then it becomes the gift that keeps on giving. An industrial *evolution*. Isn't that what you said? World Economy 2.0?"

"Our case for liability is crumbling. That *60 Minutes* with the BioTeatro team did damage to our contamination timeline."

"Nah, those eggheads were too technical. If your Average Joe understood the difference between synthetic and quantum biology, we'd be in trouble. But they don't, so we're not."

"Faith in the blissful ignorance of the masses is what gets me through the day," Dimond nodded. "But *still*. There's the Constitutional arguments, too."

"We planned for that. We'll draw it out, long as possible."

"Yes, but the ground is getting shaky faster than expected," Dimond grumbled. "If we lose the *Right of Capture*, we lose our monopoly on the tech. If real competition is about to start, we have to be first on the control mechanisms."

"All teams are working around the clock, boss," Spencer reminded.

"Not right now they aren't," Dimond spat, nodding toward the open gravesite. "If I can't get Elbowoods up and running I might as well offer myself up to a streamer and ride the whole thing out in oblivion."

Either Spencer's well of optimism had run dry, or he realized there was no point in trying to argue Dimond out of his lousy mood. They watched the crews work in silence.

When the crane finally lifted the giant sycamore that marked Nuñez's temporary grave, Dimond climbed over the mounds of debris to get to her side. He should say something to mark the occasion, so he slowed his steps to give himself time to retrieve an appropriate quotation from memory. On arrival, though, he wouldn't bother to give a speech.

Nuñez was frozen in mangled perfection. Beneath her bloodied and tattered clothing, her skin glowed from the sheer coating of bioshell. Her black hair fell over her luminous dead eyes, shielded by the strange sheen. Fatal wounds filled with bioshell looked like dark veins running under a topcoat finish. She was dead but entirely preserved, reconstructed even, by the bioshell.

Dimond was surprised at himself for not recognizing the familiar scene he'd been witnessing. He'd felt wasted here, taxed by a so-called duty to his employees. But that's not what today was about, after all. This was an excavation site like so many other exploratory boreholes and drill sites, and his patience had just been rewarded with an unexpected discovery, not unlike the archeological finds that once lined the shelves of his library. Of course none of his sites had ever revealed an actual mummy, but that's what came to mind while he studied her appearance. Mummification requires organ removal and embalming fluids, but none of those things had happened to poor Amaranta. She was preserved intact by a substance they knew little about, except for its origin. A streamer. Who knew what properties bioshell might possess? What potential might exist in this macabre combination of dead brain and smart goop? The same instinct that had drawn him to the Gorey children now led him down another path. A much darker one.

No reverent speeches of admiration for Amaranta today. Her family would go home empty-hearted and empty-handed.

Amaranta Nuñez was dead and gone.

This was something new.

Maybe even something he could use against those runaway brats.

He said simply, "Take it to the lab."

PART WALT_0001

WHEN THE FLUORESCENT LIGHTING ON THE commuter train flickered and died, Walt wondered if his bioshell scars would make him glow in the dark, like a cartoon character exposed to cartoon radiation. Berit had assured him that bioshell wasn't radioactive, but Walt was unconvinced. Her reasoning was that unsafe levels had never been detected in a streamer, so why would its skin be different? But it's not like she had a pocket Geiger counter. The truth was, she didn't know.

Ironic. This was exactly the kind of thing his dad had been trying to protect him from.

If he was aglow, no one noticed. Some commuters watched out the windows, but most were glued to the news on their screens. Streamers and vaks gave good video. The lights popped back on, but with a weak show of confidence they'd stay on. Again, no one seemed to care. Light or no light, reality was not what it used to be.

Griff sat a few rows behind Walt. He and Walt weren't plastered all over the news like Berit and Cross and Felix were after Dimond's press conference, but it's still possible that Walt's dad had arranged for "a BOLO on the DL," as Griff had put it. Griff was all about acronyms. If authorities *were* on the lookout for Walt, Griff didn't want to risk being seen with him on security cameras. Griff guarded his anonymity with an extreme level of care. He hadn't asked to join this team of fugitives. He'd been swept up in its wake, just like U.A. when his nephews were taken by a streamer in the Texas desert, and Matthias on that river in West Virginia. Griff was a casualty, in search of the only thing that could make him whole again. His wife and son. So he and Walt traveled separately on this joint mission, wearing Red Sox hats with faces tilted down, just in case things went sour.

The train to South Station wasn't as full as it should be this time of day, but the reason for that was obvious. Most people chose to stay home, find their bearings in the new world. The few on the train had no doubt checked to see that the commuting schedules were affected about the same as a snowstorm and decided to stick to their routine. They'd bury themselves in work, even if none of it mattered anymore. His mom would have been on this train today.

The way the woman in front of him wore her hair reminded him of his mother. Swept up in back and held together tightly, no strand left behind. Looked like a shiny helmet. He'd shared this observation with his mom once, and it had made her laugh. "I need a helmet some days," she'd said.

When he was small, she'd bring him on the commuter rail to her Boston office during school break. "I like to show you off once in a while," she'd say. "Remind the rest of them I'm a human capable of love." Her version of a lawyer joke. She'd embarrass him by introducing him to her colleagues as "her little man," and they'd take turns asking him questions like "What law school do you plan to attend?" and "What's your opinion of the new Chief Justice?" He took the teasing with a good-natured smile, even while feeling mildly sickened by the assumption that he wanted into their exclusive club. That it was inevitable he'd join their ranks someday.

Look at him now. He was a member of an exclusive club all right. Not one headquartered in a glass tower at the center of the city, boasting of billionaire clients, no. But exclusive—endangered, even. Hunted down under the terms of the corporate liability law his very own mother had helped write for Bradley Dimond and Furst Enterprises. Of course, Walt wasn't the one being hunted. His influential parents had made sure to exclude him from the publicized phase of the hunt, part of their ongoing promise to protect him. His future. That protective service, ironically, put his membership in this exclusive team on probation. Even though Walt was a founding member, the others didn't trust him. No, it was worse than that. They didn't take him seriously.

On the cross-country dash from the West Coast silo escape to the East Coast retreat, Walt had raised objections over keeping Matthias. He'd argued that the right thing to do was to drop him at a hospital as they passed through his home state of West Virginia. All the adults, every last one, had dismissed that idea as naïve. Berit was unwilling to let Matthias go before gathering her "data points" on his experiences both inside the streamer and during the violent release. Cross argued Matthias was a threat because he could identify U.A. and Griff, and U.A. and Griff went along with that because neither of them wanted to be identified. In the end, Berit's research and their cover were more important than reuniting a man with his family. It was only a matter of time before that strategy blew up in their faces, so Walt sped that along by getting the truck keys to Matthias when Berit sent him upstairs for the amp.

No one suspected his betrayal because Walt's insignificance to the team kept him above suspicion. He was an inconvenience, at best. They'd sent him on this mission with Griff for one reason only. He knew the person they were seeking. She might talk to him. Might.

At South Station, Walt and Griff took the stairs, separately, down to the Red Line. When a train came, Griff got in a different car. Opposite of the buddy system, this plan. It made him anxious. If he lost contact with Griff out here, Walt would have no way of knowing how to get back to Roan, and that was by design. Cross and Felix were relocating Roan and Judge to a secret place only Griff knew, and U.A. and Berit were carting a busload of bioshell somewhere west of here. That's all he knew. The grown-ups considered him a flight risk, so they were keeping the master plan to themselves. Odds were high that after Walt played his part in the mission, Griff might even try to ditch him out here. Slap him on the back with a quick "it's for the best, kid" and disappear into a crowd.

There was a critical problem with that plan. None of them knew Roan Gorey like he did. None of them had known Roan's parents, either, or made a promise to them to help her, however he could. Not one of them knew *his* parents, and how it was killing him to know that they were at the core of all this wrong. How determined that made him to do right. Now that Sophia and Paul Gorey were gone, his promise to them meant even more. He didn't intend to walk away from that, no matter how hard he was pushed aside.

Walt watched their progress to the MIT/Kendall stop from under the brim of his hat. Everybody kept their head down on the T, so he fit right in. It was the assumed position of people forced within uncomfortable inches of each other. Standing, Walt caught an upside down glimpse of a *Boston Globe* article about BioTeatro, the local biotech company Dimond had claimed was the true source of Roan and Judge.

"Bound to happen," the passenger reading the paper muttered. "Mucking around with nature like that."

He could shout at the whole train that it was a lie. Dimond had told him himself it wasn't true. But exposing the truth wasn't the goal today. Recruitment was.

Their target was Dr. Kendra Jackson, an Army veteran, a practicing burn unit surgeon, and a full-time professor of bioengineering at MIT. A few years back, she tried to add United States Senator to that list by running against his dad in a special election. Two political rookies vying for a seat left vacant after the sitting Senator became incapacitated from a stroke—it was a volatile race that got a lot of national attention. Dr. Jackson took sabbatical and dropped her on-call hospital status. Why? As she put it in her campaign ads, "I believe it is a citizen's duty to serve." Walt's dad, on the other hand, thought if he was in the Senate he could free up some of the State's conservation areas for development. Plus, he liked the sound of *Senator* Nathan Hale.

A quick check of the campus map outside the T exit showed them they were just a block away. Walt did a double take when he saw the dedication carved into the cornerstone of Dr. Jackson's building: *Bradley Dimond Cancer Research Center*.

"Holy shit," Walt said. "No way. He's everywhere."

"It's just a name on a building," Griff said, but after Walt ducked inside the door he held open, he added, "But keep your head down."

Inside, a gallery of circular screens projected photographs of deep space galaxies and nebulae, like the ones on his Hubble telescope calendar at home. A sideways glance at the labels next to each image corrected his assumption. Not galaxies, cells. Not nebulae, bacteria. One image of something called a bacteriophage looked so much like an alien from *War of the Worlds*, Walt decided that whatever was going on inside of Roan and Judge shouldn't be too much of a surprise, not to people who deal with things that look like *that*.

The stairwell was locked so they took the elevator. Dr. Jackson's lab was on the third floor. A group of young people were clustered around the TV in the common area. Most weren't too much older than he was. A couple more years and he'd be in college, too—or at least that was the old plan. Now he may never go, not unless he could work his fugitive experience into his college application essay. That brief thought made him sadder than he had time to process.

Walt located Dr. Jackson toward the back of the group, eyes glued to the live report of a streamer attack like everyone else. Walt was drawn to the report, too. Drone footage of a city at night. Shanghai, according to the graphics. A streamer octopus tumbled out of the river to wrap itself around a skyscraper, then peeled off in a nose dive into the narrow streets as a pigeon, before transforming into a giant rat that wreaked havoc on a marketplace.

Griff nudged Walt back into focus, so Walt weaved his way to Dr. Jackson's side, where he said *hello* so softly his voice caught. During the campaign Walt had met his father's political opponent more than a few times, but he'd never managed to speak a coherent sentence to her. Dr. Jackson was intimidatingly striking, and the intensity of her current stare only added to Walt's hesitance. Her piercing eyes matched her coffee dark skin, and a sleeveless shirt revealed shoulders like a boxer's.

Griff took over, impatient.

"Dr. Jackson? Excuse me, but we have an appointment with you."

"I doubt that," she said, her focus staying on the video.

"My son here," Griff continued, practically shoving Walt into her line of view, "is going to be studying with you this fall."

Dr. Jackson's spine straightened when she recognized Walt. A flash of anger crossed her face—seeing any member of the Hale family no doubt raised unpleasant memories—and she gave Griff a quick inspection, verifying he was definitely *not* Walt's father. So, a liar.

Walt's pulse quickened, but Griff waited calmly for her to decide how to react to their cover story. They didn't have long to wait. She said a quick "Come with me," and they followed her through the growing crowd around the TV to her office, her boot heels clicking commandingly on the stone tile. Walt still hadn't managed to eke out a *hello* at an audible level. It wasn't just how formidable Dr. Jackson was. His guilt by association was crippling him. His dad's campaign won only because of claims of financial corruption at her burn clinic, *false* claims that surfaced on certain "news" sites weeks before the election. His dad said he didn't know anything about the disinformation attack, but that hardly mattered. It didn't take brain surgery to figure out who was behind it all. Dimond needed Nathan Hale in office to pass the *Right of Capture* legislation. Dr. Jackson was an obstacle to that goal.

As soon as Griff cleared the door, she closed them in. "I'd say I'm surprised to see you here, Walt," she started, "but I'm all fresh out of surprise. It's been a hell of a 24 hours, wouldn't you say? Even seeing it with your own eyes doesn't convince."

"Depends on how close you get," Griff grumbled.

She pivoted to Griff and demanded, "Why are you pretending to be this boy's father?"

"Because I didn't want anyone to hear me introduce myself," Griff explained. His shoulders squared to attention when he announced his real identity, "Staff Sergeant Marshall Griffith," but dropped again when he added, "In another life, anyway."

"I know you," Dr. Jackson said, trying to recall how she knew him. "We didn't serve together. I'm sure of that at least."

"No, ma'am, we didn't. Three tours, Afghanistan, so we might've shared the same shit sandwich once or twice, but we never crossed paths." Griff moved to the window that overlooked the street below and did a business-like recon of the surroundings. Or maybe he just didn't want to face her as he explained how he got tangled up in this mess. "Two years ago, I was on leave, and I took my family to the Big E. Fun day at the fair. Let my boy Ollie pet some sheep, ride a pony. Eat junk food. Ride the Ferris Wheel. He loved that the most. We ran out of tickets he loved it so much. On that last ride, we only had two tickets left. I was going to take him, you know. I wanted to. But he's so attached to his mother. He hasn't seen me too much. I've been away more than half his life. So Laney took him, for one last ride, and then we were going to go home. We never went home, Dr. Jackson."

"The first streamer attack," Dr. Jackson said. "You were there. You saw it. My god."

"It took my wife and son," Griff said, his voice trembling until he clamped his jaw shut and punched the sill of the window so hard the tempered glass shuddered. "They said it was a tornado. That I was suffering from PTSD. I was the only one telling the truth about what happened. I was discharged."

"A Dear John letter after three combat tours?" Dr. Jackson shook her head. "That's the power of public defamation for you. Bradley Dimond's calling card."

"They discredited me to shut me up," Griff said. "They said you were corrupt to make sure Dimond's man got into office."

"So you and I were buried in the same pile of shit," she said, sinking into the leather chair behind her desk like she was sinking into the past. "So what? That still doesn't explain why you're here. I don't have time for revenge plots."

"It's not about revenge," Walt finally spoke up. "We need your help."

"Does your real father know you're here?"

"No."

"What about your mom?"

"She left my dad months ago. I don't know where she is. Nobody does."

Dr. Jackson looked sympathetic for a moment, but refreshed to her standard hard look.

"Well that's too bad, but I don't know why you're here or what kind of help you think I can offer you," she started. "In case you haven't noticed, the world is just about to lose its collective mind. I came in today to make sure my lab members have all made plans to be with their families, and then I was going to go home and be with mine."

"You're acting like this is the end of the world."

"The world as we know it, yes. Panic is coming, Mr. Hale. Massive worldwide panic. And there's nothing I can do about that, but try to keep my people safe, and my family."

"What if there was something you *could* do?"

Dr. Jackson could have seared a hole into him she was staring so hard.

"All right," she said unexpectedly. "I'm listening."

PART MATTHIAS_0002

TEN DAYS. THAT'S HOW LONG MATTHIAS FIGURED it would take him to get to Trev, now that the Chevy had gone and died on him. As long as he didn't run into weather, and he didn't get lost, or injured, ten days ought to do it.

He'd always wanted to hike the Appalachian Trail *with* Trev, not as a covert way back home to him, but choice and timing never were very cooperative in his experience. Griff had loaded the Chevy full of camping supplies, including a serious backpack, extra clothes, a sleeping bag, canteen, and dehydrated food packets. Matthias estimated the hike at 400 miles or so. Just south of Dingmans Ferry, the Trail followed the Kittattinny down toward the Susquehanna. He'd have to improvise around Harrisburg to keep himself west of the Alleghenys, but Griff had a collection of topographical maps in the glovebox that could guide him across North America.

There were faster ways home, but none safer. If he hitchhiked, he'd have to lie to whoever picked him up. He wasn't above lying, especially if it meant getting home to Trev sooner, but he was a lousy liar. In the Skaggs home, there wasn't a secret he hadn't spoiled. He could steal another vehicle, but that was more likely to get him arrested than get him home. He did not possess a criminal mind. Any interaction he had with anyone—helpful or not so much—would bring them into this mess, to one degree or another. That just didn't seem right.

So Matthias slept in the Chevy until it was light enough to

start walking, and then he started walking. Just as simple as that. One foot in front of the other, and he'd get himself home to Trev. Ten days. Maybe eleven.

PART ROAN_0002

REDEMPTION ROCK WAS THE NAME GIVEN TO a massive glacial boulder in the forest near Wachusett Mountain where a ransom of twenty pounds sterling was paid nearly 350 years ago for the return of kidnapped colonist Mary Rowlandson. The Wampanoag had taken her and her children during a violent raid of their farmhouse in retaliation for colonial settlements moving west during King Philip's War. Real estate and injustice, hand in hand as usual.

The story had always captured Roan's imagination, and once upon a time in her own life, if she'd discovered Bunker 318, the earthen mound she now called home, she would have allowed herself to daydream that she was one of those stolen children, brought back to Redemption Rock from a harrowing trial in the wilderness. She might've even imagined herself the kind of kid who would've preferred the harrowing wilderness. But now her reality trumped daydreaming. Letting her mind wander even a little seemed irresponsible.

She'd already returned from capture, and she wasn't seeking redemption.

In the last few days, Roan had come to a few new conclusions. First, there was no going back. It was a simple enough concept, but she'd been fighting it tooth and nail. She had to give up on the idea that sending Judge away would magically reset things to normal. He'd done away with her mom and dad, so normal was never coming back.

Second, she may never be able to stop the streamers from coming. Berit and her lackey researchers had never determined what triggered a streamer. Even while she lay on a bed of pine needles shed by the grove that sprouted from the inches of earth covering Bunker 318, she created more streamers. Sometimes she was aware of a new presence, a fleeting ghost in the corner of her eye. Streamers weren't interested in sticking around. The new world was coming through her, but leaving her behind like a doormat.

Judge wasn't going away, and streamers wouldn't stop coming. Both must be managed somehow. There was no hope for direct communication with her brother. If carving up his own parents didn't put a dent in that blank one-eyed stare, nothing would. She had felt the drag of him even before he was born. His absence of feeling, inability to love, condensed into a black hole at the end of that invisible tether that bound them. No. No hope there.

She needed to build a trap. One he could never escape. Fortunately, traps were her thing. She'd kept him locked up in another dimension for twelve years on pure instinct alone, and now she was a bona fide trap factory. Each streamer she produced was an interdimensional prison strong enough to hold her mistake of a brother, but she had no quality control. Everyone was on the menu when she called a streamer, and a prison can't truly be secured if it wanders off, like a streamer does. If she could only focus—really focus—to gain the power she needed over them.

The problem was the fog. It crept in and settled in her brain, keeping her thoughts random and disconnected. The same thing happened back in school during MCAS, torturous standardized tests given every spring just to ruin the fact that winter was over. Trying to work out how to control streamers, she might as well be sitting at a desk with a bunch of word problems and a bubble answer sheet. *If Bradley Dimond is 3,000 miles away but has every law enforcement agency within 10 miles at his disposal, and you are hiding on a decommissioned army base with some people you trust and some you don't, and your evil twin brother is no more than 50 feet away at any time, how long before everything falls apart and you have to cut and run? A) Any second now B) Any second now C) Any second now D) All of the above*

Roan exhaled so loudly it was more like a groan. She needed a break, so she closed her eyes and enjoyed the sound of wind in the trees and the gentle lap of waves on the pond.

Only a few days had passed since Griff had relocated them to the abandoned Fort Devens Annex, but everyone had managed to accomplish something. Everyone, except for her. Berit and U.A. had set off on a secret mission. Walt and Griff had convinced Dr. Jackson to perform the jetkill surgery on Judge, and Cross and Felix were prepping Judge's bunker for the operation.

Before splitting off from the group with U.A., Berit had cornered her in the *Knotty Bits* bus to spew information at her with the volume and intensity of a firehose dousing a fire. Roan nearly drowned in the info dump. If Berit had ever tried to get to know Roan during their time at the silo, she would have known how Roan's brain shut down when lectured. It wasn't intentional. It just happened. Roan wore her listening face, but nothing much stuck, except for one thing Berit said.

"I said I'm not your Yoda," Berit repeated, when Roan asked her to. And then she veered off into "possible motility mechanisms of a streamer," something about "false feet like a single cell organism, or the tumble and run method of a bacterial cell." Berit wrapped it up with the Insightful Moment of the Year: "Roan, you have to do this on your own."

No shit. Really?

And then Berit was gone, taking all the crazy science talk (and a bus full of bio-blubber) to wherever it was needed more. Funny that she didn't bother mentioning *that*. Big picture stuff was clearly above Roan's paygrade.

It didn't matter. Roan had overheard enough to put together that Berit was overseeing the construction of a station, of sorts. One that would allow Roan to release a streamer without getting anyone inside—or out—killed in the process. How the hub would work, and where it was located were kept from her. Evidently it was a widely-held belief that she tended to wreak havoc wherever she went, so until the hub was operational, Berit didn't want her around. Instead, Roan was stuck with the worst camp counselors on the planet, with homework to do.

The backyard bunkers were a part of Griff's family history, details of which he shared over a fire their first night, like a ghost story. His grandparents owned the land back in the 1940s, when they were forced out by the Army to make room for the Annex. The Sudbury woods became a training ground for soldiers using live explosives, and the bunkers stored munitions that would come in handy if the Nazis tried a land assault. It never came to that, but the forest along the Assabet still suffered battle scars. The spongy ground soaked up poisonous heavy metals from artillery shells, and for years the area was deemed unsafe for habitation. It was kept as a kind of military junk yard for a while. The Army turned over the land to

Fish and Wildlife at the turn of the new millennium, under a project to restore the land for public use. A notice posted about efforts to leech metals—mercury, arsenic, lead—from the forest floor, along with a health warning to trespassers, was still mounted near the front door of Bunker 318. Griff explained that they shouldn't be bothered by Fish and Wildlife because the funding had dropped off for the remediation project. His only concern for discovery of their hideout was the rare invasion by locals looking for a secluded place to get high, but they generally preferred the ruins of his grandparents' farmhouse a few hundred yards from the bunkers. For that reason—and the fact that the farmhouse was hardly more than rotted wood and mold—Griff had chosen the dry concrete bunkers for the group.

Cross and Felix with Judge. Walt and Griff with her. It had been nearly a week since they'd left the cranberry farm—and running water and beds—and no one was happy with the arrangements. Hiding out on the top of Bunker 318 was the closest she got to privacy.

Privacy, and private study. Berit had left her a study aid, a slab of what she called bioshell. Roan passed a ball of it between her hands absentmindedly, watching a light wind rustle the birch trees at the edge of the pond. She was mesmerized by how the silver white bark peeled away in a striping pattern to contrast so completely with its dark interior. She'd always liked that design, even though she couldn't say why. Just pleasing to the eye, she supposed.

She tossed the bioshell ball into the air and caught it, astonished to see the same contrasting pattern ripple across its surface.

"What the hell?" she said, and dropped the copycatting stuff. It latched onto tufts of lichen on the concrete, so when she tried to scrape it back up, it clung like a Band-Aid left on skin too long. She managed to reclaim most it, but the bioshell retained the lichen's flaky, fragile look. She wondered where the birch bark had gone, and suddenly her favorite design was back. No more lichen.

"Holy shit," Roan remarked. "It can hear my thoughts?"

Silly Putty. That's what it reminded her of. Her mom had shared the nostalgic activity with her once, because evidently her mom's childhood had been so boring that making backwards impressions of Sunday morning cartoons was a high point. Unfortunately for Roan, the only inked paper available were free coupon mailers and town newsletters, so instead of mirror images of Snoopy or Garfield, hers were limited to chimney sweep and snow plowing services ads. Lame.

This version, less so. She stretched the stuff and broke off a smaller piece, then flattened it between her palms. When she closed her eyes, her mind was flooded with images she couldn't understand. So overwhelming she felt herself shutting down. *There's that fog again*. It made her wonder, though. What if this fog wasn't the familiar signature of her inability to focus? What if this fog was an actual signal? One she was receiving at such a high frequency or transmission speed or something that the message was getting lost?

She tried slowing down everything. Her breaths. Her heartbeats. Her thoughts. The fog started to lift, just enough. An image of a feather came into focus. She felt the putty change shape in her hand. It had taken the shape of an owl feather. How she knew it was an owl feather was still a mystery, but she'd bet her life that it was.

Acorn, Roan tested. Sure enough, the feather morphed into

an acorn. *Seagrass*. Check. *Cranberry*. Check. *Firefly*. Check.

Elephant. No elephant. There had been no elephant trapped in the streamer, so its bioshell could produce no elephant. Her test was nearly complete.

Giraffe.

No way there was enough bioshell in her hand to form a full-size giraffe, but the stuff stretched like she couldn't believe. Its hoof balanced in her palm, and its head reached high into the pine grove. It was static, a full-color bioshell statue without the frenetic whiz of the spheres of light that somehow power a streamer.

The patches of brown across its hide reminded Roan of the birch pattern. As instantly as she made that mental comparison, the giraffe's fur was replaced by birch bark. She tried to figure out how she just did that, and the fog returned, even thicker this time. Instead of fighting it, she gave herself over to it. She held the harrowing wild in the palm of her hand. She paid its ransom by offering herself up for the privilege of receiving its wisdom. Suddenly, it was like she'd been given a key to a house she never even knew existed, but now she knew the exact location of every nail, screw, joist. She had the blueprint of the giraffe, and she knew how she could change things without destroying the underlying structure. She breathed *feathers* and the giraffe was shrouded in a thick coat of owl feathers, making it look more like an ostrich.

There were voices below, so she reeled in the giraffe and wiped the bioshell clean, all on pure, panicked instinct. She could feel the potential of the giraffe to rise again, but she kept a lid on it for now. She needed more practice before she revealed this trick.

She rolled onto her belly to see Cross and Felix greeting Griff as he returned in his wife's Jeep, fully-stocked from an early morning supply run.

"Have any trouble?" Cross asked.

"We're not the only ones stocking up," Griff replied. "Things are deteriorating out there. Had to go to three box stores to get everything we needed."

"But nobody recognized you."

"I'm still just another anonymous shmuck," Griff said. "Either your friend hasn't gone to the authorities—"

"—or he can't identify where he'd been held, or who had him," Cross finished his sentence. "And he was no friend of mine. Or I guess I should say, I was no friend of his."

"Does that mean it's safe to go back to the farmhouse?" Felix asked.

"No," Cross said. "With Matthias loose, it's only a matter of time."

"Not a big fan of camping?" Griff asked Felix with a smile. "This place is a four-star hotel compared to some of the places I've holed up."

"I know, I know, you're the world weary streamer hunter, and I'm the pampered techie who misses his creature comforts," Felix said, lugging a pallet of bottled waters to Judge's bunker. He added over his shoulder, pissed, "Or maybe, just maybe, I was thinking how it might be better to perform surgery on a kid some place more hygienic than a bunker in the woods."

"I think you hurt his feelings, Griff," Roan observed from above.

"Jesus!" Felix shouted, so startled he nearly dropped the water.

"Can't you put a bell around her neck or something?"

If Cross and Griff shared his surprise, they didn't show it. She dropped from the bunker, narrowly missing Walt as he emerged, giving a huge yawn. Nobody was sleeping well on the cold stone floor. Walt gave her a quick nod before shifting his path around her.

"Hey, Sleeping Beauty," teased Cross, and he heaved a pallet of water at Walt.

Walt caught the load and allowed Cross to add another. Walt noted the full Jeep and said, through another yawn, "That's a lot of stuff. How much longer are we going to be here?"

"Until Berit sends for us."

"What's she up to again?" Roan asked, just to annoy Cross. "Other than avoiding you?"

Cross didn't return volley, unless you count his vicious glare.

"With me," Griff grunted, and it took Roan a moment to realize he meant for her to follow him. She grudgingly joined him among the birches at the edge of the pond. She prepared herself for a lecture, but that's not what she got.

"Do you think Matthias regrets helping you?" Griff asked. When Roan shrugged, he continued. "I think he might, but not because it wasn't the right thing to do. I think if he has regrets, it's because he lost things as a result. His freedom. His family. Hell, even his grasp of reality. But a man like that, who offers his help when he has no good reason to, I think a man like that can overcome his resentments, but only as long as he can regain some of what he lost. I think he'll get over being snatched up by a streamer and held against his will by us. I think he'll even forgive you turning his idea of the universe inside out. But if he can't get back his family, if he's lost that forever, then I think before long you can count him among your enemies. Don't you think?"

Griff handed her a folded photograph of Helene and Oliver Griffith in a pumpkin patch. She studied their smiles. Her curly blonde hair. His pudgy, kid belly.

"If I knew how to tell one streamer from another," Roan said, trying to keep her voice steady, "if I knew how to tell *what* was inside any of them, I would find your wife and son."

When she tried to hand the photograph back to him, he waved her off with a curt "Keep it, so you know who you're looking for."

Roan carefully tucked the photo into a pocket on her flannel jacket, a jacket that had belonged to Helene Griffith. All Roan's clothes were borrowed from Griff's missing wife. It couldn't have been easy for Griff to see her wearing them, especially since it was her fault his wife and son were gone.

"I never had a chance to thank you," Roan said. "For saving my mom's life that day at the Big E."

Griff looked back at the pond, silent. The day he saved her mother was the day he lost his family. A day he clearly regretted.

Roan's gaze drifted to the bunker door opposite hers. Judge was behind that door.

"He managed to finish what he started that day," Roan said, feeling herself start to shake. "But that's my fault. I wasn't strong enough to stop him."

"You're upset about your parents," Griff said. "That's probably the most normal thing about you. But kid, you're at the center of a shitstorm. You don't have time to wallow. Be sad if you have to be, but you can't shut down. I won't allow it."

The strength of his voice made Roan shudder.

"The streamer that took Matthias followed you all the way to California," Griff said, his voice softening a little. "That's strange isn't it? I wonder why it did that."

"I have no idea."

"Any others ever do that? Follow you?"

"Not that I know of."

They pondered that mystery together in the uncomfortable silence that falls after an unsatisfying interrogation.

The algae-coated surface of Puffer Pond reminded Roan of her own Comet Pond before Mr. Hale pulled the plug and drained the land of its soupy character. Along the bank, the bright green fuzz broke only for lily pads, but further out the water was clear enough to reflect the strong mid-day sun. Blinding spots of light bounced off the contented surface like stars exploding and dying over and over, so fast the here and gone was imperceptible. A small fish jumped for a water bug with a little too much enthusiasm and disturbed the dazzling light show, an organic eclipse lasting only long enough to cause a few waves. A kestrel swooped down and hooked the poor fish, dragging it from the watery stars and into the cover of the trees.

"Well," Griff said, "that was something."

The falcon had been ready and willing to do that wetwork. Roan needed to stop flopping around on the surface, drawing attention to herself. *Come with your claws and take me away.*

She needed to become the falcon in this contest. And fast.

PART WALT_0002

WALT'S FIRST KISS HAD BEEN WITH ROAN GOREY. More like his first seven kisses. They were reenacting the marriage scene of Anakin and Padme in *Attack of the Clones*, using the Swift River as their Naboo backdrop. Roan kept calling for a retake, unsatisfied with his performance. After one kiss, she actually smacked him on the top of the head and berated him, "You're doing it *wrong*. You have to grab me—like *this*. And pull me in." He never did get it right. He wasn't trying very hard. He never signed on for a marriage scene.

It's not like he hadn't thought about kissing Roan, but he'd gotten his braces tightened that morning. His teeth were sore, mosquitoes were swarming, and his shoes kept sinking into the mushy river bank. All in all, it had been a fairly traumatic experience.

With Carmen there were no braces, no mosquitoes, and no problem with concentrating. The only thing he felt he was sinking into was her. Carmen was soft and inviting. Roan was something else.

The two girls were so different, he wasn't sure they were the same species even before Roan started pulling tricks out of her multidimensional hat. They did have one thing in common. Drama. Carmen starred in the school plays—*every* school play—and was even in a few local commercials. She was no prima donna, though. Roan, on the other hand, stuck to role playing adventures in the no-man's-land that used to be the pond between her house and Walt's, in the basements of his father's stalled real estate development. She required a controlled environment for her theatrical productions—an environment that she controlled, in other words. Roan was never good at taking direction.

He felt a pang of guilt. He shouldn't compare Roan with Carmen, especially not while spying on her like this from behind a tree.

Roan was at peace in a cathedral of pines. The spiked branches formed disconnected buttresses—tempting footholds for climbing into the sky. But she was more interested in the forest floor.

"Is this your new thing, Walt?" Roan shouted through the trees. "Spying on me for Cross?"

"Shit" he said to himself, but she smiled and called him over with a toss of her head.

Her eyes were bloodshot and puffy, and there was crusted blood on her cheek from the bad cut on her ear that was stubborn to heal. Walt resisted the urge to wipe the blood off. She was not in the mood for affection, not after catching him stalking her. Walt couldn't help notice she was still so damned pretty. In a very dangerous way.

"How long did you know I was there?"

"You're always there," Roan said.

"Harsh."

"Stalker." A smile flashed across her face like an electric pulse, and he recognized her attempt to lighten the mood.

"What are you doing out here?"

"I wish I knew," she said. "There are these patterns in my head. I can see them. Feel them, even. Patterns on top of patterns, overlapping, going on forever. I can't find an edge to it. In any direction I let myself look. It's like I'm stuck in a maze. I sound crazy, right?"

"I think you just need some sleep."

"I need to finish my homework." She pulled some of strange goo from her jacket pocket. It was the same stuff that Berit had taken with her in U.A.'s bus, the stuff she treated like it was the answer to all their problems. "Berit told me to play around with it. See what I could do."

"She told everybody else not to touch it."

"Did she? Huh. Well, I am her favorite guinea pig." She tossed the slab between her palms like she was making a hamburger patty. "Wanna see something cool?"

Walt stepped half behind a pine and nodded "Sure, okay."

She pretended not to notice his reflex to seek shelter. Roan pinched off a small piece and squeezed it in her hand a few seconds. When she revealed the result, he couldn't believe his eyes.

"What—?"

"It's a sea star," she explained.

"Is it alive?"

"No," Roan said. "It's everything but that."

"What does that mean?"

"Everything this sea star was, is here," she said, then she squashed it in her hand like an unsatisfactory Play-Doh sculpture, showed him the original shapeless slab of blubber.

"Where'd it go?"

"It's still there, just beneath the surface," Roan said. She clenched and released her hand again. This time there was a mollusk shell. "And so is this." Closed her hand, opened it again. Sand dollar. "And this." Sea cucumber. "And this." Coral.

"How are you doing that?"

"This streamer must have spent a lot of time in the ocean," Roan said, ignoring the question. "But remember the giraffe?"

The coral morphed from shades of pink to the brown spots of a giraffe.

"I can show you the giraffe, too, but it's big. One of the others might see."

"You don't have to," Walt said. "I get it. I think. Whatever was inside the streamer, the information got stuck inside that stuff. In its skin."

"Berit calls it bioshell," Roan said.

"Bioshell, right," Walt said. "It makes sense, sort of. I mean, that outer layer—the bioshell—took the shape of whatever the streamer grabbed, so information must've been passing through it. If it can do that, it makes sense that it would be able to store information, too. Like an organic database."

"And it still accepts new information," Roan said. "Watch this."

Roan pressed the bioshell against a moss-coated rock, and when she peeled it off, it looked just like a tuft of moss hanging from her fingertips. She wadded it up and the bioshell went neutral again.

"The database isn't full," Walt said. "And you can plug into it. Give it instructions. Mix and match. Giraffe spots on a chunk of coral. I mean, Roan. *How?*"

"I can't explain it," Roan shrugged. "I've never seen the world like this before. Playing around with this bioshell stuff, it's changed me."

"You didn't eat any of it, did you?"

Roan looked at Walt like he was crazy, and then they both cracked up laughing.

"No, I didn't *eat* any of it," she said.

It was so good to see Roan laugh, but it didn't last long. A cloud of grief passed over her face and wiped away the momentary happiness, as easily as she'd wiped clean the bioshell.

Roan continued, "Berit said that I'd be able to control streamers if I could figure out how they move. She mentioned a theory that streamers move like amoebas, or bacteria. Any idea how they get around?"

"None."

"I thought you might've picked something up in Biology over these past two years."

"We dissected an earthworm last year," Walt offered. "My lab partner puked from the smell."

Roan laughed again, but it was her mean laugh, the one Walt disliked.

"Anyone I know?"

Walt regretted that he brought it up, because his lab partner had been Carmen. That's how they'd gotten to know each other. He tried to change the subject.

"Just like Berit to give you an assignment without the full instructions."

"Berit thinks she knows more than everybody," Roan agreed, "but somehow she also thinks that everything she knows is common knowledge. So who was your lab partner?"

Damn. She was not going to let it go.

"Carmen DiNicola."

"Ah, the drama queen," Roan smirked. "No wonder. I always pegged her as a wuss."

"She's not a wuss," Walt said forcefully. "Her grandfather had died the week before. She said she could smell the formaldehyde at the wake. The earthworm just brought it back for her."

Roan stared at Walt for a long enough time to make him break a sweat.

"Oh, don't tell me," Roan teased. "You and *Carmen DiNicola*? I mean, I thought you would at least stick to the script your dad wrote for you and date a cheerleader. Carmen is so granola. Those sandals. Does she still wear those sandals? The whole fake hippie dippie look, *Free to Be, You and Me*. Yuck."

"Carmen is nice," Walt snapped. "You don't know her. She doesn't dress like that anymore."

"Oh please, describe her wardrobe for me. I'm dying to know."

"It doesn't matter. You've been away—"

He stopped himself, tried to steady his breathing.

"I'm sorry," Roan said. "I shouldn't have dissed your girlfriend like that."

Walt knew that she was fishing for information, feeling him out like she might try to read a slice of bioshell. She was waiting for him to correct her and say Carmen wasn't his girlfriend. But he didn't want to lie to her.

"Your girlfriend Carmen," Roan said. "Okay. Good to know."

She balled up a piece of bioshell and threw it into the woods.

"What did you just do?" Walt asked, following close on her

heels, one eye over his shoulder. He could've sworn he felt the forest floor shudder under his feet, like a distant stampede had started. "Roan? What did you do?"

PART JUDGE_0003

Subsurface living must be Judge's lot in life. First the *pre*, then the silo, Griff's basement, and now the bunker. It was never more clear that his sister's aim was to put him in his final hole in the ground, as if that would put a stop to anything. There was every reason to believe the hole behind his eye would continue to grow beyond the span of his life. He was the finite cap on an infinite well. A problem with no solution, maybe. His anonymous pen pal—the one who helped him escape the silo and continued to send him fun philosophical exercises through his ancient Nintendo DS—thought there was a shot at a permanent fix, though. In order to tackle the impossible mission ahead, he had to have a reliable jetkill. Mechanics always trump theory.

Jetkill upgrades were panic-driven events that resulted in serious infrastructure damage and minor casualties—and that was in the silo, where they had a full medical team, techs on hand to scramble for whatever, and electricity that didn't come from a gasoline-powered generator. Here in Bunker 321, the upgrade would be performed by a single surgeon who had never even seen a jetkill, and her support team included just one tech who didn't even want to be there.

The upgrade team at the silo had been working on the new install for weeks, and it turned out that Felix had had the presence of mind to steal it after Judge's escape. Felix had hoped to use it as leverage, certain he'd be blamed—and punished—for losing Judge. He never got a chance. When he got tangled up with the misfit fugitives, he kept the stolen piece of Dimond tech to himself, no doubt because he still hoped to sever ties with them. But when Walt and Griff returned with the news they'd convinced Dr. Jackson to perform the surgery, Felix finally came clean about the stolen jetkill in his possession. The reveal had gotten mixed reviews.

On her first house call, Dr. Jackson spent a couple of hours studying the jetkill with Felix guiding her through the protocols for the installation process. Judge listened in, feeling more broken computer than growing boy. When it came time for her to switch over to human wiring, Judge was surprised by how nervous he was to have her take his vitals.

"This is my first official check-up," Judge said, hoping she'd overlook how much he was shaking. "I think you'll find me surprisingly advanced for a two-year-old."

"Well, you are my first pediatric patient with a foothold in another dimension," Dr. Jackson said with a smile, "so I guess we're both in for some surprises."

She looked in his ears and his one good eye, checked his pulse and his reflexes, listened to his heart and his tummy, all in silence. Her hands were warm, but her fingertips cold. Judge thought she might be holding her breath.

When she was done, Judge quipped, "No lollipop?"

Dr. Jackson was putting her stuff in her bag. "I'm curious. How is it that you know that?"

"Know what?"

"That pediatricians give out lollipops," she said. "Well, some may have. Mine never did, and my kids get stickers after their shots. It's not the sort of thing someone who's been locked up in a missile silo his whole short life would know."

"You expect me to be more like E.T.?"

"So he let you watch movies."

"Some."

"What about books?"

"He let me borrow from his library, but he was careful."

"I bet he was. Lots of ideas in books. I'm sure he preferred to supply those himself. TV?"

"He didn't want it to rot my brain. The hole in my head was already doing that."

"Is that how he put it? That TV rots your brain?"

"That's not common knowledge?"

"I don't know, maybe. I guess I expected you to be more awkward than you are. You seem like a normal kid to me. Except for the fact that you're growing so fast I can practically hear your bones, and, of course—"

"The eye." Judge winked with his good eye, and she chuckled.

"Did you have a favorite movie?"

Judge thought for a moment and decided to give a truthful answer. "*Back to the Future*."

"Why?"

"I enjoy paradox," Judge said. "Or maybe paradox enjoys me. What's with all the questions?"

"I like to get to know my patients before I operate," she said. "Some surgeons prefer not to. Some prefer to think of their patients as meat on a table. Having a connection with a patient can make it difficult to cut them open, do what has to be done.

But I like to know who I'm fixing. And why."

"You only accept patients you like?"

"I didn't say that. But between you and me, it helps," she said. She waited for an appreciative laugh from Judge but didn't get one. "What about you? Who do you have a connection with? Your sister?" Judge humphed. "Ok then, what about Bradley Dimond? Did you like him?"

"Bradley Dimond doesn't like Bradley Dimond."

"What about Felix?"

"Meh."

"Walt?" Judge shrugged in response, so she followed up with, "Me?"

"Why is it so important for me to like anyone?"

"It's hard to destroy the things you like."

"You mean love."

"Oh, no. People destroy the things they love all the time. What we love, we hold the closest to us, so when we blow up, poof! No buffer zone. Look what you did to your parents."

"That was an accident," he said, feeling himself flinch from her directness.

"I don't doubt that. How about this bunny?" She scooped up his stuffed bunny and examined it. "Do you like this bunny?"

Judge answered by snatching it back from her. He acted without thinking, by reflex.

"I was wrong. You love that bunny," she said.

Embarrassed, he tossed it over his shoulder onto his cot and said, "No I don't. I just don't like people touching my stuff."

"Really? Well. You know what? My son had one just like it.

They were inseparable, until he lost it on a train. Would you mind if I took it home to him? It would mean so much to him, especially with all the craziness in this world right now. A real comfort, you know?"

Judge felt a lump growing in his throat, but he grabbed the bunny by its floppy ear and flung it at Dr. Jackson. She caught it, a surprised look on her face.

"You would give this up so easily? This bunny, that clearly means so much to you?" Dr. Jackson peered into his good eye. *What was she looking for?* "You're not giving this to me to make my son happy. You're throwing it away, just to hide how much you love it." She gave the bunny a close look. "You know, on second thought, my son's had white ears and a black tail. Do you think he'll notice the difference?"

Judge shrugged. He didn't want to play this game anymore. He was losing.

"Hm. I think our greatest attachments are all about the detail," Dr. Jackson said. "And you see detail, contrast, like no one before. It must be incredibly overwhelming. Or is it comforting? To measure the world by its subtlest differences, to see the connections no one else can. To have the power to separate, and the will not to. To allow the rest of us to *be*."

Judge found a spot on the floor, because he couldn't bear the intensity of her stare. He felt her press the bunny back into his chest, and he clutched it there, as if to mute the sound of his thumping heart.

"Thank you," she said sincerely, "but I think you should keep this. Your parents would want you to have it." She dropped a hand to his shoulder and lifted his chin so that he had to meet her eyes. "Don't be so ready to let go of something you love, just to prove you don't need it to go on. We all need a friend."

Dr. Jackson gave him a quick kiss on the forehead as she got up to leave.

Judge blurted out, "Conversations."

"I'm sorry?" she said, turning back.

"The techs. Engineers. Whoever. They'd have conversations around me, like I wasn't there. They never talked to me. But I listened. I guess I picked up some things. That's how I can pretend to be like the rest of you."

"Doctors and lollipops."

"And TV rots your brain."

"I enjoyed our talk today, Judge," Dr. Jackson said. "Now get some rest. We've got a long road ahead. You'll need your energy."

SEQUENCE THREE

PART KATIE_0001

You want to know how she did it, don't you? How she infiltrated Dimond's silo network in order to learn about the children he had hidden from the world, and the claim he was staking on their inner territory? How she inducted members into a society of her making, anonymous allies forging a new *wouncage* for a hybrid age of nature and technology?

I keep no power for myself.

Remember that. It will come up again later.

You've been very patient. She would have explained it all before, but honestly, she had too much going on. So go ahead. Ask. She's waiting for a message from one of the founding society members now, so she has some time on her hands.

She's there, see? On the sandy bluff overlooking Lake Saka-kawea, not far from Like-a-Fishhook village (or where it used to be), just a hop, skip, and a canoe trip across from New Town (where *she* was supposed to be). Look how the harsh wind still hot from the long summer lifts her long black hair off her back and convinces her it's safe to close her eyes.

It's ok to interrupt. She won't mind. She'll start at the beginning, even though it's not the real beginning, and she'll even break it down into parts, so that it's easier to digest. She's very good at that.

Before we start, you should know she will expect payment.

Stories are sacred, even new ones, like hers. For the Mandan, Hidatsa, and Arikara—stories *are* power. Only those who own the rights to a story can tell it, and the storyteller suffers in order to receive the power from sharing it. Power from sharing.

I keep no power for myself. There it is again. See?

Many stories have died, because many storytellers have died. Two rounds with smallpox, less than three generations apart, took thousands upon thousands. The Flood took the rest, but not by drowning. A sudden and sustained, dispiriting displacement from the world would claim them. Broken treaties, boarding schools, banned traditions. This became the drum beat of their lives, until even their very language, once spoken by all, became just another strange tongue. A story that had survived the scourge, when told in the old language, became only for the storyteller's ears. A precious artifact.

Katie could translate for you, except those stories aren't for you, and they aren't hers to tell, anyway. She doesn't own the rights, remember? She'd never be able to afford them, and many of the old stories were reserved for men to tell. So there's that.

For any good performance, props are essential, don't you think? Her people knew this well. When a story was inherited or purchased, a bundle of sacred objects came with it. Bundles contained a variety of items, depending on the kind of story they accompanied. You want some examples? Sure, anything for you, our paying customer. Most contained a robe made from buffalo or elk hide for the storyteller to wear. Elements of the story were painted on the robe. A visual aid, you know? A cluster of dried sage, because sage smells really good and many things in the bundle really do not, like the skull of a famous ancestor, or bones from a snake or coyote, raven or eagle. A necklace of bear claws, or a headdress of feathers. If it was a war story, there would be a weapon. Most often a knife, arrow, or spear. If it was a harvest story, there would be dried food. Corn, gourds, the head of a sunflower. Often a wooden pipe. A clay pot. Feathers, scalps, furs. And always a drum made from a turtle's shell, because each story had its own rhythm.

Now don't get your hopes up. If Katie were to share these stories without securing the rights first, it would bring bad luck on her *and* you, and we wouldn't want that now, would we? But she *can* share what *she* has collected for her own, personal bundle.

Most personal bundles stay personal, and aren't considered valuable for trade or sale. It's just how it is. Not everyone can be a warrior, or a guardian, or a leader, or even as interesting as a trickster. But Katie does know a whopper of an origin story, and she'll tell it to you, for a price. This origin story is set on the frontier of a New World, starring a cast of characters as strange, yet recognizable, as her own people's Lone Man, Thunderbird, and Old Woman Who Never Dies. The bundle that comes with the story, free of charge (with initial purchase, of course), contains no bones or dried plants or arrowheads, but her own tokens of nature, wild game, and sacred weapons.

Katie would want you to know exactly what you're buying. Her personal bundle consists of the following.

1. *Willow*, a programming code based on the dead language of her Mandan ancestors.
2. An encryption key for translation and security: *I keep no power for myself.*
3. A collection of wicked good video game mods.
4. A ton of sharp tools for hacking.

5. Data. Lots and lots of data.

But that's enough advertising. She's ready to spill the beans, if you're ready to listen. Don't reach for your wallets just yet. We know you're good for it.

// How Girl Who Climbs Built the Lodge //

One of the first things a Society needs is a place to meet. To exchange ideas. To debate. To plan. But Katie was as *outside* as an outsider can be when she first discovered the existence of the Gorey kids. She needed a way in to scout for a secure location for the Lodge. A subdirectory foothold in Dimond's subterranean network would do the trick. Somewhere tucked away. Nice and shady.

After weeks of scouring the network's perimeter for a back door or broken window, Katie found an underground tunnel instead, dug by one of Dimond's own people to hide, of all things, a hobby.

Stan Schoop was a creator of imaginary worlds, a fledgling game-maker trying to make his mark in the competitive universe of role-playing mods. And he was Dimond's IT guy.

Stan's latest project was a modification for *FutureBound*, a popular role-playing game centered on a family of misfits brought together by misfortune and circumstance in the wilds of the Old West. Ironic, right? As role-playing games go, *FutureBound* was expansive and still expanding. Its evolution from a free PC download to a multi-platform MMORPG sold by software giant YorReality for upwards of $69.95 was an inspiration to RPG developers like Stan who dreamed of striking it rich. Game mods for *FuBo* were welcome, and the most popular mods were purchased by YorReality for official incorporation into future version releases.

Stan Schoop spent his downtime in Dimond's SoCal silo programming expansion packs for his *FuBo* mod called Cro*xx*Roads, a transportation hack that allowed users to travel instantaneously to any of the determined locales rather than rely on the digital trains, horses, or Conestoga wagons. No doubt his proximity to the portal vaks in the warehouse had provided inspiration, but the mere fact that he continued to moonlight as a virtual world creator, even while working to catalog New World objects in his *actual* reality, raised the question of how much his heart was in his work. Pays the bills, being a minion, but it's nothing to get obsessed over. You know?

Cro*xx*Roads, on the other hand, was his baby, and his baby had stiff competition. Stan kept a working copy of his mod tucked away on Dimond's network, in a nice shady spot, so that he could make edits as they came to him. He uploaded patches and upgrades almost nightly. Forget about the co-worker kid with a black hole in his head. Download count and user reviews were the metrics he obsessed over. Successful acquisition depended on those numbers. When his hack was hacked, he generally accepted the new mods, so long as they were harmless. He did take the precaution to automatically define any piggybacking mods as user data, to avoid any IP disagreements down the road. Sharing's fine until there's a million-dollar buyout on the line.

I keep no power for myself. Stan couldn't see the virtue.

Like a barnacle on a ship coming into port, Katie hitched a ride into the silo network on Stan Schoop's *FutureBound* mod with a mod of her own. When "The Lodge" showed up in his user data, he barely noticed it. Stan unknowingly planted Katie's secret meeting place right under Dimond's nose—well, right under *all* of him, since the silo was technically Dimond's personal basement. Once there, Katie made herself at home in the neighborhood, leaving Stan to his mod development ambitions. She was much more interested in the strange children, and Dimond's plans for their powers.

Stan got himself gobbled up by a streamer not long after, so Katie did him a solid and deleted the Cro*xx*Roads files from the silo's network. No sense in drawing attention to the path she'd followed in, now was there?

So then she was sitting pretty. From her computer in the casino cashier's office, where she was tasked with reconciling M.H.A. Tribal Council Funds with the Chairman's fiscal year operating budget, Katie could roam the intranet of the silo, hunting for allies.

To hide their identities, she gave them names like *ButtonBush*, *HarrierHawk*, *Snake*, and *Coyote*. To them, she was known only as *LodgeBuilder*, because it was important for her to remain anonymous, but in fact she'd given herself a name, too. *Girl-WhoClimbs*.

And that is the story of how Katie Goodbear started to form her own family of misfits, while trying to thwart the man who was trying to take over the world.

I keep no power for myself.

+ + +

This probably comes as no surprise, but reception was generally shitpoor on the backroads of northwestern North Dakota. She was in the middle of a move, a forced relocation of sorts, and she was waiting for the cable guy, so to speak. That's why Katie hiked up here, midway between the Garrison Dam and the refinery under construction at Like-a-Fishhook, where she could find three full bars of reception. No message yet, so she still has some time.

She did promise you that origin story, after all.

It was hard to think of beginnings, when standing on the edge of an ending. Many of the old ones in her tribe still can't bear to look at the surface of the lake, knowing what lies beneath it. It causes too much pain.

Katie was born well after The Flood. She had never walked the streets of Elbowoods. Never stared vaguely out the window of the school during a lesson. Never bought a piece of hard candy from the general store, or took flowers to somebody in the hospital, or ran a game of bingo at the VA where her grandparents had met at a dance as teens. But her history was there, below that dark and choppy surface. She could follow the path down Main Street in her mind, swimming instead of strolling, among the spirits of her people.

In her mind, her ancestors had sprouted gills to breathe. For centuries the Mandan had been the people of the Heart River, but now they were *river* people. Half human, half fish. Part memory, part dream.

We've been over and over the rules about story rights, so it may shock you to learn that she only told you the rules, because she wanted you to know when she was about to break them. She's become comfortable with breaking rules lately, with stealing what isn't hers. But she has to explain, or you won't understand. If you're very superstitious, you can skip ahead. Go on. No judgment.

For the rest of you, don't be surprised if some bad luck comes your way.

// An Origin Story of the Mandan and Hidatsa//

The Mandan people came from a place under the ground, near the river, so the story goes. One of the ancestors discovered a vine growing up and out of the ground, and so the people began to climb. A girl was very pregnant and too heavy for the vine, so the others above her told her to go back. But she wanted to see the new world too much, so she kept climbing. The vine snapped behind her. No one else could follow her out of the ground.

+ + +

The point of the story, in case you missed it, is that when a girl becomes too curious, bad things happen, and no one will ever forget it was your fault. Katie had been to enough church on Sundays to know that Eve got the same bad rap for taking a bite of that sacred apple. Katie could understand how some people would see curiosity as a curse, because there is no end to curiosity, and forever mysteries can be overwhelming and scary. But being afraid to ask a question—or to start climbing that vine—seemed far worse, even if the answer led to more questions—or more climbing.

For example, that refinery over there, near the ancient site of Like-a-Fishhook village. It isn't an oil refinery at all. Not anymore. The sale of the reservation's refinery to Dimond Industries was one of the many transactions that the Tribal Chairman, her cousin Duke Paulson, directed her to *adjust* in the public records of the Tribal Council. He'd been doing that sort of thing as Chairman for several years now, but this was by far the biggest amount. More on that later.

She only mentions it now so that you understand how she came to know Bradley Dimond, a mysterious stranger with a sudden and significant presence on Fort Berthold Reservation. Overnight, the FAA declared a no-fly zone over his new property, and the whole shoreline of the lake crawled with Quarry Security, paramilitary contractors familiar with the M.H.A. Nation from past skirmishes on protest lines over pipelines and water rights, that sort of thing. It was clear Bradley Dimond knew people in high places, and low.

So Katie got curious. Started climbing. Did her research. Some snooping. Hacking. And now, full on corporate espionage.

She checked her phone again. Still nothing. *Sigh*. Even espionage had its dull moments.

Speaking of origin stories, it turns out Bradley Dimond had a knack for coming up with them. When Katie first saw Judge through the hacked security cameras at the silo, he was just a baby—not a mythological baby, but a real one who had snapped the vine from the mere weight of him entering a new world, or at least stretched it to the point of breaking. Sure enough, Dimond laid the blame on Mother Gorey. Stick with tradition where you can, you know? Helps make the rest of it easier to swallow if part of the story is familiar.

The truth of origin is infinitely curious, you see. Bradley Dimond and people like him know that, but choose to ignore it, because it's of little use. Harmful, even, to certain timelines, and milestones, and rewards. Best to carve it up into bite-sized pieces, ready for consumption.

I keep no power for myself. Or throw Mother and Father Gorey to the lions. Whatever works, right?

Two *dings* in rapid succession from her phone told Katie that two members had entered the Lodge, so in a flash she joined them. Each member had their own access point, just as if they were avatars playing a role in *FutureBound* instead of plotting against Bradley Dimond in the here and now. Anyone could start or join a conversation at any time, as long as they had means to log in. Access was key. She saw no reason to change the formatting.

> HarrierHawk has entered the lodge.

> PallidSturgeon has entered the lodge.

> LodgeBuilder has entered the lodge.

>> PallidSturgeon: It's time. He's not safe. They're going to take him today from school.

>> HarrierHawk: I'm ready. Bring him to Kaymoor. Or as close as you can get. I'll be watching for you.

> HarrierHawk has left the lodge.

So abrupt, that one. Not like Carl needed Katie's permission to act, but still.

>> LodgeBuilder: Be careful. I look forward to meeting him.

> PallidSturgeon has left the lodge.

It wasn't customary to say hello or goodbye in the Lodge. Good manners were the first to go with anonymity. The real truth was, the thought of meeting any new Lodge members, face to face, almost paralyzed her, but at least the wait was over.

Maybe this was how Dorothy's wizard felt just before that curtain was pulled back.

PART TREV_0002

Darryl Bowman was a slack-jawed, dead-eyed bully, so it was no surprise to Trev when he overheard him making a deal with Agent Selena Dohanian. She wasn't a real agent, not with the FBI anyway, but she was in charge all the same. She'd made that perfectly clear within five seconds of Bradley Dimond's final words in the most unreal press conference in the history of humans, the one that demoted every FBI agent stationed at Hawks Nest State Lodge to underlings of Furst Enterprises. To say there was a lack of enthusiasm from the FBI for their new org chart would be an understatement. Woody Owens modified Dohanian's official title of Federal Industry Agent to *Industrial Agent* because of her "caustic personality."

Trev saw Dohanian at least once a day after their first meeting in the lodge, and each time her entourage of *industrial* agents had multiplied. Meanwhile, the population of real Feds dwindled to one, and he wasn't even sure if Woody was still there on official business or if he was just hanging around to see how things played out. Real law enforcement was on strike.

Dohanian's mercenaries watched Trev wherever he went. The black sedan parked across from the Bowman's place left only to follow Trev to school and back, which meant he actually had to go to school and stay all day. No more hikes over to the lodge to sit vigil.

School was more of a joke than usual. The first few days were devoted to adjusting to the New World of pop-up monsters and backyard black holes. The school held slightly altered active shooter drills to prepare for the event of a streamer attack, and had assemblies to provide slightly altered just-say-no-to-drugs tactics in the case that somebody came across a vak. Adrenaline peaked, numbness set in, resignation reigned. Things went mostly back to normal after a week under the overwhelming realization that there was nothing they could do about any of it anyway.

Except that Trev was an orphan now. Yes, there was that extra measure of difference for him, along with the federal surveillance. Earlier that day, Dohanian herself had staked him out as he ran laps for Gym, standing with arms on hips like a coach disapproving of his performance. She'd made a point of watching him out in the open, so that everyone else could see that she was watching him, too.

A group of jocks had slowed down enough to box him in.

"Skaggs, your stalker is *hot*."

"What'd you do, Skaggs? Rob a bank?"

"Does she watch *everything* you do?"

"Does she spank you if you step out of line?"

Trev might've noticed Dohanian's good looks if she hadn't always given him a face like she wanted to disintegrate him into tiny bits. He didn't know what he'd done to piss her off, but he had a strong feeling that if she got wind of what these jerkoffs were saying about her, it wouldn't help his case one bit.

"Knock it off," he'd said between heavy breaths. His asthma had been acting up.

To his surprise, they had knocked it off. As they'd picked

up their pace to leave him behind, he'd found himself envious of the kick they still had left in them. He guessed the current climate of uncertainty took the fun out of harassing him. Darryl Bowman, however, was immune to climate change.

Darryl was the baby of the Bowman family, and he'd been a senior when Trev was just a freshman. He'd flunked out halfway through the year, but not until after he'd taunted Trev into half a dozen fights—half a dozen fights Trev had lost, most in front of a fair-sized crowd of people. As much as he'd hated all those useless cow eyes on him while he tasted blood and dirt in his mouth, Trev'd been grateful for them. As dumb as Darryl was, witnesses had probably kept him from going too far.

Not long after flunking out, Darryl got fired from the bowling alley for selling oxy behind the shoe rental counter, and he was still staying with Dave and Sally as part of his probation when they took Trev in. Darryl had pretended not to care when Sally demoted him to a sleeping bag so that Trev could take his place on the couch, but once the lights went out, the resentment radiating from his spot on the floor was like an angry space heater. To Trev's surprise, Darryl didn't try to murder him that first night, or the next. Maybe Trev's grief took the sport out of it, or maybe he was waiting for an opportunity with no witnesses.

For the past eight days Darryl tested Trev every so often to see if he was ready to receive his final pounding, like a cat toying with an injured mouse. Dave and Sally were so worried about Dave's dad, Jack, that they couldn't provide Trev with much cover. Jack Bowman spent most of his time in the back room, trying not to die of the black lung disease that was killing him, at least not until Caleb won his case against Mountain

Patriot's insurance company. As long as he was alive, it was a fight over an insurance claim. If he died before it was settled, it became a wrongful death suit against MP, and MP fought those tooth and nail. Trev didn't really understand all the details, but one thing was perfectly clear: the recent reality shift was just something else to stress out about for folks like the Bowmans, who already had a hell of a lot to stress out over. Trev wouldn't think to bother them with the small matter of Darryl wanting to smash his skull in. He'd have to deal with that on his own.

Trev was barely asleep when Darryl's phone broke into song, but he pretended to sleep through several seconds of the Katy Perry ring tone while Darryl fumbled like a drunk monkey to answer it. A couple of gruff replies, then Darryl snuck out of the house without shoes. Trev followed him to see what the hell he was up to, and there he was, making a deal with Industry Agent Selena Dohanian.

Darryl leaned against her sedan like he thought he was picking her up or something. She was giving a long hard look at the confederate flag on his tee-shirt as she handed over a thick envelope. Trev couldn't hear them from his hiding place, but he didn't need to. No matter what the deal was, it couldn't be good.

"Looks like our Darryl has just become the latest addition to Selena's illustrious list of industrial agents," said an easy going voice behind Trev.

"Maybe he'll unclog some industrial toilets. Make himself useful for once."

"Doubtful."

"What are you doing out here, Woody? Ah, never mind. I almost forgot. Secret meetings are your favorite."

"Secret meetings *at night* are really my favorite," Woody said as he stretched his back against a tree. He looked tired. "Good god. Is he actually trying to *flirt* with her?"

"Darryl would flirt with a gorilla if he thought he had half a chance." Trev moved to a tree closer to Woody to ask, "Why can't they just leave me alone?"

"Maybe it was no coincidence that your father ended up on the river with those fugitives," Woody shrugged. "Maybe he knew them before."

"I told you, he didn't."

"Maybe he had connections you didn't know about."

"The only connection he had was with that damn river. It might as well have fed straight into his bloodstream. He didn't care about much else."

"Now you're being dramatic," Woody said with an appreciative smile. "It's simple, really. Selena Dohanian is following orders, and those orders are to follow one of many leads to the whereabouts of the Gorey clan. Her path to that answer starts with your dad, and he passed that starting point down to you, whether you like it or not."

Before Trev could answer that, Woody put a finger to his own lips. Darryl was coming back, tromping through the grass with his giant troll feet. Trev and Woody stuck like glue to their chosen trees. Trev could've kicked himself. If Darryl caught him out here, Trev's life was on a countdown timer for sure. Darryl stepped on something that made him howl and put a hand right near Woody's face to steady himself. Woody eased back as Darryl knocked the broken pinecone off his foot and limped like a big baby back into the house.

Once the door was closed, Trev explained his predicament to Woody, who seemed far too complacent about it all. "I'm not on the couch. He's gonna know I was spying on him."

"No, he won't," Woody said. "Bathroom screen is broken."

Trev scurried over to the bathroom window. Woody was right. *How much time had he spent out here?* No time for wondering about that now. Trev lifted up the corner of the metal frame, and Woody gave him a leg up, launching him through. Trev caught himself on the windowsill before bouncing off the commode to the floor. Woody stuck his head through the frame to find him sprawled across the tile like a rumpled bath towel.

He sounded more amused than sympathetic when he said, "They say more accidents happen in the bathroom than any other room in the house." Trev threw a wet washcloth at him, but before he ducked back out, Woody reminded, "Don't forget to flush."

Trev flushed to cover his tracks, and sure enough, when he opened the door Darryl was blocking his way. He slapped on the light, blinding Trev.

"You jerking off in my bathroom, squirrel nuts?" Darryl barked.

"Just taking a piss."

"In the dark."

"Turn that goddamned light off," yelled old Jack Bowman from his bedroom across the hall, falling into a fit of coughing.

"Sorry, Mr. Bowman," Trev said, knocking the light switch back down.

Darryl breathed down Trev's neck in the hall, caught him by the back of his shirt before he could make it to the couch, and tossed him into the chair.

"Couch is mine for the remainder," he announced. "You've outworn your welcome here, squirrel nuts. Time you moved on."

"This ain't your house any more than it's mine," Trev said out of pure anger and stupidity. He waited for the pain, but Darryl just glared at him.

"You know what I think?"

"God, no. I can at least be grateful for that."

"I think your daddy got exactly what was coming to him. He went and stuck his nose into the wrong place this time. These people play for keeps."

Trev wanted to ask him how much was in the envelope, but he stopped himself. Keeping Darryl in the dark about what he knew was the only advantage Trev had right now.

Darryl was snoring like a congested grizzly bear within minutes. Trev wouldn't be getting back to sleep tonight. He wondered if Woody was still on watch. Could Trev trust him, if it came down to it? He was still a Fed, after all. Why on earth would Dohanian think Darryl was a good investment? What did she pay Darryl to do, exactly?

He went over things in his head, listening to Mr. Bowman's ventilator. He was jealous of the extra oxygen. His own chest felt tight, and he could hear the rattle inside from the asthma kicked up by all the excitement. He needed a new inhaler, but he wasn't on the Bowmans' insurance and they had enough to deal with. Maybe the school nurse would loan him one. He'd ask tomorrow.

If he stopped breathing between now and then, oh well.

PART ROAN_0003

DREAMS ABOUT THE SILO CAME EVERY NIGHT, no doubt induced by the familiarity of the concrete bunker. The dreams were too real, more like replayed memories. She didn't want to go to sleep. Didn't want to go back again. While the others slept she spent time outside, practicing her new kickass bioshell skills. Despite efforts to stay awake, she started to fall asleep during the day.

One such afternoon, against her will, she was swept from the darkness of sleep into the brightness of the Duomo, the largest chamber in the hamster tubes of the silo. All the equipment they'd used to peer inside her required the extra space and left her no corner to escape what she'd become. The cramped space of her old underground digs bothered her, so she willed the walls to expand. She watched the dream unfold, like scenes in a movie.

Her dream-self wore hospital scrubs and sat across from Munny at a small table, playing Euchre. Slim Munny had been her primary guard and somehow had been perpetually bored. About a month into her captivity, he'd set up a card table and undone her restraints. She resisted at first, staring blankly across from his long, hollow-eyed face while he explained the strategy and played both hands. After a while, she picked up the cards he dealt her, but only to pass the time. When his shift was over, neither of the muscle-bound morons she'd nicknamed Thing 1 and Thing 2 minded the long stretches of silence. If she complained or tried anything, they just administered a shot of sedative and out she went. At least Munny let her use her brain for something other than to keep her heart pumping.

A deep, heavily accented voice asked, "What do you know?"

Roan knew who the dream was introducing. Dr. Nilas Nygard began every conversation with that phrase. Nilas was the neuro-scientist overseeing Roan and Judge's development, and he was well-liked by most of Dimond's worker bees—all except for Munny. Munny got tense whenever the doctor visited, and that made Roan even more nervous than she already was.

Since Nilas had a Scandinavian accent, Roan had assumed the phrase was a casual greeting she wasn't familiar with… something like "How's it hanging?" But this day, the day she was dreaming about, he had challenged her for a response.

"It's not a rhetorical question, you know?" Instantly it was Nilas sitting across from her instead of Munny. Munny leaned back against the bulkhead, perturbed his game was interrupted. "What. Do. You. Know? Everybody knows at least one thing so well they can recite it, or play it, or do it blindfolded." When she was silent, he continued to encourage a response. "No? Nothing? I don't believe it. It can be a skill. Something you *know* how to do, better than most. A barber knows hair. A mechanic knows carburetors. Mr. Munny here, he knows lots of things. Tell me one thing you know, Mr. Munny."

"I know when somebody's trying to sell me something I don't need."

Nilas laughed. "Yes, yes. That is a very useful thing to know. Especially in the world in which we live. How did you come to know this, I wonder?"

"By selling people shit they didn't need."

Nilas chuckled. "Like a new vacuum? One of those miraculous juicers or blenders on TV? You don't strike me as a salesman. What did you sell that people didn't need?"

"A chance to win," Munny said, his long face curling into disdain.

"Ah, yes. That's right. I heard that about you. You were a carnival barker when Dr. Dimond discovered you. The lives we led before. It's a struggle to remember *before* sometimes, isn't it?"

"Not really," Munny said.

"*Before*, it was your vocation to convince fair-goers to play your game of chance. To win a stuffed animal. Shit they don't need. See, Roan?" Nilas turned back to her, and suddenly instead of watching from the corner, she was looking straight into his harsh, penetrating eyes. "Just that one thing he knows tells us so much about him. So tell me what you know. It can be something simple. Something small. You know how to throw a ball? You know what chocolate tastes like? You know what it feels like to stub your toe. I did that just last night. The living quarters here are so damned small."

He tried to get a smile out of her, but it didn't work.

"You know what it's like to be homesick. To miss your mother. Your father. Your own room. Your own clothes. Your freedom." Roan's eyes narrowed, and Nilas leaned back from her to cross his arms. "I can tell you what *I* know. I know how to tell a good bedtime story. Do you want to hear it?"

Roan wanted to say no, because she had already heard this bedtime story, but her dream gave her no voice in the matter.

"It's a very good one. You are in it. And your brother, too, of course. Even Mr. Munny over there. *Save the best for last,* isn't that what they say? This *is* the last bedtime story. Not just for you, or me, or Mr. Munny, our salesman of chance. It is a bedtime story for us all. The very last. And who am I? The narrator, the detached observer? The one who lives to tell the tale? No. I am the hero!"

Nilas put his fist to his sides and comically pushed out his chest. Munny coughed "Ha!" and Nilas fell back into his chair, still smiling.

"I know, I know. It's ridiculous. I mean, look at me. I don't look very heroic, do I? I'm not waving around a lightsaber or a wand, and I wouldn't know the first thing about how to burst into a room, guns blazing. No, I am a very different kind of hero. Not the sort who rescues his friends at the last possible moment, or the sort who vanquishes an evil foe against all odds. I am the hero who gives answers when others say there are none, who gathers the lost, frightened souls of this world and makes them whole again."

"I think you're confused," Munny said. "That's not a hero. That's a cult leader."

"Yes, there is some parallel there, to be sure. Cults form around the idea of impending doom, *fabricated* doom—until now—foretold by signs and symbols, predictions of the future and interpretations of ancient texts. For thousands of years, science has been the cool head in the room. Scientists like myself have warned and witnessed, created and destroyed. But there was always hope, you see. Hope that past horrors would not be repeated. Hope that humankind could learn from its mistakes. But we are beyond hope now. Beyond what science can fix— even explain. In the simplest terms, worlds have collided. The fabric of our reality has been ripped open, and we are dangling threads on the event horizon. There is no escape from this. All life will be consumed, wiped clean from the Earth—if it is not first swallowed whole into oblivion. Either fate is unavoidable. I cannot save the world. Not a single dandelion. But I can do one thing—and this one thing is what makes me a hero. I can sacrifice my own guiding principles, my own desire for hope and peace of mind, in order to save others from the horror of our near future. I can save you, Roan. I can save you from the pain of having to bear witness to the doom you have wrought simply by coming into existence. *You* are my harbinger of doom, Roan Gorey. I will offer myself up to be the final witness to the end of our universe. I will end *you*."

Nilas lunged across the table at her with a scalpel, Munny shouted in alarm, and Roan was screaming... in Bunker 318.

Walt was by her side in an instant, but she pushed past him to get outside. The sun was just starting to go down. It was cool in the evening now, so there were fewer insects buzzing around, but she could feel the presence of every single one of them. Millions of tiny little eyes locked onto her, drawn to the smell of her fear.

"Are you ok?" Walt asked for maybe the third or fourth time. "You're starting to scare me, Roan. Talk to me."

"Do you know what Berit was working on all those months at the silo?"

"The amplifier—"

"Yes, but not just that. They were designing a station. A place where I could call streamers in to release them. A safe return, from wherever they've been."

"Well, that's great, isn't it?"

"You don't understand. There are some people I don't want to bring back."

PART TREV_0003

TREV WAS IN GYM CLASS WHEN HE GOT THE urgent call to the office for dismissal. He didn't even have time to change out of his gym clothes. He knew it was a trap when he saw Darryl waiting for him in Vice Principal Cosgrove's office. Knowing what he knew about Trev's history with Darryl, and Cosgrove was ok with handing him over, like Darryl was his legal guardian. Dohanian must've paid him off, just like she'd paid Darryl. Trev could've refused to go. Raised an alarm loud enough to bring teachers and students out into the halls. But he didn't. Cosgrove and Darryl were expecting a fight from him. He could tell. So he just smiled right into their stupid faces.

"Hi Darryl," Trev said, like nothing was the matter, because why give them the satisfaction? "Mr. Cosgrove."

"Dave and Sally had to take Daddy in to the hospital," Darryl lied, sounding like a robot programmed to sound sad.

"Let's go then," Trev said, turning on his heels. When he was alone with Darryl in the hall, he added, "Making Old Mr. Bowman a part of this is wronger than wrong."

"For all I know it's true," Darryl shrugged. "Daddy's days are numbered, and once he's gone there ain't gonna be nothing left to inherit but a big pile of medical bills. I gotta look out for me, myself, and I. I make no apologies. God, I hate the smell of this place."

"Is it the clean or the learning that irks you?"

Darryl smirked and leaned in close enough for Trev to see the chewing tobacco in his teeth when he said, "I hope they do experiments on you. I hope they turn you inside out, and that you're alive and watching, the whole time."

"Damn, Darryl," Trev said. "You really gotta lay off the alien autopsy documentaries. It's skewed your take on reality."

"My reality has always been screwed," Darryl said.

"Not what I said—" Trev didn't get to finish that correction because Darryl threw him face first into the door.

Trev was stunned stupid by the pain, and he had to keep one eye shut it was tearing up so much. Darryl pulled him outside. Trev was just about to start throwing punches whether he could see or not when he heard a familiar, laid-back voice that he'd come to appreciate.

"Darryl Bowman," Woody said. "It's my distinct honor to inform you that you are officially being charged with being an ignorant asshole."

Woody moved lightning quick. He extended a baton and whacked Darryl's wrist hard enough to free Trev. When Darryl lunged after Trev, he rammed straight into the point of Woody's baton. Darryl bent over and stumbled back against the hand-rail. He checked for damage and found his confederate flag tee-shirt was ripped.

"Goddamn," he whined.

"Aw," Woody said, backing away with Trev behind him. "Flimsy fabric. I barely touched you. Mr. Skaggs, your uber driver's waiting."

Trev scanned the lot to find Caleb waving at him from his '84 Cavalier hatchback hidden behind a dumpster. If the dumpster'd had wheels it would've made for a better getaway. Caleb was shooting nervous glances at the government-issued Town Cars and Mustangs in the parking lot, knowing full well that if they didn't get a jump on that crowd, getting away was going to be about as likely as Darryl winning a Nobel Peace Prize.

Trev made it a few steps toward the hatchback before Dohanian rounded the corner of the building and leveled a shotgun at him. A cannonball hit him square in the chest, and he was on his back in the grass looking up at the sky before he even knew what had happened. Breathing became a priority, but that wasn't happening, so he distracted himself by watching the action unfold between Woody and Darryl.

One arm hooked around Woody's middle, Darryl fought for control over his holstered sidearm. Woody shut that effort down by cracking Darryl over the head with the baton, but the second that Darryl fell away, Woody took two shots close range, one in the side, one in the leg.

"Stay down Owens, and you may still have a career," Dohanian warned, advancing.

Somebody was pulling Trev across the grass, and Woody was following close behind with a profound limp. Dohanian pumped out a few more rounds at them, smashing the window of the Cavalier's door just as Woody opened it to shove Trev inside. A small black bag peeled from the spider web of glass onto the pavement, and the car was moving before the doors were shut.

Trev's diaphragm finally unclenched from the hit it took, and he exhaled nice and easy before taking a deep breath. He knew from all the hits he'd taken over the years that it hurt if you gulped air too fast. Woody seemed to be undergoing the same tender operation of breathing again. Caleb meanwhile was performing a miracle in the Cavalier, his arms a blur as he spun the steering wheel like they were a boat on water. He jumped a curb when the other vehicles attempted a blockade, and then they were on the main road, heading south toward Fayetteville.

"Am I shot?" Trev finally asked, feeling his chest for blood but finding none.

"You've been bagged," Woody responded, tossing one of the errant beanbags over to Trev to inspect. "Nonlethals. Thankfully. She has remarkable aim for corporate security."

Trev checked behind them to see a line of unmarked cars trailing close behind. They would soon pass the Cavalier and force them to stop, one way or another.

"Is this the top speed of this vehicle?" Woody asked. "Because when you said you had a plan, you failed to mention—"

"Look out!" Trev cried.

Caleb ignored him. He should've slammed the brakes on, considering the fact that straight in front of them, there was a wide-load flatbed backing across the road into Toby's Auto. Instead Caleb floored it, flying around the flatbed on the remaining inches of road. Behind them, the flatbed cut off the pursuit in a hail of screaming brake pads and a chain reaction of fenders getting bent. Caleb gave a quick wave to the flatbed's driver.

"Ok, never mind," said Woody. "Nice one."

"Dutch Harris," Caleb explained. "Former client. Owed me a big favor."

"I'd say that debt is settled. They may keep him for questioning, you know." Woody coughed, then winced. "Gosh darnit.

I think she busted up my ribs."

"Does anybody want to tell me what the hell is going on?" Trev ventured.

"Agent Owens got wind that the Indie Agents were planning an extraction today," explained Caleb, checking his rear view nervously, "so we thought we'd beat them to it."

"Why today?"

"That, I don't know," said Woody. "There could be a reason, or they could've just run out of patience."

"Why didn't you give me a warning, or something?" Trev asked. He tugged on his gym shorts. "I don't even have the clothes on my back."

"Couldn't risk Darryl getting wind and putting two and two together," Caleb said.

"Are you joking right now?"

"I have to agree, Mr. Harper," Woody said. "That does seem unlikely."

"They wanted to take you at the school to avoid a nasty fight with the Bowmans, but if Agent Dohanian knew you might make a run for it today, they would've just taken you last night from your bed. I don't think the Bowmans deserve that kind of stress. Do you?"

"Ok, ok. I get it. But damn. On the run in my gym shorts."

"We're getting off this road, right?" Woody asked. "Because fairly soon they will catch up, or set up a roadblock, and then it will all be over."

"Funny you should mention that," Caleb said, preparing for a tight turn. "Hold on."

When Caleb took State Road 7, Trev knew their options

had just narrowed to a water getaway. Trev's gut clenched. He didn't think he was ready for a trip down the New River just yet. Not after it had mistreated his father so poorly.

"Ok, Mystery Man, time to share the plan," Woody said.

"He's taking me to the Tipple," Trev answered.

"To the what?"

"Coal conveyor. Runs from the Nuttallburg Mine down to the old C&O tracks."

"Mr. Harper, do you expect our Trevor to jump a freight train out of here?"

"The C&O hasn't run for decades," Caleb answered.

"That's unfortunate. So what's the plan? I don't mean to press. It's just, they are behind us again. Did you notice?"

"He's gonna put me on the rapids," Trev said, because what else could the plan be?

Caleb glanced at him in the rear view mirror but said nothing.

"I want you to know how much it hurts my feelings that you still don't trust me enough to share your secrets," complained Woody, "especially when I shared mine, but whatever the plan is, I am in no condition for running as fast as you are going to need to run. I promise to do what I can to slow them down."

Caleb slid into a sudden stop near the old Kenney barn, and he and Trev jumped out to hide. Woody took over the driver's seat and said "Get your client out of here in one piece, Mr. Harper," before taking off down the road with a quick wave goodbye.

A caravan of chase vehicles followed the dirt cloud kicked up by Caleb's Cavalier, while Caleb and Trev tumbled down the steep yard behind the barn. Trev knew the shortcut well.

It would take them down to the Keeneys Creek Rail-Trail, but it would be a slow trek from there to Nuttallburg. Turned out, they wouldn't be hiking. Caleb pulled out two mountain bikes hidden in an old coke furnace. He typed a quick message into his phone while asking Trev the most ridiculous question ever: "Can you ride?"

In answer, Trev popped a downhill wheelie then bunny hopped over a rock. When Caleb went careening past him, wobbling like a bony bobble head, Trev shouted after him, "Can *you*?"

"Don't worry about me," Caleb said as Trev caught up and quickly passed him, "Get to the old tipple, then look toward Kaymoor."

Trev attacked the trail like a demon. It would've been down-right fun if he hadn't been aware of the un-fun party that was waiting for him at the bottom. Woody's fake-out must not've tricked Dohanian for long. A barricade of cars blocked the main access to the Keeneys, and even though Trev angled his slalom to go under the tipple itself, by the time he hit the main trail Dohanian herself was right on top of him.

She would've nabbed him, too, if Caleb hadn't slammed into her at full speed—maybe by pure accident based on his own startled face. Dohanian went sprawling into her clumsy cohorts, and somehow Caleb untangled himself to chase Trev on, his skinny scarecrow arms waving at him, shouting, "Just go! Go!"

Trev wondered why Caleb was so intent on getting cornered in a dead end, because that's all Nuttallburg was. A dead town at the end of an unused road. Downriver from Hawks Nest, Nuttallburg had been abandoned since the 50s when the last of the coal had been dug out of the mountain. Kaymoor upstream had fallen into ruin not long after. Even the footbridge across the river that had connected the two coal towns was gone. Only the pylons remained, looking like broken concrete teeth sticking out of the water to chomp on the kayakers who were crazy enough to run the Double Z rapids. The tipple itself looked part-barn, part-bridge, especially now that the park service had put a fresh coat of red paint on it as Step One of its restoration project. A rickety, covered conveyor belt snaked up the 600-foot cliff to the mouth of the mine. The trail that brought Trev into the ruins was the old C&O line that passed right under the conveyor. That's where coal miners would dump sifted coal into empty hoppers for transport to Pittsburgh, Cleveland, Chicago. Places he'd never go. He'd just reached the end of his own line, right here in the ruins of a deserted coal town. Why had Caleb even bothered? There was no boat waiting.

"What the hell?" There was no boat waiting, but there was a *helicopter*. It descended onto the New River by way of Kaymoor. No room to land, so it just hovered.

"I'm coming with you," Caleb said, giving Trev a shove. "To make sure it's safe."

"That's very reassuring," Trev replied, but he wasn't sure his sarcasm could be heard over the *fwup fwup* of the helicopter and the roar of the rapids.

Nothing about this was safe. Dohanian and her horde were nearly on top of them, but the only way to get to the helicopter was to jump across the pylons of the old footbridge. The pilot—a black guy he was pretty sure he'd never seen before—was giving him the hurry-up-and-get-over-your-fear-of-dying-a-horrible-death wave.

"Sure. Right. Hurry."

Trev felt himself on the verge of a full blown tantrum. All his life adults were telling him where to go, how to behave, what he needed to do, all with little information to back up the reason for any of it. Today was the pinnacle. The choice was clear, though, and the fact that Darryl had teamed up with Dohanian was the clincher. So Trev did what Caleb told him to do, even though every self-preservation bone in his body told him he was flat-out crazy for doing it.

The pylons by the riverbank were close enough together that it was easy to skip from one to the other. As the phantom bridge extended across the rapids though, the distance between the pylons grew quickly from a stretch of a step to an all-out jump. The currents of the New River roiled beneath him, and he thought about his father. Maybe he was under there, right now, looking up at him through eyes that can no longer see.

Trev checked behind him to see Caleb barely keeping his balance, looking terrified. Something hit Caleb's foot and knocked him so off balance he teetered on the edge. Trev grabbed his hand until he found his balance again. Dohanian aimed for Caleb again.

"Come back, or I knock him off," she said through a loud-speaker a helper goon held.

"Go!" Caleb shouted at him, knocking away his hand. "I can swim."

"Nobody can swim in this," Trev said. He didn't know what to do.

Dohanian made good on her threat and shot again, hitting the pylon just beneath Caleb.

"Hello there, assholes," Woody shouted above the fracas. His forehead sported a bad cut and his hands were zip-tied, so it was clear the chase had ended poorly for Woody, but currently he aimed his 9mm straight at Dohanian—well, as straight as the zip ties allowed. "Stop trying to kill my favorite lawyer. He doesn't have an ounce of fat on him. I fear he'd drop like a skinny anchor." Dohanian kept the bean bag shotgun pointed at Caleb, so Woody gave a stronger warning. "This gun shoots bullets, not beanie babies."

Dohanian's face contorted from anger as she relented and dropped the shotgun. Trev knew they only had seconds before her thugs got the jump on Woody and shifted the balance of power back again, so he didn't stop to think. He leapt from pylon to pylon until he could wrap his arms around the landing skid of the helicopter. His breath came hard. He thought he might pass out. He felt Caleb pushing on his legs until he was flat against the floor. The helicopter was already lifting off when he turned to help Caleb up from the skid.

Once they were both inside, the pilot ordered them to "Shut that door and buckle in."

Just before Caleb slammed the door shut, Trev heard his father call his name, clear as day. He knew it was impossible. He was just light-headed from the asthma. Hearing things.

The pilot tossed Trev an inhaler over his shoulder, and Trev sucked the medicine into his lungs greedily. *How did this guy know to have an inhaler ready? Who the hell was he?*

"I'm Carl," the guy said, a mind reader, evidently. "And you need to catch your breath."

PART MATTHIAS_0003

It wasn't the first time his house had been under surveillance. Wasn't even the second. The first time, his brother Jed was leading a union strike against MP Coal, and MP parked a sedan across from their trailer for intimidation purposes. Second was when he found contaminants in samples he took from the New, and Crowley Chemical parked a sedan in the same spot for the same purposes. After days on mountain trails hiding from he didn't know who, Matthias came home to find yet another sedan parked in that bald patch of dirt, the "watching" spot.

He didn't give two licks who was doing the watching this time. His aim was to determine if Trev was home without bringing attention to himself, so he stuck to the sycamores out back and did some watching himself. There was no sign of Trev inside, and the bus flew by without even stopping, so Matthias concluded that Dave had probably taken him in.

The Bowman place was on the way to the school complex by way of Seldom Seen, so Matthias would stop by and thank them for watching over Trev. He used just as much caution on approach to Old Jack's, and it was a good thing, too. Sure enough, there was one of those *watching* sedans parked on the Bowman easement. His paranoia was dead on lately, and that in and of itself was unsettling.

Truth be told, Matthias had been hoping for a shower and a hot meal before reuniting with his boy. He knew how embarrassed Trev got when he picked him up from school on a good day; collecting him after living in the woods for almost two weeks might be enough for Trev to claim a new family name. A pit stop at the Bowmans wasn't worth the risk, though, so Matthias kept to the woods of Seldom Seen, pushing on to the school for Trev. He'd be a sorry sight in the school office, but hopefully Trev would forgive him for at least not being dead.

Not more than a few paces up the hillside, Matthias was surprised to see his good friend Dave Bowman, trudging uphill and pushing a small crate ahead of him in a wheelbarrow. Normally he would've shouted hello and offered a hand, but unsure of who else might be watching, Matthias suppressed the urge and kept to slinking along in silence. He watched as Dave reached one of the old mine entrances and pulled aside the planks to get inside. Matthias waited for a while to make sure no one else was following, then he pulled out a flashlight.

To say his friend's behavior was bizarre wouldn't come close to the truth of it. Something was way off, and as much as he wanted to get to Trev, he couldn't abandon Dave out here without checking on him first.

Matthias entered the cool darkness, waited for his eyes to adjust. Morning light from the entrance and a stranger light coming from deeper in was enough to guide him to Dave. Whatever he'd been hauling had tumbled out of the wheelbarrow, but Dave seemed unwilling to retrieve it. Understandable, considering the crate had busted open and was leaking weird light all over.

"Need a hand?" Matthias asked, forgetting what a shock his voice might bring. Dave jumped so high he hit his head on the ceiling. Loose rocks crumbled down on both of them. "Careful now. You'll bring the whole mountain down on us."

Dave was so bewildered he couldn't speak. His lips moved, though. It was almost comical.

"I ain't a ghost, if that's what has your tongue tied," Matthias tried to help.

"They said you drowned." And then Dave grabbed him in such a bear hug Matthias felt the daylights going out. "I thought you was dead, you ol' coot. God *damn* it's good to see you."

"It's good to be seen."

"Does Trev know you're... back?"

"Not yet. I've gotten mixed up in some truly bizarre intrigue this time, Dave. I can't thank you and Sally enough for taking Trev in, but we're gonna have to go away for a while."

"Where to? Never mind, don't tell me. I have enough intrigue of my own," Dave said. "Take a look at this bullshit." Matthias studied the broken crate and the strangeness it contained. "I got a job offer," Dave explained, "from somebody who said they'd pay for all of Daddy's medical bills, all our outstanding debts, if I just do this one thing. Go over to Charleston and pick up a crate from a storage facility, bring it to one of the abandoned mines. Find a safe, dry spot."

"And then what?"

"Then I'm supposed to open it up, send a picture of where I put it as proof the job is done. That's it."

"Did they threaten you if you didn't do it?"

"No, like I said. It was a job offer. Said it was an extension of my conservation efforts with the Park Service. But what that *thing* has to do with conservation..."

"Well, let's take a look," Matthias said.

Dave took the crowbar out of his belt and pried it open. They took a few moments to let what they were seeing sink in. Black steel framed a heart of darkness. A vak, they called them. Matthias had seen only two before, and hadn't had much of a chance to study either of them, seeing as how he was running for his life at the time. Neither of them had been as tame as this one, a simple square of nothing rimmed by live wires of pure energy, set in a frame, like it was ready for hanging in a living room. The frame was secured to the inside of the crate, but the unforgiving, fiery rainbows within had managed to burn a few of the braces, leaving it off-kilter.

"I didn't think it was real," Dave said. "Not until now."

"I'm not even sure what *real* means anymore."

Handwriting on a piece of green tape stuck to the frame read *Myotis grisescens.*

"Gray bat," Matthias and David translated in unison, standing straight in surprise.

No time for discussion, because the echo of a helicopter drew their attention.

"That's coming from Nuttallburg," Dave said. "You sure you want to go that way?"

"Go ahead and take your picture, send it on," Matthias said. "I think I have a pretty good idea of what that's meant for, and if I'm right, it's not a bad thing. Not a bad thing at all. I'll see you on the other side, brother."

Matthias wasn't much for long goodbyes, and he didn't want to give Dave an opening to offer to come along, so he scuttled into the darkness toward Nuttallburg. Dave had his dying father to care for, and Matthias didn't want to drag him any further into this mess. Besides, he had a feeling of urgency about that helicopter.

At the mouth of the old Nuttallburg conveyor, he broke through some rotting wood just in time to see Trev fly past on a mountain bike, ducking under the stilts of the conveyor belt. Matthias called out to him like a madman, but he was too far away. Trev slid down the gravel hillside all the way to the bottom, and that's where he almost got tackled by some aggressive suits. Caleb Harper came tearing down out of control and knocked them all over like bowling pins, god bless him.

Matthias was trapped up there. He had to bust through planks that had been reinforced by the Park Service, and by the time he made it to the conveyor belt, Trev was already hopping the Kaymoor footbridge to the helicopter. *What the hell was he running from to make him so desperate to do such a damned foolish thing?*

Matthias was never much of a daredevil, but seeing his only son chased by professional goons into danger turned him into one. There was a slow way down the 600-foot cliff—the stairs—and the fast way—the conveyor. He didn't take the stairs.

The gravity rollers were rusted enough some of them didn't roll, but enough of them behaved to carry him down the hill at an alarming rate. Matthias hadn't considered how he was going to stop until he got to the bottom and it suddenly became a pressing requirement. He tried grabbing a lever as he flew past, but it just broke off in his hand. The floor dropped out beneath him before he had a chance to grab onto anything else. The broken lever in his hand got caught on the old coal chute, and he swung from it like the last rung of the monkey bars. He dropped the ten feet to the ground and felt something go wrong in his ankle.

He shouted Trev's name one more time, then watched him take off in the helicopter.

PART DOHANIAN_0001

No one watched the Little Bird lift off with the kid and the lawyer. No one paid any attention to Agent Owens, even though he still trained his weapon on her. All eyes were on the newly arrived Matthias Skaggs. Pack on his back, hair unwashed. A man straight out of the wilderness.

"Mr. Skaggs?" Owens ventured, lowering his 9mm. Selena took the opportunity to unload another round into his leg. Probably not necessary, but it made Selena feel better to hear him howl in pain. It registered with Skaggs that he was surrounded by people who weren't his friends, and he made a break for it. Her people closed in to prevent an escape. Owens gathered himself without falling over—pretty impressive, Selena thought—and after holstering his Glock, offered Skaggs his zip-tied hands in a weird double-handed handshake. "I'm Federal agent Woody Owens. Pleasure to meet you." Selena disarmed Owens and punched him in the stomach, dropping him to his knees. He deserved at least that. He added with difficulty, "Don't mind her, Mr. Skaggs. She's a little irritated with me. Disagreement over the welfare of your son."

"Where the heck is he going to?" Skaggs asked, sounding pathetic.

"That doesn't matter now," Selena said.

"It matters to me."

"You've been hiding from us, Matthias. That's not something

innocent people do," she pointed out, hoping to make him nervous. He'd be more likely to talk if he was nervous. "You're coming with us. Cuff him."

"There's no reason for that. He's no threat," Owens protested. He brandished the baton she forgot that he still had. He poked the nearest man in the gut and kicked the other one away from Skaggs. He surprised Selena by offering up his baton to her. "And neither am I. Much."

"Bullshit," Selena said, swiping away his baton. "You put that boy's life at risk."

"Again, we disagree. You're the one with the itchy trigger finger. Look, I am still the FBI Liaison attached to this industrial goon squad, and by law you have to have at least one. Until my home office replaces me, I'm it." Owens stood by Skaggs and added, "Wherever you take Mr. Skaggs, I'm his travel buddy. *Right of Capture* gives you custody of Roan and Judge Gorey, if you manage to get your hands on them, but anyone else you pick up along the way is in my custody, technically. So, you want to cut me loose?"

Selena slashed the air with her trusty Ka-bar centimeters from Woody's beard. "One wrong move…"

"Hey! Watch the beard," Woody whined, as she reluctantly cut his zipties. "Thank you kindly. See? Friends already."

Selena kept as close to Skaggs as she could stand on the trek back to the cars. His b.o. would've made a bloodhound weep.

"Where is Caleb Harper taking my son?" she heard him ask Woody.

"Away from these people. That's all I know."

"And who the heck are these people?"

"In my professional opinion, they are a bunch of assholes." Woody had raised his voice instead of lowered it when he said that, so one of her toughs gave him a harsh shove. Woody spun around to return the favor, but Selena barked an order to "Knock it off" and he obliged.

Home base at Hawks Nest Lodge was the next stop, where Selena reported her catch to Pirret, Owens reported his mistreatment to his home office, and Skaggs took a much-needed shower. Skaggs returned under escort dressed in clean clothes he must've had stored in his locker. He'd been a river tour guide here before the Gorey girl showed up and ruined his life, although judging by his general appearance, it had probably been ruined already. Skaggs sulked about his son while he drank coffee and ate muffins brought to him by the desk clerk. The news played on a massive wall TV with terrible resolution.

"I count *six* times you shot me," Owens said, sidling up to her with a cup of coffee, "half at close range, and yet not one apology."

"I'm sorry I didn't use real bullets," she said.

"My goodness, you are mean-spirited."

She wouldn't try to change his mind. On the giant non-HD TV, there was footage of devastation from one of the first known streamer attacks, two-year-old images of a state fairground torn up by what had been called a tornado and a collection of interviews with eyewitnesses. The topic of discussion among the talking heads was government cover-up conspiracies of early streamer encounters.

"Have you seen one?" Selena asked. "And I don't mean on TV. Up close, in person?"

"I wasn't aware you could get up close and still be a person."

"Well I have. I've lost friends. I've lost more than you can imagine," Selena said, hearing her own voice crack. She stowed her emotions and continued, "Seeing a streamer is enough to paralyze you. And vaks—well, it makes you physically ill to look at them. Our brains can't handle it. What does that tell you? What do you think we're up against here?"

"The Skaggs boy was not one of them. I know you're new to this job, so a word of advice—"

"I don't need advice from you—"

"—when you have a target, stay focused."

"And here's some advice for you, Agent Owens," Selena said. "You seem to have a soft spot for kids. Don't think of Roan Gorey as one. She's not like us. She's something else, from somewhere else, using kid camouflage, because it works on chumps like you."

"Personally, I think all kids are a little on the creepy side. *Redrum. They're heeeere,*" Agent Owens followed up his movie impersonations by pointing at the graphic on TV that read 'Are the Goreys an Alien Species?' and commenting, "I mean, if you're talking undercover alien invasion, they might have chosen wiser than a couple of creepy ass kids. What about a butterfly? Earthworm? I mean, who would suspect?"

"You think this is funny. When you lose someone you care about, you won't."

"I have lost many people I care about, Selena," Woody said, his Andy Griffith demeanor suddenly gone. "And it is my stellar sense of humor that has kept me from plummeting off the edge of this miserable existence into a netherworld of despair. Speaking of which, I saw a sign outside advertising a 'Lover's Leap' right next to a truly divine sudden drop." He held his hand out to her with a diabolical smile, and gave a nod toward the door. "Come. Join me."

Selena back away from his outstretched hand, then noticed another. Matthias was pointing a shaking finger at the TV.

"That's one of them right there," he said.

Footage of one streamer survivor in particular just became the key to finding the Goreys. Selena got Pirret back on the phone. "Tell Dr. Dimond our prime suspect is Staff Sergeant Marshall Griffith," she said. She listened to Pirret's response, then pushed Agent Owens aside.

"Raincheck then?" he said, sounding sullen.

Selena took note of the shiny scars across Matthias' hand like slug tracks on a sidewalk after the rain. "Congratulations, Mr. Skaggs. The boss wants to thank you. In person."

PART JUDGE_0004

AN ACORN. A FURRY SEED. AND A TINY JELLY-fish. Stolen goods, in Judge's possession. Tools of war, crafted by the Spaghetti Monster herself, in the open air workshop on top of Bunker 318.

She'd been toying with that goo since they arrived at the bunkers. While he was undergoing repairs, she was crafting weapons, perfecting her bioshell voodoo. What secrets the seeds and spore held was a mystery, but what they had in common was a clue to her intentions. Seeds and spores spread genetic information.

On the eve of his surgery, Judge had snuck into her bunker to steal anything she might use against him while he was under the knife, at his most vulnerable. The three strange seed sculptures had remained inert when he picked them up with his bare hands. That was stupid, admittedly. She could have booby trapped them, coded them to his touch or something. But his theft went off without a hitch, and now her manufactured infobombs were bumping pleasantly around in his bag, like marbles.

She hadn't noticed them missing yet. She was back from her morning prowl within the perimeter, perched as usual on Bunker 318, legs dangling over the blast door. The gaze she sent his way while he waited for his bunker to be transformed into a surgery room was not exactly the "Get Well Soon" variety.

"Bring a friend?" Dr. Jackson asked, beckoning him into to Bunker 321.

Judge pulled Bunny from his messenger bag, and she gave Bunny a quick salute. She draped an arm across Judge's shoulders and lead him inside. Surgical lamps powered by the chugging gasoline generator outside put a spotlight on his cot that had been raised to the appropriate height for an operating table. Next to it was a tray with scary looking tools, some of which looked more like what a car mechanic might use than a surgeon.

"Meet your new jetkill," Felix said proudly, holding the equipment in his gloved hand. "Your skull was nearly adult-sized last time, so the elastic polymer rim we constructed should have expanded with the bone structure of your face. The new shutter mechanism is made of salt water resistant metal alloy this time."

Felix winked at Judge over that one. Judge had managed to damage the jetkill by forcing corrosive tears into the electrical components. Creating chaos had been his only way out of Dimond's trap. Judge didn't acknowledge Felix's attempt at good-natured nostalgia, mainly because there'd been very little good nature about Felix's role at the silo. That, and Judge was quickly becoming overwhelmed by dread.

"As you know, we can't just cap the well, because the longer you go between vaks the faster the hole in your face grows. You have to vent in order not to blow, just like a gas pipe under pressure. The good news is that the new mechanism will work with the same remote, and should the jetkill sustain damage again, there's a secondary mechanism to prevent accidental misfires, here." Felix pointed to the switch on the jetkill, then to his own temple. "The surgery will take place in three phases.

Removal. Capping. Replacement. The three phases will last a total of 10 seconds. Any more than that, and we're all gone. That's why all the practice runs. First, I remove the hinges to prepare the damaged jetkill for lift off. At the silo we had a robot do this part, but Dr. Jackson is going to use forceps. Walt will assist. Good luck to you both. You're going to need it. Once the jetkill is removed, the clock starts. I'll cap the well with the vak shield that doubles as the delivery platform for the new jetkill. In those seconds it takes to move the new jetkill into place, the well will be open. We've given you lots of targets to occupy you."

The ceiling of the bunker was covered in glow-in-the-dark star stickers. Walt had been working on that for days.

"I remove the shield like pulling a tablecloth out from under place settings, without disturbing the new jetkill, and then I hook up the electrical components, including the latest in battery technology, thanks to Dr. Jackson, for the remote capabilities."

"I think we got it, Felix," Dr. Jackson said.

"Do we?" Felix challenged. "Because I think another practice run might be a good idea."

Dr. Jackson patted the cot, and Judge carefully hopped up.

"Nervous?"

"For you," he nodded.

"Don't worry. I'm very good under pressure. Felix said no pain meds until the new jetkill's in place. Are you sure?"

"I need to be able to focus."

"Pain can get in the way of that."

"Not for me."

"Judge, I'm not going to let this go south on us. You're going to be ok."

She took his hand and squeezed. Judge wanted to give a sarcastic response, roll his eye, sigh like it bored him to hear stuff like that, but he didn't. He squeezed her hand back.

"Ok, everybody ready?"

Walt looked like he might pass out.

"Places. Deep breath. Here we go."

PART GRIFF_0001

From Dust We Were Made… From Dust We Will Return.

CROSS THREW A ROCK AT THE GRAMMATICALLY-challenged graffiti on the bunker as he declared, "Idiot. If you go to the effort of spray painting a wall, at least get the saying right."

"Then again," Griff remarked, "to and from are getting to be confusing concepts."

Throwing rocks at bunker graffiti was a poor distraction. Judge was getting a new face, and all they could do was wait and see if it worked. The first sign that it hadn't would probably be the last thing they'd see, so yeah. They threw rocks at a wall.

A high and wide from Cross landed in the woods with an unnatural crunch, like it had smashed through a windshield instead of a pile of pine needles.

"What the hell?"

Griff and Cross moved into the woods, nice and slow, to investigate. Not more than a few steps in, the ground crunched underfoot. Something shiny covered the forest floor, a glossy lichen sheet under its moss comforter. Griff shared a disconcerted look with Cross, then crouched to knock pine needles and moss aside. Veins in the flaky film carried a silver liquid.

"Is that mercury?" Cross wondered. "It looks like mercury."

"You did this?" Griff shouted back at Roan, where she paced between bunkers. She shrugged. "You pulled this poison out of the ground. Why?"

"I have to be able to defend myself, don't I?"

"You were supposed to be learning how to *control* your first freakish creations," Cross reminded. "Not invent new ones."

"I've been working on both."

"You think this is a game?" Griff challenged, feeling the sudden heat in his face. He motioned to the woods all around him, the second parcel of land that had meant something to his family that she'd desecrated, and added, "You think this is all yours to toy with? It's not."

"It's a training ground, isn't it?" Roan asked. "I'm training."

Griff kicked at a patch of the glowing lichen stuff, and it drifted like dandruff until settling on the orange bed of pine needles.

"This crap isn't going to bring my family back," Griff said. "You *have* to focus."

"I *am*," she said forcefully.

"Shut up, both of you," Cross shouted, indicating he'd heard something.

Griff snapped to attention. Something was hunting them. Something big. All around them, the mercury-laden lichen crunched. Birds flew off in fright. No time to shout a warning.

Griff tackled Roan to the ground just as a concussion grenade landed. Humvees rumbled up the dirt road and blocked any chance of vehicular escape. The dead-end bunkers had provided seclusion, but now that they were under attack, they had fewer choices for evac.

"Get her to the escape pod," Griff ordered Cross.

The escape pod wasn't really a pod, but Griff preferred calling it that. The idea of jumping into a black wall of nothing and trusting he'd come out the other side was unsettling, even for him, even after all he'd seen. The transporting property of vaks hadn't been shared by Dimond in his world announcement, so hard to say if this particular unit had been clued in to the fact that their targets might scramble for an instantaneous escape route, as effective as vanishing into thin air. Each vak Judge produced, no matter the size or shape, was either a WayIn or a WayOut, a one-way portal. Judge's latest made-to-order vak gateway presented a tactical advantage only if its location remained hidden—nothing to keep their hunters from continuing their pursuit and jumping right in after them—so they'd installed it in the crawlspace under the abandoned house. By the time the vak portal was discovered, they would have had time to get away on the other side. That was the theory, anyway.

Cross yanked Roan into a race to retrieve her gear from Bunker 318 before they were overrun. Griff sprinted toward her brother's quarters. Something hit him in the back, and he went down mid-stride, sliding down Bunker 321's steps and face planting in the mud. Keeping to his knees, he threw open the door to announce what those inside already knew: "They found us!"

Felix bolted over him like a jack rabbit in surgical booties and hightailed it into the woods. Walt and Dr. Jackson helped Judge down from the surgical cot. Felix had knocked over the lamps, so they were left mostly in the dark. A planetarium of vak-stars on the ceiling provided the only light. Evidence of the surgery's completion.

More concussions, far enough from the two bunkers to

avoid killing or maiming, but close enough to give a warning: *We know your location. Don't move.* The enemy was closing in. Griff slammed his fist into the bunker wall, angry at himself. What good would he be to Laney and Ollie if he was dead or in prison when they came back?

Jackson and Walt were at the door with Judge between them when a strong wind knocked them back. Roan's starched lichen blanket lifted off in the gust, broke into shards against the pines and drifted toward the line of Humvees. Shimmering sails of toxins, the stuff splintered into smaller and smaller pieces. The strange glitter provided the perfect cover. Nobody wanted anything to do with it. Soldiers and agents alike stayed put in their vehicles.

Walt scooped up the barely conscious Judge, and Jackson and Griff followed him into the pines. Roan and Cross were pinned down, but she was providing her own cover. A shadow passed over—a big one in a birdlike shape. The kestrel streamer swooped down to grip the concrete door frame in its talons, like a giant gargoyle that had her six. She *had* been training.

"We have your family, Dr. Jackson," a man's voice called out on a loudspeaker. "Want to see them again? Surrender now."

"It's a bluff," Griff said, urging Jackson to keep running.

"Probably," she agreed, but he could see how the threat had really pissed her off.

"That's Pirret," Walt said, equal parts fear and anger on his face. Then he noticed that Roan had fashioned a bird body-guard for herself the size of a T-Rex and said, "Wow. Is she controlling that thing? That's new."

"Your friend has hidden talents," Jackson observed. "But Judge needs you now. Please. Go. We'll draw their fire so you have a chance to get away."

Walt nodded and adjusted the patient onto his shoulder before rushing toward the house. Griff didn't question Jackson's call. He'd been thinking the same thing, but that didn't make it any easier to turn away from their only escape route. A barrage of concussion grenades chased them through the pines. Griff took a split second to check on Roan and Cross back at the bunkers, just as a grenade landed close enough to throw Roan against the bunker wall.

In seconds, her streamer was off leash. It shrunk into a slug, slid off the bunker, then morphed into a clump of moss. Cross attempted to rouse Roan, and a huge agent who looked like solid muscle from the chin down took advantage of his turned back. The muscle pinned Cross's arms, and Cross kicked against the bunker to knock the guy off balance. It worked—too well. They both went straight into the moss streamer. *Gone.* The streamer flashed the combined figures of the struggling men— two heads, four arms—before switching to a gnat to a robin to a fisher cat that chased after a swarm of insects.

"Incoming," warned Griff, as a flurry of mock wings and tails came their way.

An intense updraft carried Griff and Jackson, screaming, into the air. Branches like ladder rungs caught them in uncomfortable places, showing no sympathy for the reluctantly airborne. *Ooph* and *ugh* and *sweet Jesus* later, they'd stopped, not too far apart. At least the trees made up for the bad catch by offering a foothold and a view. Down below, Griff thought he saw Walt slide Judge into the crawlspace, just before Roan's streamer toppled a family of pines onto the dilapidated house. Leveled in seconds. No sign of Walt or Judge. Maybe they made it through. Griff couldn't do anything for them either way. They were on their own.

And just like that, Roan regained her senses and recalled her streamer. The wind died so quickly, Griff nearly lost his grip from the sudden adjustment. The falcon again, the streamer swiped away another muscle-bound guy who got too close, then became a point of light that streaked past them. In its wobbly and warped wake was Roan, backpack on and trumpet case in one hand, other hand gripped around an invisible cord, like she was skiing behind a meteor. She disappeared into thin air. Griff could have sworn he saw a ghost of her image a second after she was gone, like a puff of pollen from a shaken tree.

Must've just been his eyes playing tricks.

PART WALT_0003

THE ESCAPE POD WAS HELENE GRIFFITH'S hardtop Jeep with a built-in WayOut where a sun roof might be. For those in need of a fast getaway, it was a customization must-have.

Walt sat next to Judge on a stone foundation that might've once been a structure from colonial times—there were lots of colonial ruins in the woods around here—or maybe it was leftover from another abandoned military annex. Walt was no expert. All he knew was that the stone was solid beneath him. It was real. He needed that reassurance right now, that there was still something solid. Something real.

He'd traveled by vak before, but it turns out, re-entry through a WayOut coated with bioshell was a very different experience. They'd come through cocooned, packed in something like Styrofoam. For a few very long seconds he hadn't been able to move or breathe, until the stiff foam evaporated, leaving him and Judge crumpled in the backseat of the Jeep like a couple of thawing steaks. Judge remained barely conscious, so Walt had carefully moved him outside, where they recovered from the trip. Walt had time to notice that all his bioshell scars were gone. He was bleeding from old scratches and scrapes as if they were fresh.

Small complaints, compared to the state Judge was in. Dr. Jackson had administered pain meds as soon as Felix had implanted the new jetkill, so thankfully Judge was asleep during the last phase of the surgery, where she grafted his face back together over the metal contraption. Judge had been awake through the rest of it, though. This was Judge's thirteenth jetkill. To think the kid had been through that so many times made Walt shudder with pity.

"Pretty gruesome, huh?" Judge said. Walt hadn't realized he was staring, so he looked away. Good timing. The sight of the wound was making his stomach turn. Judge made it to his knees and scooted over to the Jeep's side mirror to check out Dr. Jackson's handiwork. The metal was shiny as a new toaster where his eye should have been, but speckled with drying blood. Judge retrieved alcohol wipes from his bag and started to clean his wound, saying lightheartedly, "Needs a good polish."

When Walt ventured to look again, Judge was wrapping gauze over his jetkill and around his head. His arms lost their strength, so Walt took the roll from him and finished the job.

"What are we waiting for?" Judge asked when he was done.

"The others."

"They're not coming."

"We don't know that." But after nearly an hour more of waiting with no sign of anyone, Walt had to admit it looked unlikely their fellowship remained intact. He'd been worried they'd try to ditch him, but it worked out the other way around. He'd run and now he was cut off, on the verge of leaving them all behind. He tried to sound upbeat, for Judge's sake, when he announced, "You know, it won't be a bad thing if we're on the road already when they make it through."

"They're not coming," Judge repeated.

Walt helped Judge in, then climbed into the driver's seat,

found the keys, and something else. Gearshift. The Jeep was a manual.

"Oh, come on. I can't drive stick," Walt said. "Mom said she'd teach me, but she never got around to it."

"Too busy writing legislation legalizing corporate slavery?"

"Just shut up. Let me think." Walt couldn't believe his luck. Back at Comet Pond, the getaway Saab had thrown him with the ignition between the seats, and now this. Was it too hard to make the getaway car easy to get away in? "It's ok. I can do this."

Walt felt out the clutch. Eased the Jeep into first. It jerked forward and died. Tried again. Same thing. A few more tries. A few more fails.

"This is fun," Judge said, grinding his teeth. "Especially after having my face carved out like a pumpkin."

Walt finally got the Jeep moving, but at a crawl. The engine's high whining urged him to shift into second, but he chose to keep it slow and steady, in first. The dirt road was pocked with holes anyway. And it's not like that implant in Judge's head that kept him from swallowing up the world was under any kind of warranty.

"I don't think this is ramming speed," Judge said sarcastically, pointing ahead.

The road was blocked by a fallen tree. Walt let the Jeep stall out, then he punched the dashboard until his fist hurt, cursing his luck with each blow. Judge unbuckled, gathered his stuff.

"Hey, I'm sorry," Walt said, trying to keep him from leaving. "We'll go around. I'll move the tree. I'll figure this out."

"Maybe you should take this as a sign from the universe.

Time for you to walk away. Go back to your dad. He can't be rotten all the way through. We all have our dark spots."

"You gave me the same brush off in the silo when I was trying to help you."

"You didn't help me then, and you can't help me now."

Judge eased himself out of the Jeep onto wobbly legs. He was talking tough, but he looked so small and vulnerable it made Walt's throat clench in sympathy. Judge was right. He hadn't been able to help Judge back at the silo, because Dimond's security had intervened. But he could help him now. He owed it to Judge's parents to at least try.

Judge had already taken one backpack full of supplies, so Walt filled another. He checked the glove compartment and found a map and a few hundred in cash. He waited a few more seconds for Dr. Jackson, or Griff, even Felix, to drop from the WayOut, but as usual the universe did not bend to his will. That was the Gorey family business, not his.

He didn't have far to run to catch up. Judge was moving slowly. Walt lifted the backpack from Judge's shoulder and added it to his own. "I can carry your other bag, too" Walt offered, but Judge clenched his fist around the messenger bag strap. "Or not."

The walking served to calm Walt's nerves, but also gave him time to worry about the others. Roan's streamer had been under control, then out of it, so either she was hurt or she'd just unleashed it on everyone, regardless of who might get swept up. Like Cross. That would hit Berit hard, wherever she was. And where was Griff? Dr. Jackson? In custody? On the run, like Felix?

"Where are we headed?" Walt voiced the last worry on his

list. Judge didn't answer. "You act like you have a plan. Want to share?" No answer. "Is it within walking distance? Can you at least tell me that?" Judge still didn't answer. "Do you even have a plan?"

"I plan to ignore you until you give up and go away."

"Nice."

Walt tried not to take it personally. The kid was in pain, so much that Walt couldn't imagine. So he decided not to pester him with questions. He wasn't going to abandon Judge, no matter how hard Judge tried to push him away. Walt just couldn't do that.

Maybe it was wishful thinking, but he thought the path was starting to look familiar. The forest was thinning, and before long they were walking on gravel. Suddenly, Walt felt a million times better.

"Why are you so happy?" Judge asked, grim and cranky.

"Because I know where we are," Walt said, pointing through the trees at the football field of his own high school. Judge wasn't impressed, so Walt explained. "We need a car. That's where we get one."

PART JUDGE_0005

Pain was familiar. It was one of his least favorite side effects of existence. He'd taught himself to compartmentalize at a very young age, but the exquisite pain of the latest installation was unrelenting. It was all he could do to put one foot in front of the other.

He wondered if the Spaghetti Monster knew this level of pain, or if his end of the rope was burdened more heavily in that regard. Only fair to share.

They'd waited for school to let out, but Judge kept his hood up in case they bumped into anyone. Maybe it was the dungeon-like operating room he'd just survived, followed by hours of quality time with the uber-normal Walter Hale, but he never felt more Frankenstein.

Walt led him through locker-lined hallways of a school Judge might have attended himself, had he been born in an alternate reality where his reality was less alternative. He didn't allow himself to wonder what that life might have been like. No point to it. But he did allow himself to hate being here now. With every fiber of his being.

Judge ran a hand along the hanging locks, making them swing in his wake until Walt admonished him with a curt "Cut it out!" over his shoulder.

"Look at you, giving orders," Judge said. "Two seconds back in your natural habitat and you're the alpha again. Don't let the gauze fool you. I could still erase this whole place."

"Sounds like Judge the Destroyer needs a nap," Walt said.

Judge almost reached for his remote out of spite. Laughter stopped him—loud stupid cackling that made Judge's already throbbing head hurt so bad he ducked, as if he could avoid the pain. Walt swept him effortlessly into the lockers behind him and flattened himself as a group of girls rounded the corner. Crowded around a phone, they bumped heads in order to share each frame of fun, giggling as they went by, never once looking up.

"What could be so funny?" Judge wondered out loud. What he really meant, was how could *anything* be funny. Didn't they know how close it all was to an end?

"Come on," Walt said. "This way."

Walt passed by a set of open doors to an auditorium and stopped when he heard a voice. There, on stage, was a girl who looked disturbing enough to be a part of Judge's story. She was split down the middle, half monster in tattered clothing, half princess. She spoke in a form of English Judge had never heard before, so strange and musical, it momentarily distracted him from his pain and drew him in. Three others joined her on stage, two girls who wore beards and were dressed something like pirates, and a guy in all black except for white feathers on his shoulders. The guy in all black was bouncing around like he was invisible to everyone.

The monster-princess favored her monster side and said to the girl pirates, "As I told thee before, I am subject to a tyrant, a sorcerer, that by his cunning hath cheated me of the island."

The invisible guy in black stopped bouncing around long enough to accuse, "Thou liest."

To which the monster replied—to the pirates, "Thou liest, thou jesting monkey, thou: I would my valiant master would destroy thee! I do not lie."

And one of the pirate dudettes said, "Trinculo, if you trouble him any more in's tale, by this hand, I will supplant some of your teeth."

Pirate girl named Trinculo seemed all taken aback. "Why, I said nothing."

"Mum, then, and no more. Proceed."

And the monster-princess took up again, "I say, by sorcery he got this isle; From me he got it. If thy greatness will Revenge it on him,—wait, hold on. Everybody take fifteen!"

The sudden change in demeanor of the monster-princess caught Walt off-guard until she ran off the stage straight at him. He said a quick, "Oh shit. Let's go," but she'd chased him down before he even got a few steps from the auditorium.

"Wait! Walt, is that you?" Her costume looked even stranger in the harsh fluorescent lighting. Her dramatic make-up was forcing this reunion into melodrama so fast Judge almost wanted to laugh, if he weren't so concerned his own face might split in two from the pain—without the help of clever cosmetics. "Oh my god! It is you!"

She threw her arms around him, and he walked with her attached like that into the nearest bathroom, which happened to be for girls. Judge followed, uncomfortable on so many levels.

"Please, Carmen," Walt pleaded, "Keep your voice down."

"Right! So sorry," she said, dropping to a whisper. "Inside, hiding-in-the-bathroom voice." She jumped into his arms again and kissed him. "I've been so scared for you. You must be freaking out."

"I'm ok. No. That's a lie. But I don't have time to explain…"

"Oh, my," she said, seeming to notice Judge for the first time. "Is that…?"

She approached him to get a better look. He pulled his hoodie further over his jetkill and tried to back away, but his back was already to the wall.

"Carmen, don't," Walt warned, but Carmen had already pushed Judge's hoodie back from his face. She flinched when she saw his bandages, either in commiseration or revulsion.

"Hi Judge," she said. "I'm a friend of your sister's."

"Doubtful," Judge said.

"Well, I always wanted to be her friend. Let's put it that way."

"She's good at keeping people at a distance," Judge said. He turned to Walt, "Is this why we came here? So you could suck face with your girlfriend? I think I'll be on my way."

Judge started for the door, but got so dizzy he had to put a hand on the wall.

"Oh my gosh," Carmen said, catching him before he fell. "Are you ok?"

"He just had surgery," Walt explained.

"Oh, to fix him? That's great."

"I don't *need* fixing."

"I'm sorry, I didn't mean to insult you," Carmen said. "I can't say anything right."

"Carmen, it's great to see you," Walt said. "It really is. You have no idea. But I came here because we need a car."

Carmen looked hurt, but only for a split second. "My mom

always drops me. You know that. Where are you going—?"

"I was going to borrow one from Driver's Ed."

"Good idea. Mr. Davis is still here," she said. "I saw him just a few minutes ago in his office. I'll distract him while you get the keys."

"No, I can't ask you to do that. They'll know you helped us."

"Good. They should know that people want to help you."

"You don't understand," Walt said, but she was already marching out of the bathroom, head held high. "You could get in a lot of trouble."

"So? Roan Gorey can't have *all* the trouble in the world."

If Judge's face hadn't felt like it was falling off, he might have smiled. The monster-princess held Walt's hand and practically skipped her way down the corridor. Judge had never considered that level of cheerfulness possible.

Mr. Davis had a dual role, too, evidently. Driver's Ed and basketball coach. His office was opposite the gymnasium, where the sounds of shoes squeaking on the wood floor was almost as excruciating as the girl giggling had been earlier. Carmen left them by the equipment room to duck inside and start distracting by nearly giving poor Mr. Davis a heart attack. Her get-up really was startling, especially when you're in the middle of reading a newspaper article about supernaturally freaky kids.

"WHAT THE HELL—"

"Sorry, Mr. Davis! It's just me, Carmen DiNicola. Dress rehearsal. Shakespeare?" And when he managed to calm down, "Sorry to bother you, but somebody bumped into the emergency exit and now the stupid buzzer. It's *impossible* to focus." She really was a good actor.

"Can't you find the janitor? Maybe give him a heart attack while you're at it?"

"I wouldn't want to do that!" Carmen laughed. "Sorry, you're the only adult around."

Then she knocked some papers off his desk with a swish of her costume, followed by yet another "Sorry!" When she took advantage of his turned back, Judge half-expected her to say, *Sorry, I just stole this key from your desk drawer while you weren't looking*, but she kept that one to herself.

Carmen tossed the key to Walt with a wink from the princess side, before following Davis down the hall toward the auditorium. Walt waited for them to turn the corner, then used the stolen key to open the Driver's Ed cabinet, locking it again once he'd grabbed a fob. Walt returned the cabinet key to the desk drawer.

"You two may have a lucrative career in crime ahead of you," Judge said.

He'd meant it as a compliment, but Walt didn't look complimented. He ushered Judge out a side door into the parking lot. Of course the stolen key matched the crappiest looking car of them all. Walt really had a gift.

No sooner were Walt and Judge inside than Carmen jumped into the back. Before Walt could protest, she gave directions, "Take me to the ATM. I want to contribute to the cause."

"The cause? What are you talking about?"

"A corporation declares the right to own a couple of kids because they have special DNA, and that doesn't start a rebellion? Are you kidding me? Now let's go. If he doesn't notice the car missing you can have the whole weekend before they know how to find you."

"We have cash," Walt said as he started to back out. "You don't have to do this."

"You might be on the road awhile, right?"

"I have no idea," Walt said, shooting a glance at Judge.

"Then every little bit helps. I mean, it's not much. Just what I've saved from babysitting and working at Orange Leaf this summer. Darn, I have $50 more at home from my grandma. But we can't risk going there. They've been watching my house."

"Who has?"

"Well, I don't know exactly. They haven't introduced themselves. But there's two people in a car on our street, watching the house, 24/7."

"Why?"

"Because they know about us, silly. I've thought a lot about what I would do if you came back, you know. I could insist on coming with you. You wouldn't be able to stop me."

"Good grief," interjected Judge.

"But I won't. First of all, I couldn't do that to my parents. They need me at home. The stress of all this has made my mom's MS flare up pretty bad."

"I'm sorry to hear that."

"I know. It really sucks. But the other reason I won't be coming, I think I can do more for the cause if I'm not hiding from the police."

Judge wasn't sure if Carmen was delusional or for real. He wasn't getting many clues from Walt on that score, either.

"Have you seen my mom or Lucy?" he asked her when

stopped at a light.

"No. They're still missing?"

Walt nodded, and Carmen placed a gentle hand on his shoulder and said, "I'm sure they're ok."

Carmen caught Judge puzzling at her in the rear view mirror. She craned her neck to show her monster face.

"You like my makeup? I did it myself." Judge shrugged, and she showed him the blush and eye shadow of princess. "We're doing Shakespeare. *The Tempest*. You know it?"

"Can't say that I do."

"It's fantastic. The problem is, most of the cast have quit the show. Lots of kids haven't come back to school since the announcement. You know, the one about you?" Judge didn't know how to respond to that, so he didn't. High school dramas weren't high on his list of concerns. "Like they're any safer at home. I mean, they say that the reason we haven't seen streamers until now is that they spend most of their time in the miles and miles of earth, ocean, and sky becoming bugs and bacteria. If they can come at you from above and below at any second, what does it matter *where* you are? So I'm playing Caliban—" she turned to show him just her monster side"— "and Miranda"—and then just princess. "It's turned into a total farce, but we're running with it. Beats sitting at home on the couch, waiting for the world to end."

Walt pulled up to the bank, and Carmen hopped out with a quick "Be right back."

"You wish she'd come with us, don't you?"

Walt gripped the steering wheel tightly, then answered, "No."

Carmen returned with a pile of twenties and kissed Walt

through the open window. She'd transferred some of her monster paint, so she wiped it off with a nervous laugh.

"Don't forget about me out there, Walt," she said. "I know I can be ridiculous. I can't believe I'm saying goodbye to you looking like this. But at least I get a chance to say: I really do love you." Walt sank into his seat like she'd just dropped a hundred-pound weight on his chest. She hugged him awkwardly through the window and whispered, "It's ok. You don't have to say it back. I just don't want to regret anything, in case we don't see each other for a while." She unexpectedly took Judge's hand and said, "If you see Roan, let her know we miss her at school?"

"It'll be the first thing I mention," Judge said, feeling a flash of anger cross his face.

"I'm sorry you've had it so rough," Carmen said. "It's never fair when Nature picks on you, but we have to make the best of it. That's what my mom always says, anyway. Take care of Walt for me, would you? He tends to think about everyone else before himself." Probably not a good time to mention he planned on ditching Walt at the first possible opportunity. She noticed he was withholding information, so she said, "You remind me of your sister when you look at me like that."

"Two sides of the same coin," Judge shrugged.

Carmen pointed to either side of her hybrid face, adding, "Aren't we all?"

Walt choked on his goodbye and drove off. Carmen's sudden presence had been so overwhelming, her equally sudden absence left them in a silence doubly intense. After a few moments, Walt lifted the weight of the quiet and challenged Judge's hope for solitude.

"So, where to?"

PART KATIE_0002

YOU MAY BE WONDERING ABOUT THE TIMING of Katie Goodbear's relocation, or where she moved to, or for that matter, where she had been living. Or maybe you don't worry about that sort of thing at all. Not like it's your problem. Sorry, that sounded judgmental. You have your own problems. That better?

She's had some time to settle in, and yes, the "cable guy" showed up, so she's been back in the game, full tilt, without need for hiking the bluffs to find a good signal. Right now, though, she's back to waiting—this time for the arrival of guests. She's nervous. See how she's keeping herself busy? There's nothing more to do inside her new home to make it hospitable, so she's on a wobbly ladder outside, touching up where some paint got scratched during the move.

If you want to know more about her recent move, she can tell you. It's from her personal bundle, so no theft involved. Well, that's not exactly, true. There *is* theft involved. Quite a bit of it. Just not the sort that brings bad luck courtesy of disgruntled ancestors.

Don't worry about distracting her while she's on a ladder. She can do two things at once.

Side note: She's keeping track of how much you owe for the stories. If it's one thing Katie knows how to do, it's to balance a ledger.

// How GirlWhoClimbs Stole the Cache //

Storage of valuables has always been problematic, whether what you're storing is food for winter, sacred bundles, or a luxury yacht. Long ago, Katie's people had solved the problem of food and bundle storage by digging a hole in the lodge called a cache pit and delegating guard duty to someone respectable, and sedentary. Hiding something as big as a 94-foot yacht would require a hell of a big cache pit, and more than Grandmother on the payroll to watch over it.

So where would you hide your yacht? It sounds like a silly hypothetical, but in this case, it's not. It's a real problem, involving a real yacht. Maybe it would help to know why you'd be hiding it, and who from. Duke's purchase of a personal luxury yacht using the Nation's funds was no secret to the tribe, so Duke wasn't hiding it from them. The Tribal Council had looked the other way for years, because as Chairman, Duke had overseen the transformation of the M.H.A. Nation from a struggling, dwindling community to the fastest-growing economy in the U.S.A. Hydraulic fracturing techniques had opened up the shale oil squarely under Fort Berthold Reservation, and the fracking boom was seen by many as the answer to their prayers.

Prosperity was a stranger on the prairie. Self-sufficiency had always been the way of life here, and sure, that made life hard sometimes. Very hard. But her people were inseparable from the land, and not just because of their traditions. The M.H.A. was a sovereign nation with legal rights to the land and the resources found beneath it—legal rights that were complicated, but protected.

Maybe you've felt a strong connection to a place, too. If you have, you might understand the conflict that comes from wanting the best for your people, but wanting the landscape to stay the same—wanting something good and pure in this world to survive for you to share with the next generation to come. It's an old conflict, one unique to our species.

I keep no power for myself.

Fracking turned the Reservation into a beacon to those in search of steady work and those seeking an easy windfall, both, and in the tradition of all boom towns, that sticky combination sent crime through the roof. Lack of housing led to man camps springing up from Bismarck to Williston. Prostitution and drugs followed, and the tribal police couldn't keep up no matter how much O.T. they worked. Truck traffic clogged the two-lane country roads and dug deep ruts into the asphalt. Where the roads weren't paved, the trucks kicked up so much dirt you could imagine you were Dorothy hitching a ride out of Kansas.

To top it all off, grasslands that once felt the thunder of millions of buffalo were set on fire. Flaring natural gas stacks were strange trees planted wherever They struck oil—which was pretty much everywhere. The oil was the point of it all, see. The natural gas was just in the way. Getting at what you want sometimes means burning through a lot of stuff you don't.

All of this was tolerated, because the money kept rolling in, and as long as the money is flowing your direction, you'd be bonkers to put on the brakes, wouldn't you? Duke thought so. He'd knock back his Stetson and smile his wide, bright-white toothy smile and chalk it all up to growing pains. Temporary inconveniences for bringing the M.H.A. into the 21st century. He even went so far as to say that his people *deserved* this, after all the hardships they had endured. How it was all part of a grand plan, this *gift* to the Nation.

Concerns among tribe members were rarely shared directly with the Chairman. As the CEO of the Spotted Eagle Piping Company that manufactured the piping for most fracking operations in the area, part owner of Thunder Butte Trucking that provided the lion's share of the water trucks for most fracking operations in the area, and the Founder of the Medicine Rock Lodge and Casino, Duke Paulson was not a man you wanted against you. For those few whose paycheck didn't depend on Duke Paulson, you can bet they had family who did. Besides, Duke surrounded himself with a collection of jaw-busters and leg-breakers who served as very effective complaint deterrents.

So when Duke christened his new yacht the *Lady Luck of the Lake* as part of his plan to expand gambling business onto the water, the Tribal Council gave its grudging approval. To his surprise, before Duke even had a chance to take the *Lady* out for her maiden high-roller voyage, the North Dakota Gaming Commission showed up in town to levy some hefty fines. Normally permissive with their reservation casino licenses, the Commission had the unpleasant task of pointing out that gambling was only allowed on reservation *land*. While Lake Sakakawea covered tribal land—in fact, the tribal *homeland*—it was still under jurisdiction of the Army Corps of Engineers, who built the dam that created the lake that drowned the town. Duke wasn't about to pay any fines to the State, no sirree. The Nation was already getting killed by taxes on their oil revenue. So he pulled the *Lady Luck* out of the lake and dry docked her on one of his truck lots.

"It's not a floating casino if it ain't floating," he'd said defiantly, and he saved the Nation from paying those insulting fines. What a hero, right? Just like the Chiefs of old.

Some trouble maker on the inside at the casino—you can probably guess who (it was Katie, if you don't like to guess)—had gone and given the U.S. Coast Guard a holler, too. Evidently to operate a 94-foot yacht, you need all kinds of paperwork. Paperwork was not Duke's strong point. That's why he kept Katie around.

Which brings us to why Katie was around Duke to begin with. Well, it's a sad story. You probably could have guessed that, too. Her parents died within a year of each other: father of complications from diabetes; mother of heart disease. Katie was only eleven when orphaned, and her cousin Duke accepted the role of her caretaker. Katie was close with Duke's son Edgar, but that's not why he agreed to take her in.

Katie was "good with numbers." That's how Duke put it. His narrow assessment of her skills was enough to qualify her to do his personal accounting after school, as a sort of part-time job, the sort that doesn't pay. Well, unless you count the room and board she was given, which was how Duke justified it. She lived in that hole in a wall behind the casino cashier's office for five years until a few days ago, when Duke gave her quarters to someone new. Not an indentured servant like herself, but someone who required a serious demotion. Any guesses?

Anyway, *accounting* implies reconciling budget lines with revenue and expenses, but that's not really what Duke had Katie doing. See, there was so much money coming in, and so many deals being made, that Duke found himself in a pickle. He couldn't actually *account* for where a lot of that money was coming from, but he still wanted to be able to spend it. That's where having a casino comes in handy. It was that sort of *accounting*. Money laundering, in case you're new to that sort of thing.

You might be thinking to yourself that Katie shouldn't have gone along with it, especially when Duke started to dig into tribal funds to cover his debts and other sordid personal dealings, and Katie would agree with you. But Katie liked to eat. Do you like to eat? And she also liked to have a place to sleep, even if it's just a cot in a tiny room adjacent to an office. Whenever Katie raised the slightest amount of concern for what Duke instructed her to do, he was quick to threaten to send her away. As isolated as she was after Edgar, her closest friend, went off to join the Marines, Katie couldn't bear the thought of leaving the reservation. She really thought it would kill her.

So Katie did Duke's dirty paperwork, and after a while she expanded her computer skills to get a more complete picture of Duke's dealings. When Edgar came home on leave from the 2nd Intelligence Battalion at Camp Lejeune, he gave her a crash course in encryption and hacking methods. Not long after, Edgar drove his car into the lake. You'll hear about that later.

With oil prices plummeting and the sale of the refinery site to Bradley Dimond, all signs pointed to Duke looking for a way out. Katie knew it was only a matter of time before he saw her as nothing more than a loose thread, so she'd been making plans to move out even before he gave her living and working space to none other than Gwen Hale and her little girl.

At least Mother Hale had the decency to act appalled when she realized Katie was being displaced by her arrival. Or maybe she was just appalled by the conditions of her new quarters. Either way, Duke must've thought he was being so clever with this housing exchange, killing two birds with one stone:

demoting Gwen Hale to the degree Dimond required, while kicking Katie to the curb.

In truth, this move was a major upgrade for Katie, her Cinderella moment—that is, if Cinderella had hot-wired that magic pumpkin herself, instead of waiting for fairy godmothers to do it for her.

Lady Luck of the Lake sat on cinder blocks among the water trucks on Duke's lot outside Makoti. That luxury yacht was living in insult among the worker bees, just like poor upper class Mother Hale shacking up in Katie's old digs. *Lady Luck* was begging to be stolen, and Katie was happy to come to the rescue. The question was, where to put it?

So you see, that wasn't a joke about needing a giant cache pit to hide a yacht. In fact, she'd already found one.

The fish hatchery at the Garrison Dam was on the verge of being shut down. Only thirteen of its sixty-four rearing ponds were populated, and the skeleton crew who operated the place had been on furlough so many times they lost count. The last straw was the burbot. Sports fishing enthusiasts in the state government didn't much care for the fact that the state-run Garrison Hatchery had selected the endangered fish as their focus this season. The whole purpose of a hatchery was to keep marketable fish in Lake Sakakawea, not raise a bunch of slimy eel-like fish, untouchable in every way. So what if the burbot had been part of the river's ecosystem since the Mammoths roamed the prairie, until the dam had blocked its spawning run?

An anonymous donation from Duke's personal accounts, courtesy of Katie's fine-tuned *accounting* methods, kept the hatchery doors open and ponds rearing baby burbots. Around the same time, an old friend at the hatchery gave her private access to one of the empty rearing ponds for renovation into a hidden dry dock. Not a quid pro quo set up, though she could see how you might think that.

Under cover of night and with Carl Shock's help, Katie had Robin-Hooded both the yacht and the truck that hauled it. Backing the yacht down the custom dirt ramp into the rearing pond, Carl cut the turn too close and scraped the side of the yacht, right through the flowery lettering of its name *Lady Luck of the Lake*.

In his own defense, Shock had reminded her, "I'm a pilot. Not a driver."

A massive tarp tented over the yacht kept it hidden, and modifications to the dry dock connected the *Lady Luck of the Lake* to the hatchery's power and water treatment system. A/C and running water was just as important as an internet connection in this cache pit. Not much of an H.Q. of Operations otherwise.

That's the story of how Katie Goodbear became a land pirate and buried herself with her treasure.

+ + +

"What the heck is a *Lota Lota*?" a Southern-accented boy's voice asked above her. He was peering down at her through the tarp that billowed with hot afternoon wind. He'd arrived a little sooner than she expected, but that was ok.

She leaned back from her paint job to assess its impact. She was glad he could read it. She'd kept the two flowery "L"s from *Lady Luck* and used them for her new name.

"It's the genus and species of the burbot," she replied up to him.

"The *what* of the *what*?"

"It's a fish. The Lota lota is a fish."

"Oh. Well why didn't you just say so?"

"She likes naming things after fish," said a man's voice, as his face joined the boy's under the tarp. A gaunt, worried face. Had to be *PallidSturgeon* from the Lodge.

She turned on her wobbly ladder, and almost lost her balance when she opened her arms in a grand, welcoming gesture.

"Trevor Skaggs, Caleb Harper," she announced, "you have permission to come aboard."

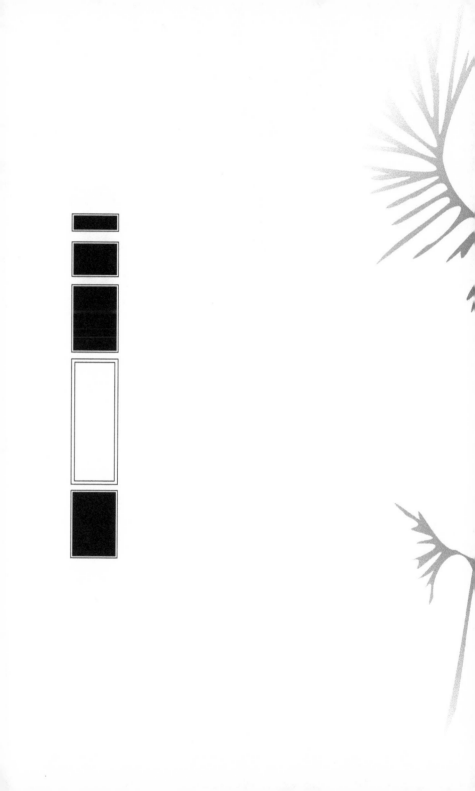

SEQUENCE FOUR

PART EMMETT_0001

"Why so sad?"

This guy, this Bradley Dimond his sister worked for, he was a piece of work. The question he asked couldn't be answered, because the guy he was asking was in no condition to reply. Just a guy in a photograph on the wall behind the bartender. Probably dead and buried now. His double-breasted, pin-striped suit reminded Emmett of old gangster movies, but the scene of this photograph was too dull for gangsters. Other men in suits huddled around a desk to witness something official being signed, all except for the one guy who covered his face, sobbing, and Bradley Dimond in the here and now, mocking him with a fake frown on his face, like he thought it was funny, asking him why he was *so sad*. What a dick.

This other guy, Dillard Pick, he was a real meathead. He must've been paid to laugh at whatever Dimond said, if you can call it laughing. Huh huh huh. Sounded more like the grunt he'd make lifting 250. Side glances to Dimond as he laughed, just to make sure he was reading Dimond right. Huh huh huh.

Emmett had worked in enough casinos to recognize dumb and dangerous when he saw it. That was Dillard Pick. But this Dimond guy, his level of mean was on a whole different scale.

Emmett resented the intrusion more than the behavior. He was having a drink alone after a particularly trying twenty-four hours. He'd started the day asleep on his own couch because he'd given his bed to his sister Gwen and her daughter Lucy. Pick and his crew had shown up on his doorstep to deliver a message from this Dimond guy for Gwen to come back to work, or else he'd plaster Walt's face all over the news and torpedo whatever future he might have left. Long, tense hours of travel later, Gwen was trying to get Lucy to sleep in the backroom of the cashier's office, and Emmett was at the bar in this cave of a casino, looking for a way out of this mess with the help of his usual strategic partner, Jim Beam. And Dimond and Pick plant themselves on either side of him, like they were old friends who'd made a plan to meet.

"You know what that picture is about, don't you?" Dimond asked him. In fact Emmett did know, because he'd thought it was a curious picture to hang above a bar in a casino and so he'd asked the bartender, who'd told him. The guy who was crying was George Gillette, a lawyer for the tribes around these parts, and he was crying because he'd just lost the fight with the U.S. government over the dam they wanted to build on the reservation. But Emmett didn't tell Dimond that. He just shrugged, so Dimond went on, "Sure you do. You're a third generation steel worker, am I right?"

"Not really," Emmett said with a swig. "By the time I showed up, most of the work was about shutting down the furnace. Not keeping it hot."

"That's what I mean," Dimond said. "You witnessed the end of an era. The great cool down of Bethlehem Steel. You must've seen *that face*—" Dimond pointed at the broken picture of Gillette—"a hundred times over. Maybe even in the mirror."

Emmett turned suddenly enough in Dimond's direction to warrant a meaty hand on his shoulder. Pick might've been dumb as dirt, but he had quick reflexes.

"I didn't mean any disrespect," Dimond insisted. The guy didn't even flinch. He must be used to guys like Emmett wanting to knock him on his ass. Emmett swept Pick's hand from his shoulder and went back to his drink. "Gwen thinks I'm disrespecting her, too, but I'm not. The accommodations here, I assure you, are not an intentional punishment. I know she left her husband, not me. I didn't take her absence personally. She needed a hiatus, so she took one. She'd earned it."

"That's one version of events," Emmett said.

"It's the preferable version," Dimond said, "for everyone involved. My point is, your sister and niece really are safest down here, locked up with the money. The Medicine Rock Lodge is temporary housing for oil workers and law enforcement trainees, and I don't recommend room sharing, not with the ratio of men to women around here."

Thin ice, this guy. Very thin ice. Emmett worked over his empty whiskey glass like he used to work over his fast ball before he launched it. Huh huh huh from Dillard Pick. Who the hell named anybody *Dillard* anyway?

"I can't imagine Gwen was any happier at your place," Dimond said. "What a surprise it must have been to see her back home, after all those years. You'd had a falling out, hadn't you?"

"That's none of your business."

"No, of course not. I'm just saying, what a trouper you were, taking them in like that," Dimond said, slapping him on the back so that he spilled his own drink. "Bachelor like you. Must have cramped your style."

"I've never been one for *styles*."

Emmett tried to get up to leave, but Pick shouldered him back into his seat.

"You and I are talking past one another," Dimond observed. "Have you noticed? We're not making a connection. Like we're in the ring, but dancing around our own corners."

"Sorry, I'm no boxer. Baseball was my game. A little hockey here and there."

"My point is, Mr. Ridley," Dimond said, no trace of a smile anymore, "You know what it's like to fight for a way of life that could never be yours, just like Mr. Gillette there in that sad old picture, and now your sister has made you a part of another fight that isn't yours at all. I'm here to offer you an opportunity that puts *your* interests first. I think you deserve it."

"My *interests* are sleeping on cots in your cashier's office store room."

"Family always comes first, of course. You can play babysitter to your niece while Gwen works for me—" huh huh huh came from Pick—"or you can turn your life around and get a job of your own. A *real* job, with a *real* future. I'm giving you the chance to be ahead of the curve, for once in your life, to learn skills that no one else will have. We are at the starting point of a new technological path forward. What I'm building here, Mr. Ridley, has never been seen before, and I need men like you." A smile came with this last part. Probably meant to be sincere, but came off wicked as hell. "Men of steel."

This guy. Emmett had only just met the man, but the truth was, he'd known this guy his whole life.

PART ROAN_0004

THE LAST TIME ROAN HAD STOWED AWAY ON A streamer, she'd landed so hard in the Texas desert she'd knocked herself out cold. She vowed never to repeat the ride, but at the bunkers she saw no other choice. Overzealous with his self-defense moves, Cross had ended up inside the streamer himself, and just like that, she was on her own. Everybody else had gone with Judge. Even Walt. That stung, but there was no time for hurt feelings.

She had a streamer kestrel to fly.

Having no destination made her flight plan pretty fucking arbitrary. Not like she could hit any target she wanted anyway. Zero visibility during streamer flight, and even if she could see the land below, she'd always sucked at Geography.

She put the brakes on after just a few moments of flight time. The trumpet case flew out of her hand, and she bounced across the kestrel's back, right over the edge of its spread wings. She didn't like the idea of falling, so she told the kestrel streamer to catch her. One of its talons hooked her by the strap of her backpack, and she dangled there mid-air, her brain sloshing around in her skull. It gave her a chance to admire her ride and the buzz of activity inside.

The streamer kestrel was as big as a two-story house and steady as a statue, even on one foot. Transparent skin covered an expanse of black, limitless as the night sky, full of those frantic blue lights that were its engine. A moveable constellation. Cross was in there somewhere, hidden behind whatever veil still remained between worlds.

He wasn't in there alone, though. Her streamer had swallowed up Thing 1 and Thing 2, the bodybuilding assholes who'd shared shifts with Munny in the silo. Shame she couldn't order Cross à la carte, leave those two off the plate, but with a streamer release it was all or nothing.

"Ok, so where the hell am I?"

The kestrel streamer gave no direct reply of course, but she swiveled herself around to see that she was in a swamp. Not too far from civilization, because there was a wooden boardwalk winding through the flooded trees. Probably a state park, or a wildlife refuge. Good thing she hadn't hit the water. She wasn't sure if the amp was water proof, and there were other items tucked inside her backpack that would not react well to swamp. Specialty items, like the lichen she'd grown back at the bunkers.

She directed the streamer to do a fly-by for the floating trumpet case before setting her down on the boardwalk, pleased by how much control she'd gained in such a short time. She'd made a discovery in the woods of the Fort Devens Annex, and it wasn't just about programming bioshell. No, this discovery was about herself. Concentration—sustained concentration—had always been a major fail for her. Trying to control a streamer was no different. She'd tense up, get lousy results, and then be fried. But something about playing around with bioshell had revealed to her she needed to adjust *her* controls, like she was a car radio picking up random stations on a road trip. Play with the volume levels, speaker balance, even change channels. Controlling streamers had nothing to do with muscle—or anything physical, really. Streamer schematics were accessible on a new channel, one that was so overwhelming it had seemed like nothing more than static at first, unorganized by language or sequence, but she was learning how to interpret it. To read. To build. To drive.

She wasn't dying to bring Cross back, so her first attempts were fairly apathetic, like homework she didn't want to do. But without him, she didn't know where to go. Hell, she still didn't even know where she *was*.

"All right," she said, irritated with herself, "Enough of this half-assed bullshit."

She swung, ducked, and thread herself through knots of cosmic gossamer until she managed to sever the trace. The explosion knocked her off the boardwalk, treating her to a healthy helping of pond scum for breakfast. While choking on that, she overlooked the other pond scum that had landed behind her.

"Gotcha!" right in her ear, said that voice too high for a man his size, simultaneous with sweaty paws clamping down on her arms.

Too bad she'd dropped Riven in the muck or she could have made him a head shorter. Instead she aimed a head butt at his nose. She missed, hitting her eye socket against his chin. She felt the split in her skin and the trickle of blood down her cheek. A physical struggle was pointless. Thing 1 and Thing 2 were too practiced at keeping her subdued. For two years at the silo, they'd treated it like a sport.

Cross was wrestling with Thing 2 in waist deep muck, until Thing 1 got his attention.

"Hey!" he shouted. "Cool it, or I break her arm."

Thing 1 twisted her arm until her shoulder felt like it was going to pop loose. The pain took her breath away. She watched Cross weigh how much he cared about Roan's discomfort. Not enough to keep from throwing one last shot. Roan's arm nearly snapped with the increased torque applied by her Thing, and a loud cry escaped her lips. Cross threw his hands in the air, and his Thing quickly put him in a headlock, shoving his face into the water.

"We don't need this one," Thing 2 said. "Any objections?"

"Disloyal asshole," Thing 1 responded, giving his thumb's down for Cross's fate.

"Are you Thing 1 or Thing 2?" Roan asked. He hadn't let up on her arm, so it was hard to be snarky. Her streamer channel was at full volume, too, but she couldn't resist. "I could never tell the two of you apart."

"That's hurtful," Thing 1 said. "We've known each other for years, and you never bothered to learn my name. It's Mi—"

At her command, the streamer algae she'd invited folded over Mi— before he finished.

"Sorry," Roan said, not sorry at all. "Didn't catch that."

As she rubbed the pain from her shoulder, she sent streamer Mi— rushing at his partner, creating a tidal wave of algae before slamming into him with the force of the entire NFL. Together they made an epic splash.

Cross came up cussing out more than he was breathing in. When he realized that she'd saved him, did he say thanks? Of course not.

"Stay right there," he ordered her. He slogged through the

swamp to the boardwalk, keeping an eye on the streamer. She let out its leash to keep Cross guessing about whether she'd let it collect him again, too. He should have said thank you.

To her horror the streamer turned into a child. How? There was no kid out there. It then pulsed from child to old man to woman and then cycled through so many bodies and faces Roan had to look away. What had she done? Where did all those people come from?

"What did you do?" Cross said, his voice strained by pain.

She tried to read the situation. Information flooded over her. Insects. Algae. Bacteria. Bear. Beaver. Deer. And people. So many people.

"I don't know," she said, and then she couldn't take any more. "Stop!"

The streamer paused midway between a young man and an eight-point buck, creating something like a minotaur.

"There's nobody there," a man in camo said behind them. He was frozen in terror on the boardwalk, holding a fishing pole and doing his best to blend into the trees. "Them's the Chickasaw. Gotta be. New Madrid quake. 1811. Mississippi flowed backward, flooded this valley. Drowned a whole village."

"So those people..." Roan started, barely daring to look at the half-boy, half-deer.

"Have been dead for two centuries," Cross said.

The man's fishing line gave a sharp jerk, but he didn't react.

"You got a bite," Cross pointed out.

For a moment the fisherman forgot his fear and checked his line with routine interest. One glance at the hybrid human-deer reminded him this was anything but routine, and his flight reflex finally kicked in. He dropped his pole and ran.

"I know the feeling," Cross said in commiseration, as he pulled himself up onto the boardwalk and flopped onto the wood like a fish giving up its fight. He said "Uh oh" when he noticed how much he was bleeding. A lot. "Well, shit." He lifted his shirt to discover his old wound looking fresh. "That's perfect. I lost my bioshell Band-aid. Just perfect."

"There's more around," Roan offered. "I can dig some up…"

"No!" Cross said. "I need stitches, not spackle."

"Ok, ok. You're welcome, by the way. For busting you out."

"Kid, the day I thank you for anything is the day I've lost all perspective."

Roan left him to spit and cuss while she gathered her shit together, starting to regret her decision to bring him back. She followed Riven's glow to its hiding spot under the thick algae blanket, fished it out. She snapped it back into its makeshift case, hoping the gross water didn't damage the eagle feathers. Before returning the water-logged amplifier to her backpack, she checked on her secret weapons, those specialty items she made, custom-designed for Judge.

They weren't there. She dug through her pack, feeling the panic rise, searching every pocket, every bunched-up seam. They were gone.

"Did you take them?" she accused Cross.

"Take what?"

An acorn, a pod seed, and a spore. Practice attempts at removing the unnatural, namely Judge. Cross didn't seem to know what she was talking about, so no need to clue him in. He wouldn't approve. Judge must have stolen them, aware her product testing was for his benefit. He'd always been a despicable shadow, following her around to steal what was hers when she was distracted. Her parents. Her life. And now her arts and crafts projects. No biggie. Plenty more where that came from. Maybe she'd get lucky and one of them would blow up in his face.

"Nothing," she mumbled, shoving the amp into the pack and hanging a strap from her shoulder. She offered a hand up to Cross but he'd rather give more orders.

"Fish that pole back out. We might need it." Roan gave her most irritated sigh, but she did it anyway. The fisherman's pole was stuck on the exposed root of a tree, so reaching it wasn't a big deal. There was still a fish on the line. "Reel it in," Cross directed, even though she was already doing that. "Not too fast. The line will break."

"My dad taught me how to fish." To make her point, she posed with the struggling fish.

"Remove the hook," Cross said, not impressed.

"My dad always did that part."

"The Spaghetti Monster is squeamish?"

"Don't call me that," she said, grabbing the fish and dislodging the hook from its jaw in one swift movement. She continued to hold the fish, feeling its scales against her flesh, its information flow strong through the direct connection. The dormant egg it once was, the diseased liver full of toxins, the hundreds of eggs she carried inside. Its potential, its doom, its legacy.

"Too bad we don't have a cooler," Cross said. "That could've been lunch."

Roan gently dropped the fish back into the water. Cross

nodded toward the streamer. "Ok, so what are you going to do with *that*?"

Behind her, in a blinding show of light and fine spray of water, the streamer vanished. The sudden rush of wind knocked Cross's hair back.

"Holy shit," Cross said. "Where'd it go?"

Roan showed a single finger, pointing up.

PART KENDRA_0001

"Don't feel bad," commiserated Spencer Pirret. He missed his sincerity mark by about a mile. "Everybody freezes up the first time they see one. It's one thing to see a streamer on TV. Up close... it's enough to make you shit your pants. Even if you've done time on the battlefield."

Kendra Jackson placed her manicured hands, manacled at the wrists, on the steel table between them. The cuffs made an unpleasant scratching sound, intensified by the concrete walls surrounding them. He didn't like that sound. She knew he wouldn't. It was one of those sounds that makes skin crawl. That's why she did it. He was trying to make her uncomfortable, so she'd make his skin crawl. At the same time, she wanted this man to see her hands, the hands that had saved Judge Gorey and in saving Judge Gorey, saved the world. Hands that he'd chosen to put in cuffs, like she'd robbed a convenience store.

The truth was, *she'd* been robbed—of her last grip on reality—but what Pirret said was also true, about her being paralyzed. She thought she'd be prepared for seeing a streamer, but she hadn't been. Being stuck fifteen feet high in a pine tree at the time hadn't helped matters. Sergeant Griffith had been captured, too. He could've fought his way out. He was armed and capable, and his neurons were still firing. He'd already had his streamer moment, the day one took his wife and child. But the kids were gone by then—Judge and Walt had disappeared one way, Roan another—so maybe he hadn't seen the point of running.

The National Guard troops had taken her and Griff in separate vehicles to the closest government building, the Massachusetts Firefighters Academy in Stow. The soldiers were working their shock, but the suits who were calling the shots pretended nothing out of the ordinary had happened. One particular suit—Spencer Pirret—the man who had threatened her family, or at least threatened her access to them—had escorted her into this room and ordered everyone else out. Intimidation technique, to make it seem like anything could happen in this room. No witnesses.

Pirret was all about intimidation. His cold hard stare. Clenched jaw. Even the leg injury, or more specifically, his tough guy attitude toward injury: *Nothing will derail me.* But she'd derailed men like him before. It took patience and guile, and a really good instinct for finding pressure points. Every man has them.

"The distraction factor," Pirret continued. Despite the fact that he said she shouldn't feel bad for freezing up, he wanted her to feel bad for freezing up. "Nothing gets you killed faster."

"Or stuck in a cast," she said with a smile.

Pirret chuckled with a feigned good nature and rapped his knuckles on the plastic coated cast halfway up his femur.

"A good reminder to never let my guard down," he said. "It does make getting around a pain in the ass."

"What's the prognosis?"

"Few more weeks in the cast. Months of rehab. Nothing I haven't been through before. Old injury, I'm afraid."

"Surgery?"

"Don't think so."

"I can take a look at the x-rays. Give you a second opinion."

"I thought you were a burn specialist."

"No specialists on the front line. Broken bones, torn muscles, busted insides, burnt outsides, these hands have healed them all."

She spread her hands as much as possible in the cuffs, then dropped them again on the table, making that awful scratching that made Pirret wince.

"Such a forgiving person," he said, "to offer me help."

"Not really. I just like to fix things."

"Is that why you agreed to help Walter Hale?"

"I agreed to help Judge Gorey. Walter Hale just happened to be the person who asked."

"And you said yes," Pirret said, looking incredulous. "Even after his daddy ran that smear campaign against you. That seems forgiving to me."

"Again, you're mistaken," Kendra said. "Let me explain. I'll speak slowly, so that you can keep up." Pirret bristled, but forced another chuckle to cover up his anger. "Let's start with what you're trying to do, right now, and why it's not going to work. And then we can discuss my history with the Hale family."

"What am I trying to do, Dr. Jackson? We're just talking about your future. Your family's future."

"In a burn room."

"It was convenient."

"No. An intentional choice. To set the scene. To send a message. I can smell the soot. I can see the burn marks. I can feel the greasy residue in the air. And you have me shackled."

"A precaution. We know your training."

"You know my training. I see. Is that why you think you understand the trauma of my experience—my *expertise*? You think interrogating me in this *burn* room is going to intimidate me, trigger a subconscious reaction of anxiety that makes me pliable to pressure, because I've seen what fire does to human flesh? What you've overlooked, Mr. Pirret, is that I've *chosen* to be close to fire, to witness the cruelty of it. You think you frighten me by bringing me here? No, sir. Mr. Pirret, you are in *my* house."

"Maybe I was just trying to be ironic," Pirret said, shrugging with a nonchalance that made her itch to slap him. "We may be in your house, Dr. Jackson. You're the healer. But I'm the fire-starter. I set your life on fire during that campaign. Remember that? I'd bet my good leg you still have colleagues who believe those alternative facts we spread about your clinic." Kendra sighed, because it was true. "That's the beauty of it. Fires change a landscape for good. And they are so easy to start."

"Like the one you told about Sergeant Griffith to discredit him?"

"Unfortunate, but necessary. We needed time, time to understand the significance of our discovery, and the Sergeant was making a lot of noise."

"Your discovery. His loss."

"*You* still have a lot to lose," he said.

"What about the Gorey family? Haven't they lost enough?"

"Blame the universe for that, not me."

"That runs counter to your own propaganda," she said, and he shrugged again. "How much time did you spend with Judge in that dungeon?"

"As little as possible," said Pirret.

"Why? Did he make you miss your kids?"

"No. Because he gave me the creeps. He's a creepy kid."

"He's a little boy who deserves to be loved."

"Good grief," Pirret leaned back with an exasperated sigh. "How can somebody so smart be so dumb? Why are you even here? What did they offer you in return for your services?"

Kendra laughed. "I considered this a volunteer opportunity."

"Another chance to serve your country?"

"A chance to serve all life as we know it."

"The ship has sailed on the *life as we know it* concept, don't you think?" Pirret waited for a response, but this time it was Kendra who shrugged. She was still digesting what she'd seen out there. "But let's jump to the inevitable page in this story where we get our Gorey kids back, safe and sound, and *life as we know it* can take hold again, in one shape or another. If you give us every bit of information you have to help us fast forward through all this running around bullshit, you can go home. If you don't help us, you're not going home. What's the smart choice?"

"When was the last time you saw your children, Mr. Pirret?" Kendra asked.

"I never said I had kids."

"You never said you didn't. So you do." She winked at him. "They must be scared, with everything going on in the world, and their daddy's not home to make them feel safe." Pirret slammed his hand down on the steel table, grinding his teeth so loudly Kendra could hear it. There it was. She had him. "Hey, I get it. Sometimes we make tough choices to be apart from our families, even in dangerous times like these. But I have to admit, I'm jealous of you. At least you can leave this room and give them a call. You're not going to let me do that. Because I'm not going to tell you *shit* about *anything*."

"How many years are you willing to spend away from them, Dr. Jackson?"

"I've committed no crime. I performed life-saving surgery."

"You think I need to charge you with a crime to hold you?"

"We still have laws."

"We do? Last I checked, the laws of nature and physics went out the window. But you think the laws of *man* still have a role to play?"

"I couldn't have said it better," Kendra said.

"Suit yourself," Pirret sighed, pushing himself to the door on one crutch, pounding his fist against it to announce the interview over. "Sergeant Griffith is already talking."

"Give him my best," Kendra said. "And same goes for those kids of yours."

Pirret clenched his fist as he wobbled out of the room. Kendra dropped her head in relief when he was gone. She knew she was likely on camera, being watched, so she didn't give them any more than that. A few moments of her silent, steady breathing, and she was surprised when the door opened again. Even more surprised by who walked through it.

"Dr. Jackson," Nathan Hale whispered, with that stupid *whassup* nod of the head he'd given her the night of their last debate, "Let's get you the hell out of here." She didn't move. It had to be a trap. "No, seriously," he said, and suddenly he lacked all of that posturing from the campaign. He just looked scared. "He'll be back any minute. We don't have much time."

"Are you setting me up to get shot, Senator?"

Nathan snorted through an awkward laugh, but then said seriously, "No. Of course not. My god. Why does everyone have such a low opinion of me?"

"It's a real mystery."

"We don't have time for this," he said, rushing in. When he tried to pull her from her chair, she wrenched his arm with her cuffed hands, knocked his leg out from under him and planted his face on the steel table.

"You are the last person on this planet who should presume to lay hands on me," she said steadily. "What's your game?"

Another man in a suit—Secret Service probably—pulled her off him and together with a suited woman also wearing an earpiece, practically carried her out of the room. Kendra considered whether elbows and knees to nerve centers would be warranted at this point, but she decided out of the burn room was better than in it, even if in the company of Nathan Hale.

"Ok, ok. I'm sorry. Jeez." Nathan followed them down the corridor, trying and failing to strike the right tone for his apology. "You saw my son? You saw Walt?"

"I did."

"Does he—" Nathan was cut off when Secret Service shushed him to avoid some of Pirret's people in an adjoining hallway. When they were past the danger, he continued, "Does he still hate me?"

"It didn't come up."

"Right."

"Where exactly are you taking me, Senator?"

"Oh, nowhere. I mean, you're on your own. Once we get out of here. Best I could do."

"On my own is just fine," Kendra said. "Can you get me out of these cuffs, though?"

"As soon as we're in the car," the Secret Service woman said.

"Will Sergeant Griffith be joining us?"

"You didn't hear?" Nathan said. "He escaped on the drive here."

As they hurried out a side exit, Kendra asked one more question. "Where's Pirret?"

The man listened to his earpiece and relayed, "Still on his phone outside."

Kendra smiled. "Talking with his kids."

PART ROAN_0005

It was clear Cross didn't know what was more painful: his open belly wound or the fact that he had to admit he needed Roan's help.

Roan was tucked under Cross's arm like a crutch, trumpet case bumping between them as they navigated the narrow boardwalk. An awkward way to walk, made more awkward by Cross growling at her each step she buckled under his weight. He balked at her plea to slow down.

"Keep moving" was his repeated order, and so that's what they did. They followed trail markers to a parking lot just in time to see the sheriff's deputy pull in, lights on, no siren. The deputy parked perpendicular to black skid marks made, no doubt, by the fisherman who skedaddled without his catch. They'd heard the peel out several minutes before.

Nowhere to hide, and no way Cross was running. He looked to her, waiting to see what she would do. Bring another streamer, swallow him up again for another ride to who-knows-where for another release? She wasn't sure he'd survive.

"You need a doctor," she said.

"I'm ok," he said, but he was leaning on her more and more.

The young deputy exited his car, hand over his holstered gun, and directed in a pleasant Southern accent, "Hands where I can see them." Cross could barely raise his; Roan raised Riven's case with hers, prompting the deputy to ask: "What's in the case?"

"Not a trumpet," she offered as a compromise with the truth.

"I didn't ask what it wasn't. Put it down. Nice and slow."

Cross faltered before she could comply, and Roan swung around to catch him, dropping the case. After the beating it had recently taken, it was no surprise when the case popped open. Riven bounced free and skittered across the asphalt. The deputy hopped over the deadly fidget spinner just before it sliced through his back tire and settled under his car.

The deputy heard the tire hissing, took a peek at Riven glowing under his chassis, and knocked his hat back.

"Whoops" was all she could offer.

Cross, meanwhile, was in a pile at her feet, moaning. She'd managed to keep his head from hitting pavement, but the rest of him had gone down hard. The deputy approached cautiously to inspect Cross's wound, keeping a wary eye on Roan.

"Nasty wound. How did that happen?"

"It's a long story." An accusing look from him made her defensive. "*I* didn't do it."

"Stay right there. Keep your hands where I can see them." He popped his trunk and retrieved a first aid kit. He packed a bunch of gauze onto Cross's abdomen before zip-tying his hands. "Keep pressure on that," he said, and she reluctantly pressed her hands over the gauze. He backed away to inspect his damaged tire with a solemn assessment, "That's a shame." A siren sounded, not too far off, and the prospect of having company seemed to prompt him to crouch and reach for Riven.

"Careful," Roan warned. "Don't let the light touch you."

He extracted Riven by its handle, then stared at the axehead-vak in wonder. "That is one hell of a mind bender."

"Hurts your brain to look at it, doesn't it?"

He tucked Riven's case into the trunk in exchange for a spare, jack, and tire iron, just as an ambulance bounced into the parking lot. Two EMTs jumped out, both women, both athletic. The older woman was stout with short gray hair and looked like she could win Gold in shot put. The other was young and slim like a track star.

"Hey Wanda," the deputy said, and the older woman nodded back and said "Hey Tim."

"What do we have here?" the younger EMT asked, pulling gloves on.

"Lacerated tire," Deputy Tim said, deadpan, then pointed to Cross and added, "Lacerated belly."

The EMTs gently pushed Roan away, and the deputy beckoned her over. "You're with me. You've got a task to do."

"You want me to change your tire?" She'd helped her mom change a tire once on the side of the interstate. The thought of her mom stabbed her in the heart. "Seriously?"

"I'll supervise," the deputy said. "First things first. Backpack, off. Slowly."

He checked inside it quickly, then tossed it into his front seat. Either he hadn't seen the amplifier, or he didn't recognize what it was. Why would he?

Wanda, on the other hand, had just recognized Cross. "Hey, this guy's on the news."

"Yep," Deputy Tim responded, knocking the jack into place with his boot. "Hence the restraints."

"Watch him, Tina," Wanda warned her partner as they rolled Cross onto an orange backboard.

"Unresponsive," Tina said, checking whatever EMTs check. "We need to move."

As the EMTs yanked a gurney from the ambulance, Wanda sent a curious look Roan's way. Roan ducked her head, following Deputy Tim's instructions.

"Is that *her*?"

"Yep," Deputy Tim said again.

"Holy shit."

"Yep."

"Why the heck is she here?"

"I don't know. I didn't ask." He nudged Roan with his side of his boot. "Why are you here?"

"To ruin your day, obviously."

"Well, mission accomplished," he said with a disarming smile. Deputy Tim certainly had a way about him. Wasn't bad to look at, either. Not that she noticed.

Wanda and Tina lifted Cross to the gurney and rolled him to the back of the ambulance.

"You think it's a good idea to give her a tire iron?" Tina asked.

"I'm pretty sure the tire iron is irrelevant in this case," Deputy Tim said, leaning against his patrol car while Roan twisted off lug nuts.

"You should call for backup," Wanda suggested.

"Maybe *I* should call for backup," Roan mumbled. She pierced the following silence by dropping another loose lug nut into the wheel cover.

"No need for any backup," Deputy Tim reassured.

"Did you see one of those... *things*?" Wanda asked him, as

if Roan couldn't hear.

"Nope."

"Shouldn't you be getting him to the hospital?" Roan asked loudly. The longer they stared at her like that, the more she wanted to clear the air. So to speak.

"Look at you, telling me how to do my job," Wanda said, pushing her fists against her thick waist. "I got a cousin over in Dyer County, lost two cows in a storm few weeks back. And I mean, *lost*. Nowhere to be found, dead or alive. You know anything about that?"

Roan was primed to give one of her trademark sarcastic replies, but Deputy Tim beat her to it.

"Wanda, are you accusing my suspect of being a cattle rustler?"

Wanda humphed and retreated to the ambulance with her partner. Deputy Tim raised a hand goodbye as they drove away, siren wailing.

He finished the instructions for attaching the new tire, plain and calm as if he was teaching his own kid. When she was done, he gave all the lug nuts one more tightening, and said, "Good job."

He rolled the damaged tire to the trunk, and Roan followed. She lurched for Riven's case, but Deputy Tim slammed the trunk closed so fast she had to snatch her hand out of the way.

"I'm going to need that back," she said.

"Is that so?" he replied, casually holding open the back door for her.

"Am I under arrest?"

"Honestly, I don't know what we're calling this," he sighed. The combination of polite and commanding in his demeanor was almost hypnotic. "For now, let's call it a ride to the hospital."

"Then why do I have to sit in the back?" she said, ducking in.

"Because I am a cautious man," he answered and shut the door. Once in the driver's seat, he met her eyes in the rear view mirror and added, "When Earl called in, he said there were two guys who attacked you out there, but then they weren't there anymore. Any reason I should send a party out there to find them?"

"Nope."

PART SHOCK_0001

FLOW DYNAMICS. THAT WAS TERI'S EXPERTISE. Knowing how things moved under pressure kept *her* moving to construction sites all over the country. Whatever was being moved—oil, gas, water, waste—Teri was the consulting engineer at the top of every corporate HR wish list. It wasn't just because she knew her shit. She knew how to talk to people without pissing them off and how to fix problems without creating enemies. An industrial diplomat.

Carl Shock followed Teri wherever she went. She had agreed to marry him, so it was the least he could do. That was the dynamics of their flow. She led the way. He followed.

When Bella came along, Carl stayed home with her. Teri's parents were back in South Africa, and his own mother had passed years ago, so it's not like they had a lot of options, outside of a nanny. Not many nannies can uproot with a family as many times as Teri's work required. His dad "didn't do babies," so he gave Carl a lot of grief over his choice to "play house." It wasn't easy staying out of the cockpit, but spending the time with his infant daughter felt right.

Teri was worried that Bella wouldn't learn speech with Carl as her primary caregiver, because, well, he didn't talk. Much. But something about Bella brought out the words. He didn't just talk to her. Uh unh. He sang. Even when he didn't know the words. Beatboxing did the trick. Bella's raspberries were pure inspiration.

Once Bella was primed for preschool, he started flying charter again. He hated being away from home, but it was good for them all. Winged creatures need to fly, or they start to pull out their own feathers, make a racket in the cage. Bella had wings, too. He could see them in her eyes, way in the back, fluttering. He took to the sky again so that one day, she'd know it was ok to fly away, too.

They were in Bismarck when Bella started school. Teri was on contract with the Three Affiliated Tribes to oversee construction of the first refinery built on U.S. soil in decades. At first, Teri was excited about the job. A unique opportunity to work with indigenous people, empowered to reap the benefits of resources so bountiful. But things went sour almost from the start. The Chairman of the T.A.T., Duke Paulson, pressured her to change her infrastructure specs in order to increase the length of piping required, material that was being supplied by Spotted Eagle Piping Company—*his* company. His corruption was only the tip of the iceberg.

She came home one day to drop a bomb on the kitchen table. The two-inch binder had made such a loud *smack* that Bella spilled her milk down her front, started to cry. "Sorry, baby," Teri'd said, scooping her up to change her shirt. Carl had flipped through the binder, recognizing drafts of her design for the refinery.

"What does he want you to change now?" he'd asked, figuring she was upset over more of the same bullshit.

"All of it," she'd answered, and launched into a breathless tirade over a management takeover. The refinery had been scrapped. Site sold to Dimond Industries. They'd discovered a new form of energy, and she'd been roped into building their beta power plant, something called the Elbowoods Capture and Generation Project. CA/GE for short. "I could go public, but they made me sign a new non-disclosure to keep my contract, so they'd sue me and they'd win. It's bullshit."

"That's a bad word," Bella had pointed out.

"I could've said worse."

"Why would you want to go public?" he'd asked. She'd navigated drastic changes in management before. He couldn't remember ever seeing her so worked up. She prided herself on keeping an even keel in the crappiest of circumstances.

"The material they brought in for this project," Teri began with a shaking voice that scared him more than anything ever had, "is not possible."

"What do you mean?"

"I mean it's not possible. Not in this world. Not with our rules." She'd rapped her knuckles against the table, and Bella'd given the conditioned response, "Who's there?"

"It's not a joke, baby."

"It's not a joke baby who?"

Teri had laughed, and Carl had felt better for a moment, until she'd burst into tears.

"The worst part, Carl," she'd whispered. "I haven't told you the worst part. The rumor is that this construction material, this *impossible* machine they want us to build, and the energy it's supposed to contain, is manufactured by children. *Children.*"

The look that came over Teri's face told him she had a plan. Of course she had a plan. She could see twists and turns so far ahead, she probably already had *backup* plans.

"What do you want me to do?" he'd asked.

"Fly for them. You've already done a few jobs for Dimond. You're vetted."

It was true. He'd been flying execs and security teams in and out for months now.

"You have to find out what they've made me a part of," Teri had said. "And if the rumors are true, what we can do to stop it."

For months Teri worked on the CA/GE while Carl gained the trust of Spencer Pirret enough to become Dimond's personal pilot. They acted the parts of loyal employees who kept their mouths shut. How big this development turned out to be frightened them both, and as each day passed it became increasingly unclear how they could undermine anything Bradley Dimond was doing, short of total sabotage. Carl considered crashing his plane into the side of the Rockies, and he knew Teri well enough that she'd considered a similar kind of sacrifice at the construction site. It became an unspoken, nuclear option that neither of them would take. There was Bella, after all.

To keep her clear of immediate danger, the summer before the *Right of Capture* became law, Carl and Teri sent their baby girl away to relatives in South Africa. Dimond had interests in South Africa, too, but the security surrounding her relatives was not the kind easily infiltrated. Bella would be safe there, but being apart from her was killing them both.

Getting rid of Bradley Dimond or his CA/GE would not rid the world of streamers and vaks, or of people who would find ways to exploit them. Teri and Carl, therefore, set sabotage aside, and struck out to find someone who could provide an alternate vision of this new world, one that hopefully wouldn't include technological domination or threat of annihilation. They didn't find someone. Someone found them.

Katie invited them into the Lodge as founding members HarrierHawk and OrbWeaver, and when disenchanted members of the silo research team started to sign on, they knew they'd found a path forward that hopefully wouldn't involve killing or blowing stuff up. A plan began to take form for a construction project of their own, but the materials required were contraband, held in the same vault that housed those world-changing anti-kids. With no way of smuggling anything out of the silo without detection, their heist called for a major distraction, a distraction that would come in the form of the kind of breach in security that would overshadow their own. Roan Gorey was lured back to the silo to retrieve the amp, hidden in the warehouse, accessible by partner WayIn and WayOut vaks buried in the hillside. Her break-in would be the cover for their break-out.

To everyone's amazement, it had worked. They'd stolen scores of custom-made vaks, and Carl had commandeered a Dimond Industries helicopter to relocate them. Since then, he'd been operating clandestine charter getaways, pro bono.

"Wires!" shouted his current passenger.

That snapped Carl out of his ruminations real quick. He swept up and over the wire with inches to spare. He was ground-hugging to avoid RADAR detection. Goddamn obstacle course.

"Apologies for the bumpy flight, Dr. Jackson," Carl replied. "I've been up for 36 hours straight, helping friends move."

PART ROAN_0006

Cross was bad off enough that he required emergency surgery, so Roan had a couple of hours to wait. She had to admit, she was a little curious what it would be like, to be among strangers who knew her name. Who knew *what* she was, at least what Bradley Dimond told them she was. She hadn't expected a red carpet, but she'd expected more of a reception than she got.

Deputy Tim was responsible for the disappointing public debut. He brought her into the hospital through the isolated basement garage elevator, straight to a staff locker room.

"Why are you hiding me? What's the point?"

"I'm trying to avoid a panic," Deputy Tim said. "People get stupid when they panic. People get hurt."

A young Hispanic woman slipped into the room, making the tight space even tighter. She introduced herself—*Jasmine*—and then she pulled Deputy Tim outside the room where she proceeded to rip into him for everything he'd done wrong. It was a long list. He took too many chances. He shouldn't have involved her in this. He should have locked Roan up instead of bringing her here. *And* he forgot it was her birthday. Deputy Tim's response was too quiet for Roan to hear, but it had a tranquilizing effect on Jasmine. She re-entered the room without a word, pulled some clothes from a locker and opened a door to a bathroom that had a shower.

Roan washed algae out of her hair with Jasmine's shampoo, then changed into clothes left for her on the sink. Jeans and a well-worn tee-shirt with a cartoon pig in a chef's hat sitting on fat graphics that read *Corky's Ribs and BBQ of Memphis*. Classy.

Jasmine smiled in approval when Roan emerged and said, "Now you look like a local." She patted the bench for Roan to sit down, then tended to her scratches and bruises. Roan wished they'd stop treating her so decently. It was making her feel guilty for what she'd have to do once Cross was out of surgery. "You could have a concussion," Jasmine surmised. "We should get an x-ray of that shoulder. And they'll probably want to run a few more tests..."

"That's not going to happen," Roan said.

"We're just trying to help."

"You can help by giving me back my stuff."

"Stuff? What stuff?" Jasmine asked, looking at Deputy Tim.

"A crazy glow-*around*-the-dark tomahawk and some kind of ghostbusting gizmo," he said, and then pointedly to Roan, "*That's* not going to happen."

"So the plan is to keep me tucked away in here until the real fire power shows up to take me off your hands?"

"The only plan I have is to keep the people in this hospital from getting all worked up."

"What did he say to you out there," Roan asked Jasmine, "to get you to help me?"

"He said that he brought you to me because I'm the one person in this whole goddamned county he trusts to do the right thing," Jasmine said.

"Wow. That's sweet."

"He's a sweet guy."

"I'm not that sweet," Deputy Tim said, and he held the door open for Jasmine to leave. "Let me know when the other suspect is out of surgery."

"Magic word?"

"*Please* let me know when the other suspect is out of surgery."

Jasmine pecked Deputy Tim on the cheek, and Roan just managed to squeeze in a quick "Happy Birthday" before the door closed behind her. Jasmine turned back to respond, but Deputy Tim closed the door.

"Forgetting your girlfriend's birthday," Roan said. "That's a no-no."

"You can stay here while your friend is in surgery, or in a jail cell across the street," Deputy Tim said. "I'm beginning to care less and less which it is, but you should know that I brought you here because I have a feeling my colleagues might decide to re-enact the Salem witch trials right here in Tennessee if they get their hands on you, so if I were you, I'd withhold the sarcasm. You're starting to irritate me."

"Yeah," Roan said, laying back on the bench and closing her eyes. "I get that a lot."

A crackle of a voice speaking Southern drawl on the radio yanked her from a deep sleep. Her arms and legs had draped over the edges of the locker room bench like she was melting ice cream with a spine. She didn't wake up fast enough to catch the meaning of the drawl, but whatever it was had Deputy Tim standing over her, looking determined.

"Time to go," he said.

"Is Cross out of surgery?"

"Your ride home is almost here," Deputy Tim explained. "We rendezvous outside of town in fifteen."

"My ride *home*?" she echoed. There was no place like home for her anymore. Whatever ride he'd arranged would be to somewhere she didn't want to go. "Where's Cross?"

"Don't worry about him," Deputy Tim said, rapping the underside of the bench with his boot to urge her up. His impatience was growing. "They'll take care of him."

"Oh sure, *They* will. Who the hell do you think sliced him open in the first place?"

"I got to be honest with you, kid," Deputy Tim said. "I don't care. I just want you both out of my town."

"Take me to him," she insisted. There was a scream outside the door, followed by the noise of a tray getting dropped. "Now."

Deputy Tim moved a hand to his holster and slowly inched open the door. The streamer waiting for him was a pile of fuzzy, dimpled capsules. The fuzz quivered, and the connected rods backed up enough to let Tim and Roan out of the room, where they saw it was Jasmine who'd been startled into dropping the dinner tray. She was plastered to the wall, staring with wide eyes at the magnified version of a germ she'd done battle with plenty of times, no doubt, but had never seen eye to eye. Or eye to wiggly antennae.

"That's—" she stuttered, "that's E. coli."

"It's what I have to work with," Roan said. "Your hospital really needs a deep clean."

Jasmine took offense at that, but kept her response to herself. Deputy Tim had thrown a protective arm in front of her. Sweet.

"Cross?" Roan pressed.

No response. Deputy Tim was in streamer coma mode.

"No one will miss this bacteria," Roan continued, "but there are things in this hospital that would be missed. Should I change channels to something more familiar?"

One of the rods extended to be within inches of Jasmine's face, and she closed her eyes with a tiny shriek.

"No!" Deputy Tim shouted, and Roan pulled the rod back, making the E. coli streamer mirror her raised hands.

"I don't want to hurt anybody," Roan said, checking over her shoulder to see armed guards round the corner of the hall, guns raised by shaking hands, "but you should probably let your friends know that if something happens to me, this thing is going to take everybody in this building, and then everybody in this town, and then everybody in the next town, and so on and so on."

"Back off," Deputy Tim ordered the guards, and they were visibly relieved to comply.

"Ok, good. You're with me again. Where's Cross?"

Deputy Tim nodded at Jasmine and she answered, "Recovery. On 4. I don't know the room number, I swear."

Roan motioned for Deputy Tim to lead the way, and the E. coli streamer followed close behind. Jasmine recoiled from the revolting sight of the bacteria feeling its way down the hall. Roan wanted to apologize for being so scary, but she might as well apologize for having green eyes. People were going to look at her how they were going to look at her, and there wasn't anything she could do about it. U.A. was right. People were never charitable that way.

At the elevator, Deputy Tim pressed the up button, waving off two more security guards. The elevator opened to reveal a pregnant woman in a wheelchair, huffing loudly, red-faced. In labor. The expectant father jumped in front of her and furiously punched the door close button.

As the doors pinched closed in front of her nose, Roan offered her "Congratulations," then suggested to Deputy Tim: "Stairs?"

"Roger that," Deputy Tim agreed and held the door open for her, watching in horror as the streamer buckled and folded up the stairs after her, as if on a leash. "That thing does whatever you say?"

"E," she whistled, and made the E. coli streamer tumble up to her. "Heel."

Deputy Tim had nearly jumped over the railing to make way for E's stupid pet trick, but said, casual as ever, "Sure, ok." Then he retched. She and E continued up to the fourth floor, and to his credit, Deputy Tim was right with them when she pushed through the door. It took them a few tries to find the right room, and Roan felt bad for those intrusions. She really did. Nobody deserved to come out of the fog of anesthesia to see a pile of E. coli the size of a St. Bernard standing next to his bed. Well, nobody except for maybe Sebastian Cross.

"Holy shit!" was his appropriate response.

"Relax," Roan said. "You'll pop your stitches."

PART CROSS_0002

"**What the hell is that thing?**"

"The nurse said it was E. coli," Roan answered. "I figure she should know."

"You're threatening me with a bacteria balloon?" Cross asked. "You've reached new lows."

"Why would I threaten you? I brought you here so they could fix you. You must still be loopy from the drugs."

He had to admit, he did feel fuzzy, but the sight of Roan's fuzzy friend in such close quarters was sobering him up real quick.

"I'm surprised you stuck around," he said, rubbing his face.

"Where would I go without you?"

"She wasn't entirely free to go," said the deputy.

"Trust me," said Cross, "She didn't stay because of you."

Sirens outside reached a crescendo, and Roan stepped over to the window to take a look.

"That would be the entire Sheriff's Departments from just about every county in Western Tennessee and Eastern Missouri," the deputy announced, sounding glum. "National Guard has been dispatched, too."

"I can see that," she said. "Looks like a real circus down there."

"This is amusing to you?" the deputy asked. He took a step toward Roan, but the E. coli streamer quivered its flagella, and he took twice as many steps back. "Maybe you should consider the downsides of holding a hospital hostage."

"Do you think you can walk?" Roan asked Cross.

Cross threw the covers off, planted his bare feet on the cold floor, and stood. He thought he might crumble to the floor, but he didn't. "Looks within the realm."

"Then get dressed," she said. "We have to go. The villagers are getting up the courage to storm the castle."

Cross looked for his clothes but couldn't find them. On the run in his tighty whities? That wouldn't do.

"Deputy?" Roan started. "You mind?"

He seemed confused about what she was asking, but then he noticed how Cross was eyeing his uniform. He said simply "No."

"You can hand over your uniform, or E can remove you from it," Roan said. "Your choice."

"Oh, brother," Cross said. "You're naming them now? What else changed while I was unconscious?"

E quivered and tumbled close to the deputy until he backed into a corner. He started to unbutton his shirt, and she caught the full force of his glare before turning away to give him privacy.

"I should've shot you when I had the chance."

"I hear you," Cross said in commiseration.

"You don't get to take the shirt off my back and pretend to be on *my* side," the deputy shot back.

"Fair enough."

Cross dressed in the reverse order that the deputy undressed. Cross probably would've felt sorrier about the situation if the pharmaceuticals in his veins hadn't been blocking most of what he should've been feeling. He could tell from the pressure in his belly that when the drugs wore off he was going to be hurting, big time.

"What's going on out there?" Cross asked Roan.

"A helicopter just landed across the street," Roan reported, and then she groaned. "The Twin is here."

Cross sighed. "Her name is Selena."

"She hates my guts."

"Well, you killed her brother."

"I didn't—" Roan stopped herself. "He fell."

"Keep telling yourself that," Cross said. "Cuff yourself to the bed, Deputy."

The deputy's eyes were daggers, but he followed instructions. Cross picked up the deputy's gun belt when Roan said, "No. Leave it."

"They may not shoot at *you* out there," Cross said. "But if they get a clear shot, they'll sure as hell shoot at *me*."

"They won't get a clear shot," Roan said. "I promise. Leave it."

If Cross hadn't been so impaired, her bossing him around might've gotten a rise out of him. As it was, compliance was a reflex until he had his full range of thought and motion back. Besides, guns weren't his style. He asked the deputy, "You have a taser?"

"Not on me."

Cross couldn't tell if he was trying to be funny, since he was down to his skivvies, or if he meant he kept his taser in his cruiser. Either way, Cross was leaving the hospital room unarmed and uneasy.

"Thanks for the lift, Tim," Roan said, shadowing her streamer into the hall.

"Go to hell" was his response, followed by a sincere threat, "If you hurt a single person in my town, I'll hunt you down myself!"

"Another friend for life," congratulated Cross, joining the queen of anti-social behavior in the hall behind the shelter of her streamer. "Do you know where he parked?"

"Basement garage," she said, calling the elevator.

Ding. Empty. Good. Roan held the open door button for E to join them, crowding Cross into a corner.

"That thing has to come with us in here?" he asked, trying to keep his voice in an appropriately manly octave. "Can't it just go through the floors and walls and shit?"

"It's locked in," she said, giving the bacteria streamer a good kick to show how solid it was. "It can only go through stuff when it's in flux. Relax. It can't collect you as long as I keep it locked."

"You can do that now?" Cross asked. "Control them. Lock them. Fly them."

"I told you, I've been practicing."

"Of course you have," Cross said. "Push Lobby. We need to pick up supplies."

E shot a rod out to push "L". Cross gave Roan a look, and she smiled. Actually smiled.

At lobby level, they followed signs to the pharmacy. Cross filled a basket with OTC painkillers, protein bars, and water.

"We're just going to steal this stuff?" Roan asked.

Cross answered the stupid question by sending an incredulous stare at her over the water bottle he was downing, so she shrugged with a defensive, "Ok, ok, we're hurting for cash, I get it." She packed her pockets with candy and chose a pair of sunglasses. She leaned over to the cowering cashier to say, "My brother's the one you should be afraid of," and she tried on the sunglasses. "I'm not so bad."

Cross found the pharmacist behind a counter in the back and said "Hi."

She said "Hi" back, her voice shaking.

"Do you have penicillin back there? Amoxicillin? Anything that prevents infection?"

"I just filled one for Cipro," she said, nailing him in the face with the bottle.

"That works," he winced. "Thanks."

They hurried back to the elevator. Roan tore into a candy bar on the short ride to the garage, her E. coli pal fiddling around next to her like it needed a dose of Ritalin.

"How can you eat with that thing right there?"

"I'm hungry," she answered, mouth full.

In the garage, the streamer tumbled across the pavement ahead of them as Roan traced her way back to where the deputy had parked. He tried not to look at E directly. It made him want to puke. Cross used the deputy's key remote to unlock the cruiser, and she snatched the backpack from the front seat, checking to make sure the amp was still there. It was.

"Where's the—" Cross said, making an axing motion with his hand. Words were too much effort.

"Trunk."

A booming voice yelled, "Stop! Don't move!"

Cross jumped into the car just as a shot ricocheted off the concrete column next to him.

"They're shooting at me," Cross said, waiting for Roan to close her door before launching into reverse. "Did you notice?"

"Sebastian," Roan said in an affected teacherly voice, "Just because somebody shoots at you doesn't mean you have to shoot back. You *must* learn to use your words."

Cross responded by swerving the car around so fast her smirk hit the window. He also ran over the streamer. The car bounced like it had hit a curb.

"Shit."

"Nice try," Roan said, rubbing the side of her face. "but E's fine. You can't hurt it."

"Seatbelt," Cross ordered, and she complied.

The tires screeched as they headed for the spiraling exit ramp. Deputies with guns drawn scattered, less afraid of being run over by him than being eaten alive by the asphalt-skiing bacteria Roan pulled behind them.

Cross smashed through the gate arm, flew into the street, and then slammed on the brakes. E bumped into the back of the cruiser so hard Cross and Roan whiplashed forward.

"Did you just rear-end us?" he asked, head against the wheel, relieved the airbags hadn't deployed.

"What did you stop for?" she accused right back.

He pointed out the spike strips. Deputies and soldiers closed in fast, guns raised.

"Hold!" a commanding voice shouted.

Cross turned to find who'd made that call: a tall guy with the beard of a fundamentalist and the suit of a Fed next to

Selena. He might not have been in charge, but his command was heeded regardless, at least for now. Selena looked like she would go postal, as soon as she recovered from her paralyzing fury. Facing your moment of vengeance can do that to you. Cross wished he didn't know what that felt like, but he did.

The bearded Fed on the other hand, peered into the car at Roan with a look of wonder that caught Cross off guard. Everyone else looked terrified. This guy looked just plain curious. He walked toward the car calmly and was just about to open Roan's car door before Cross snapped out of it and locked the doors. Thunk. The Fed frowned, tilted his head to get a good look at Cross. Cross gave him a quick wave.

"Any chance you'll come out of there if I ask nicely?" the Fed checked.

Roan disappointed him with a quick "No."

"We're screwed," Cross said, thinking out loud. "We're in a crossfire right now, but once they sort that out, we're screwed."

"Go around them."

"There's no way around," Cross said. "We're boxed in. Armored vehicles there. Spike strips there."

A shadow fell over the car, and Cross saw something in his rear view mirror that he wished he could unsee. The E. coli streamer transformed from a clump of disorganized rods that resembled a pile of excrement, into a woven sheet of furry sticks that blocked out the setting sun.

Roan knocked on her window to get the Fed's attention. He was watching the transformation same as Cross. She suggested through the glass, "You're going to want to back up now."

He took the suggestion, just as the streamer cocooned the

cruiser.

"Not to complain," Cross said, gripping the steering wheel and trying to keep a grip on himself, "but I have to be able to see to drive."

A window appeared in the streamer cocoon over the windshield, giving him a perfect view of what happened next. Rods extended out from the cocoon, moving like nimble, notched fingers between the lines of soldiers to ram the nearest armored security vehicle. The first blow knocked the ASV back a few feet. Soldiers scrambled out of the way, and some opened fire. Bullets bounced off the locked streamer, but calls to "Hold your fire!" brought the hailstorm down to a trickle.

After a combo of streamer punches there was enough of a gap in the barricade for the cruiser to squeeze through.

"Ready?" Cross asked Roan. After all, there were two vehicles that needed to move, and he was only driving one of them.

"Ready."

Cross floored it, just as Selena stepped in his path with a shotgun. He hit the brakes, and the streamer cocoon took off the back bumper before sailing straight at her. She got off one round that was deflected by the streamer shield hurtling her way before the Fed tackled her. E somersaulted and folded over into a tunnel. Cross punched through it.

As soon as they were clear of the barricade, Roan's streamer sealed the tunnel, weaving a dome over the cluster of law enforcement and armed forces, trapping them under an umbrella of bacteria.

"Don't forget the chopper," he reminded, and seconds later, he saw the streamer stretched to the rooftop to lasso a chain of rods around one of its skids.

"They're not going anywhere," Roan announced.

"How long can you keep them trapped like that?" Cross asked, speeding out of town.

"I don't know," she said, taking a bite of another candy bar. "Let's find out."

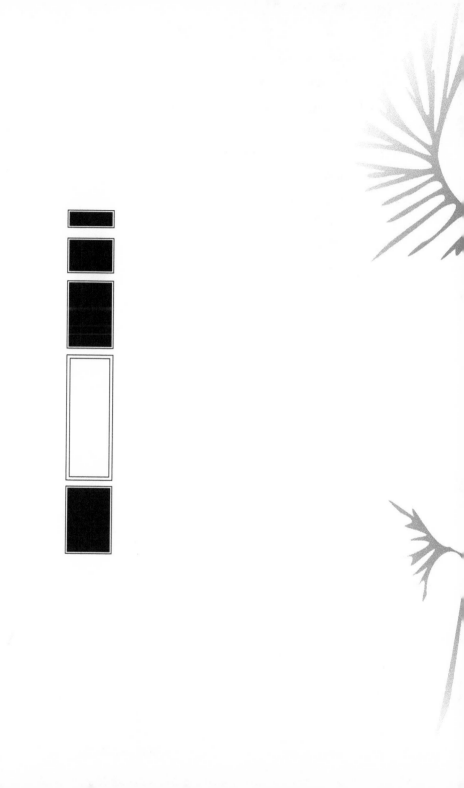

SEQUENCE FIVE

PART MATTHIAS_0004

ONLY THING WORSE THAN WONDERING IF YOU'RE still a free man, is wondering if you should give a flip about the folks who've made the answer to that question unclear. The reflexive response to that would be no, of course not. But change is constant, a point he often illustrated to his son, and shifting empathy is no exception.

After he'd identified Sergeant Griffith, the woman agent or whatever-she-was was keen on delivering him to the Man in Charge, one Bradley Dimond, and they'd fired up a helicopter on loan from the State to deliver him straight away. Woody claimed the seat next to him, after a brief tussle over it with Darryl Bowman, of all people. Agent Dohanian and the State pilot were having a disagreement of their own over whether he could transport them the whole way to Bismarck when she got the call that the girl—Roan—was in custody at a hospital in Tiptonville, Tennessee. Tennessee he could do, so off they went.

Once they were in the air, Woody located a first-aid kit and took an ice-pack for himself—he had a nasty bruise coming up on his face—and offered the other to Matthias for his sprained ankle that was starting to swell.

"Darryl Bowman," Woody said to Dohanian with a shake of his head. "Now, I understand you find yourself in need of an endless supply of knuckleheads to follow your knucklehead orders, but *Darryl Bowman*? He's more of a knuckle *dragger*, don't you think?"

She did her best to ignore Woody's criticism, texting fast and furious into her phone. Woody turned to Matthias for an ear to his personnel complaint.

"I feel like we're witnessing a rush to recruitment," he said. "The goal is to increase ranks, no matter the qualifications. To me, this is worrisome, because I can't consider an imbecile like Darryl Bowman a colleague—and trust me, I've had my share of imbecile colleagues. You know Darryl, Mr. Skaggs. What's your opinion?"

"He comes from a good family, but Darryl has always sought out kinship with the worst sort."

"There you have it!" Woody said, and then to the rest of the crew in the helicopter, he tried to raise a consensus. "Do we really want to be associated with *the worst sort*? That's not who we are."

Matthias wasn't sure, but it seemed like this Woody guy was just trying to amuse himself. Maybe hammer home the point with Matthias that he wasn't really *with* them. The zip ties he'd been in when Matthias first met him had already made that point clear enough.

"Darryl Bowman isn't your problem," Selena shot over her shoulder to shut him up.

"There you go again, *Agent* Dohanian," Woody said, "making a point of my status as an outsider. Like the safety inspector, or the auditor, or the goddamned hall monitor. I just don't see myself like that. Personally, I think your whole outfit is having an identity crisis. It can't be all about benchmarks and quotas. You've got to remember why you're in this thing in the first place. Right, boys? Now me, I took an oath to defend the Constitution from enemies foreign and domestic. What kind of oath do Federal Industry Agents take, I wonder?"

The other members of the crew just glared at him, barely able to hold back their punches.

"Is that why you were after my boy?" Matthias ventured to ask. "To recruit him?"

"We weren't after him," Dohanian said. "Not really. We want you."

"Why would you want me?"

"You must know something," Dohanian said, "because *they* want you, too."

"If folks have gotten the idea I'm the one with the answers, we're all in a lot of trouble."

Woody laughed and slapped Matthias on the back.

Later, while watching the showdown with the girl from the relative safety of the rooftop where they'd landed, Matthias considered what Woody had said about recruitment. She was definitely outnumbered, but Matthias wondered how many of that united front knew how little their numbers meant. He couldn't see her in the cruiser that emerged from the parking structure, but he recognized her tag-along monster easy enough. A squirming mass that turned Matthias' stomach, this one seemed tame compared to its New River cousin. That was, until it poofed itself out like a parachute and tented the whole block. The helicopter pilot was prepping for takeoff when a tentacle anchored his equipment to the bio-dome below. Matthias expected for the thing to gobble everyone up, but it didn't, so he left the roof to investigate. The pilot was too busy freaking out into his radio to notice, or care. Hard to blame him. It was a disconcerting vista.

The writhing dome was immovable. Matthias could hear the orders and team efforts to make a hole, or lift an edge. He thought he recognized Woody's commanding voice in there. That's where his empathy switched things up on him again.

An old man in a wheelchair joined him on the sidewalk. Judging by the cup of coffee he was sipping, he must've taken shelter in the cafe just behind where Matthias was gawking.

"You're not running," observed the old man, and thumbed into the shop to point out the barista behind the counter, "or hiding."

"No point to either."

"You've seen one before?"

"I've been inside one," Matthias said. "Inside *inside*."

The old man cocked his head in disbelief, nearly dislodging one of the nasal tubes feeding him pure oxygen. "I thought that was a one-way ticket."

"It was a helluva re-entry, let me tell you."

The old man offered his hand with his name, "Gus Freeley," and Matthias returned with his own.

"Don't you know," Gus chuckled good-naturedly, "they released me at the same time they evacuated everybody else, so I wheeled myself over here, out of the way. My daughter will be along to pick me up, once they give the all clear. I guess you and I should count ourselves lucky, considering. Oh, unless you know somebody trapped in there?"

"I don't know them all that well. I'd say they're a loose affiliation at best."

"I see," Gus said. "So, pardon me for asking, but why wait around?"

"They're my ride," Matthias said.

"Well, we can give you a ride. Where do you need to go?"

"I don't rightly know."

Gus looked at him with curiosity when Matthias was hesitant to expand on that answer. They watched the fuzzy dome in silence for a bit, and then Gus continued, "You'll have to forgive all the questions. Old habits are hard to break. I'm retired now, but for nearly 35 years, I was the owner, editor-in-chief, and lead reporter for the *Reelfoot Gazette*. Local paper. Small town stuff. Crop prices, best deals on seed and feed. Births. Weddings. Deaths. The occasional flood or drought. Lately, a few disappearances. My daughter runs the operation now, what's left of it. She's got her finger on the pulse. Started a column called *The Watchlist* for things like invasive species, pesticide drift. We're mostly an online presence now. That's how she puts it. Makes it sound like we're haunting people from the internet to me."

"You have a headline today, I'd think."

"If you really are the first *reappearance*," Gus said, looking at him through his bifocals like they were x-rays. "I'd say I do."

"I meant *that*," Matthias said, again pointing at the monstrosity outside the hospital.

"Oh, *that*. Sure, *that*. We'll cover that, but so will all the cable news outlets. They will descend and they will commentate. They'll be fast and loud, but we will do our due diligence. *You*, if you are being truthful with me, *you* are the story I'd want to tell."

Matthias was unsure how much he should share with Gus, even though there was something about him that made Matthias want to tell him everything. A handy trait for a reporter.

"That *Watchlist* of invasive species," Matthias started, "Who made top of the list?"

"Well, that'd be the Japanese carp."

"Yeah, I heard about them. Sound like a real nuisance. Well, the girl that just came through your town? She deserves top billing on that list, let me tell you. She's worse than a whole river of them carp, and I should know. I've been riding her wake since I had the misfortune of meeting her. Me and my son, both. I aim to get us out of it as soon as possible, but first I got to find him. Only way I can fish him out of this mess is by riding the current with the ones who brung me here, hope for another mixer with the group that has my boy."

"Let me make sure I'm following you. You don't have any idea where your son is? He's missing?"

Hearing the words spoken out loud was almost too much for Matthias to bear. He dropped his head and waited for the ability to speak to return to him.

"We could... run a description," Gus suggested, but before he started asking the particulars, Matthias let it all just pour out of him. How he'd first come across Roan Gorey with her companions on the side of the road outside of town one morning, and how his regrettable decision to help them led to his streamer incarceration. How he'd been blasted back into existence, etcetera, etcetera, etcetera...

"So the Gorey girl really can bust people out of those things?" Gus asked when he was finished. "Why hasn't that been reported? There are so many people who are missing loved ones, assuming the worst."

"I don't know. Maybe because it's not fail proof. Everything tumbles out at once," Matthias explained. "And I mean everything. Trees, bears, germs. It ain't exactly a soft landing. I was lucky to survive. Somebody else wasn't."

"You think we should reach a safe distance?" Gus asked, indicating the dome trap.

"That one's a different puzzle altogether," Matthias said. "These folks aren't trapped like I was."

Gus dropped his cup over an ant on the sidewalk and said, "I suppose that's the equivalency we should all get accustomed to."

"Guess so," Matthias agreed. He winced from some pain in his jaw. Maybe it was from all the talking, but it'd been nagging him since Nuttallburg. He didn't remember anyone socking him in the jaw, but that's vaguely what it felt like.

"Why does this Bradley Dimond want you, do you think?"

"He thinks I know something."

"And do you?" Gus smiled, expectantly. When Matthias was hesitant again, Gus pondered the strange traffic obstruction in his town. "Information about this new world we are all living in is a burdensome responsibility, but it's a commodity too—I get that. You're headed into the lion's den, armed only with intel to use as a bargaining chip to get your son back. But Mr. Skaggs, I hope you can see how the water's rising, all around us, same as when the Mississippi overflows her banks. It's my duty to keep my neighbors up and down this great river informed. This is a very different kind of flood headed our way, and your boy won't be on any higher ground when you get him back. We're all in this together. You have a responsibility to share your knowledge with the rest of us, so that we can prepare for the coming flood. Let me take on some of the burden of responsibility here. I'm good for it."

Matthias thought long and hard. Of course, he did know something. Something big. He'd overheard a conversation when his keepers had thought he was still unconscious.

"She's come out here for a reason," Matthias said. "I heard talk of a station. A hub they're building in a central location, a secure place for breaking those things open without killing whoever or whatever's inside." Matthias took a deep breath, and Gus waited patiently. "They plan to redistribute the contents by genus and species. They must have a network of partners all over, ready to receive whatever's sent their way."

"But how would they do that?"

Matthias had been wondering that himself, and he considered the vak he helped Ranger Dave place in the cave, the one labeled "Gray Bat." He kept that detail to himself and shrugged. He didn't want to get Dave into trouble... any more than he'd already gotten himself into, anyhow.

"They'd have to have some kind of sorting mechanism..."

In the blink of an eye, the bacteria streamer shrunk into a compact ball, revealing everyone underneath. Then the ball stretched into a stream of light, shooting off in the direction that Roan Gorey had gone. A virtual exclamation point to end their conversation.

Tiptonville looked untouched, save for the rounds of ammunition in the street from the soldiers who'd fired on the getaway car. Woody was the first to come to his senses.

"Let's do a headcount!" he shouted. "Squad leaders, make sure we're not missing anybody, then do a top to bottom of the hospital, make sure no surprises got left behind in there."

"Well, there we go," said Gus, slapping his wrinkled old hand on his knee, and he lifted the cup off the ant to let it go on its way. He shook hands with Matthias again. "I promise I'll keep your information safe, Mr. Skaggs, until I can independently verify it. At that point, I think I might just come out of retirement and share what I can with my readers. I thank you for your trust."

Matthias noticed the agents were coming his way. Gus wheeled quickly back into the café, already scribbling some notes down in a notebook he'd produced from his shirt pocket. Matthias flinched again from the pain in his jaw. Dohanian was too busy screaming profanities at their helicopter pilot who'd just taken off without them, but Woody noticed Matthias' discomfort.

"Nice to see you again, Mr. Skaggs," Woody asked. "You ok?"

Matthias stuck a finger in his mouth and pressed down on his gum where it hurt. The pressure relieved some of the pain, but it was what he found there that had him speechless.

He was growing brand new teeth.

PART ROAN_0007

Hooking around harvested cornfields at 90 mph meant that Cross spent equal time spinning wheels in grass and peeling out on pavement. It didn't help that Cross was watching the sky more than the road. Mud clods pelted the plexi barrier behind the front seat because he had his head out the window.

"Maybe I should drive," Roan suggested. "I mean, I don't know how to drive, but somehow I still think that would be better."

"We have to ditch the deputy's ride before they get eyes on us, or there's no point."

A T in the road. A sign reading "Port of Cates Landing" pointing to the left. Cross swiveled his head around like he was that possessed girl in *The Exorcist*.

"Where are all the people? Huh. They must've cleared everyone out. Or did you…"

"I didn't do anything," Roan said defensively. "Not exactly a metropolis."

Cross turned toward Cates Landing at a breakneck speed, and skidded to a halt at the abandoned dock.

"Out," he ordered Roan.

"Out, *please*?"

"We lost the spare," Cross noticed, as if that explained his bad driving. "Probably damaged it when I ran over your spiky friend back there."

"Is *anything* not my fault?"

Cross pretended to ponder the question. "No, pretty much all on you."

He popped the trunk and stood in a daze.

"What's wrong?" Roan said, stuffing the rest of the pharmacy stuff into her bag.

"You said the tomahawk was in the trunk."

Roan joined him. No trumpet case. No Riven.

"The deputy put it in here," she said. "I saw him."

Cross checked the back seat, frantic. "You said it was in the trunk!"

"I thought it was!" Roan yelled back. "Don't scream at me."

Cross joined her back at the trunk and slammed it so hard it hurt his side. He fell against the car, head hanging. "We can't go back for it. We can't risk it. Judge will have to make a new one for you. Hand me one of those rocks over there. Big as you can carry."

"Why?"

"We're going to put the cruiser in the river. Hopefully they'll waste time dredging for us. Give us a little more of a head start."

She pulled the backpack on and picked a chunk of granite from the rocky boat ramp, lugged it over to the car. Cross prepped the cruiser for its launch off the dock. Before Cross dropped the granite onto the gas pedal, Roan asked him to "Wait." The glare he gave her was classic Cross.

She did a quick sweep of the glove compartment and collected a couple things. A small book of photographs. A box wrapped with a bow. She showed it to Cross.

"Deputy Tim didn't forget his girlfriend's birthday."

"Are you fucking kidding me?"

Roan shrugged, tucking the items away. "Maybe I'll have a chance to return it."

Cross anchored the gas pedal and put the cruiser in gear. It fishtailed and knocked him over before sailing off the landing and into the river with a satisfying splash. Grimacing on his back in the dirt, he offered, "All the families you've torn apart, and you think you'll get brownie points for keeping a birthday present dry?" He struggled back to his feet as the cruiser gurgled in protest and added, "Let's get off the road."

Just as they did so, a squadron of low-flying helicopters beat the air over their heads.

They followed the river on an overgrown trail until they could no longer see the road. The number of gnats Roan ate increased as the sun dipped below the tree line. She took to breathing through her nose, even though their pace was making her breathe hard. About a mile in, the pace took its toll on Cross, too. He took a moment to lean against a tree, and she was grateful for the break. His shirt—the deputy's starched tan uniform—was dotted with blood.

He saw the look she was giving him. "I just need to catch my breath."

"Is the hub far from here?"

Cross collapsed to his knees in response. She took that as "yes, it's far."

Roan squatted on a tree root in the shade and beat back the gnats while Cross gradually capitulated to exhaustion. His chin drooped to his chest until he was fully decompressed, dead asleep. Possibly more dead than asleep.

There were a lot of dead things around them. She wasn't being morbid. It was just something Roan noticed on her streamer channel while she munched a package of salted cashews, enjoying the bug songs that grew louder as daylight faded. The pattern was interesting—the pattern of dead things. The layers bubbled out beyond the riverbank, deep into the cottonwood groves that guarded the meadows and farmland, like sentinels keeping watch. Casualties of past flooding. That's what she was reading. She was glad she didn't pick up on any human remains. She was certain the images of the drowned Chickasaw villagers back at the swamp would haunt her dreams for a good long time. A disaster of that magnitude was difficult to wrap her head around. When nature turns against you like that, what is there to do?

She turned the streamer channel down and strained her eyes in the dying light to study the book of Deputy Tim photos she'd saved from drowning. Her parents printed a few photos a year for the fridge or to add to frames in the stairwell, but only ones that really meant something, so Roan figured this photobook meant something to Deputy Tim. She was glad she'd saved it. Maybe Jasmine had made it for him. Most of the pictures were of the two of them. On a camping trip. Out with friends. A few were of a dog. A German Shepherd. One with the dog's snout out of focus as it went to lick whoever was taking the picture made Roan laugh out loud.

She was shocked when Cross snatched the photobook from her and snarled, "These don't belong to you." And he tossed them toward the river so that a few fluttered loose from their plastic sleeves, seeding the muddy bank.

"You dick!"

He pushed up, slowly, and started to walk, stiff as a zombie. She didn't follow. She climbed down to gather as many of the pictures as she could.

"Leave them," he ordered, the force of his own voice knocking him off balance. "You have no right to pretend you care."

"What's it to you? You don't have to carry them," Roan reasoned, searching for the missing pieces of the photobook in the failing light. "The deputy wasn't so bad. At least he didn't treat me like… like…"

"Like what? Like the plague that you are?" Cross towered over her as she scaled the embankment, hands full. "There's no putting things back together after *you*. You've broken the whole world. Split it in two. Now we're headed to a fantasy land where you're supposed to magically bring everything back, and you lost the one thing that made you useful. And that wasn't even something *you* made."

"I got us out of there," Roan said, struggling in the mud, "And I didn't hurt anybody."

"Too little, too late." He waved her off like he was giving up on her and staggered like a drunk through the tall weeds, alone.

Once she conquered the muddy bank, she followed behind Cross, head down, focused on reassembling the photobook and keeping the angry tears welling in her eyes from her cheeks.

There was a splash in the river and a flurry of wind. A streamer water snake glided gracefully along the surface parallel to them.

"Is that for me?" Cross asked.

"I didn't call it," she snapped. "That one's brand new."

"Here's what you need to practice," Cross suggested, "Not bringing any more of those fuckers into the world. Can you manage that? Get rid of that one."

"Fine!" she shouted, and sent the water snake into the twilight sky like a missile.

"Jesus! Can you *not* draw attention to where we are?"

Roan wanted to smash his face in, and he could see it. He squared off in front of her, like he was ready for the blow. Like he wanted her to throw a punch.

"You're in a shit mood," she said, knocking the mud and gunk off her pants instead.

"You have no idea."

They heard the aerial drumbeat of helicopters again, and instead of ducking into the trees, Cross yanked her down the embankment to a half-sunk houseboat. He tossed her through a broken cabin screen, and she landed face-down on the slimy floor. When Cross dropped in next to her, the whole boat slipped a few feet more into the river. Water sloshed in.

"Hands in. Face down. If we're lucky the mud will mask our heat."

The mud was definitely masking her heat because she was getting cold fast, but she knew that wasn't what Cross meant. The helicopters hovered with their thermal imaging tech seeking them out, until wandering off again like a flock of frustrated geese.

Cross clambered to the moldy kitchenette bench in the driest corner, while she scraped the new layer of sludge from her arms and face thanks to his rough handling. He lifted his shirt to see the bandages soaked through with blood.

"Does it hurt?" she asked, finally extricating herself from the suction of muck.

"Yes. Very much."

"Good."

"You know," he started, closing his eyes either from the pain or from exasperation, "it's a little funny to me that so many people see you as evil incarnate, when all you are is just a dumb, mean kid."

"I'm not dumb."

"Sure you are. But not as dumb as I am for thinking what I'm doing here makes any goddamned difference."

"Tell me where the hub is, and I'll leave. You're right. I should have cut you loose at the hospital."

"Berit's dumber than both of us combined. She still thinks she can get through to you. Show you all the good you can do in the world. She's just like everybody else. She sees what she wants to see."

"Oh yeah? What do you *see*?"

"A selfish mistake," Cross said. "When she sees that, too, she'll give up and come away with me."

"How sweet. You want to kill all the hope in your girlfriend."

"*Misguided* hope," Cross said. "In *you*. Hope that you can save our future. You don't even know about our past. Our collective human history. You have no interest in anything you can't easily consume. You shit all over anything that's really important, or true."

Roan got the feeling that Cross wasn't talking about her anymore, so she decided not to engage. Shortly after he wound down to an angry mutter, shivering, Cross drifted off to sleep, or maybe passed out. He hadn't taken his medicine yet. She could read the increase in bacteria around his wound. Busy little buggers. She almost felt bad about delivering their doom, especially since she probably had more in common with them than with Cross.

She stood there in the growing dark on the edge of a river, trying to make up her mind. This wasn't the first time she'd stood over an unconscious Sebastian Cross. The last time was after he'd fallen into a trap she'd set. She'd emptied his pockets and ditched him. It would be easier to leave him this time. She was already carrying everything in the backpack. No pickpocketing required.

"I know I'm going to regret this," she said to herself, and she shoved the antibiotic between his lips. The capsule fell out and onto the floor. She read the bacteria on it, shrugged, and tried to shove it back into his mouth. He resisted, knocking her hand away.

"Cross, you need to take your medicine," Roan scolded.

"Annie?"

"*Annie?*" she repeated, not sure she heard him right. "Yeah, ok. Annie wants you to take this." She put a bottle of water to his lips, and he drank, swallowing the pill. "Good boy."

Next she prepped the fresh bandages. She took a deep breath and carefully peeled off the bloody patch of gauze.

"Almost there," she talked herself through it. Suddenly, his hand shot up to grab her around the throat. Surprisingly strong for someone so close to death, he pinned her against the spongy wall. The rotting wood bowed out behind her. Water seeped in through the new breach.

"Cross, it's me," she sputtered, but then realized that wouldn't necessarily convince him to stop. She punched and kicked at him, landing a blow near his wound. He instantly caved, deflating back into the bench, eyes rolling back.

"Why do you have to be such a jerk?"

She threw the clean bandages at him, but he was so close to passing out he didn't notice. Another streamer had just appeared in the river, and she was tempted to let it take him. She could find the hub on her own. Maybe not as quickly, but she'd find it. She could make up a story about what happened to him. She used to be pretty good at making up stories. Berit would never know what she'd done. It would be so easy.

The boat shifted on the embankment, and the sudden movement prodded Cross back to consciousness. He seemed lucid again, and with one look at his shipmate became aware his fate had shifted, too.

"What's the plan, Roan?"

Their flimsy shelter shuddered as the top half of the house boat separated from the bottom. Water rushed in through the rip, but a new floor settled under their feet almost instantaneously. The streamer, locked in as a turtle as big as the house boat itself, lifted them on its back and launched into the river.

"I'm keeping us moving forward," she said. "Why don't you shut up and sleep it off?"

PART CROSS_0003

"Are you dead?"

Cross pushed Roan's face out of his own. "Sorry to disappoint." He was surprised to find clean bandages over his wound. "You did this?"

"I'm as shocked as you are." She yawned and stretched. He saw bruises on her neck.

"Looks like you got into it with somebody. They still around?"

She stared at him pointedly and said, "Unfortunately, yes."

"*I* did that?"

"Who's Annie?" she asked him.

"Don't say that name." He'd leapfrogged right over not wanting to believe he could have strangled her to wanting to strangle her.

"Just repeating what *you* said. Over and over. All night. Kept waking me up. Really annoying."

"Drop it," he said, downing some pain pills with a lukewarm Ensure. She tossed him the Cipro he'd procured from the pharmacist, and he added the meds to his breakfast cocktail. That's when he sensed that they were moving. "Hey, how are we…"

He looked down to see that his feet were resting on a luminescent shell, a shell that contained a space so vast it gave Cross that sick sinking feeling that comes from dangling on the edge of an inconceivable drop. One of those mysterious balls of bluish light slapped the underside of the shell right where his feet were, so he jerked them up. The sudden move caused so much pain he almost blacked out. The disappointed light ball slowly unraveled, revealing its broken-ladder structure before it drifted back into the void.

"Hm," said Roan, "Looks like it recognized you. You make friends in there last time?"

He ignored her, preferring not to think about his time inside the streamer. The memory gave him that same sinking feeling. Instead he looked out the mud-caked windows to see early morning light on a calm river.

"Where are we?"

"We followed the river all night," Roan said. "We had to hide under the trees a few times when the helicopters came too close. The river started to get wider, and you didn't tell me which way to go, so we've pretty much been treading water for the last few hours."

"Take us to shore. I want to see what's around that bend."

"Aye aye, Captain Jerkface," Roan said with a sarcastic salute.

She brought the heap of rotten wood to a rest, and Cross's first step from the cabin sunk right through the disgrace of a deck, dropping him a few inches onto the locked streamer. This part of it wasn't shell. It looked like a flipper, and it extended like a gangplank to a cluster of boulders. Roan slid down the flipper after his careful descent, showing off with a sort of skateboarding trick off the end. She looked really proud of herself until Cross stared her down.

"Oh my god, you are no fun," she mumbled.

From the shore, Roan's monstrosity of a vessel could pass for a shabby riverboat bobbing in the currents, as long as the flippers stayed under the surface of the water, and the giant turtle head kept obediently tucked under the bow. Cross chuckled. He couldn't help it.

"I'd like to see you do better," Roan said, taking offense.

"Sorry," he said, but she still seemed on guard. "I didn't mean to insult your maritime achievements. I do, however, think *that's* hysterical."

He pointed at the faded stenciling along the stern. *The Royal Nonesuch.*

"Oh," she said, then with furrowed brow, "What's a nonesuch?"

"*One of a kind,*" Cross answered, then corrected himself as he marched into the overgrown riverweeds. "No, it's more than that. A nonesuch is *unsurpassed in its uniqueness.* I doubt even in its heyday, if that tub qualified. 'The *Royal* Nonesuch' is a con game, played on hayseeds. Whoever owned that bucket either didn't have much respect for their fellow man, or was a big fan of Mark Twain's."

Roan didn't respond, so he turned to confirm the name had meant nothing to her. Sure enough, she was just a blank stare as she followed the path he was making through the brush.

"*The Adventures of Huckleberry…*" he prompted.

"Never read it."

"Aw," Cross said, and he felt an appropriate stab in his side as he returned to the jungle hike. "What do they have you reading in school?"

"Wouldn't know," Roan said. "I've been absent a few days."

The personal affront he'd taken from her illiteracy in the classics seemed overblown after that reminder. They trudged, tripped, and cursed the bugs for a while, equal partners in hardship. Bits and pieces of his post-surgery, adrenaline-laced fever rant were coming back to him, and with each troubled step he became increasingly surprised she hadn't abandoned him to die.

"Perfect," he muttered to himself. Now not only did he have resentments to harbor against Roan Gorey, he had to feel guilty about harboring them?

"What's that?" she asked.

"Nothing," he said. "I was just thinking we should find you something good to read in your downtime. You know, when you're busy nursing jerks like me back to health."

"Was that an attempt at an apology?" And when he shrugged, she assessed, "Lame."

He took a break in a solid patch of thistle and heather in a sunny spot and welcomed the warmth on the back of his neck. He was fairly miserable, but somehow felt better than he had in a good long time, like he'd come out the other side of a tunnel he hadn't even known he was in. Roan hung back in the shade of a cottonwood, eyeing him with suspicion. Fair enough.

"I bet you'd rather your friend Slim were here," he said, disturbing the bumblebees in the thistle as he pushed on through.

"Munny wasn't my friend any more than you are."

"He said you played cards."

"Only because he got bored," she said, but after a moment, she added a complaint. "I always lost. I think he was cheating."

"That's a solid bet. Carnival operators aren't known for their honesty," he said, daring to toss a smile at her over his shoulder. She missed it, her attention on her footing. "Dimond recruited him at the State fair, the one you crashed with your streamer."

"I know."

"He has a particular knack for reeling people in, that Bradley Dimond," Cross said, ripping a stubborn weed that was tangling him up. "I never thought I'd work for a man like him. Not in a million years."

"No? I thought you were a career thug."

Cross shook his head, "Nope."

"But you're so good at it."

"Thanks for noticing."

He thought he caught her stifling a smile that time.

"So how'd he reel you in?" she asked hesitantly. Testing the waters.

"I was in a deep, dark hole," Cross sighed, and the honesty of that made his legs heavy. "He pulled me out of it, and for a long time I was so grateful I'd do just about anything he asked."

Roan said nothing. Probably stunned he'd answered her question instead of barking at her to shut up. They walked in a shared silence, a respectful silence for once, until the tributary they'd been following reached its end by emptying into a much larger river. Barges pushed by tugs kept to lanes. Smaller vessels made their way around, navigating the currents and shallows.

"That's the Mississippi," he said, keeping hidden in the cottonwoods. "Just south of St. Louis, best guess. Gonna be tough blending in on a turtle. We may have to hop a barge."

"Or I can fly us to the hub," Roan suggested. "I just need directions."

No way was he letting her pack him inside her streamer suitcase again, but instead of shooting down her idea with prejudice, like he used to, he replied, "Slow and steady is best."

On cue, *The Royal Nonesuch* appeared in the shallows.

"So what's a hayseed?" Roan asked.

PART KATIE_0003

WHO DOESN'T LIKE A GOOD JOKE? IT DEPENDS on who's in on it, right? And the nature, or the spirit, of the joke. Sometimes, a spirit *is* the joke. The spirit animal of the coyote stars as the trickster in many stories, but for the Mandan, the coyote serves a dual purpose as a symbol of First Creator. A trickster who provides and protects.

If this sounds like a build-up to another story, it's because it is. Don't think you can afford it? Worried about your mounting debt? Think of this one like a utility bill—a necessity to keep the lights on, keep the fridge cold, keep you from freezing to death. No worries. Just like the cable company, Katie will give you a bundle discount, in appreciation for your customer loyalty. The best news—for you—is that this trickster tale comes free of warnings about bad luck. This is not a story about First Creator from the sacred Okipa Ceremony. No, this is about a different Coyote altogether—one she helped to create.

// How *GirlWhoClimbs* Tricked Her *Coyote* into Not Devouring the World //

It's not easy, the business of world-building. Creators have to decide what to bring into the light for their various characters to see and what to keep in the dark, whether to take sides in inevitable disagreements, or when to answer pleas for help. Whatever the decision, *how* a Creator chooses to communicate is crucial to the message being received. A one-on-one with an omniscient stranger can easily be misinterpreted, or manipulated. Just ask Moses.

Katie knew she wasn't really a Creator, but in *FutureBound*, she was as close as you get. Encrypted texts were her chosen method of recruitment, and she delivered them to Lodge member prospects courtesy of the backdoor Stan had left propped open in Dimond's network. She designed the messages as puzzles so that if she were to make a miscalculation and knock on the wrong employee's digital door, her motives would remain a mystery. Paranoid, you say? *You* try taking on one of the most powerful men in the world and see how fast *you* start looking over your shoulder.

But how to make contact with the children themselves—that was a real head scratcher. She'd been watching them for a while now from above, the preferred angle of benevolent Creators. She'd pulled a fast one on the silo's security cameras at the start, and she kept a live feed of the happenings at the silo as the wallpaper behind her creative accounting work. Roan was locked down, beyond all reach. Katie lost many nights of sleep over that. She rooted for Roan's every escape attempt like a fan on the sidelines, providing auxiliary by opening doors and hatches wherever she could. Despite her tenacity, her fearlessness, her agility, Roan never made it far. It was heartbreaking, you know?

Access to Judge was a different story. This one, in fact.

The early days mostly showed Judge sedated between surgeries, a helpless infant on a gurney surrounded by walking hazmat suits with iPads. Later, she'd watch him reach milestones, like taking his first step over a bulkhead. No adult ever extended a hand for him to hold in those sterile subterranean tubes, except for Bradley Dimond. That was by design, don't you think? An attempt by Dimond to enforce biological imprinting on him and no one else, like a baby duck on its mama.

When the self-proclaimed corporate nomad raided the Gorey family for their children, Dimond became the one thing he publicly vowed never to become: a father. Sure, he had more help than most new parents. Onsite daycare, for one. As the subjects of his research, Roan and Judge were under 24/7 surveillance and received the finest medical care Dimond's hush money and personalized biohazard suits could buy. But that didn't change the fact that his young interdimensional charges posed unique challenges. Roan was noncompliant and a constant flight risk. Judge was an infant with the mind of a twelve-year-old. Poor Bradley, you know? No wonder he started drinking so much.

As a rule, he avoided Roan like the plague. As far as Dimond was concerned, she'd been ruined by her "socialist" parents, so why waste time trying to convert? Isolation might bring her around, after a while. Break her spirit, in other words. Baby Judge, on the other hand, was prime for bonding. Dimond took every opportunity to make an impression, but there were only so many hours in the day, you know? Tyranny doesn't rise by itself. Like any working parent planning a planetary-wide, techno-logical overhaul, Dimond needed a method of entertainment to keep Judge occupied in his downtime, a method that required minimal oversight and provided sufficient distraction so that Judge didn't latch onto some other influence while Dimond was at work. Or, God forbid, begin to think for himself.

Enter Nintendo.

Dimond tasked Stan Schoop with providing young Judge a gaming device, and just like that, Katie had a direct link to her

Coyote. Of course Stan was eager to share Cro*xx*Roads, and who knows, maybe even get a favorable review from a rising star of the underworld, so the DSi he refurbished for Judge included *FutureBound*, along with the version of his mod that incorporated Katie's Lodge program. All Dimond's efforts to isolate and control Judge had been undermined by a single video game. He'll be kicking himself, don't you think?

To Katie's (and Stan's) disappointment, Judge showed *Future-Bound* an insulting level of indifference. Maybe he was too aware of his starring role in Dimond's strategy to appreciate the challenges of a virtual RPG. Instead he engaged with the Marios, the Sonics, the Zeldas, forcing Katie to get creative about how to attract his attention. Creators have to do that from time to time, get creative with the details. It's not all Big Bangs and Giant Vines and Cosmic Eggs. Sometimes it's puzzle games and quests for hidden treasure. Breadcrumbs, you know?

The camera on the DS gave Katie her first up close and personal view of Judge's face. You think it's creepy to spy on somebody? No argument here. Does it help to think of it like babysitting? From thousands of miles away? No? Well, tricksters do what they have to do. It's in their nature.

Katie loved everything about Judge, the way First Creator might love her. The expressions he made while he played his favorite games—the intensity in his eye, the slight jutting of his jaw. The way he powered through the pain from his surgeries to continue powering up, bonus leveling, boss defeating. She was inspired to build a unique world, just for him, and that's exactly what she did. Her trickster programs, mini-game mods in all his favorite universes, were designed to lure him into the wilds of *FutureBound*, where she could convince him to become her Coyote.

Sure, she knows that makes her sound like the Big Bad Wolf to his Little Red Riding Hoodie, but there's nothing for it. Dimond didn't know it yet (and maybe Katie wouldn't admit it herself), but they were in a competition for Judge's allegiance. Dimond was using Judge to conquer the world, one technology at a time. Katie had no use for a conqueror. *I keep no power for myself.* Conquerors, like real Creators, leave behind too much of a mess. No, Katie wanted to show Judge the reasons not to devour the world beyond the silo, a world he had never seen with his own eye. After she opened his mind, he'd see for himself the moral imperative of dismantling the threat in her own backyard, the CA/GE. What's the difference, you wonder, between Dimond's plan for Judge and Katie's hope for him? That's easy. It's the difference between training a slave and recruiting a volunteer.

Katie was winning Judge over with each new mod he mastered. With each puzzle he solved, he was rewarded with a message in a cartoon bubble, customized for his predicament. "There's a good future in life above ground" was one reward. Another was "Choice demands reason." And "You came from a place that wants you to remember it." In-game advertising for Katie's philosophy, you say? Not at all. The games were a dialogue. Judge's part of the conversation was the fact that he was playing to begin with, and the bubble format of her messaging called for short-form thought experiments. Judge wouldn't have responded to diatribes or commandments, anyway.

Finally, when she thought he was ready, she sent him an invitation to join the Lodge in *FutureBound*, under call sign *Coyote*. Judge accepted, and a barrage of questions followed.

>> Coyote: Why did this happen to me?

>> Coyote: What can I do to stop this?

>> Coyote: Why did my parents send me here?

She had no answers. Remember, she's not a real Creator. She was just a good game maker. A trickster. If she guided him straight away to the *Lota Lota* from the silo, he would only be disappointed. And besides, how can a boy who was raised in a hole in the ground understand anything about the world he was being asked to shape? He needed space to breathe once he surfaced, to see for himself which path to take. There was a risk that his path might lead him away from her, wasn't there? Sure. Maybe that's what she wanted. Katie needed his help with the CA/GE, but she was desperate to remain the *Lodge-Builder* to her *Coyote*, or even *GirlWhoClimbs*. Katie was just Katie. You know?

So she did what any trickster would do to buy herself some time. She sent her *Coyote* on a quest. Not a quest to prove his bravery or to test his skills. This was a quest for knowledge. Answers to all those questions he had, you know? Katie built the mod in *FutureBound*, complete with a treasure map that corresponded to real GPS coordinates. Judge would use this as his guide once he was beyond the silo, like the sky charts of ancient navigators of the open ocean. The virtual quest kept *LodgeBuilder* and *Coyote* tethered in the real world. The first mission directed *Coyote* to sneak into the Hale home, where Judge made off with a cache of data from Dimond Industries, files that had eluded Katie all these months. Judge's next mission was to offer this stolen data as a gift in exchange for the answers he sought, answers Katie didn't have for him. No, she'd have to send him to someone new for that, an elder of the Lodge—someone outside Dimond's silo of influence—who had spent her life in a realm where the questions were boundless, let alone answers.

Coyote carried the treasure trove on his DS hard drive and waited for the opportunity to strike out and complete his quest for answers. This has been the story of how *GirlWhoClimbs* tried to save our world from destruction by keeping *Coyote* curious.

+ + +

While we're on the subject… as masterful as a trickster has to be, there's always the risk of becoming part of a trick you didn't want to play. Like the trick that got played on Trevor Skaggs.

Katie had invited *PallidSturgeon* to join the Lodge as soon as she'd learned that Matthias had run away from the cranberry farm and was probably headed home. She would've reached out to Trev directly, if he'd had a phone or something other than an intranet school email. Caleb had made the call on the ground not to tell Trev, and without a direct link, Katie couldn't override. Like a good lawyer, Caleb's argument to withhold the information was fair, from his perspective. There'd been no report of the return in Dimond's announcement, no corroboration at all that Matthias was, in fact, alive. The tale of his return was spun by the same group who'd collectively decided *not* to return him home, for reasons unclear and with no evidence to offer in support. Without seeing Matthias with his own eyes, how could Caleb really be sure? Wouldn't it be cruel to tell Trev such a thing, and have it not be true? Almost two weeks after Caleb had been told to keep an eye out for him, Matthias still hadn't showed any signs, so even when the decision was made to pull Trev out of Selena's net, Caleb kept the fact to himself that Matthias might be alive.

These were all points made by the skilled attorney in his own defense after Katie told Trev the truth seconds after he and Caleb came aboard the *Lota Lota*. Not surprising, Trev lost his shit. Katie left them alone on the bridge, you know, so they could work it out. Reconcile, hopefully. Caleb's instinct was understandable, after all. Years of losing cases against Mountain Patriot Coal had taught him to protect his clients from inevitable disappointment. What he'd failed to see in Trevor Skaggs was an undeniable power of resilience.

After a while, Trev stopped yelling and started throwing furniture around. Katie understood. Accepting his father's upgrade from deceased to MIA was a big pill to swallow, and on top of that was the frustration of not knowing where he was. If he was ok. What he might be facing out there. She kept track of her Lodge members as best she could, but each one of them was on their own path. She could try to map things out from here, but getting from Point A to Point B, that was on them.

Safely behind her privacy curtain in the Captain's quarters, listening to the disagreement settle down on the bridge, Katie found it hard to deny the primary reason she'd sent Judge to see the elder. The more Lodge members who knew her identity, the less influence she had.

Keeping Judge at a distance maintained her mystique.

I keep no power for myself.

But that didn't mean she wanted to give it all up at once.

PART JUDGE_0006

WHITE MOONLIGHT AND ORANGE STREET LAMP competed to illuminate the bronze statue of a football player in motion, casting it in such an unreal glow that the bronze figure itself appeared to be the light source. Adding to the aura was the teenager standing at its cleats, awestruck.

It took a sculpture of a famous football player to impress Walter Hale. Judge felt insulted. In less than a millisecond he could turn that sculpture into a real work of art, one that intertwined dimensions. What would Walt think of his idol then?

"Hero of yours?" Judge asked, stretching the long drive from his limbs.

"Jim Thorpe's a legend," Walt said. "Olympic gold in the pentathlon and decathlon, pro baseball player, and one of the greatest running backs of all time."

"He could run fast and catch a ball. Awesome."

"I guess nothing much compares to what you can do," Walt sighed. "But it wasn't just about what he could do on a field."

"I could ask you to fill me in, but I really don't care," Judge said, glancing at his DS to confirm instructions. "We're supposed to leave the car here."

Walt snatched the DS from his hands in a blur. He held the DS out of Judge's reach, high above his own head. Judge allowed himself to jump for it only once. The impulse to open his jetkill was strong.

"Give it back," he ordered.

"Who's telling you what to do?" Walt demanded, voice shaking. "I need to know."

"Nobody tells *me* what to do."

"Who are these messages from?" Walt flipped the DS open to read what was there and followed up with, "Who's Lodge-Builder? How can you be sure it's not Dimond?"

"Maybe they'll make a sculpture of you someday, Walt," Judge said, trying to keep his voice steady. "I mean, just look at you. You're the stuff of legends, just like your hero up there. Master of keep away."

Walt glanced over his shoulder at the man frozen mid-stride, ball clutched in hand, face lifted in hopeful determination. Walt drooped with shame and handed Judge his DS back, with a soft explanation for his behavior. "I hate being in the dark." He waited for Judge to finish packing his messenger bag with supplies from the car before he added, "What do I have to do to get you to trust me?"

"It's not about trust. It's a matter of respect. You follow her blindly. You always have."

"Not anymore." Walt spread his arms as if to claim his current location as proof.

"I think that's what's called circumstantial evidence. Why are you *here*?"

"I have nowhere to go." Eyes on his feet, shoulders sagging.

"Then go nowhere," Judge snapped, not allowing Walt's sad confession to sink in. "Seems to work for your bronze pal up there. I'm not your new bestie. Go. Shoo."

Judge hit the sidewalk, leaving Walt alone with his idol.

Maybe it was the stillness of the air in the sleeping residential neighborhood, or the lonely sound of his small feet on the damp pavement, but Judge suddenly wished he hadn't brushed Walt off like that. He resented Walt for so many reasons. Walt could walk away from this and return to his life—or what was left of it, anyway. A sweetly overbearing girlfriend. His own personal fan club, no doubt, considering his athletic abilities and his looks. A really nice house—even with its proximity to Point Zero and the massive vak in its backyard. Walt had led a life of freedom and privilege, while Judge had spent his existence hidden in one dimension and then locked away in another. Yes, Judge resented him, but he was just beginning to understand the appeal of having him around. Walt was a calm presence amid the chaos. Probably the manifestation of his perpetual state of confusion, but it was comforting all the same. Or maybe his sudden loneliness stemmed from the cold hard fact that the only other real connection he had in this world was through the interface of a role-playing game. About five seconds after ditching Walt, Judge already missed his company.

Judge stopped in his tracks and sighed. Without turning back, he raised his DS as an offering of apology. Walt took a few moments to get over his hurt feelings before jogging to catch up, contents of his backpack jostling around noisily. Walt took the DS, and as they walked together he studied the game Judge was playing. As expected, he said "I don't get it."

"It's a map," Judge explained, and he showed Walt how to angle the screen so that the pixelated landscape in the top screen matched their own surroundings. "See, there's your hero." Judge spun Walt and the DS around to reveal the LodgeBuilder's version of the Jim Thorpe sculpture, labeled with the athlete's Native American name, Wa-Tho-Huk. A dialogue box popped up to read *Hitch your horse at Wa-Tho-Huk*. "And there's Mauch Chunk, straight ahead," Judge tutored, spinning the DS back around to face front, revealing the town ahead of them at the base of a mountain that resembled a sleeping bear. Walt focused in on the bottom screen, where a small figure moved along a highlighted route on a crude street map.

"Who's Coyote?" Walt asked.

"That's me," Judge said. "In this level I'm a prospector."

"A prospector?"

"Seeking rubies in the mountain. Well, one ruby in particular. A special ruby I guess."

"Whoever sent you this map wants you to bring him rubies?"

"It's not Dimond," Judge said, exasperated. He swiped his DS back from Walt. "You'll never get it. These games, these puzzles, they saved me."

Several minutes of distancing silence before Judge finally made up his mind and, feeling unusually anxious, ventured to ask, "Do you want to play?"

"Sure, ok," Walt shrugged, downplaying his eagerness to join in. Over Judge's shoulder, Walt craned his neck to watch Coyote's progress through the town of Jim Thorpe, closing in on a bridge that would take them to the old town center in the hollow of the mountains.

Judge could sense Walt was getting irritated by the gameplay, so he asked why.

"It's still single player," Walt complained. "When does my avatar show up? Do I get to pick my own name? Can I be Wa-Tho-Huk?"

Amused by his enthusiasm, Judge sent the membership

request to the LodgeBuilder, but set expectations low. "I don't know. Let's see."

A few minutes more of walking, and Walt was happy to see a companion appear next to Coyote on the map. He was not thrilled, however, with the name his sidekick was given.

"Sunflower?" Walt cried. "*Sunflower*?!"

Walt sulked for the rest of the walk into the old part of town, leaving Judge to keep track of their progress on his own. Their path across the bridge brought them to a two-lane road carved into the sheer rock face of Mauch Chunk Mountain. Across the ravine, Judge noticed a rail line crowded with empty coal cars that weren't going anywhere. No engine. As they followed the curve of the road, ambient light from the old town grew, along with music, heavy on the banjo and fiddle.

No sidewalk but no traffic either, so they walked in the road straight into town. No *car* traffic, anyway. The town of Jim Thorpe was bustling with people. A mix of hipsters, hippies, and hillbillies were dispersing from a party in the center of town and spilling into the narrow streets. A giant piece of coal was at the heart of the grassy commons across from a vintage train station advertising scenic rides. Historic buildings gave the town a storybook feel, but the smell of booze and other recreational chemicals was strong. The booze odor reminded Judge of Dimond, which reminded him of the silo. He started to get claustrophobic. Walt, on the other hand, was drawn to the fun like a moth to flame, conveniently forgetting they were incognito.

"This way, Sunflower," Judge reminded, tugging him back into the shadows.

"I am not answering to that name."

They steered clear of the crowds and with the help of the map on his DS screen, Judge found a broken stone staircase, narrow and steep, that took them away from the courtyard full of beanies, tie dye, and chewing tobacco. The stairs led to a decrepit graveyard that overlooked the valley. Slate tombstones tilted toward the town, and he and Walt fought the same slant that threatened to send the whole morbid operation over the edge. What an avalanche that would be. Judge tried not to think about it.

"So... this ruby we're looking for is buried in a graveyard?" Walt said. "Perfect."

Judge scoffed at that idea, but inwardly he really hoped not. The path on the DS crept along an uneven rock wall that contained the slow slide, until it ended abruptly at a hole in the wall. The real-world breach, where rocks had given in to gravity, was above an unlit alleyway—fifteen feet below.

"Looks like we're supposed to climb down," Judge said, reluctantly.

Judge was a fast healer, but his face was still aching and his legs were already shaky from the short hike here. He didn't know if he could do this without falling.

"I'll go first," Walt said.

Walt swung over without hesitation, found a foothold, and lowered himself until it was safe to drop. No one on the main street saw him, or if they did, seemed to care. Walt rubbed his hands together as if preparing to catch a football, then raised them in a *come to papa* motion to encourage Judge's descent. Judge was shaking as he threw a leg over the broken wall and immediately slipped on the wet rock. Of course. Sunflower had made it look so easy.

He had about a split second to brace for impact with alleyway asphalt. Judge cupped his hand over the new jetkill in case it popped open at the same time he got knocked silly. He'd lose some fingers, but maybe it would give him time to shut the jetkill down before the night sky became permanently darker.

No pavement. All Sunflower. They bumped heads, but the jetkill held.

"Looks like Felix did a solid job with that upgrade," Walt said, putting Judge on his feet.

"Good catch," Judge said, rubbing the back of his head. He noticed a split on Walt's lip. "You ok?"

Walt looked genuinely stunned by the lack of snark in that question. "I'll live."

Judge checked the map for their next move. The path had ended. There was only one store with an alley entrance.

"Crystal Works," Walt read the hanging sign. "Think they have rubies for sale?"

"No harm in asking," Judge replied, trying to mask his disappointment. He double-checked the game for instructions before accepting the New Agey store as his final destination. He tucked his jetkill behind his hoodie and followed Walt inside.

A few customers were milling around, so Judge and Walt feigned interest in the offerings of uncut minerals and unpolished gemstones stored in crates along the walls. When they were alone, Walt approached the young woman by the register. She was absorbed by a tattered novel, her face hidden behind a curtain of blonde curls.

"Excuse me," he said. "Do you have any rubies?"

"That is just soooooo adorable" was her cryptic response. She smiled wide enough to show the slight overbite that made her look like she was about to blow a kiss, and she closed her book, quickly locking onto Judge. "Is that you, Judge?" Relieved he was in the right place, Judge pulled his hoodie aside to reveal his jetkill, and she continued, "It's about time. I've been waiting for you."

She swept past Walt in feather-light fabric and bare feet to flip the We're Closed sign on the door. Actually, Judge noticed that it read *Our minds are always open, but we have to close the store some time.* He'd been suppressing sighs since he'd walked in, but he couldn't help that one from escaping his lungs.

"Were the instructions confusing?" she asked. "I figured it would be best to come in the back way, considering."

"*You* sent the map?" Judge asked, his heart sinking further.

"I'm not the *LodgeBuilder*, honey," she said, slipping her feet into clogs by the door. "I just provided the directions. I'm Nova." Walt was closest, so she covered her hands over his. Less of a handshake than a handhug. "In the Lodge I'm known as *HummingbirdMoth*. If you ever want to drop me a line." She winked at Walt when she said that, and he pulled his hands away.

"I'm *Coyote*," Judge said.

"I know that, silly," giggled Nova. "Who's your shy friend?"

"Don't—" Walt started, but Judge was already answering.

"This is *Sunflower*."

"Walt. My name is Walt."

She noticed his swollen lip and said, "Ouch. I have something for that." She went behind her counter like a pharmacist might check her stores and planted something in Walt's hand.

"Thanks," Walt said, showing Judge the shard of pink crystal. Judge gave a thumb's up.

"It helps the healing process," she said. "Did you hitch your horse at Wa-Tho-Huk?"

"Yes, we did," Judge answered.

"Great. I'll have my friend tow it someplace safe."

"Wait," Walt protested. "We need that car."

"It's stolen, silly. It will only get you caught, and that's no good for any of us. Now, let me get my shit together, and I'll take you to see Ruby."

Walt and Judge exchanged looks. "Ruby?"

"Yes, hon. The reason you're here? Ruby Weiss," Nova said as she gathered her beat-up book and a bunch of other useless things and shoved them into her dingy pink backpack. She shut off all the lights and led Judge by the hand outside, into the crowded street. She shouted above all the drunken chatter, "The universe is bringing people together, like the vibrations from a cymbal crashing together. Can't you feel it?"

Judge shot a look of desperation back at Walt, who answered definitively, "No, I can't."

"I can see that about you," she shouted. "You have a lot of anger inside. It's walling you off."

"So much anger, Walt," Judge leaned back to say. "Really, man. Tear down that wall."

Nova led them up a steep hill lined by brightly-colored but poorly-lit gingerbread houses with splintered picket fences around tiny yards. On the porch of one of the more dilapidated houses, a pair of unfriendly women spilled over rusty lawn chairs and eyed passersby with suspicion. A stealthy pit bull in their yard leapt up at the passing crowd so suddenly, everyone veered into the street, like a school of fish avoiding a predator.

"That dog has a lot of anger," Walt remarked.

"Meth house guard dog," Nova responded once they were clear. "Poor thing. I'd try to rescue her if I didn't think she'd bite my face off."

"Meth?" Walt asked. "Really? Here? This town seems so nice."

"It's everywhere," Nova said, slowing her pace now that the sidewalk was becoming less crowded. "And heroin. The coal still moves through this valley, but they don't pull much of it from these hills anymore. Nothing came to take its place. People get desperate when they can't see a future in a place anymore. This town is *all* about the past. Take this courthouse, for example." She turned onto a side street across from a chiseled stone building that looked more like a castle. "Even the institutions for justice in this town are monuments to injustice. They hung the Molly Maguires right here."

"Friends of yours?" Judge asked.

"No silly," she said, climbing into a parallel-parked Prius. "It's more of a ghost story than anything else, really. When I first moved here, I got a job in the gift shop. Just to get out of the house. Get to know the place. I must've heard the guide give that tour about a thousand times. I can tell you all about the Molly Maguires on the ride to see Ruby, if you like."

Judge and Walt shared a look of apprehension and resignation as they joined her in the car. As soon as she pulled away from the curb, she launched into her tour guide voice. At first Judge wanted to laugh at her dramatic interpretation, but that impulse faded pretty fast.

"In the late 1800s, Mauch Chunk was a boomtown, a company town operated entirely by one man, Frank Gowen, who owned both the coal company *and* the railroad. Gowen was employer; landlord; banker; grocer; tavern owner; executioner. Coal workers were paid in company scrip that could only be spent at company stores. Gowen set wages low and company store prices high, so that coal workers and their families were forever in debt to him." Nova's speed increased on the narrow dark country roads to match the intensity of her storytelling. Judge clung to his seatbelt. "A group of Irish coal workers banded together to protest their unsafe work conditions and unfair labor practices. They committed acts of sabotage on coal deliveries; Robin Hood theft of company banks; organized worker slow-downs and sick-outs; and yes, a violent faction among them murdered company operatives and mine foremen. To avoid retribution from company security forces led by the infamous Pinkerton Detectives, they kept their alliance a secret, under the curious name from Irish rebellion lore, the Molly Maguires. What the Mollies didn't know was that the Pinkertons had a man on the inside, gathering intel on the members and their some-times murderous deeds. With the testimony of the undercover Pinkerton and a turncoat Molly out to save his own skin, the State of Pennsylvania put the Molly Maguires on trial, right here in Mauch Chunk. The Special Prosecutor assigned was none other than the corporate king himself, Frank Gowen. Twenty men were convicted of murder and sentenced to hang. One man, Alexander Campbell, swore his innocence to the last, and on the eve of his hanging, marked his jail cell wall with a muddy handprint, vowing that it would never wash away, but forever be a reminder of the injustice of his execution. After he was hanged, the handprint was wiped away. The next day, it returned. For decades since, even though that handprint has been scrubbed away and painted over, it has always returned, perhaps the mark of an innocent man, put to death by the same company that had owned his life."

Nova timed her story perfectly. She pulled into a long driveway of a two-story farmhouse with a wrap-around porch, and put her Prius in park.

"Good story, right?" she said with a sad smile. "Now that you know something about this town, you go and say hi to Ruby. I'm going to sit here a moment and gather my thoughts."

Judge and Walt eased out of the car, unsure. Walt looked just as troubled by Nova's ghost story as Judge felt.

"You're just going to sit in the dark out here?" Walt asked.

"Just for a while," Nova said. "Coming home is different now. I'll try to explain later, but please, give me a moment." Walt closed the door, just as Nova gave another piece of advice, "Don't be surprised if she seems a little mean at first."

As they advanced on the porch, Judge's eye adjusted enough to see the outline of a large woman in a rocking chair, smoking a cigar with a shotgun across her lap. Before they got within distance to say hello, she stood up and went inside, shutting the door behind her. The deadbolt went *click*.

"Mean?" said Walt. "She didn't even try to shoot us."

PART WALT_0004

"Ruby, come on. Let us in," Nova said, banging on the door for the tenth time. "You're not really going to make us sleep outside."

From inside, Ruby answered, "I told you, no visitors. My days of hospitality are over."

Nova leaned over to Walt to say as an aside, "She's always been about as hospitable as a porcupine guarding its nest."

Walt gave her a smile, even though he didn't feel much like smiling. He'd been awake for well over 24 hours, and the better part of those were spent as surgical assistant, escape artist, car thief, and Sunflower. It was all starting to catch up to him. If he'd been of sound mind, he might've noticed how weird things were getting, particularly inside his own head, where his personal radio station was currently playing requests. Here's *Ruby* by the Kaiser Chiefs…

While he listened to lyrics that no one was singing, the porch did this odd thing where it tilted up toward him. No sensation of falling, but he did hear Judge announce, "Timmmmber."

An unappealing light made his eyes hurt before he even opened them again. He was on the floor in a kitchen, so he'd lost some time. Nova and Ruby argued in close range over him, but he didn't care. He wanted water. He *needed* water. He pushed onto his knees, fumbled for a mug from the drying rack and filled it with water. Before the mug reached his lips, Nova slapped it out of his hand. The water spilled and the mug broke into large chunks on the linoleum.

"That's poison," Nova explained calmly, as if her actions had been perfectly acceptable under the circumstance. She pulled a bottled water from the fridge and Walt drained it, feeling mostly human again. Judge sidled up to him and tugged on his sleeve.

"Don't leave me alone with them again," he pleaded in a whisper.

"Feel better?" Ruby asked. She was a heavy woman with long gray hair in two thick braids. Her scrutinizing face inches away, he felt pressured to nod yes. "Good, then you can go."

"Ruby, stop this," Nova ordered, blocking the door with her body. "They are staying here tonight, and in the morning you are going to share those beautiful ideas of yours."

"Don't talk to me like I'm a goddamned child," Ruby said so vehemently that Walt ducked when she swept past him to grab the cigar she'd left on the windowsill. "This is *my* house."

"You agreed to look at the data," Nova reminded, casually moving the shotgun leaning against the counter out of Ruby's reach.

"That was before I knew it would be hand-delivered," Ruby said between teeth clenched around the cigar as she poured herself a tumbler of red wine. She nodded at the shotgun Nova was trying to remove from the equation. "Be careful with that. The safety's off."

"Why did you even think you needed it?"

"I heard a prowler. Probably that Todd from MSO&G, snooping around. Or maybe it was just a coyote." Ruby huffed in Judge's direction, obviously aware of his call sign. "Either way, shotgun's a good deterrent as any."

"You're not going to shoot anyone." Nova followed up that statement with a reassurance to Walt and Judge, "She'd never shoot this thing, I promise."

"Would probably backfire anyway," Ruby chuckled. "Thing hasn't been cleaned in ages. Not since long before Daddy died." She downed her tumbler and closed her eyes. "Why on earth would you bring them here? How could you possibly think that was a good idea? Especially now. Now now now. Who can even tell what that means, anymore..."

Walt wished he could become invisible. He and Judge were trapped in the middle of what was escalating into the kind of fight he knew all too well from living with parents who tore into each other on a regular basis. He fell back on his best defense, making himself useful. He squatted and carefully collected the smashed pieces of mug. Judge joined him, even though it was really only a one-man job.

"Locking yourself away doesn't protect you from what's happening, Ruby. It never has."

"Who says it's me I'm protecting? *They* shouldn't be here," Ruby said, watching the clean-up operation with an inscrutable face. She reloaded with wine and a long drag of tobacco before she continued. "What a mess you've made of this, Nova. Of all the women my son could have married. You are one stupid, stupid girl."

"You don't mean that."

"Don't I?" Ruby snapped. "Look at this scene for the evidence. I have two desperate children in my kitchen, looking to me for safe harbor and comfort. You should know better than anyone, those are two things that are not to be found in this household."

Ruby waved Nova's response away before she could even give it and disappeared into the dark interior of the house, muttering angrily to herself. Nova gripped the countertop, stiff-armed, and let her curls hide her face. She sniffed, wiped away tears, and opened the cabinet door to pull out a trash can. As Walt and Judge dropped in the broken mug pieces, she assured them softly, "It's ok. It'll be ok. You boys must be hungry. Sandwiches? PB&J. Coming up."

Walt wasn't about to object to food, so she shuttled them into the dining room, ordering them to "sit and rest." The dining table was covered with documents. Nothing related to Roan and Judge, as far as Walt could see. Correspondence from Marcellus Shale Oil and Gas; The Law Firm of Dewers, Jacks, and Stipple; the Pennsylvania DEP. Reams of data sheets with red pen marks circling certain numbers and dates. Nova set their plates down on top of the uneven piles of paper, and they ate in silence.

"You'll eat. You'll sleep," she said, ducking down the hall but still telling them their near future, "and in the morning, we'll all talk."

Judge shared an observation with Walt under his peanut-butter scented breath, "She's a very positive thinker."

"Must be all the crystals," Walt concurred.

"I heard that," Nova said with a forgiving smile as she returned with bedding in her arms.

Judge claimed the couch before Nova even had a chance to put sheets on it. She covered him with an afghan, then led Walt upstairs. The bedroom she opened for him was not unlike his own back home. Music posters mixed with art prints on the walls. Dresser crowded with trophies—academic instead of sports. Shag carpet the color of sand tripped him as he dragged his feet to the bed. He was asleep before the light was out.

* * *

Sometime later, Walt woke and had a panicked few seconds of not knowing where he was. He must be in the jailhouse, awaiting trial for he-couldn't-remember-what, because on the wall there was a hand print glowing in the dark. Too tired to be terrified, he just closed his eyes again and fell back asleep.

In the morning, he woke to the smell of fresh bread, hot cinnamon, coffee. It almost masked the smell of his own b.o.. Almost. Again the room was disorienting, but at least he remembered where he was this time. No hand print near the window anymore, but when he brushed his own hand along the wall, he felt something tacky there. On the desk chair was a towel, fresh clothes, new toothbrush, bottled water, and a note:

Bathroom is down the hall. Use the bottled water to brush your teeth. Smiley face.

Walt bet his life that note wasn't from Ruby.

He took a quick hot shower—holding his breath, in case the steam was poisoned too—and dressed in the khakis and plaid button-down. The clothes must've belonged to the same person whose bed he'd slept in. Walt wondered where he was. If he'd mind the intrusion.

Downstairs, Walt found Judge showered and in fresh clothes too, stuffing his face.

"Morning sunshine," Nova said to him, and the way she smiled at him with that cute overbite made him feel warm. "I'm glad those clothes fit. I wasn't sure they would. Michael was always so thin. Healthy, but thin. Like a human hummingbird."

Nova delivered a plate piled high with pancakes to the lawsuit-themed place setting in front of Walt. He wondered if the stacks of documents had anything to do with this Michael guy, whose bed he slept in and whose clothes he wore. If they explained his absence.

"If the well water is poisoned, why do you still live here?" Judge asked, syrup dripping down his chin as he focused on reading the table.

Nova dabbed her napkin with a bottle of water to wipe the syrup from Judge's chin. He pulled back by reflex, but then allowed her to clean his face while she answered, "This place belonged to Ruby's mom and dad. She moved back here after she retired from Lehigh, and I moved in with her after Michael died. Ruby doesn't want to leave, so here we both are."

"Why doesn't she want to leave?"

"Because I like to fight," Ruby answered harshly, sipping her coffee as she joined them from the kitchen. "You see those yellow poles out back?"

Walt craned his neck to see out the kitchen window into the backyard. Bright yellow posts spaced every twenty feet or so ran the length of the yard and continued on in both directions for as far as he could see. He'd seen those posts when visiting development sites with his dad, so he could identify them with a fair amount of confidence. "Pipeline markers."

"That's right," Ruby said, impressed. Then a look came over her like she smelled something rank. "I forgot your daddy used to be in the real estate business. To your daddy, those markers showed him where his crews couldn't dig, right? Well, they meant something a little different to my folks. Piss-colored stakes, marking a claim. A yellow brick road to cemetery plots." She started flipping through papers on the table for choice documents and reams to lob at Walt at key points in her speech, as if he were to blame. "They called me out here when mamma's garden went belly up. Suspected a methane leak because of the smell. I borrowed some kits from a colleague in Chem, ran some samples. Air, water, soil. All of it came back contaminated. Sure, there was methane. But hydrocarbon cousins like benzene and toluene, too. Formaldehyde even. Nasty, nasty stuff. It killed the oak tree, too. That took more time. It still had some life in it when Michael…"

Ruby fell silent, and Walt carefully pushed the papers away from his pancakes. Why she was targeting him was a mystery. People usually liked him. He felt compelled to say, "I'm sorry."

"This is my family home, Walter Hale," Ruby continued, "and it is the scene of a crime. The chief suspect is that pipeline and the compressor station down the road, and I'm not leaving here until I can prove it." She turned to Judge and said, "You've been reading the documents from Dewey, Frackem and Howe. What do you think?"

"They're trying to bury the truth by overwhelming you with irrelevant data," Judge said.

"Oldest trick in the universe. Or in your specific case, the oldest trick *by* the universe." She gulped the last of her coffee and said, "Enough about me and my corner of misery. Let's take a look at *you*."

Ruby swooped in next to Judge and fixed his chin in her hand, swiveling his face around so that she could study his jetkill. Walt was surprised by Judge's lack of protest. Or maybe he was used to this kind of inspection.

"So you keep another dimension packed away behind that thing, do you?" Ruby said softly. "You're an astronaut on a tether, out for a spacewalk amongst us. Wanna hear something funny? You shut down my friends' work at LIGO when you showed up. They couldn't account for the new source of terrestrial interference in their data. Just about drove them out of their minds... and trust me, physicists don't have far to go. Do you feel the pull of that other place, drawing you back?"

"No," Judge said, tugging his chin away from her at last and looking away.

"Don't want to talk about it? Ok, then let's discuss the data you brought me." She pulled Judge's DS from her droopy cardigan pocket and set it on the table. If Judge was surprised that she'd taken it, he covered well. "I extracted the files you downloaded from pretty boy's computer. I've been studying them all night." The way she sniffed dismissively in Walt's direction, he knew that *he* was that pretty boy.

"Wait—*what* files?" he started, angry he was so confused. "From *my* computer?"

"I used your computer to hack into Bradley's," Judge said matter-of-factly.

"*My* computer? In *my room*?"

"Your dad had spy software installed," Judge said. "Did you know that?"

"No." Walt's face got hot so fast his hands got cold. What to be pissed about first? The breaking and entering by Judge, or his dad's spying on him? Why would he do that? He was getting good grades, on track for another good football season. There was nothing he was hiding. Maybe it was the time spent at the Goreys. Or emails to his mom after she took off with

Lucy. Walt's fist against the table almost knocked over Judge's orange juice.

"Don't act so injured," Ruby chided. "Your mystery friend is a scary good hacker, but the files we needed were behind a firewall wrapped in an enigma, hidden in the warp of a black hole. So to speak. She sent Judge on a mission to gather information for me, and your computer was an obvious access point."

"She?" Judge asked, mouth agape.

"Yes, Judge," Ruby said. "Shocking, isn't it? Your secret pen pal is a *girl*. One not much older than Walt here."

"How do you know?"

"Because I don't work with mystery people," Ruby said. "And I'm not going to play a role in some silly game when there's so much at stake. Your *LodgeBuilder* is Katie Goodbear. She lives on the Fort Berthold Reservation in North Dakota. Her cousin is the tribal leader of the Three Affiliated Tribes, and he's as crooked as they come. Guess who he's in business with?"

"Bradley," Judge said.

"A-plus to the green-eyed boy with the nice haircut. Dimond's building something there, on the reservation. It has the same footprint as a refinery, but it's not for oil or gas."

"So she wanted you to study Dimond's plans in order to stop him?"

"I can't even stop the assholes down the street," Ruby guffawed. "How am I supposed to stop some megalomaniac billionaire halfway across the country? No. Katie gave me access to the raw data on *you*."

"Oh."

"Wait," Walt said, trying to keep up. He was still wrapping

his head around the fact that she'd just revealed the identity of their anonymous leader. No drum roll. No pulling back a curtain with a *ta da*! Just a name and an address. Katie Goodbear. North Dakota. *His age.* "Why would she send Judge here? How can you help Judge? Or is Judge supposed to help you? With this?" Walt showed Ruby a fistful of the legal documents she'd tossed at him.

"Who says I need help against MSO&G?" Ruby said defensively. "That's just a hobby, you over-privileged nitwit. Small potatoes in the scheme of things."

"Ruby is a theoretical physicist," Nova said, placing a gentle hand on Walt's, releasing the papers from his grip and smoothing them out in her own lap. She whispered to him, "And she does have a call sign in the Lodge, for future reference. It's *Badger*."

When Walt turned back to Ruby, he was startled by how close her face was to his. "That's right, *Sunflower*. And you're in this badger's den, so you best show some respect."

"Ruby, he didn't mean anything," Nova started, but Ruby cut her off.

"Katie has a message for you, Sunflower," Ruby said. "All you have to do is click your heels together, and you can be on your way home. Mom, sis, uncle. They're all on the reservation. Guests of our friend Bradley."

"He's holding them prisoner," Walt said as he shot up from the table. "I knew it!"

"Don't be so naïve," Ruby snarled. "Your mom is working for him again. Must've missed that fat paycheck. Your uncle's joined the party now, too. Entry level construction job at Dimond's facility. They'll probably have your little sister on the payroll before long. We both know how loose Dimond plays it with the child labor laws."

Walt felt shame and anger boiling up inside him. He wasn't sure if he was angry at his mom and Uncle Emmett, or himself for worrying about them.

"I don't believe you," Walt said, even though the news was hard to discredit.

"If you think I'm biased, you'd be dead right," Ruby said, her face looking even meaner than before. "Quite a pair, your mom and dad, helping Dimond peddle that nonsense story about how the Gorey kids came to be. Turns my stomach, how that smarmy corporate ass-hat is building his latest monopoly on a manufactured claim of liability. Bradley Dimond couldn't have asked for better partners in crime."

"My parents aren't criminals." Walt was surprised he was defending them, but he was.

Ruby howled at that.

"Ruby, *please*," Nova said, folding her hands over Walt's to keep him from bolting.

Walt hated it here, in the Badger's den. His instinct was telling him to leave before Ruby had a chance to sink her teeth in.

"I hear you wanted your Lodge handle to be Wa-Tho-Huk," said Ruby, her voice softer.

"Jim Thorpe was always a hero of mine," Walt said in earnest, unsure of her intentions.

"Sure. Quite the athlete," Ruby said. "All those gold medals he won. I can see why someone like you would admire that. But *Jim Thorpe* was his Anglo name—his adopted name. Wa-Tho-Huk—the name *you* wanted as your Lodge call sign—was the name his parents gave him. Know what it means?" Walt shook his head. He had a feeling Ruby meant for him to feel ashamed, so he put up his guard. "It means *Bright Path*. Doesn't really fit you, I don't think. You, with your family connections, you're more of a *Bright Future*. That's what Mommy and Daddy promised you, right? A bright future."

"Ruby, for heaven's sake…" Nova started, but Ruby was on a roll. Not about to stop.

"Your hero *Jim* had to forge his own path," she went on. "One that forced him to change the name his parents gave him, for no good reason. Forced him, for no good reason, to return those gold medals you admire him so much for. Pushed him to the edge of darkness, where he drank himself to death, alone, in a dump. Forging a bright path takes a toll when the world is set like concrete in stupidity all around you."

"We don't have time for this," Walt said to Judge, leaning across Ruby's table of grievances to get Judge's full attention. "If Dimond's building something in North Dakota, we have to stop him. We have to get my family out of there."

"Sure, go there. But you won't convince them to leave, dummy," Ruby sighed. "That bright future of yours will come back into focus, and it'll blind you to everything else. No. That's not what will happen." Ruby leaned forward to get Judge's attention, too. "They'll convince *him* to *stay*. I'd bet my life on it."

SEQUENCE
SIX

PART ERNESTO_0001

WHEN IT WASN'T THE BANKS, IT WAS THE weather, or the pests, or the neighbors. With the unwelcome return of Berit Zook to his farm just outside Muscatine, Ernesto Vargas found himself in a stranglehold that was as snug and familiar as his work boots. He'd never known life without impending doom. Forty years and counting, and it finally felt like doom had landed on his doorstep. And it was his own damn fault.

There were competing conspiracies on the farm now—superweeds and fugitives—and he was helpless against both. Waterhemp could fill the soybean fields without affecting the yield—a nuisance, but not a killer—but palmer amaranth choked the crops out with a vengeance. It was everywhere. Seven feet tall, fast growing, and single-minded. Berit and her fugitives were at least self-contained—they stayed in the arena on the farm's shared perimeter with the fairgrounds—but they were just as single-minded. They were building something. A contraption that strained his grip on reality, because it was made from parts *outside* reality. He chose to focus on the amaranth. As hopeless a fight as it was, at least it was a familiar hopeless fight.

"A mess like this doesn't grow overnight," his father was fond of saying whenever a surprise took them down an unexpected path. Ernesto couldn't decide if it was his way of accepting bullshit beyond his control, or if it was a reminder of the importance to plan ahead. Ernesto had a saying, too, but it wasn't as philosophical: "Of course." Less of a saying. More of a frustrated reaction. An expanded sigh.

Of course, this mess didn't grow overnight. It took root dozens of years back and was compounded by predictable money troubles and desperate contracts. Not with the devil. Maybe his sidekick. His part-time consultant?

Berit Zook was an undergrad at Iowa State when she first visited their farm. Her department had recruited the Vargas farmland to be a part of a study, a collaboration to determine how to genetically enhance the beneficial qualities of cover crops like ryegrass. Oats. Other cereals. Ernesto's father was open-minded about bioengineering—he'd figured there wasn't much of a difference between breeding plants in the field and modifying them in a lab—and he saw the annual stipend as a good opportunity to cover his losses on a particularly bad season. The Mississippi had flooded half their acres that summer. It would take years to recover.

But—of course—the project that was supposed to have been a lifeline was nearly the thing that sunk them for good.

Dimond Industries had funded the study, and as soon as the Iowa State researchers reported on their first breakthrough, Dimond filed the patents and went on the offensive to protect their investment. They claimed exclusive ownership of the biotechnology, the new strains developed, and even the land where the bioengineered cover crops had grown. Iowa State was locked into a patent war with Dimond Industries, and the Vargas fields were the battleground. His father's health began to fail, and the only way he could see to get clear of the mess was to destroy the fields altogether. The County Fairgrounds had been after those acres for satellite parking, so Ernesto's father transformed some of the most fertile soil of his farmland into a gravel pit. Problem solved.

Berit had been only one member of the Iowa State team, but Ernesto remembered her because of her striking blonde hair and her bizarre fixation on bats. At dusk she'd sit outside in his fields with her notebook, taking notes. Her second visit to the farm, going on a year ago now, wasn't exactly welcome. He'd returned from the fields to find her on his porch, having a cup of coffee with his mother. She was offering sympathy for his father's passing and money to go with it—a lot of money—to rent out the arena he'd built on the gravel pit. She wouldn't make use of it right away, but the contract would essentially hold the space for her exclusively for twenty-four months. And she insisted on secrecy.

And, of course, Ernesto accepted. He needed the money. It was that simple.

What was happening on the farm now was far from simple. Ernesto drank his morning coffee and watched the construction in the arena with his curiosity and doubt growing in concert.

"Remind me," said a woman's voice behind him, "why did you build the arena again?"

It was Li-Wen Yang, one of Berit's researchers. She had hard eyes but always kept her mouth in a slight smile. Friendly, but Ernesto always felt like she had an ulterior motive—a directive to interact, in order to assess. Berit must've been worried Ernesto would betray them. She was right to worry.

"It was my cousin's idea," Ernesto said, knocking his cap forward to scratch the back of his head. He always scratched the back of his head when he was nervous. Li-Wen made him nervous. "Roddy got it in his head that we could hold a rodeo here."

"A rodeo?" Li-Wen said, and she laughed. "Like with cowboys and angry bulls and clowns?"

"That's right. He had partners out of Montana, looking to expand their show. Needed a permanent space."

"But it didn't work out?"

"No, it didn't work out," Ernesto confirmed, wondering how much she was laughing at him instead of with him. "Instead I got you clowns."

Li-Wen gave a full smile and looked at her feet. She and three of her young friends—Afeni, Reshma, and Scott—had arrived via helicopter about a month ago with a bunch of crates. The contents of those crates were the components of the *thing* they were now building. Ernesto's mother insisted the four of them sleep in the farmhouse instead of the unheated arena, so overnight Ernesto was running an understaffed B&B on top of a failing farm. His eight-year-old Hector enjoyed the company when he wasn't staying with Ernesto's ex in town, and his mother never turned down an opportunity to show her hospitality. For Ernesto the intrusion was too much. He spent even more time in the fields, just to avoid his own crowded kitchen.

The descent of Berit's batch was timed nearly perfectly with the news that broke the world. Bradley Dimond—the same Bradley Dimond who had nearly ruined Ernesto's family legacy—barged into his living room courtesy of cable hysteria to announce his role in the arrival of reality altering kids. When Berit's face showed up in Dimond's fugitive line-up, all Ernesto could think to say was, of course: "Of course."

At the time, Ernesto had hoped that Berit's preoccupation

with being Wanted would make her abandon whatever project she'd had planned for his farm, but this particular mess must've been in the works for months. The crates kept coming over the next several weeks, always by cover of night, always delivered by the same laconic pilot. And not long after, Berit herself showed up in a snot-filled tour bus. They didn't call it snot of course. Berit acted as if it were gold, actually. Strange, that one.

If he still had neighbors, Ernesto might've been worried the suspicious behavior would be reported. As it was, he was surrounded by giant mutes who never reported a thing. His neighbors had long since sold their fields to Avanto Corp, a recent Dimond Industries acquisition, making the Vargas farm the last family-owned land for miles. The Vargas acres were bordered by high-yield Avanto fields of corn and soybean, growing tall and proud, subservient and inflexible. Those intimidating mutes were poor sentinels.

Li-Wen noticed that Ernesto had turned to face the Avanto fields. Maybe she saw a sour look on his face, or maybe she noticed for herself the stark difference in the height and fullness of those stalks compared to his own wilting crops, strangled by amaranth. Either way, she was prompted to ask, "What's their secret?"

"Avanto fine-tunes their crops to be resistant to Avanto herbicides," Ernesto explained, happy to focus on a problem he understood. A problem he couldn't fix, but one he could at least grasp. "Then they soak the soil with herbicides. Effective."

"Apparently."

"But short-sighted," Ernesto said quickly. His face grew hot as he thought of his father, all he'd put into farming this land. "See, the Vargas philosophy was to keep crops talking. Even when making modifications, my dad saw the importance of encouraging the wild in plants. It's the wild that keeps them connected to each other."

"Keep them communicating."

"That's right."

"But what do plants talk about?"

"Insect infestation. Weeds. Disease. You name it. Plants send messages to each other. Warnings about attacks. Directions to nutrients in the soil. But when you go too far, like Avanto, you limit their instincts. You take away their language. This amaranth started in the Avanto fields. They didn't just engineer their plants to be resistant to herbicides. They created a breeding ground for weeds to grow resistant, too. When Avanto lost some fields, they just modified their seed again. And then that amaranth came knocking on *my* door. My crops never saw it coming."

"Avanto's crops didn't send a warning."

"That's right. Mum's the word."

Ernesto turned back to survey his own fields, where the amaranth carved a path like an advancing legion, stealing ground, plant by plant, diminishing his slim margin between deep debt and insurmountable debt. Background noise from the arena—banging and welding and wrenching—made Ernesto wonder which of the two invaders would be the end of him first.

And then Li-Wen reminded him he had bigger problems.

"Did you see the news?" she asked. "Streamer attack in Tennessee. Confirmation she was there, controlling it."

"Mm-hm," he replied, finishing his coffee. "Tiptonville's on the Mississippi. Not too far."

At that, Ernesto abruptly left Li-Wen to worry or hope by herself, while he headed back to work. His fields were more battleground than harvest at this point, whether Roan Gorey's wickedness landed here or not.

PART JUDGE_0007

THE GIANT DEAD OAK TREE DID NOT BEND TO the wind that rustled leaves from neighboring trees across the yard beneath it. Trespassers, flaunting their recent connection to life. Judge kicked at them, enjoying their crunchy response.

Nova had sent Ruby out here to cool down, while she stayed inside to tend to Walt's injured pride. Must've been hard for him to take that much in-your-face dislike when he's so accustomed to being teacher's pet. Maybe that wasn't fair. Ruby really was harsh with him.

"I need to have it taken down," Ruby sighed. "One big storm with a strong wind from the right direction and it's going to demolish the house. But I can't bring myself to do it. Isn't that stupid? But Michael loved that tree. Spent hours climbing it when he was a little boy."

Judge took it as an invitation and tested a low-hanging branch before swinging himself up. Ruby chuckled, watching him. He went a few branches higher, then straddled one and rested his back against the trunk to get comfortable. The view of the farmhouse and surrounding acres was surprisingly different. Ruby looked small down there as she swayed in the cool breeze, her face lifted to the tree with eyes squinting against the morning sun.

"Not many trees to climb where you're from?" she asked with a smile. Judge shook his head, even though he knew it was a rhetorical question. "You've come a long away for the story I'm about to tell you. Longer than anyone has ever traveled, in fact. I've spent my life studying other dimensions, but I've never come across the one you came from. The *pre*. I like that—names are important, you know—but it has a problem. It implies that it only existed *before*."

"For me, that's how it was."

"Perspective is everything," Ruby nodded, and then she took a deep breath. "Katie could have chosen any number of physicists to help you. There's only one reason you're here. You're here because of my son, Michael." She stopped because she had to. It was several seconds before she could continue. "Michael had allergies. Couldn't have a dog or a cat. So I let him choose a reptile, and he chose geckos. Fascinating little creatures. Sticky paws. Geckos can cling to practically any surface. Did you know that? I sure didn't. Well, those geckos were the starring attraction of every Science Fair from eighth grade on. The interest never faded. At Stanford, he developed an adhesive based on those sticky paws. Called it GeckoGlue. Became a millionaire practically overnight. So many applications for a non-toxic adhesive. Everything from ATM cash rollers to kindergarten glitter glue to biomedical applications. Targeted drug therapies could use a little help sticking to their target cells, without doing damage. It was all very exciting for him. All the good he could do in the world. All the people he could help save."

Ruby's face went dark, and Judge sensed the wind was changing. He shivered.

"Well, wouldn't you know," she started up again, "there was a contract researcher in Belarus working for arms dealers who had an idea for how my son's adhesive might be applied to a particularly vile chemical weapon. The problem with using poison gas—if you're the kind of human who desires to do such things—is that a shift of the wind can boomerang the gas back on your own people. Now imagine a sticky chemical weapon. One where each molecule of misery seeks out a surface, like a needle to a magnet, and waits for the opportunity to interact with living tissue. Skin. Lungs. Eyes. If you saw the pictures, Judge, it'd make you sick, what those monsters did. There is no depravity that has been untested by humans. Why is that? Why is *that* the direction we *always* tend to go? And they made my boy a part of it." She wiped her eyes and nose with the sleeve of her cardigan. "It was too much for him. My beautiful boy. He couldn't live with himself, knowing that something he'd created had caused so much suffering. He hung himself on that tree you're climbing."

Judge felt ice in his veins. Maybe it was the sudden awareness of being at a point of exit, of sitting on the bulkhead of a door left open to a cold eternity. He carefully lowered himself down the branches and dropped next to Ruby. For a long moment, he fought an urge to turn the tree inside out just so he wouldn't have to imagine Ruby's son swinging from it. The boy who loved geckos. The boy who created something used to kill innocents.

Judge suddenly felt the same urgency as Walt to get to North Dakota. He was being selfish, looking for answers about how to correct his own mistakes. There was no going back. Was there? *What was Dimond building?*

"You could send it away for me, couldn't you?" Ruby asked softly. "Open up that contraption a few seconds, and it'd be gone. Nothing but an oak-tree shaped hole, with that beautiful firewall of an outline."

"I will, if you want me to," Judge said, hand moving to his remote in his bag. She put her hand over his to stop him.

"Here's the thing, Judge," Ruby said. "If I thought you could actually make that dead tree disappear, I might ask you for that favor. But that's not what you do. You don't send things away. You're not making black holes. There's no warpage. No angular momentum. No gravitational pull. What do you think that means?"

"What isn't there is actually still there?"

"But how can that be?"

"It can't," Judge said.

"Bingo," she said, trying to sound encouraging but falling short. "Let's leave Michael's tree to enjoy the morning air without us stinking it up. Follow me." Ruby ambled to a small building in the back of the yard near the yellow warning signs, and with a sad glance back at the dead tree, Judge followed her in. "This is my father's workshop," she said, arms wide enough to almost reach both walls. "He dabbled in carpentry. My mother was a seamstress, and when her arthritis got bad, she turned to weaving. Have you ever seen a loom?"

"Only in a game."

"One of Katie's?"

Judge nodded, even though it felt weird thinking of her as a real person. So much easier to imagine the anonymous *Lodge-Builder* as an amorphous being with mysterious motives. He felt like he'd lost something in the exchange.

"She sent me a pattern to reconstruct using a digital loom,"

Judge explained, recalling the pleasure of directing the weave of colored thread to and fro on a blank grid.

"Ok, well, this isn't a loom," Ruby said, strumming the taught vertical threads with her fingers. "Let's get that straight, first off. *This* is a metaphor."

"For what?"

"Take a wild guess."

PART RUBY_0001

HER SLIPPERED FEET WERE GETTING COLDER by the second. A very tangible, measurable discomfort, all while she spouted intangible nonsense. She had the gall—always had—to speak with confidence. Her student this time was barely human. A tool created by the universe to wipe its memory. Who was she to school him?

But just look at the boy. He was desperate for a fix, and not the kind that comes from a bottle. *Getting low on merlot, speaking of bottles and what comes in them.*

The futility of her intervention in this mess was crystal clear. Crystal Clear was the brand of bottled spring water in the fridge. *Bottles again.* Ruby sensed a theme. Like it was all orchestrated, but for whose entertainment? *Not mine.* What else about bottles? *Don't let the genie out of the bottle.* Little late for that. *Message in a bottle.* A symbol of hope defeating statistics. What would be the opposite of that? *Futility in a bottle.* Futility has a higher power than hopes and dreams, so best contain it, or it will contaminate all action that requires a sense of meaning.

I am a perpetual motion machine, powered by perpetual thought, the sillier the better.

This inner dialogue of hers—it's what kept her going. The day she found Michael in the tree, the world stopped moving and she was shot into open space, shattered into pieces. No moorings in sight. She might have drifted apart from herself until there was nothing left. She was bound only by grief and curiosity; by immeasurable loss and the enormity of time. She knew she was only talking to herself—a one-woman show, *way*-off-Broadway—but even as the rational woman that she was, she couldn't escape the feeling there was more of an audience listening in. She even indulged, every so often, to speak to Michael by name.

Look at this boy, Michael. Is he even a boy? Becoming less all the time.

"It's only a matter of time," Ruby began, "before that tether in your head pulls too much real estate out of your face for you to function. When it starts digging into gray matter, it won't be up to you, what goes and what stays. We'll all be at the mercy of whatever's on the other end, and if there were any mercy to be had there, you wouldn't have been there for so long, all alone."

"The connection grows because I'm growing," Judge said.

"I have a feeling it's the other way around. You created the breach when you finally joined the party this side of the fence, but you didn't come through clean," Ruby said. "Your physiology includes extreme rapid growth to increase your surface area here, in our dimension, in order to counter the pull to the *pre*. Best guess, of course. The good news is, puberty should be a cinch after this."

Well, Michael, that face reminds me of the one you used to give me. He doesn't think I'm any funnier than you did.

"Equilibrium is what we seek here," Ruby continued, trying to focus on one conversation, one boy at a time. "Do you see that happening at any point?" Judge shook his head, so she asked, "Why not?"

"Because of the vaks."

"Bingo. Whenever you create a vak, there is measurable growth in the aperture's circumference."

"The more vaks I create, the sooner I die?"

"And the rest of us go down the drain." Ruby twirled her fingers around like she was stirring her coffee and then slapped her hands together. "So, simple solution. Stop making vaks."

"I can't."

"Didn't think so," Ruby said. "You're like the compressor station down the road. Its purpose is to keep the gas moving at a constant pressure through the pipeline. When the pressure builds to excess, the compressor releases gas in a blowdown. Poisons the atmosphere. Sounds like a jet engine taking off, even miles away. You can feel the pressure build up behind the jetkill, can't you?"

"Yes." Judge kicked the dirt on the floor, producing a cloud.

"So that's Problem Number One," Ruby said. "How to reach equilibrium between your existence here and in the *pre*. I don't think you'll ever be in just one or the other. But that's not the only imbalance we're dealing with."

"Roan," Judge snarled. "She's a thief. She doesn't even know what the *nots* are, but she sucks them up into her balloon animals to make them do tricks."

"Ok, so that's Problem Number Two," Ruby said. "How to keep your sister's hand out of the *pre* cookie jar. Something we should get clear. Problem Number One is my priority. *You* are the only one who can keep him alive."

"What? Who?"

Ruby felt rooted in time, in that shack surrounded by her father's dusty tools and her mother's unfinished tapestry. When she was little, this shack had been off-limits to her, and even now she felt like a trespasser. Michael's science fair experiments were tucked away in a corner, minus the geckos of course. Judge belonged here more than she did. Her whole life, she made nothing but observations, and you don't really *make* those. Not with your hands anyway. But this shack was the right place for the revelation she was about to impart to Judge Gorey.

"Did you know that the event horizon of a black hole contains the information from matter that has been sucked into the void? It is more than an echo, or trace, of what has passed through the firewall. It is measurably *there*. When it is clearly *not* there. Nothing vanishes, Judge. Not as long as there are discernible boundaries in our universe. Our place in *time* defines us before we exist and long after we are gone. We are immortal, all of us, as long as we continue to share the same limits of life and death. Nothing new can exist without what has come before. More paradoxical is the idea that the past is only possible if it is perceivable in the present. But that is the fundamental structure of *our* universe, paradox and all. Common memory has nothing to do with it. Our place in the universe is beyond consciousness. Always there, whether you look for it or not." Ruby's attention drifted to Michael's tree, barely visible through the dirt-encrusted screen and foggy window. "This place where you were, the *pre*, it doesn't have these same limitations, the same boundaries of time and space, between life and the inanimate. An *actual* black hole swallowing us up would be preferable to leaving that door open in your face. For the first time since that Big Bang started it all, our universe risks being transformed into something unrecognizable. If this *interdimensional infection* spreads beyond the two of you, we will be diminished to the sum of our parts, indistinguishable from elements in the dirt beneath our feet, or the asteroids roaming the recesses of distant galaxies. All of it doomed to mingle, forever disconnected, misaligned, decoded, along the boundary of some cold infinity. I won't let you carve up our collective universal story into nothing more than an unintelligible jumble. I won't let you."

"I don't know what to do," Judge said.

There was a time in Ruby's life when she might have been inclined to fold this boy into her arms and tell him everything would be ok. But she wouldn't make that mistake again. *This boy needs to know what is at stake.*

"Problem Number One has a two-part solution," she said. "Mitigate new damage you inflict, and repair the damage already done."

"Is that possible?"

"Time for our metaphor, if you will," Ruby said, motioning for Judge to join her by her mother's last unfinished enterprise. "This loom organizes information by layers to form a coherent picture. I believe our universe, our dimension, is built on that same basic principle. Look at this scene, for example: country road, farm house, trees. If you carve that farm house out of the picture, what's left behind looks like a hole." She took a small hook from a table and dug out a tight thread from the country scene, showing Judge the loop in the thread. "You make vaks in pairs," Ruby said. "Complementary only in that they share a pathway, and that it is a closed circuit. Step into one, you emerge from another. Assuming the size allows. Like time, movement through vak portals is in one direction only. Ever wonder why?"

"There is only one direction," he said.

"Because there is only one *side*," Ruby amended. She ducked around to the back of the tapestry, and Judge followed. She pointed out the "hole" from the loosened thread. "The information is still there. Uncompromised, but dislocated, bringing distortion to the picture."

"It looks like a hole to me," Judge challenged. "I thought you said it wasn't about holes."

Listen to that little snot, Michael! He's getting comfortable enough to sass.

"It's not about holes," Ruby said, "because you are not digging. You do some seriously heavy lifting, my friend. That gateway you carry with you has such a profound pull, information from our world gets lifted right out of it when that jetkill opens, but because of that beautiful firewall you create, it has nowhere to go except where it is. It doubles back. Folds in on itself. It looks like an empty hole. But it's not empty. Think of it like an overstuffed pocket, pockets of an overcoat that *you* are wearing. In other words, I believe they are all still connected to you."

"She's the spaghetti monster, not me. My vaks are in pairs. Closed circuits—you said that yourself. I don't have any connection to them anymore."

"Consider our metaphor again," Ruby said, sheepishly waving her hand next to the loom to draw his attention back to its design. She demonstrated the weaving process while she spoke, dust from the loom swirling around them. "The process of creating a vak is just like the warp and woof of this loom. These vertical threads are the warp, the barrier between our world and the *pre*. The woof is the thread attached to this shuttle here. That's you—or more specifically, the hole in your head. Dip the shuttle between the warp, you're in the *pre*. *Woof*, and the shuttle's back home with us. That's what you're doing when you create vaks. You're wadding up our information and stuffing it into a pocket, while weaving our two dimensions together. A tapestry of matter origami. A tapestry we'll never be able to see. The question is... can you unravel the thread, smooth out those folds? And what happens when you do?"

"You mean..." Judge stopped himself, until seemed able to ask the question. "can I retrieve what I sent away? Even my parents?"

"What do you think?"

"It's not like there's a reverse button on this thing."

"No reverse *button*, no," Ruby said, and she stared at him a long moment, waiting for him to arrive at the only conclusion she could be alluding to.

"*Me?*" Judge said, backing away from her. "*I* can't return to the *pre*. If I go through a vak without creating a WayOut first, I'm stuck."

"Sure," Ruby said. "But we happen to know somebody on this side who has a tool that's very good at collecting DNA, no matter how thin it's spread."

"Roan? You're crazy."

"No argument here," Ruby said.

"But you said yourself, the weave is only one way. I can't turn back time."

"You'd be using the same point for entrance and exit, true," Ruby said. "But that's not going backward. That's being stationary. The same way you found your way out of the *pre* the first time. Isn't it? Only this time, you'll have help."

"She won't help," Judge said, shaking his head so vigorously Ruby was a little worried he'd create an accidental vak. "She'll leave me there. Once I'm gone, she's won."

"Nonsense," Ruby said. "You're in this together. You're not the spawn of a mad scientist, or by-product of any particle collider experiment. You are a natural born disaster—a sublime creation of the multiverse—and your sister is the only possible partner you have on this planet. You need to stop fighting each other and figure that out. Now, let's talk about something really important. Tell me about these things you call the *nots*."

PART ARCHIE_0001

THE DRIVE FROM THE BUNKERS TO THE HUB was the loneliest road trip in the history of road trips. Berit sequestered herself in the back to work out the kinks in her design, so U.A. kept himself alert with an unhealthy fuel of energy drinks and anxiety. Each petrol stop was a check on his anonymity, so that was a fun gamble. He'd been criss-crossing the country with this crew, so it was only a matter of time before his connection to this catastrophe became public knowledge. Somehow, though, they made it to the heart of the Heartland without being recognized. Midwesterners must've been more concerned with keeping a look-out for monsters in their backyards than for an Englishman in a tour bus carting a renegade scientist and her gloopy cargo.

"Well done us," U.A. self-congratulated upon their safe arrival, but Berit didn't have time for congratulations. She disembarked the bus without ceremony to reunite with her crew from the silo, launching into the construction work as soon as her feet hit the ground.

The drive here should have been nostalgic for him. U.A. hadn't been behind the wheel this much since the band had first started to tour. But instead the drive, in particular Berit's instant dismissal upon arrival, was a painful reminder of how much he'd lost in that desert weeks ago. Being on tour with his boys was a raucous adventure that at times had strained his patience, but his purpose had been clear: to develop their sound and their confidence; to steer them clear of the usual pitfalls. He was the authority, in other words.

Here, he was superfluous, only useful because of the cover he could provide during transport. While he watched the operations inside the arena, however, U.A. began to see a need he could fulfill. The base of Berit's machine was fully constructed, a solid platform on which grew the cradle of a sphere made from welded-together vaks. At present it looked like a jagged, Escher-inspired lotus flower. Berit directed her people to apply the bioshell to the vaks, making the handling of them much safer, but even then it was painfully obvious to U.A. that this group lacked the skills to complete the project. As lab researchers, structural engineering was not their forte, and besides that, they simply needed more hands.

U.A. considered the consequences of mixing his old crew up with this trouble and had to acknowledge he'd receive more of a tongue-lashing if he continued to leave them out of it. Shortly after Henry and the boys and their driver Oscar had all been stolen away inside the desert streamer, he'd phoned to tell the crew leader to cancel the rest of the tour and to breakdown the set in Tucson, because the boys were going on a stint in rehab. Zee hadn't believed that for a second, but without any more details, she had no choice but to spread the lie to the rest of the crew and to all the Knotty Bits fans. She might never forgive him for that. He should have just told her the truth, but the truth hadn't been all that easy for him to swallow at the time. Difficult to share something that is impossible for your own brain to believe as fact.

Zee was cold when she answered his call, so furious she treated him like nothing more than a work colleague who'd been away on holiday, taking down details of their new gig with the sterile voice of an assistant. She repeated back to him the equipment he told her to bring, some of it so unlike the usual inventory that the list should have elicited some curiosity on her part, but she offered none. She said she'd see him soon. Never even asked *Why Iowa?*

A few days later, the lorries rolled up with roadies and gear, and Zee dropped from the cab of the lead caravan, the weight of her severity making the buckles on her boots buckle.

"How did you hide it from me?" she asked. No *Hello*. No *How are you?*

"Hide what?" he returned, coming in for a conciliatory hug. She punched him in the arm, hard. "Ow! You know, I've forgotten what a bully are you. God, I've missed you."

"Don't do that," Zee said, tears welling, even though he was the one smarting from a fresh bruise. "Don't act like what you did was *nothing. How* did you do it? And not how *morally*— how *logistically*? How much time each day on your precious *she-jewel* did you devote to keeping me in the dark about the trouble the boys were in?" She always mocked his English accent when she was really pissed. "I mean, you're an organized guy, Archie. Your *deceit* was designed."

"They aren't in rehab, Zee," U.A. explained.

"What do you mean?" Zee asked.

"I lied to you," he said, and she started slapping him all over like she was putting out a fire. It would have been comical if it hadn't stung. He kept his hands up in defense. He could hear Bruno and the others chuckle but he knew if he made light of this, Zee may really lose it.

"Why would you do that?" she kept saying in time with the light beating. "Why tell me that? Why? Why?"

"Because they're gone," U.A. said, and he no longer felt any danger of joining in with Bruno's laughter because his heart was dropping on an elevator into his shoes. Telling Zee the truth was going to be so much harder than lying to her.

"Where the hell did they go? If this has been a publicity stunt, so help me—"

"It's no stunt."

"Did they fire you?"

"God no," U.A. said, a little angry she'd think that. "There's a vocabulary for where they are and for what took them, but I can't seem to say it out loud."

Zee stared at him for a long moment, recognizing how miserable he looked. She wiped her eyes and nodded her head, as if she finally understood. "One of those things? One of those things grabbed our boys? All of them?"

"And Oscar, too."

"Oscar, too."

"My god." She started to walk in circles between the caravan and the arena. She did that when she was thinking. She'd cut her hair since he'd last seen her. Dyed it a new shade of purple. So dark, it was almost black. "I mean, I knew they were real, because why would the government freak the world out if those things weren't real, but how do you accept something like that without seeing it for yourself?" She stopped circling to ask, "Did you see it happen?" U.A. could only nod in reply. Words would not have worked for him at that moment. "Why didn't you tell me? How could you bring me here, like it's just another show? How could you do that? To *me*?"

"Honestly, once this all got started, I'm not sure how I even put one foot in front of the other," U.A. said.

"That's not a good enough answer, Archie," Zee replied, choking back a quiver. U.A. couldn't bear the thought of losing her, so he rushed forward to grab her hands.

"I couldn't tell you the truth, because that would have made it real," U.A. pleaded, pulling her into the arena to show her Berit's operations. "The girl can bring them back, Zee."

"Shit, is she here?"

"No, not at present. She's still in transit."

"So I've heard," Zee trailed off, gaping at the beginning of Berit's design. U.A. waited for her to recover from the shock of seeing a bunch of vaks for the first time.

"Bringing things back, it's a messy affair," U.A. began. "Dangerous. Deadly, even. That machine should make the return safer. Fewer things knocking about on their way out. Make sure we get them all back in one piece." As if on cue, Li-Wen and Scott finished welding a large vak onto the broken eggshell frame, only to have the structure fail and peel back. U.A. whispered to Zee, "I really don't think they know what they're doing. And we're under a serious time crunch."

"When aren't we?" Zee replied with sarcasm.

Sonny, Howie, Tulip, Gregorio, Fiona, and Bruno, all fanned out behind Zee and U.A., loops of cables slung over their shoulders, tools on belts. Ready to work, except for the fact that they were all frozen in place. This was a show unlike any other.

"So are we doing magic tricks now?" Bruno asked, derisively. "I fucking hate magic tricks."

PART JUDGE_0008

"YOU'RE CONFUSING *PSYCHOTIC* AND *ZYGOTIC*," Ruby said, and she winked. She *winked*.

"I'm telling you," Judge said, trying to keep steady as he argued with Ruby about her proposal. "I was in the *pre* because *she* sent me there. Going back would be suicide."

He immediately regretted what he said. Ruby flinched, but stayed focused.

"You and your sister were nothing more than zygotes. Zygotes aren't known for their wicked motivations," Ruby said. "Whatever cosmic collision happened between the two of you knocked you clean out of existence. Attributing your banishment to Roan is nothing but a myth you've created."

"Just a myth, huh?" Judge said. "You wouldn't say that if you knew her."

"Look, I get it. You're not simpatico. Welcome to the club of brothers and sisters. The fact that the two of you don't get along may be the least unique thing about you. That being said, after the accident with your folks—and I do believe it was an accident—the burden is yours to convince *her* you're not the enemy. You'll have to make the first move."

"I already have," Judge said. "I disarmed her."

Judge opened his messenger bag to reveal the bioshell seeds he'd stolen. They were alabaster and luminescent in the recesses of his bag, like pearls tucked away inside a clam. One was in the shape of an acorn, but the others were more alien. The strangest one looked like a miniature jellyfish. The other like a furry bean.

"Oooh my," Ruby said, a childlike look of wonder on her face. "Your sister has been playing around, hasn't she? What do they do?"

"I don't know exactly," Judge said. "I watched her throw one into the woods."

"And what happened?"

"It grew on the surface, like lichen," Judge said. "The whole forest was covered with it by the time we were attacked."

"You were hiding on a decommissioned military base, weren't you?"

"It was off-limits to the public," Judge nodded. "Environmental hazard site. Griff must've figured we'd fit right in."

"Did it look like normal lichen?"

"I'm not really a lichen expert," Judge said, but Ruby was still waiting for an answer so he expanded, "It was full of silvery stuff."

"Mercury, then," Ruby said. "Lichen produce phytochelatin, a protein that binds with metals." Judge must've been giving Ruby a look, because she glanced at him and said in explanation, "This means that bioshell is programmable, and your sister is practicing with remediation. Makes sense, right? She wants to get rid of you. Doesn't want to hurt anybody else. So she's trying her hand at creating these—what should we call them… synthetic plant life with a real punch… *blastoids*… yes, blastoids—to target what she wants to remove. I doubt they're very specific," Ruby started to trail off, "but maybe she's learned enough to target mutagens. Like mercury. In that case maybe even benzene. Formaldehyde. Radioactive material. Whatever nasty stuff that's lying about in large amounts after there's been some serious pollution…"

"The lab workers called us pollutants," Judge offered after she trailed off.

"Well, damn," Ruby said. "That's probably where she got the idea. Good ideas have nasty beginnings sometimes."

PART WALT_0005

SOMETHING UGLY WAS GROWING INSIDE OF Walt. It had taken root back at the bunkers, but after learning the mystery puppet master was his own age, an intense anger branched out into each new thought. The same group who'd kept *him* sidelined as an expendable third-stringer, spoon-feeding bites of information only when it was convenient for them, had been taking their own cues from a teen. He both resented Katie Goodbear and was jealous of her. He'd not only been painted with the "kid" brush, he'd been stuck carrying the baggage with the Hale nametag. Anonymity hadn't been an option for him.

He wasn't just pissed at the so-called adults, either. Roan had started to keep secrets from him at the bunker, and now Judge was with Ruby in the shed, collecting his own. Whatever the private lesson was about, Walt bet it wasn't Dimond's "refinery" project. Ruby'd made it clear she wasn't interested in that. As for Walt, that's all he cared about now.

This machine Dimond was building had to be dangerous, and his family was right in its path. Well, not his whole family. His dad was safe in D.C., giving government assurances that all was being done to contain the Gorey twins. Walt and Nova drank coffee in the kitchen and watched Senator Hale's press conference on her laptop. His speech was full of "uhs" and "wells" and lots of repeated phrases he'd no doubt been instructed to hammer home.

"Your dad looks tired," Nova said. "He reminds me of a pencil that's been worn down to a nub."

"He was never that sharp to begin with," Walt responded, and Nova snorted into her coffee.

"That's a mean thing to say about your own dad."

"Trust me, I could be a lot meaner," Walt said.

Nova nodded and slapped the laptop closed. Seeing his dad's face disappear like that was both a relief and a kick to the gut. Nova placed a warm hand on top of his wrist and led him upstairs.

"I want to show you something before you go," she said. "But I have a feeling you've already seen it." Walt threw a nervous glance out the window for Judge, wondering if he'd return in time for a rescue from any oncoming awkwardness. "Don't worry. They have a lot to talk about. There's time."

Her path ended at Michael's door. Walt hung back while Nova moved in to lower the blind, shutting out the strong morning sun. As soon as the light dimmed, Walt could see a glowing handprint on the wall. It was the same one he'd seen during his fitful night of sleep.

"I thought that was a dream," he said.

"For a long time, I wondered why he didn't leave a note," Nova said, tracing the fingers on the glowing hand, "but then I realized this *was* his note. It's Gecko-Glo. Another one of Michael's inventions. Phosphorescent glue. Fun, right?"

"Sure, but I don't understand."

"Michael's biomedical project glowed in the dark, too. He was helping doctors see drugs reaching targeted cells in real-time. Ruby was a subject in one of the trials."

"Ruby's sick?"

"Ruby is dying."

"Oh," Walt said, nodding, because suddenly things made more sense. He'd been wondering why Nova put up with the abuse. "I'm sorry to hear that."

"When Ruby dies, she'll be remembered for a lifetime of achievements," Nova said. "Michael should be remembered for all the good he did, too. He did so much." She placed her hand on Michael's handprint and dropped her head with a sob. "That story I told you about the coal miner, the one who left a handprint on a wall in a jail cell as a mark of his innocence? Michael meant this as a mark of his own shame. A guilt he could never wash away or forgive. But Walt, he did nothing wrong. He just created something new. Something new that was used to do a horrible, horrible thing. I mean, what's the answer to that? How can you make certain that what you create doesn't do harm? How could he have known?"

Nova gripped the crystal around her neck as if it were the only thing keeping her from sinking into fathoms.

The sound of wheels crunching over the gravel outside distracted her, to Walt's immense relief. He knew she wasn't really looking to him for answers, but her questions were so big they'd sent him into an uneasy spiral.

Nova pulled back the shade, and when she saw who it was said, "Shit. Not today."

"Who is it?"

"Someone with really bad timing," Nova explained without explaining anything.

She swept past him, with a quick motion to a bag in the hall.

"I packed more of Michael's clothes for you in that duffel. Along with some other things."

Walt took that as a warning that they might have to make a quick exit, so he grabbed his backpack and brought the duffel downstairs, too. He dropped it by the front door and listened in to the conversation outside.

Nova intercepted the man who got out of a car marked by the same logo he recognized from documents on Ruby's dining table. Marcellus Shale Oil & Gas.

"You know I enjoy talking with you, Nova," said the man in a sleazy way, "but I really need to speak with Ruby. How is she doing?"

"She has good days and bad, Todd."

"Well, that's why I'm here, sweetheart. We'd like to make sure she has more good days than bad from here on out," Todd said, his body language reminding Walt of his dad before he launched into a pitch. "It doesn't do anyone any good, stirring up all that trouble and worry, spreading rumors about toxins in the air and the well water."

"Rumors? You mean lab results, don't you, *sweetheart*?"

"We all know the history of this valley," Todd continued, not missing a beat. "Those numbers can't be traced to the compressor station up the road any more than I can trace my ancestry to George Washington. There's rumors we're related, but that's all we got. Nobody doubts the toxins are there. Nobody doubts that. Which is why MSO&G's been so generous in its offer to buy Ruby's land."

"Ruby doesn't want to move," Nova said. "Not until MSO&G cleans up its mess and protects the land and water from further damage."

"What about your neighbors? We can't move forward with any more buyouts until this lawsuit is resolved. They aren't so lucky to have your unlimited resources. They're relying on our buyout to put food on the table—"

"Lucky?" Nova said, her fist clenching. "Did you just say *lucky*?"

"Oh now, Nova, I didn't mean any disrespect to Michael—"

"You didn't know him," Nova interjected. "Don't talk about him like you knew him."

"All I meant," Todd restarted, carefully, but with a tone of condescension, "Was that you were fortunate to have had a husband who provided so well for you. You could live anywhere you want."

"My mother's garden was right here," Ruby said with her booming voice, standing between the shed and the oak tree. "Mamma thought she was growing tomatoes and zucchinis. Turned out she was growing toxins, planted there by your leaching pipes. Acute Leukemia took them both. I watched them die, Todd, and it matters to me, who killed them."

"We know the history of this valley," Todd repeated, doing what salesmen do when challenged, falling back on his spiel for support. "They've been digging coal out of the mountain and hauling it through Carbon County for centuries. But you want to blame a pipeline that's only been in the ground for a few years. You've got no proof, Ruby."

Ruby was rolling something around in her hand. Walt noticed that it glowed. Uh oh.

"It's true," she conceded, tossing the glowing ball once in her hand and catching it with a cheery smile. "Tracing the source of hydrocarbons is like tracing the wind from a whisper. And you're right, we've got plenty of potential of pollution in the hollers of Pennsylvania. But *your* gas pipeline runs through *this* yard, Todd, and *it* comes straight from *your* compressor station up the road. You were here when I ran the last tests. You remember how the process works?"

"You said it was like putting a sponge in the ground," Todd said. "A sponge that attracts certain molecules."

"That's right," Ruby said. "That special sponge soaked up the answers to why my parents were dying. But it can't lead us to the source. It only reveals concentration. And you've got *your* environmental samples and *your* results, too, however you obtained them. So you're right. I can't prove that your pipeline poisoned Mamma and Daddy."

"I'm so relieved you've come to your senses, Ruby. After all, you're sitting on top of the Marcellus Shale," Todd said. "There's been hydrocarbons in the soil for a lot longer than you and I have been around."

"I can't prove it until *now*," Ruby said, and she revealed the glowing thing in her hand. It was the acorn from Judge's bag. The one he'd stolen from Roan's private collection. "Around the same time my parents died, the old oak here started dropping acorns by the hundreds. Trees do that when they know they're dying. One last hurrah to spread their genetic information before they become nothing more than lumber, ready to be chopped down for firewood. Nothing to lose, in other words."

Ruby dropped the glowing acorn into the grass, where it sank into the ground with the purpose of a heat-seeking torpedo. The oak tree shuddered before it split apart, right down the center. Something grew inside the trunk, glowing with the same intensity as the acorn. Branches snapped and popped like wood crackling in a fire, but no flames overtook it.

"What the hell is going on?" Todd shouted, backing toward his car and tripping over a root tunneling under him.

Roots were boring just under the surface toward the house, like giant, crazed groundhogs. Walt braced himself. Windows rattled and floorboards bounced as the earth bucked under the foundation in protest. The sound of a thousand rats scurrying in the walls turned out to be tendrils of roots filling the pipes to bursting. Wrenching apart rusted joints, the tendrils sent explosions of water into Ruby's house from every corner, dousing her piles of data with the forceful imprecision of uncontrolled fire hoses. Walt tossed his bags onto the porch, just as the whole house was raised several feet by the growing mound beneath it. The ground floor snapped like the bulkhead of a ship hitting an iceberg and sent Walt tumbling out the front door and down the steps of the porch.

Walt face-planted in the churned-up earth, but he couldn't stay put. Large chunks of bark were sloughing off the dead tree to make room for its glowing replica, pulsing larger and larger. Widowmakers fell like thunder around him. He rolled out of harm's way one way, then back the other. He lunged for his bags, despite Nova screaming at him to "Just get out of there!"

She might as well have been urging Judge. Walt saw him dive out of Ruby's shed a split second before it collapsed. A tidal wave of glowing tree roots yanked the foundation right out from under it on its way toward those yellow posts planted in the backyard—the ones that marked the buried pipeline. The luminescent fingers churned the dark earth around the pipeline like a mixer. The earth mound over the pipeline bulged from the attention, and that groundswell branched out from Ruby's land, taking with it the clamor of all that rooting. All that seeking.

There was still enough noise from the deconstruction of Ruby's house to make it impossible to hear exactly what Todd was mumbling about, but Walt could guess he thought this was beyond his paygrade as a company pitchman. Todd was tapping his smartphone with shaking hands. Nova cut short his call for help by snatching the phone away from him and lobbing it onto the buckling roof. Roots popped out from the plumbing on the top floor, and the attic cracked open, swallowing up the device.

"Your house just ate my phone," Todd complained.

"And I'm stealing your car," Nova said, grabbing his keys from his hand. "Walt, honey, let's go."

Before he had a chance to ask where Judge was, he saw Ruby flying out of the driveway in Nova's Prius, Judge in the passenger seat, bracing himself against the dash. Walt threw his bags into the back of Todd's Crown Vic and then Todd threw himself on top of them.

"You're not leaving me here," he said, too freaked out to care how undignified he looked.

Walt jumped in on the passenger side, and Nova spun out in the gravel to catch up to Ruby. Glowing roots tunneled near the surface of fields on both sides of the main road, but Ruby was on the trail of the largest concentration—the massive earth mound that followed the yellow posts of the pipeline.

"What the hell is that thing?" Todd shouted from the backseat. "Is that something Michael left behind?"

"No," Nova said with irritation, and after a quick glance at Walt for confirmation, she added, "Of course not."

"It's following the pipeline," Todd observed.

"Yes, it is."

"Well, you know that pipeline goes under the road just up ahead…" Todd reminded.

Nova increased her speed to match Ruby's, as they both raced the mound in the field next to them to reach the intersection with the yellow posts first. Ruby managed to win the race, but Nova came in third. When the roots cut under the country road, the pavement plumed up and sent Todd's company Crown Vic airborne. When they found asphalt again, Nova struggled to keep control, swerving all over the road until coming to a rest on the shoulder in a cloud of dirt and smell of burnt rubber. Ruby kept going. Walt doubted she even glanced behind to see if they were ok.

Chasing Ruby as she single-mindedly traced the roots of her misery made Walt consider how his own ambition to settle his growing list of grievances compared.

Yep. He was an amateur.

PART RUBY_0002

"You can't talk about anything without a vocabulary," Ruby explained as she kept the gas pedal on the floor. "I've always been good at naming things. *Blastoids*. Woo-ee! Look at it go! Just one perk of being there when new things are discovered. Naming rights."

"I can't believe you just tossed it into the ground," Judge said, sounding disgruntled.

"You think I put you in danger?" Ruby asked. She barely registered the shrug he gave. "Fair enough. She's engineered these with the hope of getting rid of you, after all. But see, you've handled them all this time, and nothing's happened to you. Same for me. Nothing happened until that blastoid hit dirt, and that was by design, no doubt about it. She's engineered a safety measure to prevent the invasion of a living organism. God knows I've got enough toxins in me to attract a remediation effort, but of course, that kind of intrusion would kill me, so… that's considerate. She's interested in limiting collateral damage, Judge. It's an encouraging sign."

Another farmhouse they passed was being overtaken by the thirsty roots of the tree. Lifted from its foundation. Dropped. *Were those screams?*

"That didn't sound encouraging," Judge observed.

"The property damage will be extensive," Ruby said. "But here's the thing, Judge. The damage was already there. We just couldn't see it."

"I doubt that will be much of a comfort."

"I didn't say it would be. Having the truth shoved in your face is almost never comfortable. Oh, look! We're coming to the station. This is where things get interesting."

A cluster of compressor units were planted in a gravel patch behind a barbed-wire security fence back from the road a bit. Just as Ruby slowed to make the turn, a blast from an exhaust valve greeted them. Judge threw his hands over his ears.

"Hello to you, too," Ruby responded.

It was the usual blowdown, only this one lasted mere seconds. Luminescent roots broke free from the earth like arms of a leviathan from the deep and wrapped the compressor station in an aggressive embrace. Pipes bent, valves popped open, machinery grinded. Greedy for those gaseous toxins being ejected, the roots chased after them into the atmosphere, fingers of an angry hand, giving a massive insult to the sky. *Just look at that! I wish you were here to see this, my boy.*

"One thing your sister hasn't quite worked out, I don't think," Ruby said, "is a saturation point."

As the compressor station became one with the blastoid sprout, the explosions erupted. Impressive, but not a surprise, considering the disruption to the pressure flow and the regulatory processes of the station. The roots weren't bothered by the flames, continuing their work as if the eruptions were blooms of a different sort. After a particularly rambunctious *kaboom*, Ruby threw a protective arm in front of Judge, slightly aware that what she did was more dangerous than tickling the chin of a crocodile.

Thunder of distant disruptions in homes and farms all along the pipeline were a mild distraction to Ruby's victory at the compressor station. Her vindication. Here, the nature of the growth intensified, as if the blastoid was drinking up the toxins through a straw. By the time the compressor station gave up the ghost, the roots resembled an anaconda after engulfing a herd of bull elephants.

Nova joined them in Todd's stupid Crown Vic, and it was amusing to watch him freak out about the state of his company property.

"Look what you did!" he cried.

"Yes, Todd. Look what I did."

Over the hilly horizon, Ruby could see the crown of Michael's oak tree, rising in time with each pulse of growth. They were miles away now, so if they could see the tree from here, that meant her house and everything in it was gone. The base of the tree must have taken over the entire acreage of her family farm. Maybe even the neighbor's.

"It's beautiful," Nova gasped, daring to take her hand.

"My very own beanstalk," Ruby said, giving Nova's hand a tight squeeze. "Look at that. It's a goddamned flight hazard!"

"This—this is an alien takeover!" Todd spurted. "It's the work of devils."

"Aliens and devils," Ruby said. "They'd be hard pressed to do worse than humans, Todd. Let's give the Goreys a chance."

Ruby motioned toward Judge, whose hood had fallen back to reveal the jetkill. Judge gave him a quick wave hello, and Todd bolted back to his car, taking off in a cloud of dust. *Look at him go!*

"He'll report that Judge is here," Walt said, throwing his back-pack on and carrying an old duffel bag of Michael's. "We've got to get out of here."

"The Lehigh should still be running, as long as the tracks haven't been knocked out," Ruby said. "It'll take you as far as Chicago."

"Why Chicago?" Walt asked.

"No reason, except that it's on the way to North Dakota from here," Ruby said. "You said yourself you're on a rescue mission, and Katie seems to think she needs Judge's help, so there you have it, *Bright Future*." Ruby pointed to the yellow posts leading away from the compressor station into the night. "Just follow the yellow brick road, dummy."

PART JUDGE_0009

THE YELLOW POSTS THAT RUBY TOLD THEM TO follow led to the Black Diamond rail line. There was no train in sight. Judge and Walt followed the tracks north, away from Michael's tree, but Michael's tree kept up with them. Glowing roots worked against the current of the nearby shallow stream, rolling clumps of mossy rocks out of the way. The tumbling sound was almost pleasant.

"How far is that thing going to go?" Walt wondered.

Judge shrugged. "I don't think she built them to stop."

Only an hour alone with Walt made Judge miss Ruby and Nova. Ridiculous to miss people he'd just met, but he had so many questions, and Ruby was the only one who'd offered anything approaching answers. Nova, well, it wasn't difficult to figure out why he missed her.

Walt kept checking over his shoulder, presumably because he missed them, too.

"You don't have to come, if you don't want," Judge reminded him.

"I'm watching for the train," Walt explained. "I don't want to get flattened out here." Judge didn't buy it, and Walt could tell. "Because I have so many options, right? I could just walk away. My whole *bright future* is still ahead of me. Whereas you… there's only the mission. To get your parents back."

"You heard us talking?"

"I didn't need to. Of course you want them back. What about after that?"

"There is no after that," he said. "There *is* only that. If it's even possible."

"Well, I have to get my mom back, too. And she's the kind of person who can help with the *after*."

"I'm not sure I'm her kind of client."

"I think you are exactly her kind of client," Walt said, switching up his voice to sound like an announcement. "*Massive chemical spill giving you class action headaches?* Contact Gwyneth Hale and Associates. Your product kills and maims? No worries. Gwen Hale has your back."

"Except I'm not a corporation. I doubt I can afford her."

"She'll take your case," Walt said. "She has to. It's the right thing to do."

"Is she known for that sort of thing?"

Judge regretted how much snark he'd used to deliver that last dig, but he didn't have long to regret it. The tracks vibrated from an oncoming train. When he turned to face the train, an unexpected thing happened. He couldn't move a muscle.

It was late on a gray-clouded day, so the engine light was blinding even though it hadn't settled directly on him yet. The sharp cone of light fired up the bare forest, but it would be only a matter of seconds before the train came full around the bend and focused that spotlight on Judge.

Walt scooped up Judge and carried him off the tracks into the cover of the woods.

"Are you ok?" he asked over the thunder of the engine as it passed.

Judge nodded, even though he wasn't so sure. Had he been surprised by the suddenness, or by the size of the train? How inevitable its path? Standing in the way of something so unforgiving, so unstoppable, had frozen him to the core.

"That's the first time I've seen you scared," Walt said, almost smiling.

"You get some satisfaction from that?"

"It's just good to know it can happen," Walt shrugged. "*You.* Afraid." He left Judge to recover and studied the train cars. Each car that rumbled past carried the corporate tag of Black Diamond Freight, a simple geometric diamond, black on white. No imagination spent here. "It's going so slow. That's good. Too risky inside the box cars. We could get trapped. Probably locked anyway. Those hopper cars are probably our best bet." Walt pointed out the open space at the front of the car behind the ladders. The slanted design provided a shelter, something like a stoop. "Are you ready?"

"Nothing to hide behind," Judge complained.

"It'll be dark soon," Walt said with finality. He rushed onto a ladder and swung himself easily into the stoop, reaching his hand down to Judge. Judge grabbed a rung on the ladder instead, and Walt backed away with the comment, "You're more like your sister than you think."

They crouched down, waiting for any sign that they'd been seen. The train kept moving, so they settled in, as best they could. The front of the hopper was angled and uncomfortable to lean against. They braced their backs against the side ladders instead, facing each other.

"Probably a good time to connect with your digital friend," Walt said, thumping the Black Diamond logo and tracking label. "Give her the number on this car. I bet she can make sure we're going the right direction."

"Way ahead of you," Judge said. He'd already powered up his DS and signed on as Coyote in *FutureBound*.

```
> Coyote has entered the lodge.
> LodgeBuilder has entered the lodge.
>> Coyote: Black Diamond 736890271.
```

And he waited. Felt silly using an avatar now that he knew who she really was, but this was still their only means of communication. A few more seconds of waiting, and he realized returning to the game like this made him happy, in a weird way. Nostalgic for anonymity, maybe? For a simpler game play.

```
>> LodgeBuilder: You should be in Cleveland by morning.
```

Judge relayed that info to Walt, and he said, "Beautiful." Maybe the swaying of the train was getting to him, because he closed his eyes. Judge was grateful. He returned to his screen.

```
>> Coyote: We don't have to play games anymore. I
   know who you are.
>> LodgeBuilder: We were never playing games.
>> Coyote: You could have told me you were a girl.
>> LodgeBuilder: It wasn't important.
>> Coyote: Everyone is an animal, except for you.
>> LodgeBuilder: We are all animals.
>> Coyote: I mean the name you chose for us. For your-
   self. It's your own world. Why hide who you are?
>> LodgeBuilder: No world is as enlightened as you
   hope. Let's move this conversation into a private
   room.
> LodgeBuilder has left the lodge.
```

> GirlWhoClimbs has entered the lodge.

>> GirlWhoClimbs: Now it's just the two of us.

>> Coyote: GirlWhoClimbs? You're practically a whole sentence. Where are you climbing to? Where from?

>> GirlWhoClimbs: I'll tell you that story when it's time.

>> Coyote: I've got loads of time right now.

>> GirlWhoClimbs: Then it's the perfect time to do nothing. The destruction at Badger's den complicates our path forward. You must be more careful. This is not the time for storytelling. We have enough bad luck as it is.

>> Coyote: Bad luck? Since when are you superstitious?

>> GirlWhoClimbs: Superstitions can keep us from tripping on our own feet.

>> Coyote: Or keep us from taking necessary steps. Why do you call yourself GirlWhoClimbs?

>> GirlWhoClimbs: There is work to be done and allegiances made. You are weaving your way here, Coyote. Please don't leave a path of destruction behind you.

> GirlWhoClimbs has left the lodge.

Judge growled and shut down his DS. *He* wasn't the one who dropped that acorn blastoid. It hadn't mattered to Ruby that she'd destroy her own home—and countless others—as long as she found the answer she was looking for in the end. But that was a detail *GirlWhoClimbs* didn't seem to care about. He liked her better before he knew who she was. Her words had sounded like wisdom, then. Now they sounded like a lecture.

Walt's head had drooped forward. Judge pulled a trinket out of his jacket pocket that he'd had since escaping the silo. It was an old coin, smoothed by years of use, with a hole punched through the middle. Judge liked the way it felt in his fingers. He drifted off, fiddling with it.

When he woke, it was pitch black and he didn't have the coin in his hand anymore.

"Damn," he mumbled, searching around.

"It's here," Walt said, nudging Judge with his foot, holding the coin up. "This is mine. My great-grandfather gave it to my uncle Emmett. Emmett gave it to me. I never gave it to you." Walt was upset, so Judge's instinct was to admit nothing. "You don't even know what this is, do you? You just liked it because it has a hole in it."

"That's exactly why I took it," Judge said. "That wasn't the only thing I took."

He reached into his messenger back and tossed Walt the paperback one-handed with ease. *Cat's Cradle* by Kurt Vonnegut. Judge read it four times while tucked away in Griff's basement. The pages were so dog-eared the book was floppy.

"She told you to use my computer to steal Dimond's data. Did she tell you to take whatever else you wanted?"

"No."

"I guess you were just in a stealing mood." Walt was quiet for a moment. Thinking. "It was Katie Goodbear who introduced us, if you think about it. She guided me down to the basement in the silo to find you. She must've wanted us to work together."

"She motivated you to find me," Judge corrected. "She doesn't know you. She doesn't know me. She motivates avatars through a system of rewards. The harder the task, the greater the reward.

That's what I like about her."

"She leaves the human element out."

"Amen," Judge said. "Pellets, points, praise. That's how it should always work."

Walt shrugged with a curt "Ok." He flipped through *Cat's Cradle* even though it was too dark to read, then tapped the book on his knee, asking, "How'd you like it?"

"It was weird."

"Look who's talking," Walt laughed, and Judge saluted him for the burn. "Number 973. That was my great-grandfather's ID number at Bethlehem Steel. Whenever he borrowed a tool from the company, he put this check on a peg. They eventually switched over to ID cards, but he kept this as a reminder of when he was just a number on a peg on a wall."

"Maybe he liked being a number," Judge said. "Some are afraid to be more than that. Being part of something big means they only have responsibility for their small corner of things. The rest you can shut off. I saw that at the silo."

"I bet you did," Walt said. "My great-grandfather didn't leave this to Emmett—and Emmett didn't leave it for me—to discourage me from seeing the big picture. It's a point of pride. He was more than just a number. And you're more than just *Coyote*."

"She's not the same as Dimond," Judge said flatly, his voice scaring even himself.

"Judge," Walt pressed. "Why do you think she reached out to you, instead of Roan?"

"Because she knew I needed a friend."

PART CROSS_0004

CROSS STOOD AT THE WOBBLY HELM, EVEN though he knew he wasn't the Captain. *The Royal Nonesuch* had no such Captain. She also had no real hull, no rudder, and no engine—unless Roan's streamer turtle could count as an engine. In his days with the Coast Guard, he'd seen some sad spectacles, but nothing that compared to the wood-rot that was the *Nonesuch*. The pathetic part was, she was the best vessel they could hope for under the circumstances. They needed to keep moving, and nothing slowed her down. Eddies and snags didn't even register. Sandbanks that would have grounded a real vessel were little more than a speed bump to the *Nonesuch*. The turtle just crawled over them.

Roan had her head out the broken kitchenette window, her feet up on the countertop. She had that vacant look kids get when they're plugged in, except she wasn't plugged into anything. Not anything electronic, anyway. Maybe she was steering the *Nonesuch*, or maybe she was cooking up some weird shit like that silvery lichen back at the bunkers.

She noticed him staring. Tried to act nonchalant and failed. Miserably. And knew it.

"What happens in *Huck Finn*, anyway?" she asked, drawing on their previous conversation to avoid him asking what she'd been up to. "Why is it such a great book?"

"Here's an idea," he said, "how about you read it yourself

and find out?"

"Sure, I'll just pop into the local library," Roan grumbled. "Whatever. Never mind."

"Well, if you really want to know, it's... complicated," Cross began, struggling to sum up a book he knew well but hadn't thought about in ages. He drummed his hands on the spongy wheel while he dredged an answer from his former life. "It's basically a morality tale. Slavery is A-OK with people in Huck's world. He has to work it out for himself that everyone around him is messed up."

"And how does he do that?"

"His best friend is a slave. Jim. He works out what's right and wrong based on how the world treats Jim."

"Hm. I bet Jim's perspective on the subject would be less of a puzzle."

"I didn't say the book was perfect," Cross said with a shrug.

Just then, a small commercial fishing boat cruised by with its crew on deck, mouths open, eyes fixed on the *Nonesuch*. Their makeshift turtle-boat had attracted a fair amount of similar attention. There was no hiding on the open water. Cross knew it was only a matter of time before they were under siege again. He decided to enjoy the river cruise while he could. The voyage might've made him nostalgic for time spent on the river in his youth, if he allowed it to. Those memories led him to a dark place he couldn't afford to go right now, so he kept his mind in the present.

Roan was quiet for a while before she asked, "Why is it so easy for people to believe I'm the result of an industrial accident?"

He resisted his reflexive sarcastic response. Said instead,

"People were freaked out. Dimond gave them an answer when they needed one."

"His answer is a lie."

"Doesn't matter. It's still an answer."

"My parents deserve to be remembered for who they really were," Roan said.

"Sure, but digging that back up... Selling a different version..." Cross shook his head. "It'll be like taking a security blanket away from a baby. Nobody will thank you for it."

Roan fell into a sullen funk after that, occupying herself by pulling loose chunks of wood from the *Nonesuch* cabin wall and tossing them out the window.

The closer they got to St. Louis, the more signs that trouble lay ahead. Barge traffic thinned out when it should have been getting thicker. They passed fewer and fewer small vessels. Helicopters were high in the sky.

"They know where we are," Cross said.

"That's ok," she replied. "I know where they are, too."

PART GRIFF_0002

Discipline wins battles. Following unlawful orders leads to bad shit happening to civilians. The soldiers who loaded him into the carrier weren't the first to face that chain of command test, and they wouldn't be the last. He thought about pleading his case, but they'd tracked him to the bunkers, so they already knew his case. Not one of them met his eye. Not a good sign.

When their lieutenant pounded twice on the bulkhead, the carrier pulled off the road to a halt. Griff braced himself.

"Sergeant Griffith," Lieutenant Harward began, as soldiers on either side of him used wire cutters on his zip ties and one soldier flipped over his helmet to collect cash, "We're releasing you under the FUBAR Statute of the Human Genome Protection Act."

"I don't mean to sound ungrateful," Griff started, scanning the soldiers. Young faces. All colors. "But there is no such Statute, Lieutenant."

"Sure there is," the lieutenant replied casually. "I may not have the money to shove it down the government's throat, but I do have authority here. Here, the FUBAR Statute is law."

The back gate lowered, but Griff hesitated to disembark.

"Sergeant—"

"Not Sergeant," Griff cut in. "Not anymore. Just like you won't be a lieutenant anymore if you let me go."

"That's my concern," Lieutenant Harward slapped him on the back. "Not yours."

"All the same," Griff said. "I can't leave Dr. Jackson behind."

"She's got her own ride out of here," the lieutenant assured him. "A first class ticket, in fact. We figured you'd rather make your own way, considering." Lieutenant Harward handed him a packed rucksack and said, "It's not full battle rattle, but it's better than your civvie gear."

Griff pulled the rucksack over his shoulders, feeling the familiar weight on his back mix with an unfamiliar sense of gratitude. He was on his own again, and yet he wasn't. He slid down the gate, turned to pocket the cash from the extended helmet. Gave a nod of thanks to his young patrons.

"I wouldn't want to sit across a poker table from any of you. I thought you were taking me to Gitmo for sure." A few joined him in a quick laugh while others gave a *Hooah*. He offered a final warning in case they wanted to change their minds. "They'll hold you all accountable."

"Doubtful," Lieutenant Harward said. "The courts are already taking the law apart. Most local law enforcement has stopped cooperating. FBI is still tagging along, but only to obstruct."

"Some Homeland Security and National Guard are still on board though, Sergeant," one corporal offered. "So steer clear as best you can."

"Is she really the enemy, Sergeant?" a private asked. "'Cause she just looked like a scared kid to me."

"Truth is, I don't know," Griff answered. "She *is* a scared kid. But she is dangerous. All I know for sure is, the people who want her locked up don't know what the hell they're doing."

"Let's hope somebody out there does," Lieutenant Harward said. "Pucker factor is running high. Good luck out there, soldier."

Griff gave a quick wave as the carrier raised its gate and returned to the road. Griff watched them go, envious of the strong bonds he'd gone without for years. Shook it off and launched into the woods. The tasks required for solitary survival focused his mind. Attend to supplies and secure transportation, shelter. Start tracking. Before, he was chasing ghosts. Now, his target had a name: Roan Gorey. Where the hell had she gone?

The WayOut embedded in Laney's Jeep was the first point of rendezvous. No chance of finding the WayIn among all that debris back at the bunkers, and he couldn't risk hitching a ride, not with his face in the news, so Griff would have a day's hike to get there. The hope for a reunion after that much time had passed was slim to none, but he'd stick to the plan.

It had been a tactical decision to hide the Jeep near the high school both Roan and Walt knew. Those two tended to stick together when things went south, so if they had to bolt without an adult, one advantage Griff could give them was a familiar starting point. Not sharing the location of the hub with them was the only way to ensure the kids wouldn't set out on their own, but the strategy of keeping them tethered by withholding information only worked if no one else broke the tethers.

The attack had split the group in unexpected ways. Griff doubted he'd ever see Felix Kwan again. He wasn't torn up about that. Dr. Jackson had a *Get Out of Jail Free* card. Not surprising, with her connections. She'd be on her way to her family by now. Roan had flown off to God Knows Where. Cross was cargo. Griff had seen Walt and Judge scramble under the house right before the streamer tore it to pieces, so he couldn't be certain they'd even made it through the WayOut until he found the Jeep—stuck in the mud behind a fallen tree, most of the supplies and cash gone.

He followed Walt and Judge's trail to the high school, but there was no sign of them beyond that. It was no secret to Griff that Judge had plans of his own. He'd kept isolated for a reason. At least Walt was with him. Walt was a straight arrow with a lot to lose, so he could serve as a decent ballast. A big brother, maybe. Good for Judge and the universe. Maybe not so good for Walt. Griff had seen that dynamic work out plenty of times. More often than not it was the big brother who suffered the consequences of a newbie's inexperience. Walt would have to learn how to watch out for himself.

It took him the rest of the day and a fair amount of the night to free the Jeep and leverage the tree out of the way. While he worked, he listened to the radio to keep tabs on Roan. Sightings in Western Tennessee, near the Mississippi. Cross was back in the picture, but on the injured list from the sound of it. He must be leading her to the hub, so Griff set a course to intercept their path. Roan was the only one who mattered. She could bring his family back, just like she'd brought back Cross, and the hub was where she could finally do it. At least, that was the plan.

Obsessions are funny things. After losing Helene and Oliver, Griff had been consumed by the need to expose the truth. To make their loss mean something and to find who was responsible. What he found, instead, was that maybe this nightmare could end. The idea of Laney and Ollie's return wasn't the kind of impossible dream that would torture him until the end of his days. They *could* come back, but only if the strange girl with the grudge against the world waved her magic tomahawk *just so*, and only if Berit's machine kept them safe on the way back. In the meantime, if some vigilante monster hunter out there got a hold of Roan, Griff would never see his family again. Griff's new fixation was to find her again and make sure she got to the hub, safe and sound.

He knew he was on target when he saw the deadlocked traffic out of St. Louis. Only an expected visit from Roan Gorey could cause such an exodus. Griff ditched the Jeep in an abandoned church parking lot and changed into the ACU gifted to him by the rogue unit in Sudbury. The fatigues would serve as cover as long as nobody looked too closely. Give him the chance to listen in.

He fell in with a squad on civilian evac duty under new orders to fill posts along the canal. The fact that there was a canal in St. Louis was news to Griff, but if that was an area that required reinforcements, it was as good a place as any for him to be. He peeled off at a checkpoint when he caught sight of a sheriff's deputy arguing with an MP. Watched the interaction from cover of an empty warehouse.

"I was told to bring this thing to the agent in charge," the deputy said, "and now you're telling me I don't have clearance to be here. Who's running this show anyway?"

The MPs wanted to see what it was that he was delivering. The deputy reached into the passenger side of his vehicle and pulled out a trumpet case. He popped it open on his hood.

"Now," he said, sounding like a real smart ass, "Which one of you wants to take this thing off my hands?"

The MPs did want anything to do with it. They didn't even want to look at it. Typical reaction to seeing a vak for the first time. Griff cursed to himself. Roan without Riven was the Roan he'd met at the State Fair. All chaos. No control. Without Riven, Roan was incomplete. Disabled. Incapable of returning his family.

When the MPs waved the deputy through the checkpoint to meet with whoever had invited him here—whoever *wanted* that tomahawk—Griff modified his mission to stop that exchange. He cut through the warehouse and ran at breakneck speed onto the parallel alleyway to catch the deputy at the next intersection. Some squads on the move toward the canal noticed him, but must've figured he was either on orders or bugging out. Either way, nobody tried to stop him. He couldn't remember the last time he'd hauled ass this hard. By the time he burst from the alley straight into the path of the deputy's car, he had no breath left in him. The deputy had fast reflexes. Stopped just short of running him down. Griff slammed his fists on the hood.

"Aw, Christ," the deputy said, loud enough for Griff to hear. "Not another one."

"Give me five minutes to explain," Griff pleaded between gasps, pointing at the trumpet case in the passenger seat, "why you can't hand that over."

PART ROAN_0008

"CATFISH AS BIG AS MY ARM DOWN THERE, I bet."

Cross leaned over the sagging ledge of the deck, watching the muddy turbulence kicked up by the turtle streamer's flipper. They'd been traveling in silence for so long, his voice startled her. The background rhythm of helicopters and drones at different elevations around them had lulled her into a strange calm, like the steady but pleasant unrest of leafy trees before a thunderstorm.

"Are catfish the ones with the massive whiskers?" Roan asked.

"Yeah."

"Then, yeah," she said. "There's a ton."

Cross peered into the murky water, but of course saw nothing.

"You're just playing with me," he said, as if stating a fact that irritated him.

"Want me to show you?" she asked, feeling defensive, and regretted what must have sounded like a threat. There's no way she could translate into words the information she was receiving. The view from the edge of two mashed-up dimensions was hers and hers alone.

"No thanks," he said, raising his hands. "One day-glo turtle is enough. You say you can see catfish through all that muck, I believe you."

The more she struggled to explain what she was experiencing, the clearer the connection between her and those invisible catfish became. "It's more like I am the catfish, and the catfish is me."

"That's very zen," Cross scoffed. "Is that the same for your bacteria friend? You are the E. *coli* and the E. *coli* is you?"

"No," she said, slumping. How do you explain something so unlike anything else that there are literally no words that work? She was about to give up when she practically blurted, "I'm *streaming* them!"

"Streaming?" Cross said, mulling it over. "You mean, you have a new sense?"

"Maybe. I don't know. It's so hard to explain," she said, growing increasingly frustrated. To her surprise, no sarcasm came her way this time. The look he gave was different from his usual glower. Was that *interest*? It felt uncomfortable and weird, but she attempted to talk to Cross as if he were an actual human being. "It's like when my cat used to get under the covers on my bed. I could still see the shape of him under there. I knew that the lump was him, without lifting the covers to see him. But now, I'd know more than just the shape of him. I'd know what makes him a black cat with white paws and a crooked tail. I'd see the instructions that make him a cat."

"You can see DNA?"

"Don't think so. It doesn't look like what I'd expect DNA to look like."

"What would you expect DNA to look like?"

"You know, the spiral thingy. Like a ladder. A twisted staircase."

"So no ladder. No staircase. What do you see?"

"A soccer ball," Roan said, feeling silly for even saying it, but she was surprised by the rush of relief that passed through her. She expected to be laughed at. Taunted.

"So… a geometrical structure with many sides?" Cross asked. Was he actually trying to help her figure this out instead of making her feel like a freak? Who was this guy?

"Yes," she said, excitement growing. "And it has layers upon layers inward. So many I can't see the center. And it's flexible, not rigid."

"Changeable."

"Yes."

"Makes sense. In a weird way," Cross said, leaning on the warped wall of the *Nonesuch* and sinking into it a little. He was so engrossed by the soccer-ball idea, he didn't seem to notice. "I mean, you *are* looking under a blanket, right? Seeing how life ticks. How would your brain be able to comprehend all that information? You'd create a structure to keep it organized."

"I think I'm seeing something that's already there," Roan disagreed.

"Why's that?" Cross stretched his side a little and winced.

"Because there's a difference in the information from the dead and the living—at least, out here. Dead things look flat, like train tracks coming at me."

"Train tracks instead of a soccer ball."

"With breaks in the track along the way, depending on how long it's been dead," she said. "But inside a streamer, it all looks the same, dead or alive. Like the turtle here. I used part of a cracked shell to make it, from a dead one on the bottom of the river. But now that it's inside a streamer, I can't tell that it's dead anymore."

"But it *is* still dead," Cross said, wary. "Right?"

"It has to be," Roan said, scoffing. "I can't bring things back from the dead."

"That's not exactly true," Cross said, thumping his heel against the turtle beneath them. "You can bring back the shell of them."

"That's not the same," she said, but the chill that went through her felt like a warning. "There's more," she continued, feeling an urgency now to share. "Something's etched on the sides of the ball. A code, maybe. But it's not a code of numbers, or any alphabet I've ever seen. You know those weird dot pictures they show you at the eye doctor to see if you can see color? A circle of dots one color, around a roman numeral built of dots of another color?"

"The color blind test, sure. If you can see the number, you're not color blind. At least to those colors."

"Right. Well, each side looks something like that, but instead of colored dots and numbers, it's lines of code and symbols I don't recognize. When I can see the symbol, I know that the code underneath is active. It's switched *on*. In streamers, I can move those windows around. Play with them. Switch codes on and off."

"You're learning the language. Or maybe you're writing it."

"I know it sounds crazy."

"Nothing's crazy anymore." He scratched the stubble on his face and squinted at her sideways. "You see me that way? Like a soccer ball?"

"Yeah, but it's on a separate screen," she said, motioning to her head like it was an antenna. "A different channel."

"You can tune in or out. That's good. Wouldn't want you too

distracted while you're steering the *Nonesuch*," Cross said. He spread his arms with a good-natured smile. Who would have thought there could be anything good-natured about him? "See anything interesting?"

"Brown eyes," Roan said, after a second.

"Too easy," Cross said. "Anyone can see that."

"You have the code for green eyes, too. But it's not switched on."

"My mom had green eyes," Cross said.

"Well, she's in there. For what that means."

Cross returned to the decaying rail, careful not to lean too heavily while he pondered the murky Mississippi again, mulling over what she'd shared. Roan suddenly regretted opening up to Cross. Trusting him with anything was so stupid, considering their past.

"You can really read all the decaying stuff down there?" he asked.

"Yes."

"Your own personal database of the Dead," he said, his usual dark mood clouding over his face. "That's a hell of a burden to carry." He was quiet a few moments before his voice shifted yet again. His tone reminded her, oddly enough, of her dad's when he was teaching her about something. "People used to drown in this river all the time back in Mark Twain's day. All sorts of superstitions about how to get dead bodies to rise, you know, for a proper burial. Shoot a cannon over the water to make the gall bladder burst. Sink a loaf of bread soaked in mercury. They thought mercury was drawn to the dead for some crazy reason." Cross nearly faltered when he asked, "You could make those bodies rise right now, couldn't you?"

"No."

"Yes, you could. You said that you can *stream* everything that's dead."

"That doesn't mean I can make everything down there whole again." Roan shook her head as if to be free of the idea, inching away from him. Back away too far on the *Nonesuch*, and she'd be in the river. "And even if I could, why would I *want* to?"

"It's not about what *you* want," Cross mumbled. "It never was."

Roan didn't understand what Cross was getting at, but she wasn't surprised that their conversation had turned him sour. He could only suppress his true nature so long.

Harvested fields gave way to city buildings. Anchored barges ten or fifteen deep on either side of the river kept their path narrow past Downtown as they speed-turtled by. Cross continued to sulk while she managed to enjoy the view of the St. Louis Arch. It was much taller than she'd expected. And shinier.

Just north of the Downtown area, soldiers lined the shores. Cross urged her back inside. One soldier aimed a phone her way, and she gave a friendly wave before ducking into the *Nonesuch*. Was that a smile on the soldier's face? Maybe a nervous smile. She'd hoped her nonlethal defensive techniques back at the hospital would gain her some sympathy, but that was probably overly optimistic. She'd always be famous for being a freak. Crowds she drew would always be ready for a fight.

The thwump thwump of helicopters multiplied, and Cross ordered, "Shields up."

Roan extended the flippers over the *Nonesuch* to create an arc of protection, leaving their forward momentum to the turtle's powerful back legs and tail. She wished she could see how her reptilian creation compared to the arch that had inspired her. Based on the number of surveillance drones, she and Cross were likely the only two people in the world who *couldn't* see it. The E. coli dome at the hospital was not the best way to prove to people she wasn't a monster. Her turtle was a better ambassador, if anyone in the crowd remained open to persuasion.

Ahead, they could see that the river split in two. The natural bend curved to the left, but that way was blocked by end-to-end barges stocked with soldiers taking aim. The straightaway dead ahead, however, was clear.

"They're putting us into the canal," Cross said. "That's where they'll try to trap us."

"I could take us over land," Roan suggested, but Cross pointed out that the grassy island between the canal and the wild river was packed with soldiers. Impossible for her turtle to find safe footing without squashing somebody. "Never mind."

"Can you control two of these things at once?"

"No way."

"Then get yourself the hell out of here," Cross ordered.

Roan pulled the backpack on to keep the amp safe. It felt heavy on her back, like an anchor. She considered swallowing Cross back up and dealing with his wrath afterwards, but something distracted her.

"That's weird," Roan said. "There's people in the water. Not dead ones."

Cross looked puzzled, then disturbed. He said one word: "Divers."

They were both so busy staring at the water, they didn't notice that one of the helicopters had dropped over them, a huge vak on cables swinging from its underbelly just above them. The shadow from this strange haul was like a door closing on the sun. Roan had seen a vak that big only once before—in the silo warehouse, stacked like giant billboards to advertise the coming age of Bradley Dimond. The helicopter released the vak, and the wall of blackness lined with ribbons of light splashed into the water directly behind them. So close, Roan thought the intention was to slice them in half.

"Whoah! Did they miss?"

"Something tells me no," Cross said.

The vak, as big as it was, wasn't wide enough to wedge between the canal walls, so it flopped into the canal, sinking with some harmless hissing and bubbling. A second helicopter swooped down to release a twin vak directly in their path, and what happened next gave them no time to react.

When the WayIn splashed down mere feet from the *Nonesuch*'s turtlehead, it was like someone pulled the plug in the canal. The water level dropped so fast, the *Nonesuch* was sucked toward the WayIn at a shocking speed. Roan instructed the turtle to brace against the vak frame, but the *Nonesuch* slid right off its shell. Roan hit her head, and the last sensation she had was of drowning, followed by the cold flatness of the WayIn.

PART CROSS_0005

Sucked into a whirlpool, flattened like a bug on a windshield, then spat out of a muddy, frothy geyser. This was not a ride a human being was designed to survive, especially not one with a damaged belly. Of course, whoever came up with this strategy didn't care if *he* survived or not. The trap was meant for Roan Gorey, and her *homo sapiens* classification was questionable at best.

Textured gloves grabbed him, and Cross kicked away by pure instinct. The vak sucked him back in to do it all over again. Whirlpool, flattened bug, geyser. He managed to break the surface the second time around, and he fought to stay afloat in the rapids. He made for the familiar wreckage of the *Nonesuch*—or what was left of it—as it bobbed in the backwash between the WayOut and the canal wall. Another few minutes of getting thrashed against the canal wall, and the *Nonesuch* would disintegrate. Until then it was a life buoy and a barrier between Cross and the divers in the water.

"Roan!" Cross shouted out in vain. He couldn't even hear himself.

Her streamer was missing, too. That meant it was free range. A multi-headed creature breached the surface by the wall, but it wasn't a streamer in flux. It was two divers attempting to hoist Roan's limp body out of the churning water. She looked dead. Men on the wall anchored harnesses that kept the divers free of the WayIn's pull.

Jumping Asian carp are substantial enough to knock a grown man silly. The streamer carp that leapt out of the water bowled through the line of soldiers atop the wall in a flash of fins and limbs. As it arced back toward the canal, the man-carp streamer smacked into one of the harnessed divers, and Roan slipped from his grip. The other diver tried to hold onto her, but the sudden slack in his harness swung him right into the streamer. All of them gone before Roan made a splash in the water below them.

Cross saw that she was headed for another run through the vak rapids. The Coast Guard had given him basic rescue training, but nobody was trained for conditions like this. Not even the rescue swimmers who graduated from A-School. All the same, she'd drown if he did nothing, so without thinking about it too much, he dove back into the whirlpool, grabbed her around the waist, and slammed into the WayIn for a third time. Out they came through the WayOut, gargled with the rest of the debris, and Cross kicked them free of the turbulence. The pain in his side barely registered. He was all adrenaline.

As soon as they were clear, Cross had only the killer currents of the Mississippi to contend with. The river was sweeping them toward a Coast Guard cutter, the Cheyenne. She was hitched to a small barge outfitted with a crane for installing river buoys, and her crew was scrambling to keep the intersection with their current aligned.

Meanwhile, the streamer wreaked havoc in the canal. Flopping around in that whirlpool trap as a carp turtle diver, the streamer was putting on a real show. It finally broke free of the tumble cycle and flopped onto land where it started to harass the lifeforms there. Cross heard gunfire. Explosions. Screams.

He had to ignore all of it. Their collision with the barge was imminent, and Cross was certain they'd be sucked right under if he didn't time his grab for the ladder just right. He hit even harder than expected, but strong hands grabbed him, detangled him from Roan, and dropped them both onto the deck. The medical officer wasted no time before starting CPR on Roan. Her efforts were rewarded by Roan throwing up water all over her.

If Cross wasn't still coughing up half the Mississippi himself, he would've thanked the crew. His relief was cut short, though. A horrible wrenching drew their attention to the blockade, where the streamer had become a monstrous barnacle on the side a barge. The weight of it tipped the barge over, and soldiers started to slide across the deck. The streamer detached into the water where it morphed into a patch of bluestem. The released barge flipped back from the sudden loss of ballast and couldn't recover equilibrium. For a sickening moment, the barge teetered on its side, dumping all its human cargo into the brown, churning water. So many voices it sounded like one giant wounded animal. The Cheyenne turned into the cresting wave from the lost barge, and her crew prepped for a major rescue mission, even though that meant heading straight into the streamer's territory.

"Roan," Cross said, shaking her by the shoulders, "Hey, wake up. Please. You've got to get the leash back on that thing. Come on. Wake up."

Roan's eyes fluttered until they focused in on him. It took her a few seconds to come around. Another few to realize the indescribable sounds were the screams of men and women.

"Stop," she said, and a familiar, benign turtle-streamer paddled gently up to the cutter.

"Life boat?" Cross asked the crew. A seaman pointed aft, and Cross hurried to lower the small RIB. He helped Roan in and tossed her the drenched backpack, then dropped in himself. None of the crew tried to stop them. They were focused on scooping soldiers from the water.

A helicopter swung around, taking aim at their RIB, and Cross ordered: "Shield."

A second later, the lifeboat was tucked inside the turtle shell, making the outboard motor moot. Expanded holes around the neck and flippers served as open portals. Roan held her knees tight to her chest on the floor of the boat, shivering, as Cross stood at the helm for no good reason. She guided the turtle boat straight through the new breach in the barge blockade. Soldiers thrashed about in the water, desperate to get away from the streamer, even in its unthreatening turtle form. Cross threw them every flotation device he had.

"Help's coming," Cross shouted to them. "Just keep treading water."

Roan was no help. She was too busy crying, hiding her face. Once he'd exhausted the supply of life jackets and ring buoys, Cross dug two blankets out of the supply box. He tossed her one and drew the other around himself. She sniffled until they were well away from the screaming, and then she felt silent.

"How many, do you think?"

"Drowned?" Cross asked. "Or taken?"

Roan dropped her head in her hands and said, "This is not ok."

"You're right," he said, looking back at the receding lights of St. Louis. "It's not."

That's when he noticed a buzzing sound. A quadcopter drone was following them.

"We've got a tail again," he said.

Roan lifted her head for a moment, and said, "Yes, we do."

The turtle's tail whipped up at the drone to knock it out of the sky.

PART GRIFF_0003

"TELL YOU WHAT," OFFERED THE DEPUTY. HIS Southern drawl oozed out of the side of his mouth while he slid around corners of the gravel path to the canal, "You want the tomahawk. This So-Called *Agent* Dohanian wants the tomahawk. I do *not* want the tomahawk. How about I do a toss-up and you two fight for it?"

"This isn't a game for me."

"No? Seems like you want to play keep-away to me."

"That tomahawk doesn't belong to anyone but Roan."

"That tomahawk," mocked the deputy, "is a priceless archeological artifact that had been housed in the private collection of one Bradley Dimond, our current high commander incorporated, until it was *stolen* by your friend, Miss USA Teen Witch. Now, Sergeant Griffith, I'm just a lowly deputy, but it's my humble opinion that *stealing* something doesn't give you ownership rights."

"And I'm just an Army grunt, but it's my humble opinion that claiming something you found in the dirt doesn't make it yours, either."

"OK, fair enough. But I'm not driving all the way to the Pine Ridge Reservation in South Dakota to return the artifact to the rightful owners, and even if I was so inclined, I don't think they'd want it back, considering its current condition."

"Look at you, being culturally sensitive."

"What can I say? My mama raised me right."

"That girl is the only one who can make any use of it... in its current condition," Griff argued. "By the way, that's the reason *they* don't want her to have it. They don't want her to split any more of those things open."

"But you do."

"That's right."

"Because your wife and kid are inside one," the deputy said. Griff was quick to discourage the deputy's dismissiveness. One punch to the dashboard got his point across. The deputy acknowledged the point with a succinct "Ok." Corrected his tone when he continued, "Don't you think it'd be better if there was a *machine* to bust your family out? I mean, I've seen the kid operate. She threatened my girlfriend, stole my uniform, *and* my squad car—this one is on loan from Deputy Kincaid and it smells just like he does, like French fries—then trapped my town under a bacteria dome, so yeah. Not somebody you'd want to put your faith in."

"No machine can do what she can do," Griff said.

The deputy remained unconvinced. Forced to halt at another barricade. His explanation to the Corporal in charge that he was expected by Agent Dohanian was challenged by the Corporal's explanation that Agent Dohanian had just locked the whole area down. They were encouraged to turn around. Strongly.

The deputy argued his position, but Griff had no interest in convincing the Corporal that they belonged. Something was about to happen in the canal. Something that should have everyone's undivided attention. Griff watched a squadron rush to support a small team who were manning lines dropped over the canal wall, three to a line. A pair of Chinooks hauled the biggest, most mind-disorienting vaks Griff had ever seen so low overhead that the cruiser wobbled in their wake. One after the other, the choppers dropped the vaks into the canal and broke all hell loose. Torrents of muddy water gurgled over the canal walls. Doused the team who heaved on the lines like they were pulling in a big fish.

"What the hell are they doing?" the deputy asked.

A giant fish head slapped down on the canal wall, its scales so out-of-scale they could've been windows on a skyscraper. The streamer's back and forth swishing collected whoever was in range, then reflected its catch. Almost bragging, Griff thought. The soldiers on the lines fell, but losing this game of tug-of-war meant more than falling on your ass in the mud. Erased from the world, taken back to the river.

"Holy shit!" the deputy shouted, and he threw the cruiser into gear.

When he tore around the barricade, Griff asked, "What the hell are *you* doing?"

But Griff knew what the deputy was doing. *What he was trained to do.* Griff had been following that same instinct at the fair when he'd rushed to Sophia Gorey to stop her from bleeding out instead of getting Laney and Oliver off that stupid Ferris wheel. Of course that was years ago, back when he shared the deputy's current delusion—that he could still *do* something.

By the time the deputy fishtailed close to the canal's edge, the streamer had returned to land for seconds. The deputy yanked the trumpet case out of the cruiser with him.

"You don't even know how that thing works!" Griff shouted.

A small tsunami knocked back Griff when he tried to stop

him. The deputy ignored his warnings and rushed the canal, tomahawk raised in hand.

"It doesn't work that way!" Griff yelled after him.

The streamer was an eel now. Flopped toward a squad doing their best to scatter. The deputy held his ground. Sliced into the monster eel like he was carving sushi. Each swipe, Riven just passed right through. Frustrated and confused, the deputy turned to Griff for an answer to what he was doing wrong. An answer Griff never had a chance to give. The deputy knew he was done for. The moment before he was taken, he managed to throw Riven high into the air.

The tornado-strong wind from the streamer caught it and sent it even higher. Griff blocked out all the shouting and shooting and protected his eyes from the stinging water and mud. He had to focus on Riven's path without getting collected himself. He lost sight of the damn thing in the glare of the setting sun.

It was like losing hope of ever seeing Helene and Ollie again.

SEQUENCE SEVEN

PART ROAN_0009

THE STREAMER TURTLE SHELL BLOCKED HER view of the drones, but Roan turned her head in the direction of the buzzing, anyway. Anything to avoid the look Cross was giving her.

"I know you blame me," she said. "You don't have to rub it in."

Cross sat up straighter, like he hadn't been aware of his staring. He settled back into his sourpuss face and said, "You should have split." She shrugged. She didn't want to admit that she hadn't wanted to abandon him. It seemed stupid now. "You'll never do what you're told, will you?" Cross continued. "If I told you to stay you'd…" and he made a sound like a rocket taking off. "Arrogant from top to toe. And it's always somebody else's fault."

"Looks like you popped your stitches."

"Probably when I hauled your ass out of the water."

He was hinting for a thank you, but she wasn't in the mood for giving any thanks. It was hard to even breathe, worse than when Thing 1 had her in his clamps. She massaged her sternum.

"Chest hurt?" Cross asked, and before she could answer, provided the explanation, "That's from the CPR. Coming back from the dead hurts, I'd imagine. Not everybody comes back, you know. But of course you would."

"You didn't have to save me," Roan said.

"Maybe I shouldn't have."

"Then why did you? Why didn't you just let me drown?"

"I don't know," Cross said. His honesty was a kick in the gut, and he must've known it. They looked away from each other. Trapped together beneath a star-infested turtle shell glowing red-orange from a harsh sunset, they might as well have been back in the dark depths of the silo as prisoner and guard. But when Cross began to speak, it became clear to Roan that what had happened on the river had taken Cross back much further than the silo. "My wife didn't come back like you did."

Roan was almost afraid to ask what had happened, but she heard herself ask anyway.

"What happened?" Cross repeated her question, his eyes far away. Roan felt like she was an intruder, and it frightened her, seeing how vulnerable he was. How broken. She was confused about how to react. She still hated him, in many ways. But all the same, she listened. "I was a Chief Warrant Officer serving on the Chena out of Hickman. Annie taught English at Fulton County High. One of her students—tormented kid—became obsessed with her. Followed her home from school one day and shot her on our front porch. Tried to hide what he did by dumping her body in the Muddy, then left a note in his car and shot himself. I was on duty when the call came in, dropping containment booms around a tug that was going down, leaking oil like a son-of-a-bitch…" Cross faded off and for several moments Roan wondered if he was going to finish his story. "We searched for weeks, but we never found her. My life was over. I resigned from my post. Moved North. Met Spencer. He gave me a job. The rest is history."

"Why are you telling me this?"

"Because you and I have been on a river cruise," Cross said, "while the rest of the world has been going up in flames."

"What do you mean?" Roan asked, stomach sinking. "What else has happened?"

"I don't need to see the news to know what's going on out there," Cross explained. "There are two starting points for every human reaction to shock: the random shit camp and the divine intervention camp. Those who can't admit it's all random shit choose to believe there's divine judgment behind every outcome. Some kind of mysterious purpose that we may never understand. See, that's how you protect yourself from being next on the list, by cloaking yourself in the superiority of being spared. You were *chosen* to go on."

"I think people are just scared," Roan said, "and maybe don't know how to feel."

"Bullshit," Cross said. "It's a choice. Just like the one I made. Because once you accept that random shit is what rules the universe, and you've lost what you loved to it, there's nothing left. We're close to our destination, kid, and you're about to be surrounded by a shitload of damaged people, just like me. People who don't even recognize themselves anymore. But you'll sure as hell draw followers from the camp of divine intervention, too. Trust me, once they get to know you, it won't take them long to see you're not what they had in mind for a savior. That's when they'll slap you with that *other* label."

"So I'm no knight in shining armor," Roan said. The admission made her flinch, but she finished her thought. "That doesn't mean I'm a monster."

"Keep telling yourself that. But here's the kicker," Cross said. "These two camps, they're not even your biggest problem. Bradley Dimond isn't even your biggest problem. The ones who profit from these two camps going to war are waiting in the wings. Ready to pounce. To them, you and Judge are nothing more than parts suppliers for the next great killing machine. They'll be coming for you."

A chill went right through her, as the last rays of sunshine dropped below the horizon.

"And Roan," Cross added, "the reason I saved you… my wife would have wanted me to."

PART MATTHIAS_0005

Flares from fracking wells looked like landing lights. As they descended, though, Matthias realized the actual airstrip was pitch black by comparison. As relieved as he was to be back on the ground, touching down in the middle of nowhere under a sky that looked ready to swallow him up did nothing for his nerves. Matthias was further from home than he'd ever been.

No one spoke on the short drive into town. FBI Agent Owens, who'd insisted Matthias call him Woody even though he continued to call him "Mr. Skaggs," had dropped his chatter somewhere over South Dakota. His silence was sobering and made the journey feel like a funeral procession for a distant relative.

Matthias searched out the window for Trev, even though he knew he wouldn't find him. Keeping that connection with his boy made him feel less homesick, less alone.

This place was bleak. The pale moon and the bright street-lights partnered up to make the dust that blanketed the whole town look like dirty snow. Back home, towns took on that powdered look when crews blew apart mountaintops that had the nerve to be sitting on top of a node of coal. All that dirt had to go somewhere. This coating looked more to do with heavy truck traffic. Even at this late hour, the small streets were packed with water trucks and eighteen-wheelers hauling drilling equipment.

When his bulky hosts announced Matthias would be brought to see "the boss" at the casino, he predicted their trip would end at the usual kind of obnoxious beacon for risk-takers and fun-seekers. Instead, they pulled into a gravel lot behind a boxy beige building with no ground floor windows and a plain marquee sign that read Medicine Rock Lodge and Casino. Even the casino and dog track up in Wheeling had more flash.

"Were you picturing something more like the Vegas strip?" Woody whispered to him. The guy was bent on convincing Matthias to buddy up to him, but Matthias couldn't see the benefit. Neutrality was his aim. Getting to Trev was all that mattered. Making friends did not. "Where's the neon?" Woody continued. "Neon's my favorite."

Two hulks emerged from the casino to usher Matthias inside. He was surprised, but also a little relieved, when Woody took claim on his arm, even if it was just to keep his place in the pack. Woody was far from a trusted friend, but it never hurt to have competing motivations going into unknown territory.

Bradley Dimond was waiting for them in his penthouse suite, parked in front of a whale of a TV. A news conference had Dimond's full attention, and their arrival did nothing to divide it. After getting over the fact that he was standing in a room with the most powerful man in the country, Matthias tuned into why Senator Hale's speech had the guy so wrapped up.

"...the facts are that Roan Gorey remains at large, despite recent efforts in Tennessee and St. Louis. Judge Gorey, too, has evaded capture, last seen near Jim Thorpe, Pennsylvania. I'll repeat again, my intervention in the unlawful detention of Dr. Kendra Jackson occurred *after* the Gorey children disappeared without a trace, in the manner that they do. Dr. Jackson is a respected physician and professor. A distinguished veteran. She did not deserve to be treated like a criminal. As for Sergeant Griffith's escape from custody, I had no part in that, but I believe that his apprehension was also unlawful. It is my deeply patriotic belief that I did not break any constitutionally-upheld laws by taking these actions, but if it is determined that I did, I'm willing to pay the consequences."

"Nathan Hale!" Dimond declared. "He's not going rogue... he's going full hero! I don't think that costume will fit, do you? Not any more than his Revolutionary name. He sponsored the same bill he's denouncing for Christ's sake! But then again, the public has no interest in details..." Dimond faded off. Then he snatched his phone to yell at somebody, "Spencer, I believe the courtesy we've extended to young Mr. Walter Hale has suddenly expired. Please make certain his handsome face is on every news outlet before our Senator finishes taking his bows." Dimond turned to Matthias, still shaking from anger but trying to smile. "Matthias Skaggs," he pronounced, like his name meant something. "The first to return from the great beyond. Or before. Or whatever we're calling it. How are you feeling?"

"Like a steak about to be thrown to a pack of wolves," Matthias answered.

"Heavens!" Dimond exclaimed. "What makes you think that? Hm. Maybe it's the unnecessary escort you've received from our federal friend here?"

"Agent Woodrow Owens," Woody introduced himself. "And my escort is mandated under the law you bought and paid for. I'm the FBI Liaison to your—*Industry* Agents, I believe they're called? Sorry, I'm still adjusting to the new terminology."

"Aren't we all?" Dimond said as he made himself a drink. He offered a glass to Matthias, but he declined. Dimond made a point of offering nothing to Woody.

"All of these gentlemen here are FIA?" Woody asked.

"That's almost correct," Dimond said, swishing his whiskey and ice cubes.

"You're handing out the distinction with abandon," Woody said.

"People want to be helpful."

Woody focused in on a particularly meaty guy in a funny mix of a suit jacket over sweats. A Vikings fan, by the looks of it. He'd been snarling at Woody as soon as they'd walked through the door, and Woody was finally acknowledging it. "And how do *you* help, I wonder? And by that I mean, what qualifications do you hold? What did you do *before* becoming an Agent of Industry?"

The Vikings fan checked in with Dimond, and with a mouthful of whiskey, Dimond gave him the ok to answer. He said in a gravelly voice, "I'm a contractor. For the Chairman. Transportation and Security."

When the man reached into his suit pocket, Woody's grip on Matthias' arm tightened, as if preparing to yank him down. But the Vikings fan didn't pull a gun. He pulled out a business card. He handed it to Woody, pointing at it as if that said everything he needed to know.

"There it is, in black and white," Woody said, "and raised lettering, too. My, that's fancy. Dillard Pick. Federal Industry Agent. Transportation and Security Division. A dual threat. Tell me, does that mean that you secure transportation, or that you transport security? Maybe a little of both, hm? Anybody else getting a *this-is-creepy* vibe? No? Just me?"

"Agent Owens, I understand your frustration," Dimond started, his condescension thick as slurry. "Truly, I do. You don't think federal agents like yourself should have to answer to my people. I am, in fact, very sensitive to your assertions about traditional hierarchies. But it's fascinating to me that you think you have any authority here at all. Traditionally speaking."

Woody studied the business card a moment longer, and then he read out loud, "*Liaison* Industry Agent *to the Three Affiliated Tribes.* Well. Fuck me."

"Custer's last words, I believe."

"We're on a reservation," Woody said softly out of the side of his mouth to Matthias. He looked apologetic, almost, like somebody who realized they'd just made a terrible mistake. He released Matthias' arm, and Matthias instantly felt a lot more alone.

"As a Federal agent, you have no authority here," Dimond said, sweet as pie but with daggers in his eyes, "unless someone has broken a federal law, and certainly no one here has broken any federal laws." Disturbing chuckles filled the room. "Your only role on the team was as Liaison to the FBI, and we have no need for the FBI while in the care of tribal authorities here. In other words, we have no need of you."

"I've been replaced," Woody said, flipping Pick's business card into the air. "Mr. Skaggs, I strongly encourage you to come with me, right now."

"He stays," Pick announced, but Dimond sent a glare that settled him down real quick.

"Mr. Skaggs," Dimond began, "You're free to go with Agent

Owens if you like, but I can assure you, he won't be able to help you find your son."

"I came here to see you," Matthias said, trying to keep his voice steady.

Pick took that as a cue to advance on Woody, and this time Dimond didn't yank the chain. Matthias felt guilty about that, so he avoided looking Woody in the eye.

Woody gave Matthias a protective nudge out of the way, while he bargained with Dimond, "Locking me out will only make it look like you have something to hide."

"I *do* have something to hide," Dimond said with a laugh. "Good god. Why else would *I* be *here*?"

"You're just buying yourself time," Woody stated, as if he just realized it.

"Time comes at an astronomical price, and right now, you're wasting it."

"Here comes transportation and security," Woody mumbled, just as Dillard Pick put his hand on his chest to push him back. Pick ended up with his face in the carpet. Matthias wasn't even sure how that happened, and by the look on Pick's face, neither was he.

"Federal agents using aggressive tactics toward indigenous peoples," Dimond tsked. "An old story, but a good one."

It was plain as day Woody wanted to charge Dimond, but instead he straightened himself and headed for the door, saying, "Mr. Dimond, I look forward to meeting you under different circumstances."

"We'll have a role for the FBI again, soon, Agent Owens," Dimond said. "I'll make sure to recommend you for the job."

The slammed door made Woody's departure official. "Mr. Pick, I think we might've hurt his feelings. Would you be so kind as to make sure our federal friend finds accommodations? Someplace between here and Bismarck would be good, I think."

"I know a good spot," Pick said, making it back to his feet to follow Woody out the door. A few of his friends fell in line behind him.

Matthias figured if they were dancing around something more malicious than chest-thumping, Dimond wouldn't have risked giving orders with him as a witness. Then again, Dimond tended to forget that nobodies like Matthias even existed. Either way, Woody was a big boy and could handle himself. Sticking his neck out was what got Matthias into this whole mess to begin with. He had to stay focused on Trev.

"Sorry about that," Dimond said, waving off the interaction. "Government overreach is a huge pet peeve of mine. Please, sit down."

"Why were your people after my boy?"

"They weren't," Dimond said, surprised by Matthias's bluntness. "They were after the people who were after your boy."

"Why was anyone after him?"

"We could discuss your many grievances, Mr. Skaggs," Dimond asked, "or we can get down to the business of where your son is *now*. Let me be clear. I want what you want. I want you to be reunited with your boy. I promise I can use the full force of my influence to find him. Make sure he's safe. You had a chance to go your own way in Tennessee, and yet you chose to come here. You had a chance to leave with Agent Owens, and you didn't take it. You came *here* to make a deal."

"What if I did?"

"You think you have something to offer me that I don't already know," Dimond said. "I hate to break it to you, but I already know about the machine my pathetic rivals are building—with materials they pirated from me, by the way. So that's a nonstarter. But you *can* help me, Mr. Skaggs."

"There's nothing else," Matthias said, dropping into a chair, despair washing over him.

"That couldn't be further from the truth," Dimond said. "What you can offer me is much more valuable than information. See, I have a wee bit of a PR problem. I expected a certain amount of resistance among law enforcement and the military, but our recent, very public failures have shaken all confidence in our ability to run the show. The Senator's defection is a prime example. The public will never truly be *on my side*, and I don't need them to be. But I can't have everyone *against* me. Too much headwind for our timetable. I need people to go back to seeing me as the lesser of two evils. I need you to go public and tell the world the truth: that you were held against your will by Roan and her fan club, and now they have your son. Can you do that for me?"

"It was your people who shot me with a tear gas canister," Matthias dared to say. "Your people who chased my boy away from home."

"Best to keep it simple," Dimond advised. "After you do this one thing for me, we'll be able to focus on finding your son. It's regretful how this competition has kept you from the important lives you lead. As a show of my gratitude for your cooperation, I plan to set up a scholarship for your boy, in addition to the generous compensation owed to you under our *Right of Capture* liability clause. Your son has a bright future. If you do this."

Dimond had gone from bribe to threat in the blink of an eye. Matthias took a step toward him with no clear intention of how he planned to show his own gratitude, just that he planned to show it. Dimond set his drink down in preparation of an incoming disagreement. Matthias was aware of the henchmen closing in around him, but nobody got a chance to follow through.

There was a ruckus in the hall, followed by a woman yelling, "Let me in! I want to see him, right now!"

"It's ok, let her in," Dimond shouted, eyeing Matthias with distrust.

A nice-looking woman dressed for business burst into the suite with murder in her eyes. Matthias could commiserate.

"How dare you!" she cried. "You lied to me. You said you'd keep Walt off the wanted list, and now—"

She pointed at the TV, where Walt's high school portrait filled the screen above a banner that read: *Did Senator Hale interfere to save his own son from capture?* It shook Matthias up to realize how fast Dimond made that happen.

"Your husband broke the contract," Dimond shrugged.

"But I'm here. Doesn't that count for anything?"

"Yes. If Walt is taken into custody, I can have him brought here, to you."

"He won't be prosecuted?"

"That's up to you," Dimond said. "Mr. Skaggs, this is Gwen Hale, the Senator's wife. I'm surrounded by concerned parents lately. It's heartwarming."

Despite the introduction, Gwen Hale didn't recognize his

presence in the room. The way she stomped around the room in her heels, Matthias expected her to leave puncture holes in the carpet. She was thinking through things, just like Matthias was. He felt grateful for her interruption. It prevented him from doing something that would've complicated his reasons for coming here.

"Everyone will know how involved he was," she said at last, exasperated. "His future is ruined."

"His future is *changed*," Dimond offered. "That doesn't have to be a bad thing."

"But he'll be famous. There's no changing that."

Matthias suddenly interrupted with a declaration, "I'll do it."

"Excellent!" Dimond said with happy surprise.

"He'll do what?" the woman asked, helping herself to a drink from Dimond's bar.

"The same thing you've been doing," Dimond explained, "the best thing for his son."

Matthias had changed his mind sure enough. This woman's high class hissy fit had made something extra clear. She and Dimond operated in the shadows, where becoming a known factor was the worst thing that could happen. Matthias and Trev, on the other hand, were "little" people of no consequence. No real role to play, and easy to dispose of.

Unless they were on TV.

PART EMMETT_0002

No matter how bad things got, working with his hands helped clear Emmett's mind. It was solid proof that he still lived in a world where parts could be put together to make something whole. Problem was, with this new job he landed, the pieces themselves were mind twisters.

Vaks rattled his basic comfort in knowing how things work. The ribbons of light around a vak reminded him of snakes on fire, and the inside of them—well, it was like looking at death. At the CA/GE, thirty-six of those death pillars, each as tall as the steel stacks in Bethlehem, were set in a slotted steel carousel on a grooved track built to spin. It made for deep coffee break talk.

"I stuck my hand in once, by accident," this guy Paulo had confessed in a whisper to Emmett his first day. "Felt cold, but not like any kind of cold I'd felt before. Like my body didn't know what to do, so my nerves said 'cold—we'll call that cold.'"

And after Emmett made the mistake of asking how the CA/GE worked, his foreman Leonard had berated him, "How does it *work*? This is not that kind of jobsite, pal. Did Cinderella ask how the suspension system of her pumpkin carriage handled the soft chassis problem? No, she did not. Because if you have fairy godmothers, you are no longer living in a world where a soft chassis made of pumpkin flesh might dump you out in the middle of the highway before you even get halfway to the castle. There's no privilege of understanding here. We are waving a frikkin' wand and standing back to watch what happens."

It was the most non-standard reply from a foreman Emmett had ever received. No comparison. Then again, skyscrapers were built and rockets were launched to the moon on the same tunnel vision mentality. The project had been broken down into bite-sized problems for teams to solve. The enormity of it had to be ignored at the nuts and bolts level, or nothing would get done.

The basic infrastructure for the power station had been completed under the original plans for the Like-a-Fishhook Refinery. Emmett noticed how some of the abbreviated signage had been modified from L.A.F.H. to CA/GE, but that effort had been abandoned as noncritical, leaving a mix of branding on everything from security gates to payroll forms. It gave a strong impression of haste, which in Emmett's experience was never comforting.

Emmett was a welder by trade, so he was assigned to the internal turbine system. The pipelines were in constant need of repair. Turbines built within the lines themselves provided a self-sustaining source of power for the CA/GE during the construction phase. Problem was, instead of crude oil pumping through the pipes as designed for the original refinery project, the CA/GE crew tapped into the lake. The specs were for oil, not water, and the engineers couldn't find the right pressure point, so the pipes kept popping.

It felt good to be welding again. To be building something, even if he wasn't sure what it was he was building. The last time he'd worked a welding job, Emmett's task was to cut things apart that his grandfather had welded together. Since then, he'd been doing odd jobs that barely paid rent. He'd long ago sold off his tools, so at the CA/GE, Emmett had to rent his welding torch, just like his grandfather once borrowed his from Bethlehem. Dimond Industries used a database instead of brass checks, but the system was basically the same.

The shuttle to the camp just north of Bismarck dropped him as usual on the main road to New Town. Each night he'd managed to hitch a ride back to the casino, no problem. He often waited a bit before he stuck out his thumb. He enjoyed the walk and the time alone.

The air had a bite to it tonight, and the stars were sharp as knife points. With each step, his rented blow torch clinked against the metal thermos in his backpack, making him sound like the vagabond he was. The road ahead was marked by red taillights and oncoming headlights so he could afford to walk a good ten feet off the road if he wanted. Most of the rattle-snakes stayed further away from the road than that, but even so he was pretty sure his work boots had saved him from one or two strikes.

A long stretch of elevated road over Lake Sakakawea was where Emmett chose to hitch a ride. He cursed his rotten luck when he noticed the traffic had thinned out, just as he was about to stick out his thumb. That's when he saw the accident that was no accident.

Tow trucks generally don't lose their haul, but this one dumped a sedan just in time to get creamed by the water truck following close behind. The crunch of car against guard rail was swallowed by the great expanse of sky and water. The squashed sedan barely made a sound when it hit the lake. Both trucks kept on going. Most disturbing, Emmett thought he saw a man behind the wheel of the wreck. None of it made any sense, unless the intent was murder.

He waited for the trucks to pass before investigating. If what he saw was what he thought he saw, those drivers wouldn't hesitate to run him down, too. He ran to the breach in the rail. The sedan had landed several yards out from the momentum of the impact, and it was taking on water fast. The headlights were on now, and the interior lights, too, confirming Emmett's suspicions... there was a man at the wheel. *Handcuffed* to the wheel.

"Just my luck," Emmett muttered.

He used the twisted broken guard rail like a rickety ladder down to the lake. The controlled flow at the hydropower plant made enough of a current to bring the damaged car back toward the bridge. When it collided with a pylon, Emmett dropped down from the railing onto the hood.

The man in the car was in rough shape, one eye swollen shut and a beard full of blood. He looked more than a little surprised to see Emmett. He lifted his handcuffed hands to show him how a rescue was pointless, but Emmett revealed his torch.

"Now that, kind sir, has lifted my spirits considerably!" the guy shouted.

Emmett thought he had a funny way of talking, but he wouldn't hold it against him.

It only took a couple of good kicks to the cracked windshield to get into the car. In seconds Emmett was waist deep in lake water. He fired up the torch and split the cuff, but got no thanks because the man's face was under water by that point. Emmett yanked him through the hole in the windshield, and the man coughed some water on the hood before the whole car submerged. It pivoted around the pylon and disappeared into the shadows under the bridge, sucking them along with it. The railing chose that particular moment to break free and fall on them.

As Emmett sank under the weight of the twisted metal, he saw something that couldn't have been real. The welding torch was sinking in one direction, and the sedan's flickering lights were pointed straight down at the bottom of the lake. The two sources of light were enough to reveal a submerged world. Like the wreckage of some ancient navy, broken buildings, some heaved on top of each other, sat on the lake floor. A ghost town, drowned.

The headlights of the ditched car spiraled down until disappearing into the soft wood of a house. Emmett's commute home had never been so strange.

PART KATIE_0004

Sacred stories are the source of great power, and therefore fetch a great price. Other stories that come at a great price are free. How can this be?

Bismarck News

M.H.A. Chairman Loses Son in Fatal Pursuit
New Town, ND
A high-speed chase on old Route 8 ended in a fatal crash Tuesday. Edgar Raven Looks Around Paulson, Lance Corporal, USMC, drove his vehicle into Lake Sakakawea after a brief pursuit by T.A.T. Police following a traffic violation. Attempts to retrieve his body from the submerged car resumes today. Paulson was the only son of M.H.A. Nation Tribal Chairman Duke Red Spear Paulson.

That's how.

Katie didn't know what really happened that night almost three years ago. Maybe Edgar drove into the lake on purpose out of anger, or to make a statement, and then became trapped. Or maybe he fell back into bad habits and pushed things too far with his father, and the jaw-busters and leg-breakers made him disappear. All she really knew was that he wasn't happy at Camp Lejeune, and he wasn't any happier when he came home.

The last few weeks of his life, he spent hours with Katie showing her tricks of the espionage trade, but spoke of nothing else. She didn't ask why. To question why he chose to train her would be to question his judgment, and would reflect her self-doubt of being worthy of this inheritance. There was an understanding between them regarding the payment owed to him for these lessons, his personal tech bundle. Katie would cover the debt by how she would use this knowledge. After Edgar died, the understanding expanded to include an eternal partnership clause. Whatever Katie accomplished by using Edgar's skills would be a reflection of Edgar and his life. She was bound to do right by him.

That night, standing right there on the cracked pavement of Route 8 that had guided Edgar Raven Looks Around under the surface of the water to swim the streets of his ancestral hometown, Katie shared what she could of his story with Trevor Skaggs.

"I'm not sure why I told you that," Katie offered as an epilogue.

"It's no great mystery," Trev said. "You don't want to forget about him. He's probably a big reason you're doing all this. I get it."

Katie blushed. She never blushed. Working the levers behind the curtain for two years, trying to stay ahead of Bradley Dimond while remaining invisible to him, our Katie had grown accustomed to thinking of herself as a machine, an organic machine with grand purpose. After less than two days of living in close quarters, Trev recognized her grief and assigned her another motivation. A human one. Demoting her devices to a common emotional context was insulting and insightful at the same time. So she blushed, you know?

"Or maybe you're telling me so that I'll be more sympathetic about why you brought me here?" Trev added. She snapped her face away from him to stare out over the lake, and he gave a long conciliatory sigh. "I'm sorry about your cousin. I really am. And I get why you felt bad for those kids in the silo, even if I don't share your sympathies. But why bring me here and tell me all of this? I don't have any special powers. I can't even make the goddamned football team." He took a puff from his inhaler on cue. "And please don't give me that load about all of us being *special* in our own way. Spare me that."

"You think I'm foolish for revealing myself to you? You think I've chosen poorly?"

"I didn't say that."

"But you did." Katie looked away again. Hiding out in the rearing pond meant the only time it was relatively safe to get fresh air was at night. She wished she'd worn her coat. "My people have a history of helping those who need it. It hasn't always worked out for us."

"You didn't send a helicopter rescue because of history," Trev said. "You were worried if Dimond's people got a hold of me, they might be able to draw my dad out. Use me as bait, or leverage, to get information out of him. Screw up your plans. Nabbing me first… that's not exactly helping *me*. More like helping your cause."

"One and the same."

"Bullshit. I'm sorry, but bullshit! None of this has anything to do with me, or my dad."

"You're wrong," Katie said. "We're all in the same boat now."

"So what the hell is going on, then? I deserve an explanation. A real answer."

If it's one thing Katie had a difficult time giving, it was a straight answer. And a short one. Everything was a story, you know?

"Programming is very repetitive," she finally said. He rolled his eyes to indicate he didn't appreciate the change of subject, but she lifted a hand to ask for more patience before continuing. "When you first start out, you might copy and paste a lot, it's so repetitive, but that leads to problems. Bugs, you know? Then you're playing Mr. Fix-It all over the place. So you learn how to build algorithms to do all that hard work for you. Sometimes they work. Sometimes they don't, and there you are as Mr. Fix-It again. Until finally you have the program up and running, nice and smooth."

"I'm from West Virginia, not the Middle Ages. We have computer science, even in the hills. What's your point?"

"What if that's how everything came to be? All of this. The lake. The stars. You. Me."

"I think you've spent too much time alone with your laptop."

"Please, I'm trying to answer your question."

"It really seems like you're not."

"Then you aren't listening carefully," Katie chided, and she instantly regretted her tone. She and Trev weren't that far apart in age, and their friendship would never last if she treated him like a kid. She waited for him to keep the conversation going, if he wanted to.

"You think we're all just programming?" he asked, gazing up at the stars.

"I recognize a pattern, that's all," Katie shrugged. "Lots of repetition. Systems built on other systems. Echoes of the past. Whispers from the future. Mistakes and Mr. Fix-It."

"You're talking about time now."

"And the universe."

"So my piddling, hillbilly history is a line in your *universal* code?"

"Not *my* code."

"Who wrote it then?"

"It's not the kind of code that's written. It's the kind that's grown."

"Ok, so who planted it then?"

"Not everything that grows was planted. Seeds drift on the wind." Katie nudged a weed growing out of a crack in the asphalt as a visual aid.

"You think our universe was created by pure accident, like that weed?"

"That weed couldn't grow if it didn't have soil, water, sun. You know, the basics. I don't think that's purely accidental. Do you?"

Trev released some of the tension he was holding in his shoulders, like a grudge he intended on keeping, and he withdrew into himself a few moments to think.

"So you think those kids are kind of like a bug in a program?"

"But what caused the glitch?" Katie asked in return. "Bugs can be homegrown, like a copy/paste error, or they can be seeded from outside, you know? An unforeseen, external interaction. Even an intentional, malicious attack."

"Like a virus? From… where? Out there somewhere?" He motioned to the stars, a dismissive huff like punctuation to the silliness of the idea. Or maybe he needed his inhaler.

"I don't know if it's malicious," Katie said, mindful of his breathing. "I doubt it, but you never know. Programming is language based on a fundamental geometry. It can't go beyond the basics of our hardware. I think that must be where the real problem is. The hardware."

"Can you please just spell it out for me?"

"Sure, ok," Katie said. "I think we got hit by a sledgehammer."

"A sledgehammer?"

"Sure, the equivalent of that, yes. That would do it, I think. Another dimension rammed us, like a sledgehammer. Broke our basics, you know? Right inside those kids. Crunched our hardware to bits. So the programming did a reinstall and reboot, right there where it happened. Mr. Fix-It to the rescue, patching up our instruction manual. Only it didn't quite work, did it? *Streamers*? *Vaks*? This is not the same environment. Our programming is crazy adaptable, but we could be headed for a total system crash. The *last* crash. You know?"

"Not really, no."

"We need to be really careful, and we aren't famous for being careful, are we? That's why I stuck my neck out for you, Trevor Skaggs. Because you and I are the same, even though we are so different. And I think you can see that, too. Not everyone can. Many don't even try."

"I keep no power for myself," Trev said. She was struck dumb by the comment, until he explained. "I saw it written on a post-it on your monitor. Is that what you're getting at?"

"Yes."

"Well, you chose correctly, then," Trev said, tugging on his borrowed clothes. "I have never profited from anything in my life."

They shared a laugh, and then accepted the silence that fell after.

"It's killing me," Trev said softly, gazing out over the lake. "Knowing he's out there, looking for me. No way of telling him where I am."

His hand brushed against the back of hers. By accident or design? Katie felt something stir inside of her that made her shake a little.

"Are you cold? We can go back if you're cold," Trev said. "I'd offer you my jacket, but I didn't have a chance to pack one."

Katie smiled and shook her head, "I'm not cold."

Katie had done research on Trev when his father had first been claimed by the streamer at Hawks Nest, but she hadn't expected the boy from West Virginia to be so kind, so curious, so handsome. Katie knew that other girls might think he was small with a bland face, but Katie could see his strength, and the face that he would grow into.

Trev took her hand in his, and their fingers intertwined effortlessly. He might have kissed her, if they hadn't been distracted by the sound of voices coming from the water.

"The handcuffs would've been a big clue."

"I think their priority was putting me at the bottom of the lake. Evidence—*if* I was ever found—was probably not even secondary."

"Why'd they bother putting you in a car at all? What's wrong with a block of cement?"

"I'm going to overlook the fact that you sound irritated with their method of body disposal. My guess is, they like to smash things with trucks, and this was an excellent opportunity to smash something with a truck. Everybody has their favorite things."

The two men were walking out of the water toward them, up the submerged road, as if they'd just come from having a drink in town. Katie tugged on Trev's arm to pull him back into the dark before they were seen, but he was staying put.

"Agent Owens?" Trev asked.

The bearded man wiped his face of water and blood and said, "That is not Trevor Skaggs. It can't be. My universe is not that ordered."

Several moments of humans being astonished at paths crossing in unexpected ways. Stories exchanged. Handshakes and introductions. Time enough for Katie to put a few things together and distraction enough for her to text Teri and Carl to steer clear of the *Lota Lota* for now. If you think a Federal agent emerging from the drowned streets of Elbowoods could be taken as a sign of good things to come, you haven't been paying attention. The arrival of Agent Owens would mean the departure of Trev. For that reason alone, she wasn't thrilled to meet him.

"Trev, I have some tremendous news for you..." Owens started.

"Is it about my dad?"

"Why, how'd you guess that?" Owens wondered, but then was racked by shivers. "On second thought, hold that answer. Would you happen to have access to some towels nearby? It's a little nippy out here."

"Sure," Trev replied. "Just up this way..."

Katie watched Trev lead Owens up the hill to the path that would reveal their fishery hideout. Nothing she could do. Katie stayed back with the other man, Emmett. He was reluctant to leave the lakeshore, too. He stared at the black surface like he was puzzling something out.

"I lost my torch out there," Emmett pined. "They'll be taking that out of my pay."

PART TREV_004

N<small>EWS</small> <small>COVERAGE OF HIS FATHER'S DEMISE BY</small> rogue wind freak accident had been presented with mean humor, a variety of local yokel story that made the Darwin Awards, or got millions of hits on YouTube. To the world before it knew about streamers, his dad was a victim of his own stupidity, performing a stunt on the river akin to "look ma, no hands!"

So the news conference starring his father—a man declared dead and gone—was like a dream, if dreams were simultaneously broadcast to the world. The yacht's entertainment system on the bridge was a high-end platform for his return. Graphics placed him in New Town, ND.

"He's here!"

"He is," Agent Owens confirmed. "We shared a ride, in fact, until we were… separated."

"Let's go then!" Trev said, but Woody grabbed him before he could go anywhere. Trev almost hauled off and punched him, but the look Woody gave him changed his mind.

"You and I are friends, but I would discourage you from pushing me tonight," Woody warned. "You can't go. Not yet."

"He's right," Katie said. "They'll move your dad the second the cameras are off. If you go now, they'll use him as leverage to gain information from you."

"That's still all you care about?" Trev asked, sounding more hurt than he'd wanted to let on. "I won't tell them anything about you."

"How about you tell me?" Woody requested. "I would *love* to know how you came to be here, in a yacht buried in a fish hatchery. The twists and turns, I can't begin to imagine."

"You can't afford my story," Katie disappointed him.

"Hm. Can I afford *his* part of it?" Woody asked, nodding toward Trev. Katie offered only silence, so Trev followed suit. Woody continued to towel-dry his hair, turned to Caleb and said, "It's good to see you landed on your feet, Mr. Harper. *You* have anything to share?"

"Only that if you have questions for my clients," Caleb started, "we'll need to come to terms before any interview takes place."

"Clients?" Woody laughed. "You've drummed up business along the way? That's excellent. You know what? Never mind to all of you. It truly is still the Wild West out here, and I can only deal with one calamity at a time. If it weren't for the outstanding heroics of my new best friend Emmett here, I would have been finished this evening, and that's not something I take lightly. I plan on making a triumphant return to that casino to impart some goddamned justice on one Dillard Pick and his associates. But first, I need to call the cavalry." He winked at Katie, but she didn't acknowledge the attempt at humor. "No offense."

He felt in his coat pocket for his phone, but of course it was gone.

"Use mine," Caleb offered.

"Why thank you, sir," Woody said, punching in numbers.

"Dill doesn't usually sink people in the lake," Katie said while Woody waited for the call to be verified and for the secure connection to be made. "You must've really pissed him off."

"Well, that was the plan," Woody said, working his bruised jaw. "I needed him to assault me so that I could have a federal crime to investigate. That way I'd have cause to stick around. I underestimated his enthusiasm."

"That's entrapment," Caleb accused.

"Is it?" he asked sarcastically, and then back into the phone, "Sorry for being tardy on my daily, but I was busy getting the tar beaten out of me. That's right. It's come to that. I'm going to need backup, and some arrest warrants, and a whole barrel of monkeys by morning. Rendezvous point will be the Medicine Rock Casino. No stopping to play the slots."

Woody gave a few more details, then disconnected.

"You're gonna get my dad out first," Trev said, getting right in his face.

"Here's the problem: he's not a prisoner who needs springing," Woody explained. "He came here voluntarily. He stayed with them voluntarily."

"But that's only because—"

"You and I don't know his reasons," Woody cut him off.

"You still think he knew the Goreys from the start?" Trev cried. "That's just crazy!"

"All I mean is," Woody said carefully, "when all this is over, he'll need debriefing on some discrepancies… and curiosities."

"I'll need to be present for that," Caleb interjected.

"He's not accused of any crimes," Woody assured, and then he smiled as he shared, "He's growing his teeth back in. That's an interesting side effect of visiting another dimension, don't you think? We'll need to keep an eye on him to make sure nothing *unnatural* decides to grow out of him."

"You think there's something wrong with my dad?"

"He seems perfectly fine to me. I'm just trying to be honest about what to expect. If I'm able to extract him, I'll make sure you see him. It's those reunions I live for, truly. But you won't be able to go straight home."

"He means quarantine," Katie said flatly.

She was most definitely not charmed by Agent Owens. It put Trev on guard.

"You are a very suspicious young lady," Woody said with a smile.

"I have my reasons."

"I honestly don't know if quarantine will be necessary. That's not my department."

"Maybe I'll go ahead of you," Trev said, trying to make it past him.

"Not going to happen," Woody said, blocking the hall with his arm.

Trev punched the wall and retreated to Katie's cabin. Katie followed him, and as soon as they were alone, he said urgently, "I'm going. Come with me." He felt a connection to this girl, something he'd never felt before.

"I can't," she said. "I've set things in motion. Judge is coming. I have to stay."

"The FBI is standing in your headquarters, Katie," Trev said. "It's over."

"Trev, don't you remember what I told you?" Katie asked. "The FBI can't fix what the sledgehammer has broken."

PART ERNESTO_0002

Saturdays in the summer, the Vargas farm would host a cookout for the field workers to thank them for a hard week's work. Ernesto and his son Hector would man the grill, while his mother worked her magic on the greens and corn. Dessert was their prized melon. U.A.'s roadies reminded Ernesto of those migrant workers, so it wasn't much of a surprise to him that his mother shared the sentiment and aimed to show their new guests the same hospitality.

Even though Ernesto was against it at first—it just didn't seem like good timing—he had to admit, the routine of the cookout and the familiar smells and sounds were a welcome oasis from all the strangeness on the farm lately. Hector couldn't have been happier. He'd spent the last several weeks being ordered out of the way and told the arena was off limits, but now that the structure was complete, Ernesto could see no harm in letting him admire it like everyone else while they ate.

Well, not everyone. Instead of taking a break to socialize, Berit stood still as a statue with her laptop propped on her forearm in front of a giant projection on the arena wall. The projection showed a series of branched lines with unpronounceable labels like *Chiroptera, Microchiroptera, Vespertilionidae*. Or *Fungi, Basidiomycota, Agaricomycotina*. Ernesto had looked these up on his laptop. Bats. Mushrooms. What bats and mushrooms had to do with this machine and those monsters, Ernesto could only guess. Another mystery was the goopy stuff they called bioshell, stacked in transparent tubs and coolers. The stuff reminded Ernesto of the canisters of goo his son liked to buy at the dollar store. Ernesto hated that stuff.

The plate Ernesto had made for Berit remained untouched. Part of him wondered if she was making a point of not joining in, as a message to her team. Or to him? To drive home that she was no friend. To remind them not to get attached? After all, he knew that she took breaks. Ernesto had found her stretching her legs in his unharvested fields, ripping weeds out by hand like it was therapy for her frustrating work. She'd passed him on her way back to the arena, waving handfuls of weeds, remarking casually, "You've got an amaranth problem." No shit.

"So what's her story?" Zee asked, nodding Berit's way as she licked her fingers.

"Berit is a machine," U.A. replied, more interested in eating than answering.

"She knows her way around a farm," Ernesto added.

"I think she ran away from one," U.A. offered.

Zee bumped shoulders with him playfully and said, "We're all runaways then."

"Not all of us," Li-Wen said, with a nod to Ernesto.

"That's right. I'm all about roots. I should've been a tree."

"That's what that thing looks like," Zee said, pointing at the wall projection. "Tree roots."

"That's exactly what it is," Li-Wen said. "The Tree of Life."

"Hm," Zee said. "Biblical."

"Scientific."

"Cool," Hector said.

"Can I give him a closer look?" Li-Wen asked in Ernesto's ear, her breath making his neck tickle. He nodded, and Li-Wen wiped her hands before offering one to Hector, "Come here, I'll show you." Ernesto shadowed them, hoping for an explanation himself. "Hector, this thing that looks like a tree is called a cladogram. All life on our planet is related, because all life is made from the same building blocks. But not all life looks or acts the same, right? A kangaroo's not the same as a bumble bee. A pine tree doesn't move like a rattlesnake."

"No way," Hector said, giggling.

"The cladogram shows those differences," Li-Wen continued, moving closer to the projection so that she could point to certain branches, "where one species of life has branched out from another. For example, the group Berit's studying: *Carnivora.* There's two branches: *Feliformia* and *Caniformia.*"

"Felines and canines," Ernesto said to himself. He was a little embarrassed that he said it loud enough for Li-Wen to hear him, but she smiled.

"That's right," Li-Wen said, and then back to Hector, "You can find some pretty interesting surprises along these paths. Would you have guessed that bears are related to dogs? Or weasels? Or walrus, even? Physical differences, big and small, stem from variations in the genome."

"In the DNA," said Zee, and only then did Ernesto realize that she and U.A.—and all of their roadie crew—were listening to Li-Wen's lesson with as much interest as he and Hector.

"So you have a database of the DNA for all the life on that tree?"

"Well, it's not *our* database," Li-Wen said. "It's available to everybody."

"Something Bradley Dimond doesn't own?" U.A. mused.

"Not yet anyway," Zee frowned.

"With our DNA printers over there," Li-Wen explained, pointing to the bank of equipment tucked away inside what was designed to be a ticket office for the rodeo, "we can synthesize key sequences of DNA that map to specific differences in species, for each branch on the tree. The same information that's on that cladogram is in our cladosphere." Li-Wen turned toward the unearthly glowing dome that was the centerpiece of the arena now. "Variations in DNA sequences are the foundation for this machine. You have helped us build a giant sorting box."

"I have one of those for my Legos," Hector said proudly.

"Pretty much the same idea," Li-Wen said with so much encouragement, Hector blushed and hid behind his dad. Li-Wen smiled at him and continued, "I bet your box has different sized holes that only let certain sized Legos drop through, right?"

"Yeah," Ernesto said. "The smallest ones fall through all the way to the bottom, and the biggest ones stay on top."

"Awesome," Li-Wen said, and then she turned to the rest of the group waiting for a more detailed explanation. "We've always known that if it were to become possible for Roan to release a streamer, managing the organic content would be problematic. We tried to program membranes to allow passage to only matching sequences, but our success rate was dismal."

"We had a chassis problem," Berit interjected so suddenly that half of them jumped from surprise. "Yeast doesn't like being told what to do any more than anything else does."

"But then *this*," Li-Wen said, lifting the top of a bioshell container to show the weird goo.

Hector stepped forward to get a better look, but Ernesto pulled him back with a quick warning, "Don't touch that."

"Bioshell," Li-Wen said. "Streamer skin. Like no material known on this planet. Versatile. Programmable. Benign. We think. It latches onto organics, but only at points of structural breach, to mimic what's missing. Fill in the gaps. It also solves our deadly firewall problem." Li-Wen crossed to the cladosphere and touched an insulated vak to prove her point. She then swiped her hand across the bioshell film that covered the window to nowhere, as if she were petting the sleek fur of a docile animal instead of flirting with a cold and infinite pit. "And last, but certainly not least, bioshell gives us the capability to program. This screen, for example, will absorb the special fragment of DNA we've identified for members of the *Caniformia* family, coupled with a path-finding program designed to select for *only* that parameter. Any other organic material will be repelled, as if bouncing on a trampoline. This is how we will sort canines from all other species." She leaned over to remind Hector, "Just like sorting your Legos."

Zee wandered closer to the cladosphere, and the group followed, showing a new appreciation for the machine that they'd been helping to build since their arrival. Ernesto was still skeptical. The structure was enormous, but not big enough for the job Li-Wen was describing. Not even close.

"Each one of those windows is for a separate species?" he asked.

"No. We don't have enough vaks for that," Li-Wen explained. "The cladosphere is programmed to do the first sort."

"Ok, that makes more sense," Ernesto nodded. "But in case you haven't noticed, I don't have enough acres to hold the zoo that's gonna pour out of this thing. If it works."

"You don't have to worry about that," Berit said in a tone Ernesto didn't like. "Only humans will be released in the arena."

Li-Wen shot Berit a harsh look but quickly covered with a smile to ease Ernesto's concern. It wasn't the first time he'd noticed tension between Li-Wen and Berit, but that was the sharpest moment yet.

"You know how vaks work?" she asked, and Ernesto nodded. "The cladosphere is mostly WayIns. The partner WayOuts were sent to multiple locations. Sorting stations, operated by other collaborators, like you."

"I'm a collaborator now?" Ernesto raised his eyebrows. "Nah, I'm just a farmer who was stupid enough to get into the landlord business."

"We have other farmers working with us," Li-Wen explained. "And park rangers. Biologists. Epidemiologists. Foresters. Research scientists at the Insectorium in Montreal. Woods Hole is taking the marine mammals. Hatcheries for the fresh water fish. Aviary in Pittsburgh. Ranches and shelters for domesticated breeds. Roan often expressed regret about all those lost pets."

"Seems like she'd have regret over more than that," Ernesto said.

"I don't know," Zee said. "When I was a kid, I had more empathy for animals than people."

"You still do," U.A. mumbled.

"Maybe," Zee shrugged. "My point is, she's a kid. Kids don't generally do regret."

"I guess so," Li-Wen acquiesced, as if she'd never really thought about it before. "Anyway, preparations have been ongoing for nearly two years. By now everyone should have received their vaks, and their instructions to stand by."

"That's a logistical nightmare," U.A. whistled. "How do you know which WayIn goes to which WayOut?"

"If there's one piece of wisdom I learned while working for Bradley Dimond, it was this: *Know your inventory*," Li-Wen said. "At the silo we barcoded each vak frame to keep track. The anonymous benefactor who started all this kept that data secure for us until we needed it."

"An anonymous benefactor," Ernesto smirked. "Must be nice to have one of those."

"Too creepy," Zee said, shaking her head. "I like knowing who signs my paychecks."

"Each of us in the silo relied on our anonymity at the start," Li-Wen explained, and then lowered her voice to a whisper, "We all figured the leader was Berit. Part of me still wonders if it *is* her." Berit raised her head as if she heard her name, so Li-Wen returned to her spiel. "Want a tour of the inside now that it's complete?"

Li-Wen stepped into the cladosphere, and the others followed. Ernesto let Hector go to the top step before placing his hands on his shoulders to indicate that was far enough.

"Careful of the large vak in the center of the base," Li-Wen warned as the group fanned out. "That one is unprogrammed. Anything that doesn't find its corresponding WayIn on the first round gets another chance. Its partner is *way* up there, for max opportunity on the second go."

"Welcome to the pinball machine," said Li-Wen's lanky colleague Scott, from his perch on a vak platform high above them.

"Don't call it that!" Berit yelled from outside. As hard as she was trying not to join their group, she still aimed to control the conversation. Li-Wen was visibly irritated.

Ernesto thought *soap bubble* when he'd first looked inside the sphere, but after studying its design, he could see why Scott called it a pinball machine. Angled vaks above them looked like bumpers, and ramps made of vaks spiraled down the interior to guide what gravity would draw down. No spring launcher, though. The game would start when the girl broke the streamer open in here, like a piñata. The softened glow of the firewalls created an artificial light that reminded Ernesto of time in the arcade as a kid. To think that creatures great and small would be the pinballs in this machine made Ernesto cringe.

"The bumpers in the center are programmed for humans," Li-Wen said. "The diamond shaped nut in the center—that's for plant life."

"But it's so small," Zee said. "Won't the trees break apart?"

"How to protect from trees was our greatest concern," Li-Wen said, "considering what happened to Amaranta Nuñez. Once again, bioshell to the rescue. Exposed firewall is known for being extremely unforgiving. We all have the scars to prove it. But with a bioshell coating, a vak gains flexibility. Material much larger than the vak's aperture passes right through, as if the organism itself is made smaller."

"Compression of data during transport," the tattooed-all-over roadie Bruno said. "Bitchin'."

"Yes," Li-Wen said. "We think it's something like that."

"It'll be the world's worst mosh pit in there," said Zee. "Bound to be massive casualties."

"We thought so, too," Li-Wen said. "But something very interesting happens when traveling through a vak with a bioshell screen. Can I give them a demo, Boss?"

"Go ahead," Berit responded. "But don't break anything."

Li-Wen winked at Ernesto. "Pretty sure she means the sphere."

At that, she jumped up, grabbed her knees and landed on the unprogrammed screen like she was making a cannonball splash in a pool. Except there was no splash. Less than a second later, she landed on a padded part of the arena, a good fifty feet away.

A collective "Whoah!" from the roadies.

It was a race to join her. Hector beat them all, so Ernesto shouted to him to "Wait!"

Li-Wen was covered in a strange foam, like she'd been packed in a Styrofoam peanut. As she slowly stood, the foam evaporated into a thin mist. Li-Wen was a little shaky, but had the kind of smile on her face that teens wore after an afternoon on the midway rides.

"That was awesome!" Hector shouted. "How did you do that?"

"Wanna see?" Li-Wen asked, and she led Hector to a monitor where they watched a slo-mo replay of her stunt. Frame by frame, Ernesto watched her journey from the base leap to her reappearance from the apex, where she dropped onto angled panels coded for humans, and popped out the exit in the corner of the arena.

While they watched, Li-Wen blew her nose.

"Get some of that foam stuff up your nose?" Ernesto asked.

"No," she said, wiping her nose again. "Allergies."

"It's the ragweed," Ernesto commiserated. "Bad this time

of year."

Li-Wen's energy was low after her trip, and Berit must have been paying enough attention to notice. She joined them at the monitor, and Li-Wen stepped aside to let Berit give the closer.

"This prototype was designed to maximize human survival during a release," said Berit with pride, "but with the protection offered by the bioshell, we have the opportunity to increase the survivability across all species. While you were helping us with the construction, you may have noticed how my design created open joints at certain welding points. That's because our next step is to drill holes in the hollow frames and install our injection pump and oxygenator."

"Sounds like you're adding an irrigation system," Ernesto mused.

"We are," Li-Wen confirmed. "Instead of water for crops, we'll be filling the sphere with bioshell bubbles before each release. That should increase the buffer between organics by an order of magnitude."

"If we can prove that Roan can release a streamer without killing anyone," Berit said, her voice strained, like she was in competition with Li-Wen, "and actually manage to protect some of the wildlife and domesticated creatures at the same time, we'll have the public on our side for the first time. They'll demand that we continue working at this. But only if they see results."

"It won't be enough to *show* them," Li-Wen said. "We need to be able to shift the conversation—"

Suddenly, they were all startled by a loud shout of "Geronimo!"

Ernesto spun around just in time to see Bruno jump into the base vak. He popped out another human exit point on the other side of the arena. By the time they reached him, he was thawing from the foam shell.

"Woo-hoo!" he hollered, squiggling on the ground like a happy worm.

"Dude," Zee laughed. "Your tats are gone!"

In a panic, Bruno checked his arms, and when he discovered his elaborate tattoos wiped clean, he wailed, "Ah, no."

"Come on, man, perspective!" Zee commiserated, patting him on his back. "You just rocked another dimension!"

PART ROAN_0010

IF SHE CLOSED HER EYES, SHE COULD IMAGINE she was in her old school gymnasium on a rainy day—not her favorite place to think about, but compared to where she was and what she'd just been through, she'd take a memory of anywhere from before. Anything to help her forget all those screams. The rain drops hitting the turtle shell canopy could've been a downpour against the metal roof of her school; the musty smell of the inflatable Coast Guard raft, the rubber balls stored in the utility closet. The weird twang twang of those red balls on the basketball court was a memory more like a dream of someone from another world.

She was that someone from that world. But she was this someone in this one, too. How is that even possible? To be two someones, so different from one another, in the same body?

"Are we almost there?" she asked, for the millionth time.

"Can't see in this sleet," Cross grumped. He was shivering, maybe from the cold, maybe from the pain. The new blood stains on the deputy's uniform made Roan queasy. The meds had been ruined by their muddy water bath. For once, he wasn't blaming her. He didn't have to.

White caps on the river started to slosh over the bow, and the wind howled loud enough to drown the buzz of the drones that still followed them. Cross didn't seem to notice the worsening weather. He was preoccupied by looking for their exit.

"There it is! Port Louisa Refuge," Cross announced, pointing at a small green sign hidden by tall grass.

She aimed the Coast Guard Yertle at the inlet. It looked little more than a stream between clusters of trees. The wind picked up again, and this time kept picking up. Cross finally noticed.

"What the hell are you *doing*?" Cross asked, spine going stiff.

Roan couldn't answer. Her attention was on the two colliding storm fronts inside her. She thought she heard gunshots just as they entered the refuge, tall trees hiding them from the river.

"Another trap?" Cross wondered, searching for the source of gunfire.

A man in a flannel jacket burst through the tall grass above them and came tumbling down a steep gravel boat launch.

A woman's voice shouted from far away, "Ernesto! It's coming!"

A warning wasn't required. From the look on his face, this Ernesto guy knew he was being hunted, and knew that the shotgun he carried wouldn't make a difference. As he slid, a streamer in the shape of massive plant roots grew like snakes from the side of the hill. He twisted away from them and rolled onto his belly in the gravel and mud.

Roan met his eyes just before the streamer roots enfolded around him—and froze into something like a mini cathedral. No time to admire her architecture. She was busy sucking water up her nose in the capsized raft. Taking control over the plant streamer had forced her to give up Yertle. No longer a turtle, it flopped around in the inlet as fish algae frog bug bug bug frog fish.

Port Louisa was shallow but the current was swift, sweeping the Coast Guard raft back toward the Mississippi on the choppy surface. When the fish streamer decided to evolve and struck out for the shore, the raft made like a Frisbee and got stuck in a tree.

Meanwhile, Ernesto had extricated himself from the streamer cathedral. Cross and Roan were in danger of becoming one with Yertle in the shallows, so Roan froze it as a tadpole. The switch of her attention flipped the plant streamer on again. Ernesto swung around with his shotgun and fired at the pearly tentacles.

"Don't bother!" Cross yelled at him, and then to Roan, "Send one of them...*up*....why don't you?"

"That was one," she said sparingly. Hard to concentrate as it was. "This is two."

He tossed her the backpack, suggesting, "See if the amp helps."

As she harnessed the amp around her waist and the glove on her hand, Roan bounced her attention back and forth between the plant streamer and Yertle, knocking each back a few yards when one got too close. The amp lit up, and she felt the cold run through her like the sleet outside had found a vein. She could see the traces of gossamer between her and each streamer, but neither was very bright. It was like someone had dimmed the lights.

One of them had to go. The strain was starting to wear her down.

She had to keep Yertle close, due to the high count of people it had collected back in St. Louis. She targeted the plant streamer, trying to whiplash it up into the atmosphere, like she'd done before. It was pitiful. The plant streamer got snagged in a clump of cottonwoods, and the flurry of debris whipped them in the face. Lamest throw ever.

"Go go go," Cross ordered, pushing her up the path that Ernesto had tumbled down.

Roan kept Yertle at bay as they scrambled over muddy rocks to reach the top of the hill. There was a canal on the other side, and fields of tall crops as far as she could see in both directions. A line of destruction marked the plant streamer's path through one of the fields. Ernesto led them across a small footbridge over the canal, but the cottonwood streamer bounced in random streamer style to block their path. Nearby, an ornate wrought-iron sign painted white read *Port Louisa Cemetery*. Without a second thought, she pushed the streamer through the gates, where it became consumed by a rich environment. Roan dragged Yertle past the cemetery, trying not to look. The streamer settled into the soil and rolled around in the graves, uprooting markers as it churned the ground, sprouting the occasional body part from the newly-tilled earth.

Ernesto made an awful kind of whimper right before he parked himself in Roan's path, leveling the shotgun at her, pleading, "Let them be. Just let them be."

Cross knocked the shotgun aside and said, "Better them than us."

"This way!" a woman's voice called. The same one from before.

Waving to them from further down the dirt road was a woman Roan thought she recognized from the silo. Lee something. If it was her. It looked like her. The long straight black hair that framed the narrow moon-white face. Roan felt a strong ambiguity about their successful arrival at a hub run by the same people who'd kept her prisoner at the silo.

Yertle kept pace with them in the fields, a blue-black shadow that filled in the space between the crop rows like liquid finding a groove. Roan's fatigue kept her from locking Yertle, so it became the crops weeds bugs bacteria.

Behind them, the other streamer departed the cemetery and took flight as a pelican. It buzzed them in the field, then dove back into the crops. It took an acre of corn before Roan gave it a shove out of their way.

Her shift of focus brought a new revelation that made her cuss herself out. Now that the new streamer had collected Port Louisa Cemetery, she could no longer tell the difference between the two. They both contained human information. Their relative whereabouts were all that kept them distinct in her mind. As if she didn't have enough to keep track of.

Clear of the crops, Roan could see their destination, the large building that Lee-whatever was running towards.

"The cladosphere," she shouted above the wind. "It's in there!"

The arena reminded Roan of the hangers at the Big E that housed the large animal exhibits. Thinking of her helplessness that day at the fair—the day she'd been taken from her family—made Roan sink to her knees. She was being led to the cladosphere to make quick work of these streamers, but it was impossible. Riven *was lost*. This long detour was all for nothing. The surprise appearance of this second streamer would be the end of them all.

Cross seemed to realize the futility of it, too, and in Sebastian Cross fashion, he placed all the blame on her.

"Why'd you have to call another one here?" he asked. "Why'd you go and do that?"

"I didn't call it," Roan said. "I didn't, I swear."

"Then how the hell did it get here?" he screamed at her.

Ernesto tripped over Roan in his distraction. "My family," he kept saying as he gauged if he could run to the farmhouse without getting snatched by the streamer lurking in the fields. He turned once to Roan for emphasis, "This is my life here."

As if taking that as an invitation, a streamer made a dash for the farmhouse as a pheasant. Roan pulled it back into the field, where it took on the shape of another plant, a monstrous one in size and appetite.

"Amaranth," Ernesto shuddered.

Free to roam, Yertle streamed crops bugs birds bacteria, allowing Roan to notice a new ingredient being added to this disaster.

Police sirens and flashing lights. The deputy's car made the sharp turn onto the Vargas farm just in time to get knocked into a ditch, courtesy of a strong gust of streamer wind. The siren warped into a pathetic complaint about the rude treatment, and the spinning wheels of the deputy's car spat mud in all directions. The amaranth streamer flailed like a leafy octopus as it crept from the crops. Roan slapped back its spiraling sprouts to give whoever was in the car a chance to run for it. As if there were anywhere to run at this point.

A drone on their trail from the Mississippi got caught in a downdraft and torpedoed the deputy's windshield, exploding into flames.

"That's unfortunate," Cross cringed.

Screams got Roan's attention back on Yertle as it threatened to collect a group of people running from the arena. She yanked Yertle's chain just in time. More screams from the farmhouse, and Roan swung around to deny weedy fingers from snatching a little boy who ran to Ernesto. The fingers detoured into the dirt instead, and the whole streamer became a massive grub.

Roan banished it back to the fields where it mimicked corn stalks before returning as the giant weed. It preferred being amaranth.

"Sebastian!" Berit shouted, waving to them from the open hangar doors of the arena for them to join her. "In here! Bring her in here!"

"You have to try," Cross said, tugging on Roan's arm. "We came all this way."

"Try with what?" Roan asked, showing him empty hands, feeling weaker all the time.

"We need a vak!" Cross shouted back to Berit. She looked puzzled.

A fast-tunneling streamer root knocked Cross into Roan. His head bumped her nose, and she felt a burst of pain and the taste of blood in the back of her throat. In that moment, she lost tabs of both streamers. They were so close together now, there was no distinguishing one from the other. One had dozens, maybe hundreds of men and women. The other only bones. The blue streak of curse words that came next were under no more of her control than either streamer.

When she opened her eyes, she had to squint from the bright light from the firewall in her face. She jerked back her head, certain she was about to be split in two.

But it wasn't Judge standing there, holding Riven inches from her nose.

It was Griff.

"That's a fine thank you," he said, pretending to wince from the impact of her cussing. "I think this is yours."

PART BERIT_0001

HER INVENTION WAS ABOUT TO BE BETA TESTED in view of the whole world by a surly teenage girl who was, in many ways, Berit's nightmare.

A squadron of surveillance drones formed a ring around the farm, marking the circumference of the streamer windstorm. Drawing a bullseye on their location in the sky. Their collective broadcast of Roan's journey here would end with success, or failure, of Berit's design. If successful, their work had just begun. If the cladosphere failed, there would be no second chance. A far cry from sterile lab experiments where results were published after months of peer review. This prototype was built on a dirt floor by roadies, supported by insecure scientists, and review was instantaneous, global gladiator-style.

As usual with Roan, she brought unexpected complications. Interference. The amplifier was a tool based on guesswork as much as theory, and even in theory it was only expected to read one signal, from *one streamer*. Two streamers would cause interference, confusing feedback. Only Roan would be able to sort that out. So far, she was not sorting it out.

At least she hadn't lost the amp like she'd apparently lost Riven. It was fortuitous that Berit had been in the dark about Roan's separation from the tomahawk-vak. If she'd known, she would have devoted time to altering one of the unscreened vaks into a viable replacement, and that was time they didn't have. No matter. Sergeant Griffith had solved that crisis on his own.

Reunited with Riven in hand, Roan's demeanor changed. She went from hopeless to charged with purpose as quickly as if she'd been struck by a lightning bolt.

"Ah ha!" she cried happily, rising to her feet and raising Riven high in triumph.

Roan raced into the arena, dragging both streamers behind her in turn like uneven tails of a kite. Berit ran ahead of her to the ticket office where she would monitor the test.

"Berit!" Sebastian yelled after her. "Get out of there!"

The bioshell bubble blower was operating at high capacity, the superfast *thunk thunk thunk* of the compressor barely audible above the wind from the competing streamers. With each *thunk*, the luminescent Escher mind game of the cladopshere transformed into an eternal disco ball within a disco ball. Berit didn't have to check to know that Roan was close behind with her streamers. The sides of the arena bowed in and out from the pressure, and a panel of sheet metal roofing peeled back to reveal sky. A reckless drone got sucked inside the hole and buzzed around in the rafters a few seconds before going haywire in the maelstrom. Berit took cover in the ticket office just as it did a kamikaze dive into a corner, bursting into flames.

"Aaaahh!" Scott screamed.

Berit thought she was the only one crazy enough to stay behind. Scott recovered his senses and grabbed a fire extinguisher. One streamer—as an aphid—split its shell and nearly collected Scott with its spreading wings. He spun around, screamed again, and sprayed the streamer with foam. It took flight and swept up everything that wasn't bolted down in its wake, including the projector that displayed the cladogram. For a brief moment, the labelled branches were illuminated on the shell of the streamer itself.

Roan brought the aphid streamer back under control, and the field mouse streamer bolted for the door. Scott screamed as it scurried past and sprayed it with extinguisher foam, too. As if that made any difference.

"Release it inside the sphere," Berit instructed Roan from the office, "as close to the center as possible."

Roan didn't acknowledge the direction, but as she began her strange dance with the aphid streamer, Berit could see she was drawing it toward the cladosphere. Roan wound the invisible gossamer around the amp, seeking that special point of disconnection, and seconds after the streamer floated inside, she swiped decisively with Riven. The violence of the streamer explosion sent Roan head over heels outside the arena.

"Oooh," commiserated Scott. "That looked like it hurt."

Berit watched in hushed wonder as soldiers poured from six exit points in the arena. Each packaged in bioshell foam, they rolled off one another, like misshapen eggs. Within seconds the foam evaporated, creating a mirage of mist in the arena, giving the returned a ghostly environs. Most of them moved within a few moments, but some came through injured, and some lay so still Berit worried there were fatalities. Many were still soaking wet. Berit wished she had time to interview each of them, find out if their injuries were sustained before they'd been collected or if the cladosphere hadn't protected them as much as she'd hoped.

"Welcome back!" Scott slapped one of the rising soldiers on the arm enthusiastically.

The soldiers were understandably freaked. Many still gripped their weapons. Not unexpected. Both Matthias and Amaranta had been returned fully-clothed, and Matthias still had change in his pocket.

"We're not the enemy," Berit said, approaching them with raised hands.

Some lowered their weapons, but when they heard the other streamer outside, still ripping things apart, they raised them again. Divided from their usual squads, the soldiers attempted to regroup in order to face the monster outside, even if on shaky legs. Berit was impressed by their resilience, but wished they would be a little less gung-ho at the moment.

Berit squeezed through them to check on Roan, still flat on her back. Riven was stuck in the ground up to its handle, like an axe cleaving wood.

"Roan," Berit said, "you did it. But our guests are a little antsy. So this would be a good time to—"

"Yeah, yeah, I know," Roan coughed before she could finish.

She summoned the streamer, keeping it in the shape of the Amaranth weed but shrinking it to toddler size. The wind stopped so suddenly Berit fell to a knee. That's when she noticed Sebastian hovering behind her, guarding her from soldiers who filed out of the arena in formation, weapons aimed at the streamer. When they saw the weed under her control, the soldiers didn't know what to do. Drones droned overhead.

"It's over," Sebastian said to them. "She's got this. You shoot at us, try to take her again, it all starts up again. Please, think beyond your orders. I've had a hell of a forty-eight hours, and you just got back from another dimension. None of us are in shape for another round."

The soldiers and guardsmen, dazed, lowered their weapons

one after another. Some took a knee. Others crumpled to the ground completely.

Berit rose to greet Sebastian with a hug that made him wince. Wounded again. Or the same wound, not healing. "It worked," Berit whispered in his ear. "The cladosphere works."

"It's good to see you, too," he said.

"Yack," Roan said from the ground.

Sebastian sent her a glare over Berit's shoulder and made a request, "Please don't ever make me chaperone again."

"I promise," Berit said, and then despite her personal distaste for public affection, she planted a whopper of a kiss on him. They melted together right there, in front of all those soldiers and drones.

"Aw," said a man's voice behind them, pretending to be affected by their reunion. "Isn't that sweet."

"Uh oh," Sebastian said.

"That's right," said the sheriff's deputy, lifting handcuffs up for them to see, "Stop kissing the scientist and put your hands behind your back. Asshole."

"Hi, Deputy Tim," Roan said, still flat on her back. "Welcome back. Have a nice trip?"

"Shut up," he said, and then he noticed the squad car in the ditch, smoldering from the drone strike. "Goddamn. Is that my cruiser?"

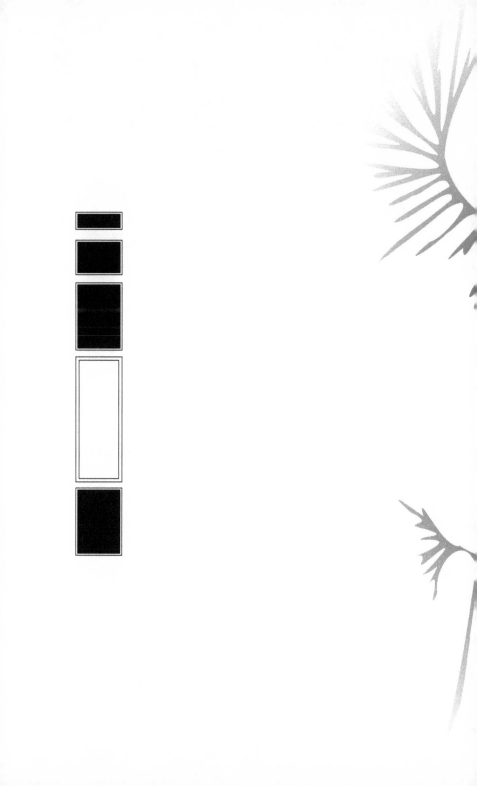

SEQUENCE EIGHT

PART CROSS_0006

CROSS WAS TOO EXHAUSTED TO CARE HOW LONG he'd spend in prison. Whatever cell they'd throw him into for the crimes he'd committed along the way wouldn't compare to where Roan could still send all of them, if she wanted to, so it was hard to give a damn.

He'd delivered Roan here—or she'd delivered herself under his supervision—and thanks to Griff she was able to do her crazy dance with the devil to bring this nightmare of a journey to an end. Or if not to an end, to a brief intermission. The deputy wasn't as sound on his feet as he tried to look, but Cross had no intention of taking advantage. No fight left in him.

Among the squads, crews, and agents in the arena were civilians—some with press badges still around their necks—and those who weren't injured were self-organizing in a daze. Medics did their best to triage, first directing resuscitation efforts on those who drowned in the Mississippi thanks to Roan's streamer. Once those patients were coughing up water, the medics moved on to broken bones.

Roan's streamer was reorganizing, too. Locked as a weed, its glowing roots dug into the earth next to her. The thick stalk twisted around itself and formed dozens of thin stems that began to weave around each other too, then it all shrank back down to a single stalk and started over. She was fiddling, like a kid mindlessly playing with a yo-yo.

"You did it!" Griff hollered, startling them all as he emerged from cover of soybeans. He did a quick scan of the relative calm in the arena, and he slapped his hands together. "Outstanding! Looks like everybody made it out ok?" He slapped the deputy on his shoulder to congratulate him on his arrest: "Deputy, I see you got your man. Good to see you again." Then Griff smacked Cross on the cheek with affection and said, "You too, Cross. You look like shit."

"Thanks," Cross grumbled.

"It's great to see everybody!" Griff said, his face almost cracking from his smile. He gave Roan a friendly pat on the back and said with manic excitement, "OK, so what's next? You call the streamers here, one by one? Assembly-line style? Chop, chop. Everybody goes home?"

"No!" Cross yelled, but not in response to Griff.

It was happening too fast, and he was cuffed anyway so there was nothing he could do to stop it. A face in that crowd he hadn't seen soon enough was hurtling toward them, screwed tight by rage. Selena Dohanian was rushing at Roan with a pitchfork leveled like a bayonet.

Griff yanked Roan behind him in a flash, leaving himself exposed for a skewering.

"Hey!" Deputy Tim shouted, reaching for his sidearm, but not fast enough.

Roan's streamer wound its weedy fingers around the pitchfork in a blur of stitching in mid-air, creating a luminescent bramble as quick as lightning that stopped Selena's momentum, the tines centimeters from Griff's chest. He stepped back to exhale without impaling himself, and stared Selena down with a look that conveyed his disbelief.

"That was extreme," the deputy observed in his patented casual style.

Selena howled in anger, fighting the pulsing hedge for control of the pitchfork. A young man in a suit that didn't suit him ran to her side to help, but that just seemed to enrage her more.

"Back off, Bowman," she ordered. "When I need your help, I'll ask for it."

Roan's streamer pulled the pitchfork out of Selena's hands so fast she probably got splinters. The overzealous Bowman kid lurched for it.

"I got it!" he declared, but he didn't. The genius ended up with an arm stuck in the locked tangle of streamer weeds, his hand clenching the pitchfork on Roan's side of the hedge. He screamed in fear like a stuck pig.

"Let him go, you disgusting freak," Selena ordered.

Griff slapped the pitchfork out of Bowman's hand, and Roan's streamer spat him back out at Selena's feet. Bowman popped to his feet with a comic amount of machismo that almost—*almost*—softened the moment. Cross took note that if jokers like this guy were Dimond's new recruits, he must've been getting desperate for pawns.

"Of course you'd choose a *weed*," Selena snarled at Roan. "That's what you are. A *weed* that needs to be pulled and thrown in the fire."

Selena's hands were shaking, so what she tried to do next looked clumsy and desperate. She spun and attempted to disarm a baby-faced private. It didn't go well. For her. That baby-face knocked her back with enough force that she fell. Then he said "Shit." Because of course the chain of command under Dimond's *Right of Capture* included the woman he just knocked on her ass. He swiveled around for orders, but the highest ranking officers, a National Guard Lieutenant and a Coast Guard Captain, were focused on regrouping their people.

"Lieutenant!" another soldier shouted. "We have a situation out here."

"I'm well aware of that, Specialist," the lieutenant responded. But then she checked over her shoulder to see that this particular *situation* involved one of her own. She joined the Specialist and baby-faced private outside the arena to take stock of the enraged Industry Agent finding her feet again and the glowing hedge row designed to embargo or trap. Hard to tell.

"Give me that weapon!" Selena screamed at the baby-faced private. "You're under my command, soldier."

"Ma'am," the lieutenant said sharply, "with all due respect, your authority as a strategic consultant does not extend to active tactical. I am ordering a retreat."

"Retreat? She's right there! Just shoot her. Shoot her, and all of this will be over."

"Selena, you know that's not true," Berit said.

"*You* say it's not true," Selena spat. "All you can see is what you're trying to sell. Or start. She is nothing more to you than a generator. A spark plug. And *you*," she turned to Cross, "you traitor. I knew Munny was a moron, but I thought you knew what was at stake."

"Munny was smarter than us both," Cross replied. "He figured out how insane Nilas was before everyone. Well," he gave Berit an apologetic smile, "almost everyone."

"Nilas wasn't insane," Selena countered. "He was the only

one brave enough to face up to what needs to be done, before it's too late."

"Killing them won't make any of this go away," Berit said.

"We'll never know if we don't try."

"Wow," the deputy whistled. "And I thought *I* had a grudge."

"You're wrong about Nilas," Roan said, and all eyes went to her. "He didn't think that killing me would bring an end to anything. He thought I was in the way. Of the true beginning."

"Begin," Selena said, almost sweetly, "and end. That was once our story. But you have taken that away from us. Nilas saw what you've done, and he would've have stopped you, if that moron Munny had just done what he was told to do." Selena paced the hedge row in front of Roan like a caged animal, as Roan raised the height between them. "You'd like to bring Munny back, wouldn't you? He was your pal."

"I didn't have *pals* in the silo."

"Bring Munny back, and you bring Nilas, too," Selena said in a sing-song taunt. "And that's the day I'm waiting for."

"Everything is coming back," Roan announced, despite her obvious distress from the idea, "and everyone." She locked eyes with Griff to add, "That's a promise."

"Can you bring back my brother?" Selena shouted. "Can you bring back Erik?"

"You know I can't."

"Wait," Berit interjected, "I thought he was in the group that got swept up in that streamer attack in the silo?"

Cross was embarrassed for Berit. He really was. "No, honey," he said gently, leaning over to whisper, "Erik was the one who *fell*."

"Oh," Berit said, as if she'd just had her math corrected instead of the life and death status of a human she'd once known. "Well, come on. That was an accident."

"*She's* the accident," Selena barked back.

"Agent Dohanian," said the lieutenant sternly, "we are setting up triage on the county fairgrounds. I strongly suggest you come with us."

Soldiers and coasties filed out of the arena, dragging their feet like they'd just walked the length of the Mississippi to get here, but staying on guard all the same. Civilians made a separate path toward the fairgrounds, using the military parade as a buffer, taking video as they left. Cross wondered why they bothered. There were enough drones overhead to capture every angle.

Selena, however, stayed behind, still staring Roan down across the weedy barrier. Roan could have blocked her from view completely, but she didn't. Glutton for punishment, that one.

"You have a twin brother," Selena said after a while, her voice sounding almost normal again. "You hate him so much you denied him his place in this world. You tore a hole in the fabric of our existence because you didn't want to *share*. How can you be human, and act that way toward your own flesh and blood? Everything about you is unnatural. Whatever it is that's inside you—it's rotting away your soul."

With murder still in her eyes, Selena joined the march to the fairgrounds, her new recruit obediently at her heels.

"You leave an ugly history wherever you go, don't you, kid?" Deputy Tim observed.

"That's not fair," Cross said, barely believing he said it. "She didn't ask for this."

"Buddy, I've been in your shoes," said Griff to the deputy. "Trust me. You're gonna want to hear the whole story before you decide your next move."

"My next move is taking this suspect up the chain in command," Deputy Tim replied without wavering, "on the other side of *that*. And then I go home."

That, of course, was Roan's streamer weed wall. As if in response, a stem broke away from the wall and extended straight into Deputy Tim's face. He dodged it, but it wasn't aiming for him after all. Roan planted it at his feet and grew a new hedge in angles all around them, closing them off from the others until it looked like they were in the center of a maze. The streamer hedge stifled all the noise from the arena and the retreating army.

"Well goddamn," Tim exhaled when it finally seemed to be winding down. They were completely isolated from the others.

"Impressive, right?" Cross offered.

"Impressed is *not* how I'm feeling right now," Tim disagreed.

"Roan," Cross called out. "I appreciate the effort, but no. Stand down."

He heard Berit counter his order, "Roan, don't you dare."

"Honey—" started Cross, but he didn't get far with that.

"Bluch," Roan said loud enough as a warning. "I *will* stand down if I hear any more of *that*."

"No you *won't*," Berit insisted, and then she raised her voice to reach Cross in the maze, "This isn't a joke. Seb, if he takes you, they'll turn you over to Bradley, and he'll have Spencer hurt you for information. Just like before."

"Well that's what's great about being the muscle," Cross shouted back. "I don't know a damned thing."

"Deputy," Berit said, a disembodied plea. "She brought you back. And because of the work we've done, we brought you all back *safely*. I hope you can see the magnitude of that."

"She gets zero points for bringing back what she stole in the first place," the deputy said, but only loud enough for Cross to hear. Cross could tell the confines of the streamer maze were starting to get to him. Frankly, it was starting to get to Cross. Even though he probably realized the futility of it, the deputy started to move through the maze, careful not to touch the sides.

"If you take him," Berit continued, "We could lose everything we've built here. They will use him to get to me. Bradley knows how much he means to me."

"That's very touching," Deputy Tim said sarcastically to Cross. "I'm almost convinced."

Suddenly, something emerged from the maze wall right in front of them. A tangle of weeds carried a package through, and as the delicate tendrils peeled back, Cross could see what it was. The streamer was offering a present—the wrapped present that Roan had saved from the deputy's glove box before they'd sunk the deputy's car.

"Sorry about the mud," Roan said with a raised voice.

Tim carefully accepted the gift and pondered it quietly for a few moments before saying softly, "Well, the Mississippi is mostly mud around St. Louis."

"She nearly drowned because of the trap they set for us," Cross said.

"Is that so?" Tim said, still distracted by the gift she'd returned.

"Sorry," he finally added, "Just trying to remember if I still had the receipt." And then he raised his voice to reach Roan to say, "Hey—super weirdo? How about you part the green sea here so that we can talk?"

Almost instantly, the luminescent hedge maze disappeared, its retreating stalks sucked back into the original barrier, extending its reach around the arena and farmhouse. The deputy squared up across from Roan and raised the present as if it were a question all to itself.

"I saved some pictures, too," she explained, "but the river destroyed them. Sorry."

"One question," Tim began, and Cross knew his fate depended on what came next. "Will you let me pass with my prisoner to join the others?"

Roan looked to Cross, and Cross gave her an affirmative nod. She looked stricken. Hurt. But she kept it together. Out of the corner of his eye, Cross could see Berit reaching for a piece of debris behind Tim. Griff had seen her plan of surprise attack, too, and he nipped it in the bud. Griff swept the wood out of her hand and tossed it aside, giving her a stern shake of the head to deter any similar course of action. Berit looked on the verge of losing it.

If the deputy had noticed any of those exchanges during the long pause after his question, he didn't let on that he had. He focused on Roan and her response.

"If that's what he wants," Roan said.

"Ok, then," Tim said, and Cross felt the cuffs fall from his wrists. "Don't read too much into this. It doesn't mean you get a free pass or anything. I just means that I don't care much for people who try to murder kids—even if that kid is *really* annoying. Fact is, right now, I'm not military. I'm not corporate. I'm on my own out here, and my options are dim: take you in and side with Vlad the Impaler's little sister or don't take you in and side with the DNA whisperer. And then it hit me. You're just the accomplice. The comic sidekick. She's the big fish."

"No argument there," Cross said, winking at Roan, and a second later, he felt Berit's arms around his waist and her head against his chest. He kissed her forehead and whispered, "Please don't try to murder anybody on my behalf. It's not your style."

She humored him with a soft rumination of "Mm."

"I *do*, however," Deputy Tim continued, "want you out of that uniform pronto, because it pisses me off seeing you in it." His legs buckled, and Griff lent an arm. "I also need to sit down."

"Is that just going to keep growing," said a voice behind them, "just like the real thing?"

It was the man in plaid who they'd first met while running from the streamer, his shotgun now resting in the crook of his arm and his young son tucked protectively under the other.

"Roan, this is Ernesto," Berit introduced, pulling away from Cross sooner than he'd like. "Your streamer is currently displaying the *Amaranthus Palmeri* that was collected from his fields. It's a super weed, created by the overuse of pesticides on those corporate farms across the street. He's lost acres to it. In other words, you've invited his worst enemy to the party."

"Oh, my bad," Roan said, and in a brief flurry of wind, the streamer hedge shrank and pulsed back to a blob of E. coli.

"Ah, nuts," the deputy said, and then he puked.

Ernesto joined him.

Cross, on the other hand, said, "Good to see you again, E."

PART ROAN_0011

"AN ACTUAL PITCHFORK," U.A. REMARKED, CASU-ally leaning against the same tool Selena had tried to spear her with.

"I know," Roan said grumpily. "I saw it up close."

"If you recall," he said, "I warned you this would happen if we didn't get in front of the story."

A striking girl with short dyed-black hair whacked him over the head and said, "If *you* recall, I don't date guys who say '*I told you so*'."

"This is Zee, by the way," introduced U.A., rubbing his head. "My better half."

With her angled hair and her black, tight everything, Zee looked every part a rebel. Roan suddenly felt super self-conscious about her own lame clothing, which currently still included Jasmine's borrowed tee-shirt advertising a BBQ place in Memphis, now stained the deep mud-red of the Mississippi. The hard look Zee wore came off as more accessory than scrutiny.

The farmer's hard look was all scrutiny. She didn't blame him. Roan tried a smile at his little boy to show she wasn't scary, but Ernesto shielded him even from that interaction.

"Go back inside to Mama CeCe," Ernesto urged his son, and the boy ran to a plump grey-haired woman on the farmhouse porch who was helping Berit get Deputy Tim and Cross inside. They both needed a nap.

Meanwhile, others emerged from the storm cellar and various hiding places to gawk at her and E. Some faces she vaguely recognized, like Scott and Lee-something, from the silo. Most were new and wore jaded faces like Zee's and tattoos all over, except for one of them who looked naked by comparison. He must've felt naked, too, the way he was giving himself a hug.

"We've been waiting for you," Zee said.

"Truth be told," Ernesto said, "I hoped you wouldn't make it."

"Not many people are happy to see me these days," said Roan.

"A hazard of living life on the road," U.A. opined, twirling the pitchfork around. "My boys were nothing but havoc and distress on tour, and we traveled in relative luxury. Wouldn't you say, Zee?"

"Oh sure," Zee said flatly. "This is *nothing*. National Guard, Coast Guard, and bacteria the size of a house? That's the Knotty Bits on a *good* day."

"There's no need to get sarcastic," U.A. griped.

"Then don't make ridiculous comparisons," Zee said, and she turned to Roan with genuine awe, "Sorry, girl, but the Knotty Bits have nothing on you. *That* was an entrance! You nearly wipe out everybody, then dump a bunch of surprised guys with machine guns on the lawn, and pick a fight with a genuine psychopath. All while playing puppet with *that* thing, whatever it is. I mean, Jesus! *HELLO*."

Zee slapped the farmer's arm in commiseration, but Ernesto's shrug was a clue that his assessment of her arrival was a little more complicated.

"This is my land," Ernesto said, his tone immediately tampering Zee's enthusiasm. "It was my father's land before.

And his before that. Generations of the Vargas family have worked the same ground we're standing on. And those same generations were buried together at Port Louisa. Until today."

"I'm so sorry about that," Roan said, and she meant it.

"Oh Roan," U.A. chided. "You didn't?"

"I couldn't help it." How could Roan explain she'd been pushed to her limits out there? That tossing a streamer into a cemetery had bought them all time to escape? That none of them would be standing here if she hadn't made that split-second decision? She couldn't explain it, so she just looked at her feet instead.

"Are they in that one?" Ernesto asked, nodding at E.

"Yes," Roan said, pained. She hadn't meant to test Berit's machine on so many living humans, but they wouldn't understand that mix-up, either. "Signals got confusing at the end."

"Yes, I imagine it is confusing," said Ernesto, doing his best to keep his temper. "Now that things have quieted down, can you please return them so they can rest in peace?"

"More like *pieces* at this point, man," said the un-tattooed associate of Zee's. A young woman with a neck tattoo of a snake punched him in the arm, so he added, "Sorry. Intense situations turn me into an asshole. I miss my tats."

"Hold on," said Griff, his voice edgy with growing anger, "If she's taking orders, my family's priority one. Not a pile of bones." He pointed his finger in Roan's face and he ordered, "You bring the one that has them here. Now."

"I can't," Roan stuttered.

"What do you mean, you *can't?*" Griff pressed, the look in his eyes scaring her. "You just showed us that you *can.* You proved it to the world. That's what this hub, this station, is all about. Isn't it? You know what my family looks like. I gave you that photo. So bring them here. *Now.*" He reached for his wallet as he said, "If you lost it, I can give you another."

"It's not about what they look like. That's not the problem."

"Then what the hell is?"

"I can tell if a streamer has humans in it," she started, and hearing her own voice shaking made her even more nervous, "so I can definitely start with those. But I can't distinguish between living and dead—not *inside* a streamer. And I can't tell *who* is inside any of them."

Griff let that sink in, but then said pointedly, "You'll figure out how to do it, and quick. You'll bring the one that took my wife and son, and you'll let them go."

"Of course she will," said U.A., managing to work himself between Griff and Roan. "She'll bring back my boys, too. But we can't ask her to do it right now."

"Why can't we?"

"First of all," U.A. lowered his voice, "Just look at her. She's spent. It's too risky. And secondly, our audience hasn't arrived yet."

"Audience?" Griff scoffed. "What the hell are you talking about? I don't care about an audience."

"You should," U.A. said, "because the audience—" and he pointed up at the drones above them— "will decide our fate—" and he gave a thumb's up and thumb's down.

"*Her* fate," Griff said, pointing at Roan. "Not mine. I just want my family back."

"And I want my nephews," U.A. said, "but when they come

back, they won't be *ours* anymore. They've been touched by something so new, the world will fear them, maybe almost as much as they fear *her*. Your family and mine, they are unwilling astronauts. Shanghaied to a place beyond comprehension. And we are just at the start of their return. Explorers are not always welcomed home with ticker tape and parades."

"Especially when what's been discovered challenges long-held beliefs," added Lee-something. What *was* her name?

"Debriefing of civilians is limited," Griff said, unsure. "Quarantine laws…"

"…can be changed," U.A. finished his sentence. "We've seen how quickly a new law can upset the order of things, yes? And the same people who managed to push that through now have a populous that is truly terrified. Imagine what they'll be able to do now. Unless…"

"Unless what?" Griff barely let him finish.

"The next time she releases one of those things," U.A. said, "I want it to go out *live*, and not through the eyes of those drones at a distance. We need to set the stage and control the narrative. We need to show the world that they are a part of this adventure. We're all in this together. No more *us* versus *them* nonsense. Right now we're a freak show. We need to go mainstream." He paused before adding, almost as an afterthought, "We need to sell tickets."

The all-too familiar sound of helicopters got everyone's attention, and more drones swooped in, ranging in size from hummingbird to bald eagle.

"Set the perimeter," Griff ordered. "Now."

Roan didn't need to be told twice. Like a fuzzy accordion, E expanded in either direction as she sent it tumbling into the fields. She closed her eyes to concentrate on stretching and growing E until the circle was complete, encompassing the farmhouse, the arena, and as many acres of Ernesto's land as she could manage.

When she was done, it looked like the Vargas farm was in feudal times, protected by a castle wall—a wall of stacked rods and woven flagella. She figured keeping the streamer in the bacteria form would be a repellant to anyone who might consider scaling it with a grappling hook. The gag reflex was pretty strong. If helicopters tried to land, she would complete the dome, just like back at the hospital. For now, though, she'd let the sky stay the sky.

A chill ran through her. Setting borders was Judge's thing, not hers. She tried to console herself with the idea that her squiggly wall was protecting people—both within and without—while a deadly path created by Judge was built to banish everything within its boundary and to slice through anything that tried to cross it. At least her wall was made in the shape of life—a fuzzy, clever form of life. Judge carved life from existence.

She pulled Riven from the ground by its handle, and the gathering crowd backed away. Its firewall was her only weapon against streamers. Without it, she'd been useless. She vowed never to lose sight of it again. Whatever Riven's path, Roan would follow. She had no choice.

She was facing all of this alone, because of *him*. And while she was here, performing a high-wire act with strangers who expected so much of her, Judge was out there, playing with fire, without care. Unchecked.

She suddenly felt exposed, and her grip on Riven tightened.

He'd stolen her prototypes because he feared them. For that reason alone, she needed to make more.

For that reason alone, she needed an arsenal.

PART WALT_0006

Thank you, Nova. Train hopping was already the most uncomfortable form of travel Walt had ever experienced, but when the sun dropped below the trees, the misery really set in. Blankets Nova had packed made it better, but sleep would be impossible.

Judge's face reflected his discomfort. No. He was in real pain.

"You ok?" Walt asked, panic rising. What if something went wrong with Judge out here? What would he do? What *could* he do?

Judge seemed surprised by the question. Maybe he thought Walt couldn't see him in the dark. Maybe when he thought nobody could see him, he let the pain show. Judge put on his usual stone mask and shrugged it off, saying, "It's making its presence known. Claiming space in my face. Pressuring me to grow too fast."

"It's a real bully," Walt commiserated. After a moment, he asked, "What is *it* anyway? Is it really a black hole?"

"A black hole is absence." Judge pointed to his face. "*This* is presence. It's proof."

"Proof of what?"

"That there's more. Or less. An after. Or a before. This hole in my face is the end of the debate."

"Or maybe it's the beginning of a whole new one?"

"Nah," Judge smirked. "Starting stuff—that's Roan's domain. I'm more about… termination." Judge's smile faded. Maybe he was in too much pain to smile, or maybe it had just registered that his joke was more of a threat. "Want to know what Ruby told me today?"

"Only if it was good news," Walt shivered. "It's too cold for bad news."

"She told me if I wanted to bring back my parents, I'd need Roan's help."

"How?"

"It's complicated," Judge said, waving him off. "She'd never help me, so it doesn't matter."

"My god, you two are so stupid," Walt shook his head. Judge was caught off-guard by that, straightened his back in a show of defense. "You and Roan are locked into this epic challenge, like the universe was created just so the two of you could duke it out. You are *literally* tied together. You are *connected* in ways that no other human beings ever have been, and all you want to do is kill each other. It's goddamn depressing."

"She's the one who—"

"Please don't say '*She started it.*' I swear I'll lose it."

"She is insignificant," Judge growled. "She started *nothing*. I fought my way here. *I* did that. Alone. I don't need *her*. It's a joke."

"Ok. It's a joke. Sure," Walt said, pulling the blanket around his own shoulders and turning away in anger. He fumed in silence a few minutes before adding, hesitantly, "You know, if you want, *I* could help. With her, I mean. Olive branch, that sort of thing."

"You'll come in handy," Judge replied, his voice sounding colder than the air between them, "As a human shield, maybe. Not an olive branch."

Walt considered jumping from the train, taking the duffel bag and all the snacks and blankets with him. It satisfied Walt to imagine Judge, teeth chattering on the train, starving, facing the journey to North Dakota alone, full of regret about dismissing Walt, yet again. But after a few seconds, Walt recognized how his own crappy mood was a result of anxiety and aching joints. Judge was being pissy again, that's all. Some quiet would do them both good.

The grumpy quiet lasted through Rochester and carried them all the way to the train yard in Buffalo, just before dawn. Judge had received a message from Katie Goodbear, and he relayed it to Walt with a kick to his leg, "We're decoupling."

Walt didn't understand at first, but when Judge climbed the ladder to hide on top of the hopper car, Walt quickly packed their duffel to follow him. A rail yard engineer supervised the coupling of their car to a new engine, and by the time the sun was coming up, they were watching Buffalo recede into the distance. The train followed the shore of a large body of water that stretched as far as they could see. Judge wanted to stay on top longer, but Walt was afraid they'd get scraped off by signals.

Once back on their stoop under their blankets, Judge asked, "Was that the ocean?"

"No," Walt answered. "It's one of the Great Lakes. Lake Erie, I think."

"That's a *lake*?"

"Our world bigger than you thought?"

Judge didn't answer. They watched the play of morning light on the lake through the blur of trees. Judge looked tired, but less anguished. Maybe it was time to try again.

"You talk like you know Roan," Walt said, "but you don't."

"You're the expert?"

"Well, looking back on it," Walt said, "I think I was the guinea pig. She was practicing adventures on me. How to play hero. God, I was always in so much trouble."

"Then why be her friend?"

"Good question," Walt said honestly. The answer wasn't easy to give. "I was lonely."

"You? *Lonely?*" Judge said, incredulous. "But you're *the guy.*"

"That's the problem with seeming like you have your shit together," Walt shrugged. "You become a finished project. My parents figured I was set. Ready to launch. On autopilot. And I went along with it. My mom still needed to be needed, so she adopted Lucy. Focused on home improvement projects. Work."

"You had other friends. Carmen. She was nice."

"Nobody was like Roan," Walt said. "She was so bossy. Controlling. Selfish. Contrary."

"She sounds great," Judge said sarcastically. "I've really missed out."

"Adventure seems like kid stuff, long before it should," Walt tried to explain. "Especially when you have parents who are always talking about the real world. *'The real world is right around the corner.' 'You're almost a part of the real world now.' 'Soon enough, you'll see how the real world operates.'* For Roan, the real world was still far away. I liked that. I needed it."

"And she made you suffer for it," Judge said.

"Not all the time," Walt said, and he fell silent for a while, memories dragging him back to Comet Pond and basement adventures and mischief. "I really miss it, actually. I miss *her*. And my family. I never thought I would, but…"

Walt stared at his hands to avoid looking up because he was afraid he might lose it if he did. He heard Judge digging for something, and then a butterfly hair clip landed in Walt's lap.

"I may have visited Lucy's room, too," Judge confessed.

"What, are you a clepto or something?"

Judge shrugged. "I'm a sucker for souvenirs."

Walt worked the clip over in his hand, feeling a lump rise in his throat. "Lucy hasn't worn this one in a long time. Said it was too babyish." He clenched it so tightly it dug into his palm as he added, "I wasn't a very good big brother to her."

"We could start a club."

"You think of yourself as a big brother?"

"I don't think of myself as a little one."

The day became brighter and warmer, and Walt shielded his eyes. He wished Nova had packed sunglasses. The swaying and constant speed of the train made him drift off, his grandfather's brass check in one hand, Lucy's butterfly clip in the other.

Screeching airbrakes woke him up. His face hit the side of the ladder they stopped so fast. He pocketed his recently returned heirlooms. Probably shouldn't have been a priority, but all the same, that's what he did first. Judge looked just as startled. He'd obviously fallen asleep, too. It hadn't even occurred to Walt that one of them should stay awake to keep an eye out. Being a fugitive was hard work, and he was still learning the ropes.

"Is this Chicago?" Judge asked, sounding like he already knew the answer was no.

"Don't think so," Walt answered.

A quick check of the tracks revealed they were stuck on a trestle, high above a narrow canal. A loud buzz announced the arrival of a quadcopter drone, and Walt instinctively ducked behind the hopper's fin.

"Shit."

"I agree," Judge said.

A man's voice they both recognized shouted over a loud-speaker: "Judge Gorey. Walter Hale."

"Pirret," Walt grumbled, and he made a fist even though he wasn't in range.

"Welcome to the lovely city of Cleveland, Ohio," Pirret announced. "A.K.A., in *so* many respects, the end of the line."

"Too far to jump," Walt assessed the drop to the canal below, and then he was choking. Someone had him in headlock.

Across their stowaway stoop, Judge managed to squirm out of a similar grip. Walt's assailant was either stronger or more determined not to let him go. Or it could be the fear-of-touching-an-actual-monster differential. Whatever it was, Judge had a few seconds to dig in his bag for something before the guy grabbed him again. No way Walt could free himself, so he decided to give Judge a chance. Maybe he could climb down to the trestle. Or across to the next car and escape that way. Walt kicked Judge's attacker in the face, knocking him off the stoop. He was harnessed to the train, though, so he didn't fall far. In seconds, he was already climbing back up, looking pissed now that his face was bloodied.

Judge hadn't made a move. Maybe the height had him frozen,

just like the oncoming train yesterday. Even when the guy grabbed him by the back of his neck and nearly hoisted him off the hopper car, Judge stayed fixated on the canal below, waiting for something. Walt clawed at the arm across his throat, desperate for air. Spots danced in front of his eyes.

Judge could take a shot that would end this, if he wanted. What was he waiting for?

"Judge," Walt said with the last of his air, "Little help?"

"I don't do little," Judge replied, wrapping his arms around the ladder. "Hold on."

Walt was too close to blacking out to hold onto anything. Something big hit the underside of the trestle and knocked their car off the track. The guy who'd been choking him lost his balance and swung away on his harness empty-handed, dumping Walt into open air.

Walt registered that he was falling at the same time he was pulling air into his lungs again. His body arched on instinct. He'd hit head first. *Probably better that way*, he thought—an observation that somehow shared its limited time and space with the surprise of how unexpected an end this was.

Best friend to Roan Gorey. Human shield to Judge Gorey. *So long, Sunflower*. He was much more important to the story than this. Wasn't he?

A rusty roof was fast approaching, and Walt had one last thought. *This is going to hurt.*

Then everything went black.

PART JUDGE_0010

LILY PADS ON THE SURFACE OF THE POND NEXT to his bunker at the military annex had been the most delicate thing Judge had ever seen—on this side of the *pre*, anyway. No doubt they were Roan's inspiration, but these lily pads launched from the blastoid dropped into the canal were far from delicate.

After slamming into the train trestle, the massive, floppy pad flipped the hopper off the tracks like a dog's tongue knocking a scoop of ice cream from a cone. As Walt fell, Judge made a quick adjustment, then leapt from the stoop to the pad and flattened himself against its slick, rubbery skin. The screams of the men harnessed to the hopper reached him as he rose, but he didn't care about them. Judge searched below him for Walt but couldn't see him anymore. He felt sick inside and closed his eyes.

"Hey, nutjob," Pirret over the loudspeaker again as the lily pad elevator reached the height of his helicopter. "That's the Cuyahoga down there. You know what you've done?"

Judge threw a dismissive salute as he passed him by. The edge fluttered enough for Judge to see glimpses below, static scenes caught between waves of motion. The derailed hopper car hung in mid-air above the canal, threatening to drag the other cars down with it. Pirret's men dangled from it like angry tassels. No clear view of Walt's landing.

Judge had his own problems. The lily pad's skyward growth

wasn't stopping.

And it was blooming. This lily flower wasn't the silky white of the pads back on the Annex pond. It glittered with flecks of metal. A sculpted snow globe of toxins. It fed not on the morning sun, but on whatever poison was in the water below.

"Who knew Cleveland rivers were so polluted?" Judge marveled, securing some relative safety inside the shimmering charcoal flower.

The lily pad kept carrying him up. The pad itself had grown so wide, he could no longer see over the edge. He was starting to get cold. He didn't know how to stop it. He didn't know how to get off. He had no idea what to do.

His climb from the *pre* had taken him years, but most of that time had been spent seeking where to start. In mere seconds, Judge was rising into the heavens of this new world on the surface of a blastoid designed to remove him from existence.

Maybe this was how she'd planned to get revenge all along— not *inside* a blastoid. On the back of one.

Well, Judge thought, freezing. *Bravo.*

PART KATIE_0005

STORYTELLER'S REMORSE IS SIMILAR TO BUYER'S remorse. Instead of regretting that 90-foot yacht in your dry dock, it's the story you gave away, or the time you spent giving it.

Katie was aware she was both storyteller and player, but there's nothing new about that. You can't be separate from a story any more than your thoughts can be separate from you, or you from the universe. Parts to a whole, you know? No way around it. It's just how things work.

But all this time explaining things to you, catching you up and connecting the dots for you—she has to be honest—it's been a distraction, and her work has suffered. Her path forward had been clear.

Stop the construction at Like-a-Fishhook.

Expose Duke's crimes.

Honor Edgar Raven Looks Around.

But none of those things has happened yet. They are local concerns. It doesn't matter how important they are to her. The world was on monster watch and makings plans of its own. The world was full of local concerns.

She had to admit, she'd been swept up herself. It was hard not to be, when almost everything that happened reeked of meaning. Of myth. When what you're living feels like a storyline from legend, how are you supposed to keep your eye on logistics?

>> Buttonbush: Everything came back.

That was the message for the Lodge after Roan's successful test of the cladosphere. A simple enough sentence, right? Especially considering it came from Berit, who lately was using the Lodge as her personal forum for her own grand plans to save the world. But if you were Katie, you would hear that phrase and consider how close it sounds to the final day of the Okipa ceremony, Everything Comes Back Day, the most sacred of Mandan traditions.

Everything Comes Back Day recreates the legend of Hoita who trapped all the animals and then was tricked by Lone Man into releasing them. Katie can't tell you whole story, but you get the gist. Like Noah and his arc, with more humor, less rain.

Why can you know details of one story, and not another? The Okipa is a summer ceremony, and it's not summer. Tell a story out of season, you're just asking for trouble. Besides, Katie doesn't own the rights, and even if she did—and you *weren't* the outsider you are—you wouldn't understand a word because it's told in a dead language. The only way the Everything Comes Back Day can truly exist is if you bring the Mandan language back from the dead. Can *you* do that?

Consider this. Maybe the whole universe is on borrowed time, written in a code no one understands anymore. Maybe that explains looking up at the stars and feeling special and insignificant at the same time. Something is speaking to us, but we lack the vocab, so all that vast information just washes over us. We are a part of a masterpiece we can never translate into our own language. We can listen, but never understand.

Or maybe Coyote is just having a good laugh at our expense. Who knows?

You can imagine, that's exactly how Katie felt when she was

sharing a real moment with Trev by the lake, and Federal Agent Owens came walking out of it, like he owned the place. What kind of Creator would reward all her hard work that way? A trickster, that's what kind. She should have seen it coming. All stories have an element of the unexpected. The improbable. Life has those elements, too. A story without them is just a grocery list. An itinerary.

That perfectly timed appearance of Trev's federal friend was so clearly orchestrated to fluster her that she couldn't help but take it personally. She was the master, here. You know?

And now on the TV screen in her cabin, Katie watched as Judge soared toward the stratosphere on a giant lily pad in Cleveland.

You can't make this stuff up.

She needed Judge. She could see a way down for him, but she knew he must be terrified. She was terrified, too. If he didn't get off that beanstalk and find his way here, her plans would fall apart. Her story was already unraveling, diluted by forces beyond her control. Diminishing her power. Belittling her history. The outside world was rushing in like a tsunami, and all her local concerns were as endangered as Noah's animals. Fortunately, Katie had built herself an ark.

She wondered if there was wi-fi all the way up there on that lily pad.

```
> GirlWhoClimbs has entered the lodge.
> Coyote has entered the lodge.
>> GirlWhoClimbs: Jump.
>> Coyote: I can't.
>> GirlWhoClimbs: I'll catch you.
```

>> Coyote: That's a lie. I'll fall.

>> GirlWhoClimbs: You'll fall until I catch you. Jump toward the rising sun.

>> Coyote: This isn't a game. I could die.

>> GirlWhoClimbs: If you die, we all die. You're not alone.

>> Coyote: But I am alone.

>> GirlWhoClimbs: No one is alone.

Katie lost the connection there. No way to know if Judge got her last message, or if it would mean anything to him if he had. In the *pre*, he'd been alone. Or at least, the only one of his kind. He knew what it felt like, and that memory might be the end of us all.

Or maybe he would trust her, one more time, and jump. Katie watched the TV as if her life depended on it.

Who knows, maybe the Creator would throw us a bone.

ACKNOWLEDGMENTS

I'd like to thank my husband Sam and boys Nick, Charlie, and Leo for their humor, patience, and support.

To all the writers, historians, teachers, artists and activists in my life who through their own endeavors and passion remind me the work is worth doing: Sam Deese, Charlotte Beeler, Mark Givens, Marcia Ross, Mariann Murray, Martha Deese, Rupert T. Deese, Tamara Snihurowycz Beeler, Marielle Risse, Terry King, Dee Beeler Jones, David Atkinson, Jennifer Henry, Mohit Bhasin, Ben Deese, Frank Deese, Aran Parillo, Louise Lepera, Michael Lepera, Laura Martin, Cindy Hill-Williams, John Rudd, Larissa Sasgen, Tom Dietzel, and Howard Drucker.

To all the scientists and researchers who have inspired and supported me: Natalie Kuldell, Forest White, Michael Birnbaum, Christopher Voigt, Michael Yaffe, Vasilena Gocheva, Mary Ann Brow, Dave Brow, Heather Thomson, Ty Thomson, Barry Canton, Reshma Shetty, Jason Kelly, Austin Che, Tom Knight, Sophia Roosth, Kenneth Oye, Alexandra Naba, Joe Davis, Felix Moser, Samantha Sutton, Meagan Lizarazo, and Drew Endy.

Thanks also to John Beeler, Jess Deese, Bernice Beeler, D.J. Weicker, Patrick Weicker, Julie Roush McKinney, Tanya Karapurkar Bhasin, Alison Gabel, Charity Tabol, Feni Ricard, and Rachel Deese, for being pillars of perseverance in dark times.

Special thanks to Natalie Kuldell, founder of the BioBuilder Educational Foundation, Richard Curtis of Richard Curtis Associates, Inc., and Mark Givens at Pelekinesis Press for believing in me and the value of this story.

Lots of gratitude goes to the MIT Science Fiction Society and MIT Artists Beyond the Desk.

I'd like to acknowledge the naturalists, conservationists, and rangers whose work at the following locations informed the various paths taken in this book: Assabet River National Wildlife Refuge, Massachusetts; New River Gorge National River, Nuttallburg Tipple, and Hawks Nest State Park, West Virginia; SteelStacks of Bethlehem, National Museum of Industrial History, Pennsylvania; Delaware and Lehigh National Heritage Corridor, Pennsylvania; Delaware Water Gap National Recreation Area, New Jersey; Reelfoot Lake State Park, Tennessee; Chain of Rocks Canal and Lock, Missouri River Water Trail, Missouri; Port Louisa National Wildlife Refuge, Iowa; Ohio and Erie Canalway National Heritage Area and Cuyahoga Valley National Park, Ohio; Knife River Indian Villages National Historical Site, North Dakota; and Garrison Dam National Fish Hatchery, North Dakota.

Through their original research and writing, personal interviews, and assistance with access to research materials, I acknowledge: Alfred Bowers, *Mandan Social and Ceremonial Organization*; Frances Densmore, *The Little River Women Society*; Elizabeth Fenn, *Encounters at the Heart of the World: A History of the Mandan People*; Edwin Benson, the last fluent speaker of Mandan; Calvin Grinnell and Joseph Jastrzembski, "In the Words of Our Ancestors: The Mandan Language and Oral Traditions Preservation Project"; Sara Trechter, CSU Chico, for her translation of Edwin Benson's oral histories; Raymond Cross, law professor at the University of Montana, *Development's Victim or Its Beneficiary?: The Impact of Oil and Gas Development on the Fort Berthold Indian Reservation*; Paul Van Develder, *Coyote Warrior: One Man, Three Tribes, and the*

Trial that Forged a Nation; Kimberly Jondahl, State Historical Society of North Dakota; Three Affiliated Tribes Museum, *Excerpts from the House Joint Resolution 33 dealing with the construction of the Garrison Dam, North Dakota*; Prairie Public Broadcasting, *Faces of the Oil Patch*; and Mary Baker, intern for the Ancestral Lands Program at Knife River Indian Villages National Historical Site, North Dakota.

Because I reference this photograph, I wanted to acknowledge its actual existence:

George Gillette covers his face as Washington D.C. legislators take over 150,000 acres of reservation land from the Three Affiliated Tribes for the site of the Garrison Dam on the Missouri River.

AP Photo - May 20, 1948

A portion of the proceeds of the sale of this novel goes to the Native American Rights Fund (NARF). For more information about the critical work NARF is doing: https://www.narf.org/

CPSIA information can be obtained
at www.ICGtesting.com
Printed in the USA
FSHW020512301018
53282FS

9 781938 349805